Regency
Society

MISCHIEF *in*
Regency
Society

AMANDA
McCABE

MILLS
&BOON

Published in Great Britain 2014
by Mills & Boon, an imprint of Harlequin (UK) Limited,
Eton House, 18-24 Paradise Road, Richmond, Surrey, TW9 1SR

MISCHIEF IN REGENCY SOCIETY
© 2014 Harlequin Books S.A.

To Catch a Rogue © 2008 Amanda McCabe
To Deceive a Duke © 2008 Amanda McCabe

ISBN: 978-0-263-24634-6

052-1214

Printed and bound
by CPI Group (UK) Ltd, Croydon, CR0 4YY

Amanda McCabe wrote her first romance at the age of sixteen—a vast epic, starring all her friends as the characters, written secretly during algebra class. She's never since used algebra, but her books have been nominated for many awards, including the RITA® Award, the *RT Book Reviews* Reviewers' Choice Award, the Booksellers Best, the National Readers' Choice Award and the Holt Medallion. She lives in Oklahoma, with a menagerie of two cats, a pug and a bossy miniature poodle, and loves dance classes, collecting cheesy travel souvenirs and watching the Food Network—even though she doesn't cook. Visit her at http://ammandamccabe.tripod.com and http://www.riskyregencies.blogspot.com.

To Catch a Rogue

AMANDA McCABE

To Laura Kay Gauldin,
who has been brave enough to be my friend since we were
teenagers! If not for the three Gauldin sisters there
never could have been three Chase sisters.

Prologue

"Where'er we tread 'tis haunted, holy ground;
No earth of thine is lost in vulgar mould
But one vast plain of wonder spreads around,
And all the Muses' tales seem truly told
Till the sense aches with gazing to behold
The scenes our earliest dreams have dwelt upon...

Lord Byron

Never had a night been as dark as this one.

The moon was a mere sliver high over the crooked rooftops of London, nearly obscured by scudding clouds. There were no stars at all, not even a tiny, bead-like sparkle, and an infamous London fog was creeping inward over the sluggish Thames. Heavy and greasy, a noxious grey-green, it would soon blanket the city, cutting off even the dull shimmer of that tiny moon.

But all the guests at the Marchioness of Tenbray's ball—and that was nearly everyone in the *ton* who mattered at all—cared not a whit for the ominous night outside the brilliantly lit mansion. They were far too busy moving through the crush of the ballroom, laughing, dancing, trading the latest *on dits* behind silken fans, drinking champagne, stealing kisses under concealment of the terrace's potted palms. All the world seemed compressed into this one marble-and-gilt room, a swirl of music and chatter and clinking crystal rising up and up with no care for the dark chill outside.

Not one of them—not even the marchioness herself, deeply preoccupied by a sudden shortage of lobster tarts— noticed a window in the library sliding silently open.

Someone else was taking full advantage of the darkness, and not for surreptitious caresses on the terrace. No, this person had something far more important, far more devious, in mind.

As the window swung all the way open, this person, tall and slim, muffled and masked all in black, climbed inside and hopped lightly to the Aubusson carpet laid over polished parquet. The figure made no sound, as soft as cat's paws on the silken weave. It went automatically down into a low crouch, breath held as bright eyes, revealed through the slits of the satin mask, darted from left to right. The library, as expected, was deserted, lit by only one small Colza lamp on the polished desk. It cast a circle of golden glow, flickering, sweetly scented, and all the far corners were deep in gloom. Bookshelves rose to the ceiling, crowded with leather-bound volumes that looked scarcely touched, let alone read and loved.

Well, thought the intruder. *Old Lady Tenbray is scarcely renowned for her brains, is she?*

Yet the late Lord Tenbray *had* been renowned for his passion for Italian antiquities, and this was what drew the black-clad figure's interest. Once assured of being alone, the intruder rose from that crouch and moved stealthily across the room. The shadows were no deterrent—the library's layout had been carefully studied, every chair and table mapped. This person knew what they sought.

At the far end of the space, on either side of the carved fireplace, were glass-topped cases, each one filled to the brim with the marquess's ill-gotten gains. In his youth, long ago, he had served as a diplomat to the kingdom of Naples. From there, he sent home crates full of statuary, jewellery, frescoes, vases. Only a small part of the collection resided in this library.

The very best part.

"Ah, yes," the intruder whispered. "There you are."

From a pocket tied around the waist came a thin piece of metal, which was carefully inserted into the case's lock. One upward twist, and the mechanism popped free.

"Lax, lax," the person murmured, lifting up the lid. Really, people who could not take care of their possessions did not deserve them.

The object of desire lay in the very centre of the display, an Etruscan diadem of gold hammered very thin and formed into the shape of delicate leaves and vines. Once, it had graced the head of a queen. Now it satisfied an old Englishwoman's vanity.

But not for long.

The figure reached for it with black-gloved hands. Even in the shadows the diadem glowed like the Italian sky, so light and perfect. It seemed so fragile, yet had survived so much for these thousands of years.

"You will soon be safe," came the reassuring whisper, as the diadem disappeared into the pocket.

As its glow vanished, there was a loud thump outside the library door. The figure's masked head whipped around, eyes wide, heart pounding.

"No, Agnes, we shouldn't!" a man groaned, his words slurred, overly loud in the quiet room.

"Oh, but we really must!" a woman answered. "We haven't got very long. My husband will soon leave the card room and be looking for me."

There was another thump, then a click of the door handle as someone, either Agnes or her drunken companion, groped for the entrance.

Time to be gone. One more object emerged from that pocket, a perfect white lily that was carefully placed in the diadem's abandoned spot. Then the figure sprinted lightly across the floor, jumping up on to the window ledge. Just as the door flew open, the thief was gone, disappearing into the gloomy night.

The Lily Thief had struck again.

Chapter One

"I call this meeting of the Ladies Artistic Society to order," announced Calliope Chase, sounding her gavel on the table in front of her. "Our secretary, Miss Clio Chase, will take the minutes."

Slowly, all the teacups and plates of cakes were lowered to laps and tabletops, and the members of the Society turned their attention to their founder and president. Bright sunlight flowed from the tall windows of the drawing room of the Chases' townhouse, warm and bright after the chilly misery of the night before, casting pastel spencers and muslin gowns in a brilliant light. Everything in the fashionably appointed room was just as expected—the ladies seated in pretty groupings of chairs and settees, china tea sets, silver services, hovering housemaids, the soft sound of Mozart from the pianoforte in the corner.

All expected and proper. Except for one thing. Behind Calliope, set high on its pedestal, was a marble statue of Apollo. An anatomically correct, completely naked statue of Apollo.

But then, what else could be looked for in a house belonging to the famous scholar of Greek history, Sir Walter Chase? A house where his nine daughters, named after the Greek Muses, resided and pursued their own, not always completely ladylike, interests.

Calliope, the eldest of the Chase Muses at age twenty-one, was also not all that was expected. She was quite attractive, taking after her late mother's French family with her black hair and brown eyes, her flawless fair skin; and those good looks—with the Chase fortune—had attracted more than a few offers from very eligible *partis*. Yet she had turned them all down. "They just don't care about history and antiquities," she told her father, and he immediately agreed that those young men would never do for one of the Chase Muses.

She also cared little for fashion or for dancing or cards, preferring to spend her time in study, or in conversation *about* her studies with like-minded people.

That was why she founded the Ladies Artistic Society in the first place, so that she and her sisters could reach out to other females with more on their minds than hemlines and hats. "Surely there must be others like us here in London," she told her sister Clio. "You know—ladies who wish they could take books with them to pass the dull hours at Almack's."

And so there were. Their membership now included two of their friends, along with the three eldest Chase daughters (the other six still being in the schoolroom, and therefore members-in-waiting). There was also a waiting list, though Calliope suspected that many of those just wanted a glimpse of Apollo. They met once a week during the Season to talk about history, literature, art, music. Often a guest lecturer, provided by the Muses' father, would speak, or a painter would give a demonstration. Sometimes they would just discuss amongst themselves a book read or an opera seen, or Thalia, the third Chase sister and an ardent musician, would perform a scandalous, passionate Beethoven piece.

Not today, though. Today there was very serious business to discuss, and obviously everyone discerned that from the stiff set of Calliope's shoulders in her white muslin day dress. A hush fell over the bright room, all clinkings and rustlings stilled. Even Thalia ceased playing the pianoforte, swivelling around to face her sister.

Calliope lifted up a copy of the *Post*, pointing at a black, shrieking headline: *The Lily Thief Returns!*

"It has been many weeks since this criminal struck," Calliope said softly. Her voice was quiet, but she felt her cheeks burn with the force of her inner anger. Many weeks—and she had thought the Lily Thief gone, vanished like so many other ephemeral sensations in Society. A two-day scandal, and then something else, an elopement or divorce, or other such harmless trifle. "I suppose he realised that attention was drifting from his foul deeds."

Her sister Clio glanced up from the minutes, her auburn brow arched above the gilt frames of her spectacles. Clio said nothing, though. Merely went back to her note-taking. It was Lady Emmeline Saunders who spoke. "Perhaps the Lily Thief has very good reasons for what he does."

"Reasons such as profit and riches?" Thalia cried from her piano. Her golden curls, so shiny and pretty, trembled with indignation. Thalia might look like a china shepherdess, but she had the heart of a gladiator. And that accounted for the many scrapes she always found herself in. "I am sure he saw a pretty penny from the sale of Lord Egermont's Euphronios krater and the Clives' Bastet statue."

"Antiquities have more than a monetary value, you

know," Clio said quietly. "Something their previous owners seemed to have lost sight of."

"Of course they do," Calliope said. "And that is what makes the exploits of this Lily Thief so heinous. Who knows where these objects have gone, or if they will ever be seen again? We will have no access to the lessons they could teach us. It is a terrible loss to scholarship."

Clio bent her head back over her notes, murmuring low enough for only Calliope to hear, "As if there was much *scholarship* going on in Lady Tenbray's library."

"The Lily Thief does not just steal money or jewels, as a common burglar would. Objects that could easily be replaced," Calliope said. "He steals history."

The other Society members glanced at each other. Finally, Emmeline raised her hand again. "What must we do about this, Calliope? Perhaps engage a don from Cambridge to speak on cultural thefts?"

"Or tomb-raiding!" cried Miss Charlotte Price, the youngest and most excitable of the Society. She had an unfortunate predilection for reading horrid novels, but her father was a friend of Sir Walter Chase. He hoped the Society would help her expand her horizons. So far the hope was in vain, but one never knew. "I did read about a cursed tomb robber in *The Baron's Revenge*—"

"Yes, indeed," Calliope said, interrupting smoothly before Lotty could be carried off into a rambling synopsis. "But I have something rather more—personal in mind."

"Personal?" the others chorused.

"Yes." Calliope placed her palms flat on the table before her, leaning towards her audience. "We are going to catch the Lily Thief ourselves."

A great sigh went up, floating to the plaster-ceiling medallion in a wave of exclamation.

"Oh, how very thrilling!" trilled Charlotte. "Just like *The Curse of Lady Arabella*—"

"We are to turn amateur sleuths?" Thalia said, clapping her hands. "What a marvellous idea!"

"Indeed," agreed Emmeline. "Scholastic inquiry is all very well, but sometimes we need to *move*."

Clio's pen stilled, her brows drawn down in a puzzled vee. "How do you propose we go about this task, Calliope? If even the Bow Street Runners could not find the Lily Thief…"

Honestly, Calliope had not thought quite that far ahead. The idea of taking action themselves had only occurred to her at breakfast that morning, as she read the papers in mounting anger over the harmful exploits of that show-off Lily Thief. She had some vague notion that, as ladies of the *ton*, they could move about more freely and with far more stealth than those Runners. They could listen and observe with no one being the wiser, and perhaps catch the villain at a vulnerable moment.

For she was sure of one thing—the Lily Thief was a member of the *ton*. He had to be, to possess such knowledge of the houses and schedules of lords and ladies. But she was *not* entirely sure how to begin catching him in their net.

"I suggest," she said slowly, "that we begin with last night's theft of the Etruscan diadem. Was anyone at Lady Tenbray's rout?" Calliope herself had not been, turning down the invitation to what was sure to be a dull crush to attend the theatre with her father. *Macbeth*, she had thought, was sure to be more exciting. If only she had known the Lily Thief was to strike again!

Clio and Thalia were of no help, having chosen to stay home with their studies. There must have been *someone* there whose observations she could trust!

Finally, Emmeline raised her hand again. "I was there, but I noticed nothing untoward, I fear."

"No one behaving oddly at all?" Calliope asked hopefully.

"Just Freddie Mountbank," Emmeline answered. "But then, what does one expect of him? I would have been suspicious if he behaved *normally.*"

The ladies all giggled. Poor Mr Mountbank—he was so earnest, so very much in love with Emmeline, yet he had the unfortunate tendency to lose his temper and blurt out curses when he was nervous in a lady's presence (which was always). He had launched more than one dance set into disarray by knocking down all the participants. Unless Mr Mountbank was very clever indeed—and, judging by his parents, that was not likely—he was not the Lily Thief.

"Nothing else?" Calliope asked.

Emmeline shook her head regretfully. "I fear not. It was so very crowded. And my mother insisted I dance with Mr Mountbank, so I was rather distracted in dodging him."

More giggles rippled around the room, and even Calliope had to laugh at the vision of her rather tall friend ducking behind curtains and potted palms to hide from her persistent suitor.

"I'm sorry," Emmeline said. "If I had known…"

"Yes." Calliope sighed. "If only we all knew."

"What shall we do now?" asked Thalia, her tone suggesting that *she* would prefer to armour up like a Valkyrie and go marching out into Mayfair to destroy all villains in her path.

"I am not entirely sure," Calliope admitted. "But I think I *do* have an idea where the Lily Thief will strike next."

"Really?"

"Where?"

"Oh, do tell us!"

Calliope had not completely worked out all this in her mind. Yet sometimes, she thought, intuition was the best guide. "The Duke of Averton's ball."

"Oh!"

"Of course."

"The Alabaster Goddess," Thalia said. "Lud, but that is clever of you, Cal."

"I'm surprised the Lily Thief hasn't made a move towards it yet," Emmeline said.

"He is obviously growing in audacity," Calliope said, gesturing towards the newspaper. "To snatch the diadem in plain sight indicates confidence."

The Alabaster Goddess was a rather small, perfectly preserved statue of Artemis with her bow, taken only a few years ago from a ruined Greek temple on the island of Delos and purchased by the Duke of Averton (or Duke of Avarice, as he was known in certain circles) for his famous collection. She was quite unblemished for being thousands of years old, and the duke loved to show her off, strangely enough, for he was a well-known recluse. The goddess had even sparked quite a fashion in society for "Artemis" hair-styles and "Artemis" sandals. The duke had made it known she would soon be moved to his heavily fortified castle in Yorkshire. But next week she could be seen at a grand masked ball the duke was hosting. His first ball in years.

The ball had a Grecian theme, of course.

Yes, Calliope thought, suddenly sure. The Lily Thief would strike there.

"We must all go to the ball, and there we will—"

"Oh!" Calliope's instructions were cut off by a sudden cry from Lotty, who sat closest to the window. She pressed her nose to the glass, leaning forward precariously. "Oh, it is Lord Westwood! And your beau Mr Mountbank, Emmeline."

Those words, of course—Lord Westwood—caused a great rush to the windows, silks and ribbons furiously a-rustle. More noses and fingers pressed to the glass, un-heeding of smudges and dignity.

"Oh!" cried Thalia. "He is in his beautiful phaeton. I wish Father would buy one for me, I'm sure I would be a rare hand at the reins. But Westwood appears to be in some sort of altercation with Mr Mountbank. How fascinating."

Oh, what a great surprise, Calliope thought sarcastically. Where Cameron de Vere, the Earl of Westwood went, "altercations" were sure to follow.

"Cal, Clio, come, you must see this. It's too amusing," Thalia said.

Clio left off her scratching of pens and joined the others, peering down as if observing some scientific demonstration.

Calliope did not *want* to go and gawk with her friends, as if they were all silly schoolgirls who had never before seen a man rather than the intelligent, rational women they were. She did not want to give Lord Westwood the satis-faction of yet more attention. Yet, somehow, she could not help herself. It was as if a thick cord suddenly tightened around her waist, pulling her inexorably towards the window. Towards *him*.

Calliope dropped the newspaper and strolled reluctantly towards the others, peering past Thalia's shoulder to the scene below. It was indeed Lord Westwood, his bright yellow and gleaming black phaeton wedged into traffic, at a complete standstill. His matched bay horses snorted and pranced restlessly, as Mr Mountbank, in his own convey-ance, blocked Westwood's way, shouting and gesticulating, as he was wont to do. Mr Mountbank's face was an alarming shade of purple above his overly starched cravat, yet Westwood looked on with an expression of amused boredom on his ridiculously gorgeous face, as if the quarrel had nothing at all to do with him, and he merely watched the action at Drury Lane.

"Really," Calliope muttered. "Our street is hardly Gentleman Jackson's saloon."

"Oh!" Thalia exclaimed. "Do you really think they might come to blows? How terribly interesting."

"How very handsome he is," sighed Lotty. "Just like the comte in *Mademoiselle Marguerites's Fatal Secret.*"

Handsome—well, yes. Even Calliope had to admit that, albeit grudgingly. Westwood was sometimes called "the Greek God" in more florid circles, and strictly from an aesthetic viewpoint it was all too true. He could have been their Ladies Society Apollo statue come to warm, vivid, breathing life, if he were to shed his buckskin breeches and exquisite bottle-green coat. He was hatless now, despite the sunny skies, his glossy, sable-dark curls tossed by the wind until they fell in artistic disarray over his brow. His skin was always a golden-bronze, his eyes dark and maddeningly unreadable.

No, Calliope thought as she watched him now, trying to reason with Mr Mountbank with a half-grin on his lips. He was not so much a god, as a young Greek fisherman, virile, earthbound, as secret as the deepest sea. Surely he got that sense of *otherness* from his mother. Like the Chases' own mother, the late countess had hailed from more exotic climes. She came from where else but Athens, the daughter of a famous Greek scholar.

For an instant, it seemed as if Westwood would actually alight from his phaeton and face the apoplectic wrath of Mr Mountbank. The ladies at the window held their collective breath, but, alas, fisticuffs—and shirtsleeves—in Mayfair were not to be. Mountbank, faced with an opponent potentially closer than several feet away, backed off and hurried on his way, steering his carriage precariously around the corner.

The ladies, disappointed, also backed away, leaving the view to return to their seats. The drawing room was soon filled with the mingling of chatter, music, tea being poured into delicate cups. Calliope, though, could not yet leave with them. Could not break that cord. Something tightened, binding her there, staring down at Cameron de Vere.

He laughed aloud at Mountbank's precipitous retreat, his head thrown back with the unbridled freedom of his humour. His hair fell away from his chiseled face, the sharp angles of his cheekbones and nose. He leaned back easily on the cushioned seat, free as a corsair at the helm of his ship. Passers-by paused to stare at him, as if drawn by the sheer *life* of him, yet he noticed not at all, so comfortable in his own skin, his own world.

Blast him, anyway, Calliope thought wryly. Blast for being—*him*. For being all she was not. For being so free. Not bound to family responsibilities.

Calliope leaned her forehead against the cool glass, watching as Lord Westwood's laughter faded and he once again collected the loosened reins. Even his casual movements were filled with a smooth, unstudied grace.

She watched him, and remembered their first meeting, at the beginning of the Season. Was that only weeks ago? It felt a lifetime. Or mere moments. That night when...

No! No, that didn't bear thinking of. Not now. She was in the middle of a Ladies Society meeting! Her friends were nearby. Thinking of Cameron de Vere, seeing him, fantasising about him as some Greek fisherman on a beach, would only discompose her. Her friends were sure to ask questions, and that would never do. She was always collected and calm. Always in control. She had to be, her family relied on her.

Why, then, did she tremble so much, just from watching him down on the street? It was ridiculous!

Calliope reached up for the fringed edge of the satin drape, clutching at it to draw it over the window. Before she could do so, concealing herself and all her unruly emotions, Lord Westwood glanced up and saw her there. Saw her staring at him.

For an instant, it was as if a cloud passed over the Grecian sun. He frowned, his velvety brown eyes narrowing. Then, as swiftly as it came, the cloud vanished. He smiled, a wide, white Corsair grin, and gave her a jaunty salute.

Calliope gasped involuntarily, and yanked the curtain closed. *The rogue!*

She spun away from the window, wrapping her cashmere shawl tighter around her shoulders—only to find Clio observing her closely.

Calliope adored her sister, the closest to her in age and in artistic inclination, but sometimes, just sometimes, she was a bit uneasy to be faced with those unerring, unwavering green eyes.

"You should stay out of the sun, Cal," Clio said quietly. "It makes your cheeks so flushed."

Calliope Chase.

Cameron frowned as she thrust the draperies shut, as if to block out a demon from her home. To bar all laughter from the premises. To bar *him*.

He shouldn't care. He *didn't* care. Calliope Chase was beautiful, it was true. Yet London was filled with lovely ladies, most of them far less prickly and mysterious than Miss Chase. Yet somehow, ever since their first meeting—

or first clash, as he thought of it—he couldn't get her out of his mind. Was he becoming like his rather bizarre cousin Gerald, who paid lightskirts hefty sums to whip his bare backside with a riding crop, pain and aggravation equalling pleasure?

Cam laughed aloud as he guided his horses back into the flow of traffic, picturing Calliope Chase wielding a leather whip with fire in her brown eyes. It was not an unlikely vision. She was named after the wrong mythological figure, surely. She was not a Muse, changeable and capricious and seductive. She was Athena, goddess of war, marching into battle to defend what she believed in, right or wrong.

An Athena with such an intriguing sadness behind her gaze.

Cam glanced over his shoulder before he turned the corner of the street, but the Chases' house was closed up tight. There was no flash of shining raven curls, no glimpse of fair skin and sparkling eyes. Yet he knew she was in there. Could still see her in his mind.

As he headed off into the park, a shortcut to his own home, he let his horses have their head a bit. He saw Mountbank far ahead. Such a silly puppy, getting so upset because Cam had danced with Lady Emmeline Saunders! Anyone could see he was no rival for her affections. She was a pretty girl, and full of interesting conversation (unlike most of the society chits mothers were always pushing his way!). She had a quick humour, too, despite being bosom friends with Miss Chase. But there was something missing when he talked to Lady Emmeline, looked at her.

There was *always* something missing. Something so empty and hollow at the centre of his life, something that was not filled by all his pursuits—his clubs, his horses, women, even his studies. It was a cold and echoing spot, always with him. He only really forgot it, felt a new warmth spark on that ice, when he crossed swords with Calliope Chase.

Curious. Very curious indeed. And not something he cared to think about too deeply.

His horses were now a bit winded after their gallop through the park, so he eased them out of the gates towards home and their own mews. But they were blocked by an unexpected traffic obstruction, a tangled knot of vehicles and horses and pedestrians that brought all movement to a temporary standstill.

"Blast!" Cam muttered, craning his neck to try to peer past a lumbering barouche. He was meant to attend a musical evening later, one he was rather looking forward to as it featured a speculative reconstruction of ancient Greek theatrical music. "What is it now?"

Then the barouche lurched to one side, and he understood. A great crowd had gathered in front of the Marchioness of Tenbray's home, gawking up at the window where the infamous Lily Thief had climbed in to snatch away her ladyship's Etruscan diadem. The thief had been gone from society for a while; his reappearance was the latest sensation.

Cam chuckled, and sat back on the seat to wait for the crowd to clear enough for him to pass. The Lily Thief—how dramatic the moniker was! And how amusing his exploits were, tweaking the noses of some of the *ton*'s most misguided collectors. If only...

If only it was not so dangerous, and destructive. Cam was usually the first to applaud daring, to laud independence, even eccentricity. Look at his own family! Eccentrics one and all. But some things were simply too important to trifle with, including objects of immense cultural heritage. Like that diadem, or the other antiquities that fell into the Lily Thief's hands. Who knew where those precious pieces had gone? What would become of them?

And then there were objects that had not yet fallen to the Lily Thief. Objects whose fate was even more vile. Averton's Artemis, for instance.

Cam's gloved hands fisted on the reins, causing the horses to toss their heads restlessly. He forced himself to relax, murmuring to them soothingly, but by damn, there was nothing that made him more furious than the Duke of "Avarice"!

That Artemis was snatched from her home on Delos, the place where she had belonged for thousands of years. She was *Greek*, and now she was merely an object of greed for an English lord. A vile man who had no care for her true worth.

"You know of Artemis?" Cam could almost hear his mother whisper so long ago, her accent as warm and musical as her Athenian home. *"Zeus' favourite child, the goddess of the moon and the hunt, the Maiden of the Silver Bow. She races through the forest in her silver chariot, always free, never the possession of any man. Once she shot an arrow into a vast city of unjust men, and the arrow pierced all of them, never ceasing in its flight until justice was served..."*

And now she was a prisoner, locked away from the Greek moonlight for ever.

What would the learned Miss Chase say about that? For Cameron was certain she had an opinion about the Duke of "Avarice" and his newest prize, his famed Alabaster Goddess. But would she tell that opinion to *him*?

The traffic snarl finally eased a bit, letting him guide the horses through on their way home. Yes, indeed. Calliope Chase was sure to have something to say about it all. And he very much looked forward to hearing it.

Chapter Two

Calliope watched in her dressing table mirror, distracted, as her maid brushed out her hair in preparation for the evening ahead. A *musicale*, featuring not the usual young and untalented misses with their harps and pianofortes, but a recreation of music that might have been performed at plays by Aeschylus and Euripides at the great festivals of ancient times. She had been very much looking forward to it, it was just the sort of thing that most fascinated her. But now her thoughts were scattered and hazy, scudding here and there like springtime clouds.

She couldn't stop thinking about Lord Westwood. He just kept popping into her mind, the vision of him outside her window, laughing and windblown and carefree.

"Pfft," she sighed impatiently, reaching for one of the small white roses on the table and tearing at the soft petals. It was ever thus when she saw Cameron de Vere. He unsettled her, made her feel so ridiculously flustered and foolish. His smiles, so mocking, made her angry and impatient. So *disordered*.

He was an impossible man, with such incorrect ideas. But why didn't he like her?

"Miss Chase!" her maid protested. "There will be no flowers left for your hair."

Calliope glanced down, startled to see that she had destroyed two roses. "Sorry, Mary," she muttered, dropping the denuded stem.

"Shall I try that new Artemis style, miss? It's ever so popular!"

"No, thank you," Calliope said, shuddering at the thought of appearing at the party with the same coiffure as everyone else. "Just my usual."

Mary pouted a bit. She had surely long thought her talents were wasted on Calliope and her conservative tastes! But Calliope could not help it. She knew what suited her, what she liked.

And she had even dared fantasise once that Cameron de Vere would "suit her". When he first arrived back in London, after a very long voyage to Italy and Greece, rumours raced through the drawing rooms of how handsome he was, how dashing, how scandalous. But that was not what fascinated her. She was interested in the fact that he was a student of art and history, as she was. She longed to hear tales of his travels, to see the beautiful antiquities he had surely brought back with him for study and preservation.

It seemed they were destined to be friends, as their fathers had once been many years ago. Sir Walter Chase and the late Earl of Westwood were both scholars and collectors, great rivals as well as friends. The earl finally pulled the trump card in their collecting race, a bride who was actually Greek, not just French as Lady Chase was. Calliope and Cameron both grew up surrounded by the glories of the ancient world, though they never met after the de Veres departed for their incessant travels when their son was small.

When he came back to London, a grown man, the earl in his own right now, Calliope listened to the whispers about him and dared to let a tiny hope grow in her heart. Could this, then, finally be a man who could understand her? Share her passions, as none of her suitors could?

Those hopes were blighted when they at last met in person, at a reception he gave at his parents' townhouse, his house now.

From her earliest childhood, Calliope remembered an antiquity she had adored, a bust of Hermes that once graced the foyer of that house. Her father had tried to buy it, but the old earl refused all offers, much to Calliope's sadness. She loved Hermes' mischievous smile, carved to be almost lifelike in the cold marble, loved his winged helmet and the swirls of his curling hair. She was so very excited the night of that reception, so looking forward to seeing Hermes again.

But he was not there! His niche was empty, as were all the others that had once held exquisite vases and goblets. Stunned, Calliope stayed there in the foyer as her father and sisters joined the gathering in the drawing room. She stood below that empty niche, staring up as if she could *make* her Hermes appear. Her plans for this reception—seeing all the lovely antiquities, meeting the new earl, talking with him about those cherished objects and perhaps forming a bond—were completely thrown awry.

Calliope did not much like having her plans upset.

"Well," she heard a voice say, deep and velvety, faintly amused "you must be the missing Miss Chase."

Calliope glanced over her shoulder to find a man standing a few feet away, a faint half-smile on his lips, as sensual as that of her lost Hermes. He was dressed most properly, in buff breeches, a dark blue coat, and a pale grey brocade waistcoat, his cravat simply tied and skewered with a cameo pin. Yet he seemed an alien creature dropped into the sumptuous foyer, a man of bronzed skin and too-long, glossy dark curls. Of flashing, familiar brown eyes.

"The Greek god," she remembered Lotty sighing. *"Oh, Calliope, he is a veritable Greek god!"*

"And you must be Lord Westwood," she answered coolly, disconcerted by her reaction to him, to that smile of his. This was not how she pictured their meeting!

"I am indeed," he said, moving closer, graceful as a cat. He stopped close to her side, so close she could smell the faint lemony scent of his cologne, feel the heat of his skin, reaching towards her enticingly. She stepped away, closer to the reassuring chill of the marble wall.

"There used to be a bust of Hermes here," she said, swallowing hard to still the sudden tremor of her voice. "A most beautiful piece."

"Most beautiful," he answered, gazing not at the niche, but at her. Steadily. "I returned it to Greece. Where it belongs."

And *that* was when she knew they could never be friends…

"Miss Chase? What do you think?"

Calliope jumped a bit in her seat, startled out of her memories by the sudden sound of Mary's voice. She glanced into the mirror, only to find that her cheeks were flushed, her eyes too bright. As if that scene in the de Vere foyer, weeks in the past now, had only just happened.

But her hair was tidy, swept back in her usual braided knot and decorated with the remaining white roses, her curls perfectly smooth.

"It's lovely, Mary. As usual," Calliope said breathlessly.

Mary nodded, satisfied, and went about finding Calliope's shawl and slippers. Calliope reached for her pearl drop earrings, trying to forget that past evening, to focus on the soirée ahead. Cameron de Vere did not matter in the least! He was merely a misguided individual. Albeit a handsome one.

As she clasped on the earrings, there was a knock at her chamber door. "The carriage is waiting, Miss Chase," the butler announced.

"Thank you," Calliope answered. She took a deep breath, and rose slowly from her seat. It was time for the show to begin.

"If Lady Russell's plumes were any higher, I fear she would launch up into the sky like some demented parrot and leave us quite without a hostess," Clio whispered, leaning close to Calliope's ear.

Calliope pressed her gloved fingertips to her lips, trying not to laugh aloud. The hostess of the *musicale* did indeed look a bit like a bizarre parrot, with towering, multi-coloured feathers spraying forth from a purple-and-green satin turban. Clio always did this; she was so very quiet that everyone believed she had nothing to add to any conversation and thus ignored her. This was a great mistake, for her sharp green eyes observed everything, and she sometimes broke forth with startling—and acerbic—insights. Comparisons to jungle parrots were quite mild for her.

"But what of Miss Pratt-Beckworth?" Calliope whispered back. "I'm afraid someone told the poor girl that orange stripes were all the rage this season and she believed them."

"Indeed. It is better than that chartreuse creation she wore to the opera last week. Perhaps the Ladies Society needs to take her under its wing?" Clio shook her head sadly.

Calliope joined her in perusing the room, turning away from the mediocre painting of a stormy sea she and Clio had been pretending to admire. An evening of ancient Greek music would surely not sound too jolly to most of the *ton*, but Lady Russell was popular, turban or no, and tended to attract around her those of a more philosophical bent. So the room was quickly filling up, people milling about between the rows of gilt chairs, chatting and sipping lemonade—and stronger beverages—before the music began. It was not a "dreadful crush" by any means. There was no danger of overheating, or fainting, or having one's train trodden on. But the colours were vivid against Lady Russell's collection of bad paintings and very good antique statuary, a swirl of pastels, blues, greens, reds—and one orange—mingling with the hum of conversation. Talk of music and history were *de rigeur* tonight, exactly what Calliope usually loved.

But she could not entirely concentrate on the classical world. She still felt so restless. Unfocused.

Next to Calliope, Clio removed her spectacles, squinting out at the crowd as she rubbed the bridge of her nose. Unlike Calliope, who usually wore Grecian white muslin because it was the simplest choice, Clio was clad in emerald-green silk embroidered with a gold-key pattern, her auburn hair bound back by a gilded bandeau. A parrot of a far more subtle sort.

"What do you think, Cal?" she asked quietly. "Is the Lily Thief among us tonight?"

Calliope stiffened. *The Lily Thief*—how could she forget? Her gaze quickly scanned the gathering, jumping lightly from one young man to the next. There were so many there, tall, short, plain, handsome. Yet not the one she sought.

Could that possibly be the cause of her strange restlessness?

Certainly not! Calliope shrugged that away. The doings of Cameron de Vere were none of her concern. Just because she had been certain a Greek evening would appeal to him...

"I don't believe so," she said.

"Then you *do* suspect his identity?" Clio asked. "You know?"

"I don't *know*," Calliope answered impatiently. "How could I? I simply have an idea."

"Yet he is not here, your suspect?"

Calliope shook her head.

"But then how...?" Clio could not say more, though. Thalia called to her from across the room, where she was closely examining the musicians' instruments—much to their chagrin. Clio wandered away, leaving Calliope alone.

There were several friends she could join—indeed, a few people she really ought to speak to. She feared she would not be good company at the moment, not with such wild thoughts of de Vere and the Lily Thief whirling through her mind. She placed her half-empty glass on the nearest table and drifted away from the crowd towards the doors of Lady Russell's conservatory.

The glassed-in space was invitingly warm, scented with the rich, green fragrance of geraniums, lavender, mint, the earthiness of the damp soil. The room was empty now, though softly lit and furnished with scattered wrought-iron settees for visitors. Calliope welcomed the silence, the moment to collect her thoughts and become her usual calm self again.

At the far end of the conservatory was a cluster of antique statues, a stone Aphrodite and her scantily clad acolytes. They watched all the horticulture with expressions of impassive, scornful beauty. They were quite stunning, and their cold perfection drew Calliope closer.

"If only I could be like you," she whispered to the disdainful Aphrodite. "So very—certain. So unchanging. No doubts or fears."

"How very dull *that* would be," Westwood said.

"Did you follow me in here?' she asked, not surprised, glancing over at him.

"On the contrary, Miss Chase," he said, giving her one of his too-charming smiles. "I was in here enjoying a quiet moment to finish my wine…" He displayed a half-empty glass. "And here you came, talking to yourself. One couldn't help but overhear."

Calliope reached behind her to plant her palms on the cold stone base, trying to hold herself upright, to maintain some dignity. His cognac-coloured eyes, so deep and opaque, seemed to see far too much. She didn't know where to look, where to turn.

"I, too, was looking for a quiet moment," she said finally. "Before the music begins."

He nodded understandingly. "Sometimes people ask for too much. The only recourse is solitude." He took a step closer, then another. Calliope shivered in her thin gown, yet he no longer watched her. He gazed up at the statue.

"You chose a fine confidante," he said. "She looks so very—knowing. As if she has seen everything in the long years of her life."

Calliope, too, glanced up at Aphrodite, her pointed, cracked white chin, the clusters of her rippling hair. She did seem knowing, mocking even. Just as Westwood himself was. "I wonder what she makes of Lady Russell's routs? How they compare to the revels of Greece."

He laughed, that rich, rough sound that touched her to her very core. "I am sure she thinks them very tame affairs indeed! For did she not come from the inner sanctum of a temple to Aphrodite, where there were, er…"

"Orgies?"

He glanced towards her, his brow arched in sudden amusement. "Miss Chase. How very shocking."

Calliope could feel her cheeks heat under his regard, but she forced the horrid blush away. A scholar did not always have time for niceties. "My father possesses an extensive library on the ancient world. I have read much of it, including John Galt's *Letters from the Levant*. And Lady Mary Wortley Montague's narratives of her travels."

"Of course. Well, after the *orgies*, she must find musical evenings a bit tedious. I'm sure she was most happy you chose to converse with her."

Calliope reached out to touch Aphrodite's sandaled foot, the stone cold through the thin kid of her glove. This *was* the best sort of confidante—the mute sort. "If it was up to you, she would surely be sent back to moulder in the ruins of her erstwhile temple, with no one to talk to at all."

"Ah, Miss Chase." He leaned even closer to murmur in her ear, his warm breath lightly stirring the curls at her temple. "Who says all the orgies have ended?"

Calliope stared up at him, captured by his voice, his breath, his gaze—everything. It was as if she was suddenly paralysed and could not move, could not turn away. All time was suspended, and there was only *him*.

He, too, seemed startled by whatever this moment was. He watched her, his lips parted, the glass in his hand perfectly still.

"Miss Chase," he murmured. "I…"

Outside their green sanctuary, the sound of music tuning up began, and it was as if the prosaic noise burst some enchantment, some spell. He shifted back, and she turned her head away, sucking in a deep breath. She felt as though she had just run a long distance, all achy and airless.

"Shall we go in?" he said, his voice taut, even deeper.

"Of course," Calliope whispered. She spun around and marched back along the flagstone walkway, smoothing her palms over her warm cheeks. He was behind her. She could hear his steps, the soft rustle of his superfine coat, but mercifully he did not offer his arm or touch her.

She wasn't sure what she would do if he *did*.

Chapter Three

Calliope slipped into the empty chair next to Clio just as the musicians finished tuning their instruments. Her throat ached as she tried to draw in a calm, normal breath, tried to still the clamorous beating of her heart.

Clio gave her a sidelong glance as she slid a handwritten programme into Calliope's hand. "Where were you, Cal?" she whispered.

"Just in the conservatory," Calliope whispered back, resisting the urge to fan herself with the thin parchment. Why did Lady Russell insist on keeping her room so warm? "Looking at the Aphrodite statue."

Clio's expression was unreadable as she glanced at her own programme, her lips pursed. "Oh? Did you suspect she would be the next victim of the dreaded Lily Thief? Spirited away into the night for nefarious purposes?"

Calliope bit her tongue to keep from laughing aloud. "Certainly not. Aphrodite is solid marble and at least six feet tall. Unless the Lily Thief is the reincarnation of Hercules."

"One never knows. He could then lift the statue up through the skylights and…" Her words trailed away as

Lord Westwood appeared in the room, leaning carelessly against a pillar at the very periphery of the audience. His gaze met Calliope's as she watched him warily, and then, slowly, audaciously, he *winked* at her.

Blast him! Calliope's stare shot back to the front of the room, her face burning. Where was the cold marble of Aphrodite when it was truly needed?

"Were you quite alone in the conservatory, Cal?" Clio murmured.

"Lord Westwood might have wandered in just as I was leaving," Calliope answered reluctantly.

"And did you two quarrel again?"

"I never *quarrel* with people!"

"Never? With anyone?"

"You and Thalia are different. You are my sisters; I'm allowed to quarrel with you in the privacy of our home. But not with people at parties. Lord Westwood and I merely discuss our artistic differences."

"Hmm," Clio said, very non-committally. "I do believe our hostess is about to say a few words."

Calliope had seldom been more grateful to anyone than she was to Lady Russell for her timely interruption. Usually she felt she could tell Clio anything, and her sister's quiet understanding could soothe any hurt or trouble. There was no use in trying to articulate what a meeting with Cameron de Vere made her feel, though. It was a tangle of temper that could never be unwound.

Calliope hated—*hated*—to be so discomposed! The solution would be never to see him again. Yet he always popped up wherever she was! If only he would go back to Greece, and carry on with his misguided, dangerous work far away from her...

Calliope folded her gloved hands tightly in her lap to

still their trembling, staring straight ahead at Lady Russell's multi-coloured plumes, now even more lopsided than before.

"Good evening, my dear friends," Lady Russell said, holding up her hands so she did indeed seem to be a parrot about to be borne aloft. "I am so glad you could join me on this very special occasion. We will hear for the first time in centuries the strains of music last heard in ancient Greece. Using a fragment of measures copied from a work by Terence, fortunately preserved during the Renaissance and hidden away in an Italian monastery, we have reproduced a 'Delphic Hymn to Apollo'. The instruments used tonight greatly resemble the lyres, aulos and citharas seen here."

She waved her hands, and two servants appeared carrying a large blackwork krater. A gasp rose in the room. This was one of Lady Russell's greatest treasures, borne out of Greece decades ago by her grandfather. She seldom displayed the vase; it was rumoured she kept it locked up in her own bedchamber where only she could view it. It was exquisitely lovely, completely intact except for some thin cracks and a missing handle. The decoration was a party scene, graceful dancers, musicians, reclining drinkers. The ancient instruments they held did indeed resemble the gleaming new ones held by the musicians seated now in Lady Russell's drawing room.

That vase would make a prime target for the Lily Thief, Calliope thought, examining its gleaming elegance.

"Now, my dear guests," Lady Russell said. "Close your eyes and imagine you are sitting in a Grecian amphitheatre thousands of years ago..."

"I'm surprised she didn't make us all wear chitons and sandals tonight," Clio muttered. "What a sight we'd make then. Especially old Lord Erring. The poor man must weigh three hundred pounds. I doubt there would be enough white muslin in London."

Calliope laughed behind her programme. She could think of *one* man who could do a short chiton justice, and it wasn't poor old Lord Erring. She peeked at Lord Westwood over the gilded edge of the parchment. He was also watching the krater, a small frown etched across his brow. An unhappy Apollo.

What could he be thinking of?

Cameron's gaze followed the krater as it was carried from the room. How lovely it was, and how tragic it was so seldom seen. Seldom loved. Like Lady Tenbray's Etruscan diadem, it had been snatched from its home and locked away for the selfish delectation of a tiny group, its true purpose long forgotten. Lost in time. That krater was made for parties and merriment.

Yet at this moment it was not the vasc's sad fate that preoccupied him. It was the carefully etched figure of a woman along one polished curve of the krater. Her slender body, draped in the fluid, graceful folds of her robe, was bent over her lyre. Dark curls, bound by a bandeau across her forehead, sprang free around her oval face. Her expression was serious, pensive, in contrast to the merrymaking dancers gambolling around her. She seemed to hear only her own music, lost in her own thoughts and feelings.

The image was ancient, and yet the artist's model could have been Calliope Chase. The slim, dark beauty, the seriousness, the single-minded purpose—it was all Calliope.

As the music, a strange, discordant, haunting tune, filled the room, he glanced from the disappearing krater to its living embodiment. Calliope had been giggling with her sister, but now she stared raptly at the musicians, her pink lips parted and dark eyes shining as if she, too, could see things that were long dead living again, bright and vibrant. When Cameron saw ancient temples and theatres on his journeys, he saw not just the broken, silent ruins they were now, but the centres of life they once were. Places where people gathered, where they talked and laughed and loved, where they created art and beauty that were the greatest heritage of flawed mortals.

Calliope Chase shared this ability to see the vibrancy of the past, the living arc of history. He could see that in her eyes as she gazed at a sculpture or vase—as she listened to lost music roused to life again. But he could never understand her despite what they shared. If she could sense what he did, sense the true value of the heritage left to them by their ancestors, how could she advocate that these objects be locked away, unseen, far from their homes?

She *was* beautiful, just like that ancient woman with her lyre. Beautiful and intelligent and spirited. But as stubborn as a wild horse in the valleys of Greece.

Seeming to sense his regard, she glanced towards him. For a fleeting moment, she lacked the protective veil she usually drew around herself. Her gaze was open, vulnerable, gleaming with unshed tears. The eerie beauty of the music had moved her, as it did him, and for an instant they were bound together by the enchantment of the past.

Then the veil fell again, and she turned away so that he saw only her black curls, the pale curve of her neck and bare shoulder. But the magic was still there, a shimmering web of connection that urged him to press his lips to that white hollow at the nape of her neck, to trail kisses along her spine, breathing in the warm scent of her. Feeling her tremble under his touch until she cried out and that maddening veil vanished for ever, and he could see her true self.

Yet what would that true self be? A beautiful muse in truth—or a gorgon of destruction? Only a madman would take on one of the Chase Muses, and Cameron wanted to hold on to his tenuous sanity for as long as he could.

Suddenly, the music, the overheated room, the strange allure of Calliope Chase were too much for that thread of sanity. The old wildness was rising up in him like a fever. He spun around and left the room, the strains of music trailing behind him. In the foyer, the servants were placing the krater on a high pedestal where it could be viewed in distant safety after the performance.

It was too high to be touched without the stepstool the servants took when they left, yet from his vantage point Cam could clearly see the lyre player. The jewels in her headband, the delicate sandal peeking from the hem of her robe. From here she was even more like Calliope Chase. Beautiful and untouchable.

"Are you trying to decide how to steal it?" Calliope asked.

Cameron glanced back to find her standing in the drawing-room doorway, watching him with those steady brown eyes. Her face was a smooth and unreadable piece of marble, yet he could feel her tense wariness.

He should not be surprised at her suspicion. They had been at odds ever since that reception at his house, when she found Hermes missing from his niche. Their arguments only grew with every meeting after that. Yet still it hurt, like the sharp pinpricks of a tiny but fatal poisoned arrow. As he listened to the ancient music, as those strange, intimate thoughts of her neck and skin bombarded his mind, he felt so bound to her. So close to discovering the mystery of her.

But she seemed to think him a thief. The connection was not there for her. Not a muse then, or a gorgon either. Just a cold judge. The cool Athena he had once thought her.

He buried that hurt, shoving it down deep and piling other emotions on top of it—carelessness, insouciance. A chill to match her own.

"Perhaps you would care to come closer, Miss Chase, and ascertain for yourself if I carry a fresh lily in my pocket," he said lightly, as if he did not care one whit for her suspicions. He stepped forward, holding out the edges of his coat so she saw the smoothness of the silk lining.

She did not move away, but her shoulders stiffened. "I am not a fool, Lord Westwood."

"Indeed not, Miss Chase. 'Foolish' is the last word anyone could use to describe you. 'Misguided', perhaps."

Something flared deep in those unreadable eyes, a flash of some black fire. But still she did not rise to his bait. She seldom did. "I am not the one so *misguided* as to turn to crime in order to prove a point! I am not the one who holds the honour of my family or the claims of scholarship so cheap. Those of us with the advantages of education and travel have a duty—"

"And who are you, Calliope Chase, to lecture *me* on duty? Or honour?" His temper, tamped down so carefully for so long, burst out in a veritable Catherine wheel of sparks. His desire for her, her beauty and stubbornness, his frustration—it would all drive him mad, in truth!

He stalked closer to her, so close he could smell the summer scent of the roses in her hair, see the delicate blue tracery of veins under her ivory skin, the throb of her life pulse at the base of her throat. That wild urge to grab her and kiss her until her chilly frostiness thawed and flowed away, leaving only her, *them*, was nigh undeniable.

She did not turn away, just stared up at him, still and wide-eyed, that pulse beating until he swore he could hear it. Hear her heartbeat. He even reached for her, his fingers aching to clasp the smooth, bare inch of skin above her kid gloves, but some last flicker of sanity made him drop his hands, back away from her.

"How can you know me so little, Miss Chase?" he said hoarsely.

Her lips parted, yet she said nothing. For a second, a whisper of doubt floated across her face. A hint of puzzlement. Then it was gone, hidden again.

"What else am I to think?" she said. "How can I know you at all?"

Cameron could bear it no longer. He spun away from her and left the house, storming past the startled footman who appeared at the front door. The night air was chilly and clammy as he strode along the quiet street, leaving the lights and music of Lady Russell's house behind him. He could not quite leave Calliope Chase behind, though. Her quiet, accusing ghost seemed to follow him as he turned the corner.

"Infernal woman," he muttered. There was only one place he could exorcise her—the most raucous, most disreputable gaming hell he knew, far from these genteel squares and solemn prosperity. The Devil's Dice. There not even Calliope Chase's ghost could survive.

As Lady Russell's front door slammed behind Lord Westwood, Calliope sagged against the base of the krater's pillar. Every ounce of willpower that held her upright, that kept her from fleeing, flooded away in a cold rush, leaving her weak and trembling. Why did she feel this way every time she saw him? Why did they always quarrel so?

Behind her, she heard the click of the drawing room door opening and closing, the rise and fall of music, the patter of slippers against the parquet floor.

"Cal?" Clio whispered. Her steady arm went around Calliope's waist, and Calliope turned into her gratefully. "What is wrong? Are you ill?"

"No, no. I just—needed some air," Calliope answered.

"So you came out here alone?"

"I was not quite alone. But then I said something wrong, as I always do with him, and he left. Just ran out the front door into the street rather than be here with me!" Calliope realised she was not making any sense. She hardly understood herself! Why did she care at all if Cameron de Vere, a reckless probable-thief, ran away from her? She didn't want to be with him, either.

Did she?

Clio glanced towards the door, frowning. "Who ran out into the street?"

"Lord Westwood, of course."

"You mean you were speaking with Lord Westwood out here, and he became so angry he just ran off…" Clio's stare shifted to the krater above their heads, and her green eyes hardened, turning oddly intent. "Oh, no, Cal. You surely did not accuse Lord Westwood of being the Lily Thief!"

Calliope covered her hot cheeks with her gloved hands, trying to blot out the memory of his anger. Of her own impulsive ridiculousness. "I—may have."

"Cal…" Clio groaned "…whatever has come over you? I could see Thalia doing such a thing. She would challenge the devil himself to a duel! Not you. Are you ill? Do you have a fever?"

"I wish I did, then I would have some excuse."

Clio shook her head. "Poor Cal. I am sure he will not speak of it to anyone, since his father and ours were such friends."

"No, he won't speak of it. Except maybe to the governors of Bedlam."

Clio laughed. "There, you see! You made a joke. All is not lost. Perhaps next time you see him you can say you were simply overcome by the power of the music."

"Or drunk on the wine," Calliope muttered. She smoothed her hair and shook out her skirts, feeling herself slowly coming back to her usual calm presence. "I wish we never had to see him again at all."

"That's not likely, is it? Our world is so very small." Clio looked again to the krater. "But tell me, Cal, what made you suspect Lord Westwood of being the Lily Thief?"

Calliope shrugged. "It seems the sort of hot-headed thing he would do, does it not? He sent his own antiquities back to Greece; perhaps he thinks others should do the same, willy-nilly. I don't know. It was just a—a feeling."

"Now I *know* you have a fever! Calliope Chase, going by a mere feeling? Never."

Calliope laughed. "Tease all you like, Clio. I know that I usually have to carefully study a thing before I make my point…"

"Study it to death," Clio muttered.

Calliope ignored her. "I like to be certain of things. But don't the exploits of the Lily Thief just seem like something he would do? A person must be clever to get in and out of such fine houses undetected. They must be knowledgeable about art and antiquities, for only the finest and most historically important pieces are taken. They have to be sure of their cause, as Lord Westwood is. And they must be very misguided. As Lord Westwood also is."

"Why, Cal," Clio said softly. "It sounds as if you admire the Lily Thief."

Calliope considered this. Admire the Lily Thief? The most dangerous of criminals, for he stole not only objects but history itself? Absurd! "I admire his taste, perhaps, but certainly not his goals. I abhor the disappearance of such treasures. You know that."

Clio nodded. "I do know how passionate you are in your own cause, sister. But pray do not let it overcome you again when it comes to Lord Westwood! We have no proof he is the thief."

"No proof yet." Behind the closed drawing room door, the strains of music faded, replaced by the ring of applause. "It seems the concert is ending. Shall we fetch Thalia and go home? It grows late."

Chapter Four

"Good morning, Miss Calliope!" Mary sang as she drew back the bedchamber curtains, letting the greyish-yellow light of late morning flood across the room.

Calliope squeezed her eyes tighter shut, resisting the urge to draw the bedclothes over her head. How could it be time to wake up? She had only just fallen asleep. The long hours of the night she had spent tossing and turning, going over and over her hasty words to Lord Westwood. The anger she saw in his eyes.

Clio was surely right. She *was* fevered. It was the only explanation for showing her hand so early. She would never catch him now.

She needed to regroup. Strategise. It would surely all come back together at the Duke of Averton's Artemis ball. The Ladies Society would see to that.

"Did you enjoy the *musicale* last night, Miss Calliope?" Mary asked, arranging a tray of chocolate and buttered rolls on the bedside table.

"Yes, thank you, Mary," Calliope answered. She propped the pillows up against the carved headboard, pushing herself upright to face the day. No one ever won a battle lolling around! "Tell me, are my sisters up yet?"

"Miss Thalia has already departed for her music lesson," Mary said, rifling through the wardrobe. "And Miss Clio is at breakfast with your father and Miss Terpsichore. She left you a note on the tray."

As Mary organised the day's attire, Calliope munched on a roll and reached for Clio's message.

Cal, it read in Clio's bold, slashing hand. *I think we need an outing to clear our heads. Shall we take Cory to see the Elgin Marbles? She loves them so much, and we can talk there without Father overhearing.*

Calliope sighed. Perhaps Father would not overhear them at the British Museum, but the rest of London would. Still, Clio was right. They needed to clear their heads after last night, and where better than among the glorious beauties of the Parthenon sculptures? Terpsichore—Cory— was a delightful girl, just turned thirteen now and wanting so much to be a young lady, and she deserved a treat after being separated from their younger sisters, who stayed in the country with their various nurses and governesses.

And surely they wouldn't run into Lord Westwood there. The man probably didn't rise until two at the earliest, and the Elgin Marbles must represent all he abhorred: treasures taken from Greece and displayed for Londoners.

"Mary, I shall need a walking dress and warm pelisse," she said, swallowing the last of her chocolate. "And my lap desk. I need to send notes to the Ladies Society."

They had battle plans to draw up.

The Chases' *de facto* second home when in town was always the British Museum. They had been brought there since earliest childhood, escorted from artefact to artefact by their parents, instilled with a love for the past by the beauty of the pieces and by their father's vivid tales. Many of their favourites—Greek vases, Egyptian sculptures, Viking helmets—were immortalised for them in their mother's sketchbooks, kept by Clio since Lady Chase's death in birthing the youngest Muse, Polyhymnia, three years ago.

But their mother had never seen the sisters' favourite room of all, the Temporary Elgin Room—which was showing signs of becoming rather more permanent. This was where they went now, after climbing up the wide stone steps and passing through the massive pillars into the sacred hush of the museum.

"May we visit the mummies after we see the Marbles?" Cory asked eagerly.

Clio laughed. "Morbid child! You only want to scare your little sisters with gruesome tales of them in your next letter. But we can visit them, if there is time."

Cory wrinkled her nose. "There won't be. You two always spend *hours* with the Marbles."

"You enjoy them, too, silly monkey, and you know it," Calliope said. "Perhaps after the Marbles and the mummies we can have an ice at the shop across the way."

Smiling happily with the promise of dead Egyptians *and* a sweet, Cory went off to sketch her favourite sculpture yet again, the head of a horse from the chariot of the Moon, his mane and jaw drooping after an exhausting journey across the heavens. Calliope and Clio strolled over to the back wall, where the frieze depicting the procession of a Panathenaic festival was mounted. It was quiet there for the moment, despite the milling crowds, tucked behind the massive carved figures of Theseus and a draped, headless goddess.

Calliope stared up at the line of young women, all of

them gracefully poised and beautifully dressed in chitons and cloaks, bearing vessels and libation bowls as offerings to the gods. They were not as well displayed as they deserved; the room was cramped and ill lit, the walls dark. But Calliope always loved to see them, to revel in their classical beauty, in the procession that never ended. And today she was glad of the dim light, for it hid the purplish circles of her sleepless night.

"I have called for a meeting of the Ladies Society tomorrow afternoon," she told Clio.

Clio's gaze did not turn from the figure of the head girl in the procession, the one that held aloft an incense stand, but her lips curved down. "So soon? We usually only convene once a week."

"This is an emergency. The Duke of Averton's ball is coming up soon. We must be prepared for whatever might happen there."

"Do you still think you-know-who plans to snatch the Alabaster Goddess away that night?"

"I'm not sure. That is why I said we need to be prepared for anything. Even nothing. The ball might pass off quite peacefully—or as peacefully as anything could at Averton's house. The sculpture will stay in place…"

"But it will *not* stay in place!" Clio hissed. Her hand tightened on the head of her furled parasol, and for a moment Calliope feared she might stab it into the air, or at an unwary passerby. "Averton is sending it off to his infernal fortress in Yorkshire, where no one will ever see it again! He is a vile, selfish man with no care for his collections. Do you think that is a better fate for poor Artemis than to fall into the hands of the Lily Thief?"

Calliope bit her lip. "It's true that he is well named the Duke of 'Avarice'. I like him no better than you, Clio. He is a very—strange man. But at least we would know where the statue is, and one day a museum or legitimate antiquarian could acquire her. If the Lily Thief took her, she would vanish utterly! We would learn nothing from her then."

"Honestly, Cal! I do love you, but sometimes you don't seem to understand." Clio stalked away, her parasol swinging, and left Calliope standing alone.

Calliope stared up again at the carved procession, swallowing hard against her pricked feelings. She and Clio were as close as two sisters could be, drawn together by their love of history, by the need to be "mothers" to their younger sisters in the wake of their own mother's death. And she knew Clio had a temper that subsided as quickly as it flared. That did not make their little quarrels any easier, though.

What was it lately, Calliope wondered, that caused such arguments? First Lord Westwood, now her sister. Her eyes itched with unshed tears, and she rubbed at them hard. When she looked up again, she feared she was hallucinating. Lord Westwood stood right beside her, staring down at her solemnly, his glossy curls brushed carelessly from the sharp, shadowed planes of his face so that he seemed one of the sculptures himself.

She blinked—and found he was still there. She drew in a steadying breath, and offered him a tentative smile. "Lord Westwood."

"Miss Chase," he answered. "I trust you are enjoying your outing?"

"Yes, very much. My sisters and I visit the museum whenever we can." She gestured towards Cory, who was still sketching the horse's head with Clio leaning over her.

"I come here often, as well," he said.

"Do you? I—I imagine it reminds you of your mother's

homeland," she said carefully, wary of yet another quarrel. How could one speak of these controversial carvings without starting a fuss, though?

But he simply answered, "Yes. Her tales when I was a child were always of gods and goddesses, and even muses."

Calliope smiled. "Perhaps then you have an understanding of how changeable a muse can be?"

He smiled in return, a quick grin that seemed to light up their dim corner of the room. "I have heard tell of such things. One day the muse will smile on you, the next she has vanished. Perhaps that is simply part of her allure."

Allure? Did he then find her—alluring? She would have thought "prickly" or "annoying" more likely adjectives he would use. But then, did she not think the same of him? Annoying, and yet strangely alluring. She shrugged away these distracting thoughts and said, "Sometimes, too, a muse forgets her manners. Says things she should not. Then she must apologise."

"Is that what this is, Miss Chase? An apology?"

Calliope sighed. "I fear so."

He clutched at his heart, staggering back as if in profound shock. "Never!"

She laughed. "I would not have you think I was not properly brought up, Lord Westwood. I should not have said those things to you last night. My sister says I should blame it on the spell of the music or on the wine, but in truth I do not know why I said them. I was just rather out of sorts."

"I suppose I have been out of sorts with you in the past as well, Miss Chase. Perhaps we can start anew. Cry pax."

"Pax, then. For now."

"For now. Come, let me show you my favourite of these friezes." He offered her his arm, and though she only laid her fingertips very lightly on his fine wool sleeve, she could feel the warmth of his skin, the strength of his coiled muscle beneath the layers of cloth. His arm tensed under her touch, as if he felt it, too. That strange, gossamer tie. "There, that wasn't too hard, was it?"

"Not at all," Calliope answered.

He smiled, and led her to the end of the marble procession, where it curved around to the next wall. There was etched the very reason for the procession—Athena, seated in profile as she observed her offerings. She did not wear her usual helmet on her curled hair, but held her aegis on her lap and bore a spear in her right hand.

"She is your favourite?" Calliope asked.

"You sound surprised."

"Perhaps I imagined you preferred one of the Lapiths and centaurs from the metope, drunkenly breaking up the party. Or Dionysus over there with his leopard skin."

He laughed. "Oh, come now, Miss Chase! I do enjoy the pleasures of life, but I am hardly a centaur. Or a Dionysus. Were we not just speaking of orgies last night? His soirées tend to end so badly, with the participants tearing each other limb from limb and devouring the raw flesh. No, indeed, cannibalism is not for me."

Calliope felt herself blushing again, an embarrassing red heat flooding up her throat to her cheeks. "I never quite imagined *cannibalism* as one of your vices, Lord Westwood. But tell me why you like Athena here so very much? She seems too rational and measured for you."

"It is exactly those qualities—her rational calm, her dignity. My life has never held much of those qualities, pulled from pillar to post with my parents, and I crave them. I can find them right here, carved in this marble."

Calliope blinked in surprise. True, the two of them had

declared peace only moments before, but she could never have expected such an instance of confidence from Cameron de Vere, of all people. A wistful longing was etched on his handsome face, driving out the careless mockery.

"She is my favourite, too," she admitted.

"And so she should be, for you are very like her."

"I, like Athena?" she said, startled. "She would never have been rude to you at a *musicale*."

"No, she would have struck me down with her spear. I must feel fortunate you wield no such weapon. Your tongue is quite sharp enough."

Before Calliope could answer, there was a sudden commotion in the doorway, disturbing the church-like hush of the room. A ripple of comment, of tension. Calliope peered around the bulk of a headless goddess to see that the Duke of Averton had just made an entrance.

He was a handsome enough man, Calliope thought, she would give him that much. Tall, slim, with flowing redgold hair that fairly shimmered in the dim light, and bright green eyes that took in everything around him in one penetrating glance. The only flaw on his handsome face was a slightly crooked nose, as if it had once been broken and not healed straight. His dramatic, almost Celtic looks were emphasised by his flamboyant way of dressing—a long cape where all the other men wore wool greatcoats, a yellow satin waistcoat, tasselled boots, and jewelled rings on his fingers. Rubies and emeralds.

The duke stood there for a moment until he was certain everyone watched him, then he swung his cloak from his shoulders in a great arc and deposited it with one of the many lackeys trailing behind him. The sweep of his arm seemed to encompass and embrace all the sculptures as if they belonged to him alone.

"Ah, the glories of Greece, the ancient spirits—we meet again," he said, softly but carryingly. Then he turned and made his way towards the metope section, his entourage hurrying behind him.

Calliope almost laughed aloud. The Duke of Averton so seldom went about in town; it was part of what made his upcoming ball the talk of the *ton*. But when he did it was more amusing than Drury Lane.

"Ridiculous toad," Lord Westwood muttered darkly. "What is the purpose of such a preening display?"

Calliope glanced up at him to find him glowering towards the duke, his long fingers curled into fists. Where was the lighthearted Apollo now? Westwood resembled no one so much as the ill-tempered Hades, lurking in his black underworld, wishing he could feed the duke limb by limb to his snarling Cerberus.

Calliope had to admit she rather liked that image herself. Of all the selfish collectors in London, all the people who hoarded their treasures while denying scholars all access, Averton was the worst. He never scrupled about where or from whom he bought his treasures, and the precious objects always disappeared into his Yorkshire fortress. But she had not known that *Westwood* had a quarrel with him. Indeed, Westwood seldom seemed to dislike anyone— except her, of course.

Yet it was more than mere dislike she saw on his face now. It was dark, unadulterated hatred, raw and primitive. And very frightening.

Calliope shivered despite the warmth of the close-packed room, and edged away from him until she felt the hard edge of a stone base against her hips. He seemed to notice her wide-eyed regard, and that glimpse of jagged emotion was quickly concealed behind his usual smile.

"I did not realise you knew the duke well," she murmured.

"Not well," Lord Westwood answered. "Certainly better than I would like. We were at Cambridge together, and the Duke of Avarice has certainly not changed much since those days. Except to grow even more vicious and brainless."

Vicious and brainless? The duke was a menace, certainly, and had a reputation for eccentricity and rapaciousness. But vicious? Calliope waited, full of anticipation, for Westwood to elaborate, but of course he did not. Their brief moment of confidence was gone, and Calliope was soon distracted by the sight of the duke drawing close to Clio.

Clio did not even seem to notice the man's theatrical entrance, or his stately parade around the room as everyone cleared a path for him. She was leaning close to a goddess sculpture, frowning as she examined it through her spectacles. The duke, much to the consternation of his followers, suddenly veered from his trail to stop at her side.

As Calliope watched, puzzled and concerned, he edged closer to Clio until his bejewelled hand brushed her arm. Clio spun around, startled, bumping into the goddess.

"Your sister should have a care around that man," Westwood muttered.

"I have no idea what he could be saying to her. We hardly know him."

"That won't stop him when it comes to ladies. Even respectable ones like your sister."

Calliope saw Clio's hand edging back and up, towards the sharp pin that skewered her silk bonnet. Clio's frozen expression and demeanour never altered, yet Calliope knew she would have no compunction about driving that pin into the duke's arm. Or more sensitive areas.

Calliope took a step forward, intending to intervene, but Lord Westwood was there before her. He strode across the room, reaching out to practically shove the duke away from Clio. As the duke smirked at him, Westwood leaned in to mutter low, harsh-sounding words that carried to Calliope's ears as only the rushing noise of a stormy sea. Clio eased away from the men, her hand dropping to her side, as everyone else in the room edged closer. A quarrel between a duke and an earl in the middle of the British Museum was not something to be seen every day! This was certain to be much talked of for days to come.

If only she and her sister were not in the midst of it, Calliope thought, perturbed. Yet even she could not help but stare at the two men, Westwood so full of barely leashed anger, Averton still smirking but growing in agitation, if the spasmodic opening and closing of his fists was any indication. It was a scene that hardly belonged in civilised London. More like those Lapiths and centaurs, wrestling in ancient stone.

Calliope shook off the strange spell that urged her just to stare at the growing fight, and hurried to Clio's side. She took her sister's arm and whispered, "We should take Cory out of here, don't you think?"

Clio shuddered, as if she too were bound by some strange, wicked enchantment and only Calliope's voice shook her out of it. "Of course," she said, and rushed over to where Cory still sat sketching. Clio overcame her protests with renewed promises of mummies, and ushered her out of the Elgin Room.

As soon as they departed, Westwood and Averton broke apart, Westwood striding from the room without a glance backward. The duke straightened his waistcoat and returned to his friends, laughing as if nothing had happened.

Puzzled, Calliope stared after Westwood. How very angry he seemed! And to think, for a moment there, when they smiled and talked together so easily, she had thought herself silly for imagining him the Lily Thief.

Now, after witnessing that strange scene with Averton, she was more convinced than ever that he had to be the thief. And she was determined to prove it. One way or another.

Chapter Five

What does it matter, de Vere? The girl is a tavern wench, free for the taking!

Cameron heard the echo of Averton's voice in his mind, the laughing, mocking words from many years ago. He saw the man's smile, that knowing smirk of smug entitlement, that only vanished when Cameron had planted his fist in Averton's face, bloodying that aristocratic nose. It had been small comfort indeed to the girl, no more than sixteen years old, who had run away sobbing, her dress torn. And it was hardly a balm to Cameron's white-hot fury, for he knew he would not be there to rescue the next girl. Or the next purloined vase or sculpture.

As Cameron's friends had dragged him away, he had been able to hear Averton mutter, "Let him go. What do you expect from the son of a Greek street mouse?"

It had taken ten men to pull Cameron out of there that day, and he had soon left the suffocating confines of Cambridge to begin his travels anew. To find himself among the "street mice" of Italy and his mother's beloved Greece. Those years of wandering had erased the memories of

Averton's words, of the feeling of his fist meeting bone and flesh. Until today.

The sight of Averton hovering so close to Clio Chase, of Calliope's helpless concern, had brought back that day in the dingy tavern, that girl in the torn dress. Brought it back with a vicious immediacy that frightened him.

Averton was known as an eccentric now, a semi-recluse who only came out to show off his ancient treasures. His Alabaster Goddess. Cameron had not even seen the man since he returned to town. Yet surely the duke's vices were only hidden now, tucked away behind his stolen antiquities. Who would dare challenge him? Who would even seek out the crimes of a rich and powerful duke?

Cameron stopped at the museum gates, roughly raking his fingers through his hair until he felt his anger ebb. Cold thought was needed now, not the impulsive fisticuffs of his youth. No Dionysus. Athena was the god he required.

He stood there for a long time, the wind catching at his hair and his coat, ignoring the flow of London life around him. He thought of his mother, of her tales of great warriors like Achilles, Ajax, Hector. Their downfalls always seemed to be their tempers, their rush to battle without planning, without forethought, driven by their passions.

"You are too much like them, my son, and it will get you into trouble one day," she would say. "There are better ways to win your fights."

As he stood there, leaning against the cold metal gates, the doors of the museum opened and Calliope and Clio Chase emerged, their younger sister between them, holding their hands. She chattered brightly, but the two older Muses seemed silent and serious, as if their thoughts were far away from the windswept courtyard. Calliope kept shooting Clio concerned little glances.

Cameron ducked behind a large stone planter as they passed by. He could not speak to Calliope now; she had been taken aback by his violent behaviour, and he could not explain it to her. He could not even explain it to himself. But he fell into step several feet behind them, watching carefully until they climbed safely into their carriage and set off for home, without being accosted by the duke or any of his minions.

If Averton thought he could get away with meddling with any of the Chases, he was very much mistaken.

"Lord Mallow. Mr Wright-Helmsley. Mr Lakesly."

Calliope stared down at her list, biting the end of her pencil as she examined each name by the light of her candle. They were certainly all men of means and some intelligence, as well as collectors of antiquities. Could they really be candidates for the Lily Thief?

She tapped her chin, running through all the men of her acquaintance who were not children or infirm. Or who showed not a speck of ingenuity, like poor Freddie Mountbank. "Lord Deering. Sir Miles Gibson. Mr Smithson."

Yet, in the end, she always came back to one name. Lord Westwood.

She had begun by being so very certain it was him! He had all the necessary qualities—intelligence, interest, plus a certain recklessness, probably born of his years in Italy and Greece. He had the courage of his convictions, as misguided as those convictions were. But now something bothered her, some irritating little voice at the back of her mind that whispered doubts. Could it be—was it—that she was growing to *like* him?

"Piffle!" Calliope cried, tossing down her pencil. Of course she did not like him. How could she? That very recklessness went against all she believed was important. That voice was surely just her inborn female weakness, lured by a smile and a pair of handsome eyes.

He was still the most likely candidate for the Lily Thief. His dark, sizzling anger towards the Duke of Averton only emphasised that fact. Westwood had an edge to him, like the fire-honed blade of a dagger that was usually hidden in its velvet sheath, but could flash out and wreak destruction in only an instant. Lady Tenbray's diadem had already fallen victim to its slice. Was the Alabaster Goddess next?

Calliope stared down at her list, and slowly reached for her pencil. *Lord Westwood*, she wrote.

Her bedchamber door creaked, warning that she was no longer alone. Calliope hastily shoved the list under a pile of books and drew her shawl tighter around her shoulders.

"Are you working, Cal?" Clio said quietly, slipping into a chair next to the desk.

"Just reading a bit before I retire. I couldn't sleep."

"Me, neither." Clio fiddled with the edge of one of Calliope's notebooks. She seemed rather pale tonight, her green eyes shadowed and large without the shield of her spectacles. Calliope had noticed she didn't eat much of her dinner, either.

Blast Averton, anyway! Why did the man have to go parading through the museum today, upsetting their outing, pestering her sister? Why did he choose Clio? And why couldn't he just stay hidden away at home with his ill-gotten Alabaster Goddess?

Yet if he did that, she wouldn't have the chance to catch the Lily Thief once and for all. The Alabaster Goddess was an alluring bait like no other. If only Clio didn't have to be caught in the middle of it all.

"What did he say to you this afternoon, Clio?" Calliope asked.

Clio stared down at the notebook. "Who?"

"Averton, of course. You have been so quiet tonight. You didn't even seem to be listening when Father read from the *Aeneid* after dinner."

Clio shrugged. "I am just tired, I think. As for Averton, he is of no importance."

"But his behaviour this afternoon—"

"Is of no consequence! He is like so many men of his exalted ilk, he thinks all women are his for the asking. No, not even asking, just taking. Like an ivory box, or an alabaster statue from a Delian temple. When he meets one who wants nothing to do with him, it only makes him more determined. But I have twice the determination he does."

That Calliope knew to be true. No one was more determined, more single-minded than Clio. Expect perhaps Lord Westwood. "I did not realise you even knew the duke."

"I don't. Or about as much as I *want* to know him. I have encountered him once or twice at galleries and shops. He seems to have taken a ridiculous fancy to me of some sort."

Calliope stared at her sister in astonishment. She always thought they were as close as two sisters could be, yet she had no idea of this "fancy". "Clio, why didn't you say something?"

"I told you, Cal, it is of no importance!" Clio cried, slapping her hand down on a pile of books. The volumes toppled, revealing the list beneath. Clio reached for it. "What is this?"

"Nothing, of course," Calliope said, trying to snatch it away.

Clio held it out of her reach. "Lord Deering, Mr Smithson, Mr Lakesly. Is this a list of your suitors?"

"Certainly not!" Calliope finally succeeded in retrieving the list. She folded it in half and stuck it inside one of the books. "I would never consider a suitor like Mr Lakesly. He gambles too much."

"I noticed Lord Westwood's name on there, too. Certainly you would not call *him* a suitor, though I did notice you two were having quite a coze at the museum."

"We were discussing Greek mythology, that is all. And this list is merely something for our Ladies Society meeting tomorrow."

"Ah, yes, the meeting. What is it really all about, Cal?"

"I told you. To make plans for Averton's ball. We must all be extra-vigilant that night, so there is no repeat of Lady Tenbray's rout. Unless…"

"Unless what?"

Calliope bit her lip. "Unless you don't want to go to the ball. It would be completely understandable, given the duke's deplorable behaviour! We don't even have to talk about this any more, if you don't care to."

Clio slumped back in her chair, arms crossed and face set in stony lines. Calliope had seen that mutinous pose since childhood. "Cal, really. It's not like the man tried to slit my throat in the middle of the Elgin Room. He merely said some—words to me. Nothing I cannot manage. Surely you know better than to treat me like a piece of fragile porcelain."

Calliope smiled reluctantly. Oh, yes, she did know that. When they were children, Thalia could always outrun them all in foot races, a veritable Atalanta. But Clio was the first to climb up trees—and leap down from them as if she had wings. The first to swim streams and scramble up peaks.

The duke didn't know what he was up against.

"Of course," Calliope agreed. "No more porcelain."

"So, tell me about this list. I would guess they are your candidates for the Lily Thief."

Calliope drew the list back out, smoothing it atop the desk. "Yes. Some of them are a bit far-fetched, I know."

"A bit? Mr Emerson couldn't tell an amphora from a horseshoe. And Lord Mallow is shockingly myopic."

"Hmph." Calliope pushed the list towards her sister. "Very well, Clio, since you're so clever, who would *you* put on the list?"

Clio pursed her lips as she examined the names. "Not Mr Hanson. He would be utterly paralysed at the thought of his mama's disapproval. And not Mr Smithson—he is far too honest. What about Lord Wilmont?"

"Oh, I hadn't thought of him! That's very good. Remember that krater he had that no one had ever seen before?" Calliope added the name to the others. Now Westwood was no longer at the bottom of the list.

"And Lord Early. Remember when he nearly fought a duel with Sir Nelson Bassington when that unfortunate man declared Early's Old Kingdom stela was clearly Amarna Period?"

"What bacon-brains the two of them are. I think they should both be on this list."

They sat there long into the night, debating the merits of each suspect. Names were added; others erased. The only one that stayed in place, black and solid, was Lord Westwood.

Chapter Six

"I call this meeting of the Ladies Artistic Society to order," Calliope announced. "Miss Clio Chase will take the minutes."

The chatter and rustling among the members slowly ceased, as they put their teacups back on tabletops and faced Calliope once again. Their pretty faces were alight with curiosity.

"What is our subject today, Calliope?" Lady Emmeline Saunders asked. "It must be something very important, since this is not our regularly scheduled day to meet."

"Oh, something truly dreadful must have happened!" moaned Lotty Price. "A murder. An illness. A poisoning!"

"Someone needs to take away that girl's novels," Clio muttered under her breath.

"Do let Calliope talk, Lotty," said Emmeline.

"Indeed there hasn't been a murder, by poisoning or any other method," Calliope said. "And I hope that we may prevent one from ever happening."

Emmeline gave her a sharp glance. "You suspect a murder is about to occur?"

"I knew it!" Lotty cried. "There is a dreadful plot afoot."

Calliope sighed. "I fear Lotty is not far wrong this time."

"Whatever do you mean?" asked Thalia. "Who is to be killed? Should we not arm ourselves?"

"No, no, I don't mean it in that way," Calliope said quickly, trying to stem the rising tide of panic she sensed among her friends. "I have no knowledge of any *human* murder being planned." *Yet.* "The plot I refer to concerns the Alabaster Goddess."

The ladies subsided back into their seats, yet there was still a distinctly unsettled feeling in the air. "So, you still think the Lily Thief intends to steal her?" Emmeline said.

"Yes, probably from the duke's masquerade ball, as we discussed at our last meeting," Calliope answered. "We must formulate a plan to prevent it."

"I am ready to defend her at any moment!" Thalia cried. She leaped up from her chair, eyes aglow as she no doubt imagined herself wielding a sword against any would-be thief. "Only give me the signal and I shall do battle."

"Thalia, dear, do sit down," Clio said, shaking her head. "We don't need Boadicea and the Iceni hordes to keep an eye on one little statue."

"You never know," Thalia said, plopping back into her seat. "What if the Lily Thief has a partner? An army?"

"Even if he had a battalion—which he does not, for how could a battalion sneak into Lady Tenbray's library?—he could not get by us," Calliope said.

"What is the plan?" asked Emmeline. "What are we to do?"

"I made up a list of anyone who might even remotely be suspected of being the Lily Thief," Calliope said, holding up her list from last night's sleepless hours. "Everyone in the *ton* received an invitation to the ball, so they are sure to be there. You will each be assigned one or two names. Your task will be to ascertain what each man's costume is, and then keep an eye on them, make certain they do not try to slip away."

"I hope you do not want me to trail Freddie Mountbank," Emmeline said. "He's already made himself a nuisance in my life!"

"Mr Mountbank is not even on the list," Calliope answered, remembering the quarrel Mountbank got into with Lord Westwood right in view of these very windows. "And we must not be at all obvious about our observations. We wouldn't want to give the wrong idea."

"Perhaps we should work in pairs," Lotty suggested. "That would make it easier for us to trail anyone who might try to slip away."

"Oh, very good idea, Lotty," Calliope said. She reached for Clio's pen and quickly made the amendments to the list. "All right, then, ladies, here are your assignments."

Thalia handed out the papers to the Society members. They bent over them eagerly, laughing and exclaiming.

"Mr Emerson!" Lotty said. "It would certainly be no hardship to watch *him*. He is so handsome."

"Nor Lord Mallow," said Emmeline. "But what of Mr Hanson? I wouldn't have thought he could plot a stroll to the end of the street, let alone a theft."

Calliope rapped her gavel against the table, bringing order back to the gathering. "Now that you have your assignments, this is how we shall proceed on the night of the ball…"

"Do you think it will work?" Emmeline asked quietly, coming up next to Calliope, who stood staring out the window.

Calliope glanced back at the others, gathered around the

pianoforte as Thalia played them a Beethoven nocturne. "I don't know," she answered honestly. "The ball is sure to be a dreadful crush. How can we watch just a few people? People in disguise, no less. Yet I can't just stand here and let that statue be stolen without at least trying to do something."

"I know. We all care so very much, we want to save them all. Make sure they are all properly looked after and studied," Emmeline said. "There are only five of us, though. But we will do our very best to save the Alabaster Goddess, Calliope, never fear. She never had more devoted acolytes, even in her temple in Greece."

They were quiet for a moment, listening to Thalia's beautiful music, watching the traffic on the street below. Emmeline leaned closer to murmur, "Did you assign yourself Lord Westwood to watch, Calliope?"

Calliope looked to her, startled. "I thought Clio could do that."

"Oh, no, I really think it should be you. The two of you are always circling each other like wary hawks anyway."

"We do not!" Calliope cried. The others glanced towards them, and she hastily lowered her voice. "I do not *circle* Lord Westwood, Emmeline. Whatever do you mean?"

"Oh, Calliope dear. Everyone sees it. Whenever you are in a room together smoke practically billows. My brother even tells me you are in the books at his club."

"The books! People are *wagering* on me?" Calliope felt a sick, sour pang deep in her stomach, an ache of sinking embarrassment. "How dare they! What—what are they saying?"

"Are you sure you want to know?" Emmeline said, her eyes full of concern. "I should never have brought it up."

"Of course you should. If people are talking about me, I want to know."

"Well, half of them wager you will be married by the end of the Season. The other half wagers one of you will be in Newgate for murdering the other."

Calliope pressed her hand against her stomach. "What does your brother wager?"

"Calliope! He would never do that to a friend."

"Come now, Emmeline. He is a man. Wagering seems to be in their very veins. They cannot help themselves."

"Well, if he does he doesn't tell me about it. I was much too angry with him for not putting a stop to it."

"People are always full of such tittle-tattle. They must be desperate for gossip indeed to make up Banbury tales about such a dullard as me! Where do they find that kind of nonsense?"

Emmeline eyed her closely. "It is not entirely made of whole cloth, you know. You and Lord Westwood snap and quarrel every time you meet, or if you don't speak you glower at each other from across the room. What are people to think?"

Calliope now felt ill in earnest. She sat down heavily in the nearest chair, wrapping her arms tightly around herself.

"Calliope, dear, you really didn't know?" Emmeline asked.

"I have been so engrossed in my own studies," Calliope murmured. "Worrying about the Lily Thief. I suppose I was just oblivious. My mother always did say that living in my own little world would get me into trouble one day."

"It is hardly trouble," Emmeline said. "It's not as if you were caught kissing him! You're right, it's just silly gossip from people who have nothing better to do. It will soon be gone, replaced by something else and forgotten. My brother says they also wager on whether or not Prinny is the Lily Thief, so you see how serious their betting books are!"

Calliope laughed reluctantly. The vision of the prince, fat, red-faced and encased in a creaking corset climbing in windows and picking locks was so absurd it nearly drove out those sick feelings.

"Just ignore them, Calliope," Emmeline said. "Their ignorance deserves no response. In the meantime, why don't we go for a stroll in the park? It is too fine a day to stay indoors, and we all need time to think over our plan for the ball."

"I would like some fresh air," Calliope admitted.

"Excellent! I will tell the others."

Calliope caught Emmeline's arm as she turned away, staying her for a moment. "Emmeline, what do *you* think of Lord Westwood and me?"

Emmeline gave her a gentle smile. "How can I say? I'm just an unmarried lady like you, with Freddie Mountbank my most serious suitor. I know little of romance. You say you dislike him. Very well. But are you *sure* that's all there is to the matter? Maybe you should ask Lotty what would happen in one of her novels."

Calliope watched Emmeline walk away, more confused than ever. Antiquities she knew about; they could be studied, classified. Men never could. Especially Westwood.

Maybe she really should take up reading horrid novels, and not so much Aristotle and Thucydides. It was obvious that her powers of observation, her knowledge of modern life, of what passed for romance, was sadly lacking. Would *The Prince's Tragic Secret* fill that gap? Surely everything could be learned, with the right tools. Herodotus was no help here. Perhaps *By An Anonymous Lady* could be.

Calliope pushed herself up from her chair and made her

way resolutely towards her friends, who were gathering up their shawls and bonnets in preparation for their walk.

"Lotty," she called. "Could I speak to you for a moment?"

As it was a fair day, cool and dry after the morning's rains ceased, Hyde Park was quite crowded. Riders cantered along Rotten Row, stopping by the barriers to chat with each other, or with friends who rolled past in their open carriages, showing off their newest fashions. Nannies in starched caps and cloaks watched their charges as they sailed tiny boats on the calm, murky waters of the Serpentine or rolled hoops along the gravel pathways.

Calliope smiled as she watched them, their laughing faces turned like smooth-petaled flowers to the sun. She remembered days when her own nannies, or sometimes even her mother, would bring her and her sisters here. They would pretend the Serpentine was the Mediterranean, the trees and rocks the grove of Apollo's Oracle at Delphi, and they were Muses in truth. The fount of all art and wisdom.

Suddenly, she felt a sharp pang, a yearning for that innocence that seemed so far away now. The days when she thought any dream was possible, that she could attain any goal she longed for. Even the wisdom of the Muses. Now—well, now she wondered if somehow their father had cursed them by giving them their names!

Yes, she did wish now for childhood's blissful oblivion. For as she walked the pathways now, she imagined every person, every polite greeting, concealed smirking laughter. *There is Calliope Chase! You know, the one who is pursuing Lord Westwood.*

Emmeline linked arms with her, smiling in her cheerfully determined way. "There now! Is the fresh air not bracing?"

"Yes, indeed," Calliope answered. She could be

cheerful, too. After all, Emmeline was quite right. Any rumours about herself and Westwood were merely the product of idle minds and sure to pass soon. Especially if she gave them no more heat for their scandal broth.

"Oh, look! There is Mr Smithson. Was he not on your list of suspects?" Emmeline said.

"Hmm," Calliope said, watching the gentleman in question as he strolled past, politely doffing his hat. "I will admit he is a bit of a long shot. He's so slender, one can hardly envision him pulling himself through a window."

"And not Lord Deering over there! They do say the dowager Lady Deering is such a dragon. She would incinerate her poor son if he disgraced the family name."

Calliope laughed. "Quite so. But I think we must examine every possibility, no matter how farfetched."

"Yes. Appearances can be so deceiving."

Calliope nodded. Surely no one knew that better than herself, after all her studies of the ancient world. The ancient Greeks had such an appearance now of rationality, of cool, pale beauty. Yet in truth their statues and temples, which were so slavishly recreated now in Adam foyers and white muslin gowns, had been brightly painted. Their ideas of order, their great philosophy and tragedy, concealed a love for madness, ecstasy, the paranormal that was distinctly *irrational*.

People were like that, too, in modern London or ancient Athens and Sparta. Layer upon layer, concealing whatever truly lurked at their core. A mystery.

And the greatest mystery of all was strolling into her view. Lord Westwood himself, of course. No wonder people gossiped about the two of them, Calliope mused, for he so often appeared just where she happened to be!

Unlike when he stormed out of the British Museum, all

Hadean fire and anger, he was back to sunny Apollonian charm. A small parcel was tucked under his arm, half-hidden by the folds of his greatcoat. He smiled at the people he passed, pausing to kiss giggling ladies' hands or chat with friends.

Layer upon layer. Where was the real man?

Calliope's steps froze as he moved nearer, bringing Emmeline up short.

"What is amiss?" Her eyes widened as she followed Calliope's gaze. "Oh. The man himself, I see. And so handsome today!"

"Perhaps we should turn back," Calliope said. "We've left the others so far behind…."

"Nonsense!" Emmeline said, continuing on their path so resolutely that Calliope had no choice but to follow. "It would only fuel the gossip if you were seen avoiding Lord Westwood, Calliope. We must be polite and say hello."

When Lord Westwood saw them, Calliope thought she saw a frown between his eyes, a whisper of solemnity. But whatever it was quickly vanished, replaced by a sunny smile, a flourishing bow.

"Miss Chase, Lady Emmeline," he greeted. "A lovely day for a walk, is it not?"

"Indeed it is. We were just discussing our costumes for the Duke of Averton's ball, weren't we, Calliope?" Emmeline arched her brow at Calliope so she had no choice but to nod, even though they had been discussing no such thing. "A Grecian theme, of course, so we were hoping some of the park's statuary would inspire us."

Westwood's lips tightened. "I am sure that whatever you two ladies wear you will be the loveliest in the room."

Emmeline laughed. "Miss Chase might. She looks like a Greek statue all the time!"

He glanced at Calliope, but she could read nothing in his eyes. They were as opaque as the waters of the Serpentine. "That she does."

"Oh!" Emmeline suddenly exclaimed, detaching her arm from Calliope's. "I see someone over there I absolutely must speak to. Excuse me for a moment, Calliope. Lord Westwood."

What on earth was her friend up to? Calliope tried to catch Emmeline's hand, but she was off, dashing away like the traitor she was. Leaving Calliope alone with Lord Westwood.

Well, not entirely *alone*, of course. Not with half of London around them, and Clio and the rest of the Ladies Society not far away. Yet it felt as if they were alone. Calliope felt dizzy, her vision blurring until she saw only him, not the crowds.

She clasped her hands together, reminding herself of her purpose. Cause no scenes; act perfectly calm and normal. No scandal broth.

"So, you plan to attend Averton's ball?" he said. His voice was as unreadable as his face.

"Of course. Isn't everybody? I do long to see the Artemis again. Unless…"

"Unless?"

Calliope remembered how murderous he looked at the museum, when the duke edged so close to Clio. "Unless there is a reason it might be unsafe."

"And you think I might know that reason?"

"Perhaps. Better than some. And I would hope, Lord Westwood, that you would tell me if you know of any reason why my sister or I should not go. I know that you and I are not exactly friends…"

At last there was a glimmer of emotion, a tiny smile like

the sun peeking through grey clouds. "Are we not, Miss Chase? Friends, that is."

"I—well," Calliope said, flustered. "Perhaps we *could* be."

"If we were not both such stubborn spirits?"

Calliope took a deep breath. Infernal man! Just when she thought she had him figured out, he fooled her. Revealed another layer. He lured her from her resolve to be cool and polite. "Lord Westwood, tell me! *Is* there a reason Clio and I should not go to the ball?" A reason such as that he was planning to snatch the Alabaster Goddess while everyone else danced in oblivion?

He shrugged. "As you say, everyone will be there. Averton won't try anything in front of the entire *ton*. You should be safe enough. As long as you don't do anything rash."

"Rash?" Calliope cried. "What do you think I would do? Rashness is much more your style than mine, Lord Westwood. I merely plan to examine the statue, have a glass of the duke's fine champagne, and depart. In peace."

"Of course. As befits a Muse," he said. His smile was now that maddening full-fledged grin.

Cool and polite! Calliope berated herself. "Will you be there?"

"Oh, I wouldn't miss it. I always enjoy fine—champagne."

"Are you sure that's wise?" Calliope asked doubtfully.

"I never overly imbibe, Miss Chase. Not in polite company."

She had to resist the urge to childishly stamp her half-boot on the walkway. "You know what I mean."

"Oh, yes. You are remembering our scene in the Elgin Room. I do so often seem to show myself at my worst to you, Miss Chase, and then I have to apologise. It's true that I have no liking for the duke, or he for me. But I do know better than to cause a scene at a ball, though I've given you little cause to trust my word on that."

"I don't believe you would cause a scene at a ball," Calliope admitted, bemused. "It doesn't seem your way to turn a grand ballroom into Gentleman Jackson's parlour."

"Just a museum, eh? Well, you and your sister may attend the ball in peace. We'll all be masked, won't we? Averton himself won't even know I'm there. Neither will you." He bowed to her again, the paper of the parcel under his arm rustling. "Good day, Miss Chase. Enjoy the rest of your walk."

Calliope turned to watch him leave, to watch him greet Clio and the others, then hurry on his way, obviously a man with an errand on this fine afternoon.

Oh, but you are wrong, Lord Westwood, she thought. *For I will certainly know if you're there.*

Cameron leaned back in his chair, surveying his library. At least nominally it was "his" library, but ever since he returned from his travels to take his place as Earl of Westwood it felt like his father's library. His father's house. Everywhere Cameron looked he saw his father's furniture and carpets, the niches where his collections once resided. Their country seat was one thing; the furnishings there were old family pieces and not personal. This townhouse had been his father's, the place where he indulged his love of Greece, his passion for collecting.

But that was about to change. For too long now Cameron had lived with someone else's life. It was time to begin his own. One piece at a time.

He stood up and reached for the parcel on the desk. It was small, flat, carefully wrapped in brown paper. Cameron carried it over to the carved fireplace mantel, gazing up at the painting that hung there. It was one his father had acquired on his own Grand Tour many decades ago, an indifferently executed murky scene of Egyptian pyramids. Cameron had never much liked it, even though it hung there through his childhood. The perspective was all wrong, the colours dim, conveying no sense of the desert brightness, the mystery of the Egyptians.

He reached up and unhooked it from the picture rail, lifting it down at last. It left a pale square on the topaz-coloured silk wallpaper. Then he tore the wrapping from his new package and lifted the pyramid's replacement into its place.

Cameron stepped back to survey the image. He had seen it in that gallery window and knew it was meant to be his. Meant to hang just here, where he could see it every day as he worked at the desk.

It was an image of Athena, standing framed between the shining white pillars of her temple. The sacred fire burned behind her, outlining her slim figure in pleated white silk. One arm was outstretched, holding her grey owl, while the other hand rested on the shield propped beside her. Her golden helmet rested at her feet, and her hair, a river of glossy raven-black, flowed over her shoulders.

Her beautiful face, a pale oval set with wide-spaced grey eyes, was solemn and knowing. She was beautiful, oh so serious, set on her own course come what may.

She was, in short, Calliope Chase. Or very, very like her.

Cameron smiled up at her, not sure she would appreciate such levity. The *real* Calliope Chase certainly wouldn't appreciate knowing he had her double hanging in his library. Yet he could never have passed up this painting. It was so lovely, just as her modern counterpart was.

Why was he always so drawn to her, when their

meetings so often ended in strife or farce? He should stay far away from her, from all her family. The Chases were trouble he did not need, now most of all. He had important work to do, and couldn't afford to be distracted by a beautiful Athena with fire in her eyes. Fire just waiting to scorch him if he got too close.

Yet he never could stay away. Every time he saw her he was pulled to her side, he couldn't help himself. Lately it seemed quarrelling with her was more fun than making love to another woman would be. The thought of quarrelling *and* making love with Calliope was enough to make his head explode! Her fiery nature would surely take hold even in bed, and her pale skin and black hair against his sheets…

"Blast," Cameron cursed, spinning away from Athena's knowing gaze. The chances of Calliope Chase ending up naked in his bed were slim to none. She wouldn't even come near his house once she found out what he had done with his father's antiquities. Not even Aphrodite could help him with that Muse, no matter how much he desired her.

But he *could* keep her safe from Averton. Safe from her own folly concerning the Lily Thief, perhaps. She said she would be at Averton's ball. Well, so would he. And he would not let his Athena out of his sight.

Chapter Seven

"Oh, Miss Calliope! You look lovely," Mary said, putting the last touches on the hem of Calliope's costume.

From her perch atop a stool, Calliope surveyed herself in the mirror. "You don't think it's too much?"

"Not at all. It'll be the finest costume there."

Calliope *did* rather like it. She had worked closely with the modiste to replicate an etching her father owned of the Athena statue that had once stood in the Parthenon. The soft, thin white muslin was pleated and fastened at the shoulders with gold brooches, bound at the waist with gold cord. The sandals were also gold, and she wore antique bracelets and earrings that had once belonged to her mother. Waiting for her by the bedchamber door was a helmet, shield and spear.

Calliope fiddled with the cord, unaccountably nervous. Ordinarily she would be excited about a Grecian masquerade. Yet this was no ordinary ball.

What if the Lily Thief *did* appear? It was one thing to talk about catching criminals in her own drawing room, quite another to face a real, living thief bent on taking the

Alabaster Goddess. What if she could not stop him? What if Artemis did indeed vanish, never to be seen again?

Don't be faint-hearted! she told herself sternly. *You can't fail. This is much too important.*

She glanced towards the spear and shield. The weapons, pasteboard and glitter, would never hold against steel. But they reminded her of her purpose. She had to be Athena, and protect those in her charge from harm.

No matter who the Lily Thief was. No matter what might happen.

"Shall we finish your hair now, Miss Calliope?" Mary asked, putting away her needle and thread.

"Yes, thank you," Calliope said. She stepped down from the stool and went to her dressing table, where gold ribbons and combs waited. "We don't have much time left, the carriage is ordered for nine."

Mary had just started brushing out Calliope's hair, twisting the strands into long ringlets, when there was a quick knock at the door and Clio appeared.

"Oh!" Calliope gasped. She hadn't yet seen her sister's costume, or even known its theme, and the effect was dazzling. Dazzling and strange.

Clio was not an Olympian goddess, all pale perfection, or even the Muse of their namesakes. She was instead Medusa. Her gown was of vivid green silk, the sleeves like long wings, split and folded back from her shoulders. The green robe revealed glimpses of a gold-tissue underdress, embroidered with tiny green glass beads that winked and sparkled. An emerald kirtle, a rare medieval piece that had also been their mother's, caught the rich fabric around her waist.

But it was her headdress that was truly extraordinary—a twisting, tangled nest of gold-tissue snakes, their scales overlaid with greenish, brassy embroidery. More of the

beads formed their eyes, and they seemed to gleam malevo-
lently, as if the snakes were alive. Only a few long tendrils
of Clio's own auburn hair escaped, revealing that here was
a real woman and not a vengeful Gorgon.

"What do you think?" Clio asked, twirling around in all
her frightening splendour.

"I think there will be no one else like you at the party,"
Calliope answered, bedazzled by those snake eyes.
"Wherever did you find such a creation?"

"Madame Sophie made the gown," Clio answered, adjusting her sleeves. "And I did the headdress myself. Cory
helped me, you know she's quite the budding artist. They
look quite fearsome, don't they?"

"Terribly," Calliope said with a shiver. A frown from
Mary made her sit still again, facing the mirror so her hair
could be finished. "I doubt the duke will attempt to harass
you with *those* staring at him."

Clio laughed. "I'm not afraid of the duke!" She brand-
ished her staff, a tall gold-and-green, ribbon-wrapped pole
topped with yet another snake, a puffed-out cobra. "I shall
just turn him to stone."

"If only it was always that easy to deal with men," Calliope
muttered. "What are Thalia and Father dressed up as?"

"Thalia is Euridice, and Father is Socrates, of course."

"With his cup of hemlock?"

"Hmm, yes," Clio said. She stepped up to Calliope's
mirror to make sure her snakes were straight. "Or rather a
cup of lemonade with sprigs of mint floating in it. We
shall have to make sure he doesn't bore everyone in sight
at the ball, for he is already wandering around the drawing
room, declaiming to the furniture."

"If there is no youth to corrupt, a hassock will do. Is that
a direct quote from Socrates as he drank the hemlock? If

not, it should be." Calliope watched as Mary finished the curls and ribbons and carefully lowered the helmet over her creation. "How do I look, Clio?"

"Perfect, as always. Surely there can be no finer Athena," Clio answered. "Too bad Cory's pet owl died last year, it would have made an excellent prop."

"A prop that would fly off and get lost in the chandeliers. I told Cory a barn owl didn't want to be a domestic pet. This one here will do very well." Calliope hoisted up her shield to display the enameled owl on its face. "Shall we go?"

Athena, after all, was never late to battle.

The Duke of Averton's grand townhouse, Acropolis House, was lit up like the Colossus of Rhodes set down in the middle of London. Even from their place far back in the long line of carriages, Calliope was dazzled by the amber glow.

Acropolis House was not the usual among aristocratic townhouses. No plain white stone, no mellow red brick set in tidy rows for the duke. No. Acropolis House was like a vestige of medieval London, a fortress of solid, dark rock, turreted and many-chimneyed, the shutters of all its mullion windows thrown open to let out all that candlelight. It was set back in its own small garden, surrounded by high walls. The iron-tipped gates were usually closed and chained tight, but tonight they were open to admit the flood of carriages, the gawking curiosity seekers. As their own conveyance entered the gates, Calliope peered out to find leering gargoyles staring back at her. They topped the gates and lined the walls, discouraging the curious.

Calliope shivered and drew back into her shawl.

"You'd think the duke was Charlemagne," Thalia

sniffed. "And look at that obelisk over in the corner of the garden! Twenty feet high at least."

"Terribly pretentious," their father agreed. But Calliope thought she saw a tiny glint of envy in his eyes as he peered at the towering obelisk. "I wonder where he obtained it? The hieroglyphs are quite fine."

"Somewhere he had no business being, I'm sure," Clio said tartly.

Calliope did not answer, for their carriage at last rolled to a halt before the massive, iron-bound front doors and it was their turn to alight at last. The duke's footmen, clad in chitons and sandals for the evening, hurried forward to assist them. Calliope held tight to her spear and shield as she followed Clio's glittering green train into the very lair of the Duke of "Avarice".

The foyer, where they surrendered their cloaks to more classically garbed servants, was a soaring, octagonal space with black-and-white marble floors and walls inlaid with dark wood panels. Tall, wrought-iron candelabras provided the only light, flickering on tightly closed doors, on Minoan frescoes of slim bull jumpers, on suits of armour, and bristling maces and swords, and on two massive Assyrian lions guarding one of the doors, as if ancient Persia rested just beyond that portal.

"My, what eclectic tastes our host has," Clio muttered, as they joined the line of revellers making their way up the twisting staircase towards the ballroom.

"To say the least," Calliope answered, eyeing the treasures tucked in niches. Sculptures, vases and amphorae, even Byzantine icons. They were all impressive pieces, beautifully restored, elegantly displayed. Yet Calliope noticed something odd about them all. Unlike her father's own antiquities, which depicted the gods and Muses, wise scholars, merry parties, the finest of human endeavours, these pieces all had some element of violence about them. Battles, fights, sacrifices. Even the icons depicted martyred saints: Catherine and her wheel, Sebastian and his arrows, and St George driving his sword into the dragon.

Calliope turned away from them, disquieted.

"Or perhaps not so eclectic as all that," Clio said quietly. "Murder and bloodletting are sadly a part of every civilisation. The duke seems bent on reminding us of that fact."

"Indeed he does," Calliope said.

The higher up they went, the more the noise of the party grew, a hum that expanded into a vast river of sound as they spilled into the ballroom. Calliope usually had little use for balls and routs that earned the coveted society accolade of "dreadful crush". There was little real conversation possible amid such clamour, just overheated air and far too much noise. Tonight, though, she welcomed the crowd. It seemed a bright haven of normalcy in this very bizarre house.

The ballroom was not as eerie as the foyer and staircase, but was merely a large, bright space with white walls and gleaming parquet floor. The domed ceiling was painted with an elaborate fresco of an Olympian banquet where, thankfully, no one was killing anyone else. Around the walls were more ancient frescoes, no doubt snatched from some Italian villa, scenes of cosy domestic life. Marble statues were interspersed with the paintings of scantily clad nymphs, satyrs, gods and goddesses that echoed the costumes of the revellers.

As Calliope expected, there was no one quite like Clio among the crowds who were forming a dance set or milling among the statues, sipping champagne and nibbling on lobster patties and mushroom tarts—rather *un*Grecian hors-d'oeuvres, Calliope thought. There was a Minotaur, hulking and hairy, flirting with Ariadne and her ball of twine; several Achilles and Hectors; some giggling Aphrodites with various versions of Ares and Cupid. Their father soon joined a cluster of other philosophers in the corner to argue about how man could examine his reasons to be in harmony with the cosmos, and Thalia was swept into the dance by an Orpheus, their respective lyres deposited with a footman.

Calliope tucked her spear under her arm and reached for a glass of champagne from a passing servant's tray. It was the finest quality, of course, a rich, tart golden liquid that blended well with the exotic setting, the swirl of music and laughter. For a moment, she felt transported from London, from everyday life, and lifted into some phantasmagoric fantasy world where reality was gone, vanished amid the sea of masks.

She held the glass up to the light, wondering if the enchanting little bubbles concealed some hallucinogenic elixir, some Shakespearean "love in idleness".

"Is something amiss with the champagne, Miss Chase?" an amused voice asked.

Calliope whirled around to find their host standing behind her, a smile on his lips. He was as unusual as his house, dressed as Dionysus with a leopard skin over his chiton, his long, red-gold hair loose over his shoulders. Dionysus, the god of wine and revels. Of maddened followers who tore their victims limb from limb in their bloodlust.

Or stole treasures that did not belong to them.

Calliope stiffened under his intense regard. "Not at all, your Grace. The champagne is excellent, as are your arrangements. Your house is most—extraordinary."

"That is high praise, indeed, coming from a Chase. For you are all experts in art and antiquities, are you not?"

"I would not say *expert*. We are all students, in our own ways."

"And is *your* interest strategic warfare?" he said, gesturing towards her Athena shield.

"Or perhaps olives," she said flippantly.

"Ah, yes. For it was Athena who ordered olive trees planted on the hills of her Acropolis. The very foundations of her followers' prosperity."

"Until rapacious thieves ordered them dug up, in search of buried treasure. Now glorious Athens is just a dusty little town. Or so I hear."

The duke laughed. "My dear Miss Chase, how kind of you to defend a people you do not even know! Yet if your so-called rapacious thieves did not dig on the Acropolis, think what would be lost to us. So much beauty and learning. Is it better that these things should moulder in the ground, disintegrating in the care of people who have no regard for them?"

Calliope grudgingly had to admit that he said nothing she herself had not argued. But his smug tone of voice, his patronising smile, made her want to quarrel with him. To slap that expression off his face. She shrugged, and drained her glass of champagne.

"Come, Miss Chase, let me show you one of the treasures that would have been lost for ever," he said, taking the empty glass from her hand.

"The Alabaster Goddess?" Calliope asked.

"Are you trying to gain an early glimpse of the masterpiece of my collection? No, she will be revealed later. At the right moment."

"One last chance for her to be admired before she is shut away?"

"She is hardly a cloistered nun. She is being taken to a

place where she can be properly protected, unlike other antiquities in our fair city of late," he said. He took her arm in a light clasp, steering her around the edges of the crowd, calling jovial greetings to the noisy guests.

Calliope had to grit her teeth to resist the urge to pull away, to run from him. When Lord Westwood took her arm just so at the British Museum, it was warm and easy. The duke's touch felt like a cold shackle. She pinched her lips together and walked faster as they moved past candelabra and frescoes.

He led her to the end of the room, where tall glass doors led on to a dark terrace. The crowd was lighter here, the air cooler. Calliope almost feared he meant to lead her out on to that terrace, away from the noise and light, and then—then what? Push her off to the stone walkway far below?

Calliope almost laughed aloud at her own foolishness. He did not know of her plans to keep his Alabaster Goddess safe, to prevent her from being stolen like all those other lost pieces. To keep her from disappearing into Yorkshire, too, if she could help it at all. He did not know of her great aversion to him, of how frightened she was by his behaviour towards Clio at the museum. He couldn't know any of that.

Nevertheless, when his clasp on her arm loosened, she wasted no time in moving away.

"What do you think of this, Miss Chase?" he asked, gesturing towards another statue displayed between the glass doors.

Calliope forced herself to turn her wary attention from him, to take in a deep breath as she examined the piece. Art, as it always did, slowly worked its magic on her senses. The duke and the crowd subsided to a whisper.

It was beautiful, of course, as everything in the duke's collection was. Beautiful in a strange, violent way. This depicted not a battle or brawl, but Daphne at the very moment she was transformed into a tree by her father Peneus, after Daphne called on him to stave off Apollo's unwanted advances. She was running, her body twisted as she looked frantically back over her shoulder. Her legs and upflung arms were turning to branches. Her long hair flowed back like a river.

"What do you think, Miss Chase?" the duke asked.

"It is lovely. The sense of movement, the way the flesh of her arms transforms just here into wood—extraordinary."

"Exactly so. It is a Roman copy, of course, but still its great beauty is evident. And her face looks rather like your sister, does it not?"

Startled, Calliope stared up at the duke, shaken from the reverie the Daphne invoked. He did not watch her; all his attention was on Daphne's cold, carved face. He reached out one fingertip to touch her cheek, sliding a slow caress along the angle of her cheekbone.

It *did* look like Clio, Calliope had to admit. With that hair, and the sharp, thin angles of the face and bare shoulders. And that made his rapt attention all the more chilling.

"She has the same independent spirit, you see," the duke murmured. "But in the end, one way or another, she will belong to the gods. Run though she will."

Calliope's throat was dry, and she knew she had leave, to find Clio. She slowly backed away from the duke, who still seemed lost in his own world. His own fantasies of poor Daphne.

"Excuse me," Calliope murmured. "I see someone I must speak to."

She hurried back into the midst of the crowd. There seemed to be even more people packed into the ballroom than before, knots and skeins of humanity laughing and drinking, oblivious to any nightmarish quality this house might hold. Yet there was no Clio anywhere, not even a glimpse of her shimmering green silk. Thalia was still dancing, as she probably would do all night. Their father was nowhere to be seen. Probably he had gone off to the card room with his philosopher friends, continuing their discussion over a hand of *vingt-et-un*. She did see Emmeline, dressed as the Delphic Oracle, talking with one of her assigned possible thieves. She gave Calliope a small nod and smile. All was going as planned in that corner.

If only Calliope could say the same! She so hated when her plans went awry. But then, what could she expect from someone like the Duke of Averton? He was a strange one, to say the least, and there could be no predicting what might happen in his house. She had to stay calm. Remember her goal—to protect the Alabaster Goddess.

And surely in such a vast crowd Clio was safe enough. The duke couldn't hurt her here, couldn't turn her into a tree. He probably couldn't even find her. Still, Calliope would feel better if she could talk to her sister, warn her to be on her guard.

Hoisting her shield higher, Calliope threaded her way through the ballroom. Several friends greeted her, but there was no Clio.

"Where *are* you?" she muttered, straining on tiptoe to see over the crowd.

"I am here, grey-eyed Athena," a voice said, slightly muffled, close to her shoulder.

Half-fearing the duke had crept up on her again,

Calliope turned. There was no Dionysus, though. It was Hermes, in his winged sandals and helmet, muscled arms bare in a white chiton. The visor of the helmet was down, but Calliope recognised the unruly dark curls that escaped its golden confines. She also recognized Hermes' scent, the clean smell of citrus soap with something darker, more complex and alluring, underneath, like cinnamon or sunshine, salty sea air.

A strange sense of relief flowed over her. She was not alone in this crowd any longer! "My eyes are brown, Lord Westwood," she said, resisting the urge to hug him, to cling to those strong arms. It was surely just another measure of how bizarre this evening had become that she was so very happy to see him.

"Always so logical," he said, pushing back the visor to reveal his smile. "How did you know it was me?"

"Your soap."

"My *soap?*"

Calliope shook her head. "It's not important. Have you by any chance seen my sister?"

"Miss Clio? I don't think so, but then anything is possible in this crowd. What is her costume?"

"Oh, you couldn't miss her. She is Medusa, in a green-and-gold gown, with snakes on her headdress."

"Snakes? Never say she brought reptiles in here! But then, I would not really be surprised. You Chases always do things in your own fashion."

Calliope had to smile in spite of herself. "I dare say Clio might have brought real snakes in, if she didn't know how I dislike them. But she only has cloth snakes. With green glass eyes."

"I fear I've seen no Medusas at all. Is something amiss?"

"No, I just need to tell her something. I'm sure I will see her later. Unfortunately, I can glimpse little in this crowd."

"Did I not predict it would be a 'dreadful crush'?"

"You did. Surely what every hostess most desires."

"Or host." His expression hardened. "I saw you were speaking to Mr Dionysus."

"For a moment," Calliope answered cautiously. "He was showing me a statue of Daphne." The memory of the duke's hand on that marble cheek made her feel cold all over again, and she trembled.

"Are you cold?" Lord Westwood asked solicitously.

"Just a bit. Though I'm not sure how I could be, it's so overheated in here!"

"Such a mausoleum as this place can never be truly warm. Come, Miss Chase, dance with me. I think the exercise will do us both good."

Calliope glanced towards the dance floor to find a new set forming. Emmeline was there with Mr Smithson, as was Thalia with the strange Minotaur. Still no Clio. Yet surely a dance *would* do her good. Take her whirling thoughts from the duke and his bizarre actions, the Alabaster Goddess and the Lily Thief, and warm her chilled bones. Westwood was right—this place was a mausoleum. Only music and dancing could bring it to life again.

Especially a dance with Lord Westwood, for surely no one could be more alive than he was. His cognac eyes, the golden glow of his smooth skin, fairly breathed youth and vitality and strength. After the duke's brief, cold touch, the breath of his corruption, she craved that heat. Yearned for it. Even if it *was* with Westwood.

But he was not Westwood tonight. He was Hermes. She

was Athena. And this was not an ordinary London ball, but an Olympian revel. For the length of one dance, anyway.

"Thank you, Lord Westwood," she said. "I would be happy to dance with you."

Chapter Eight

Clio glanced back over her shoulder as she tiptoed along the narrow corridor. Empty. No one followed her. Probably they did not even notice her absence from the ballroom, not in such a crush.

Perfect.

It was silent here, unlike the roar of music and shallow conversation. So quiet it was almost like a cave, lit only by a few lamps built to resemble flickering torches. The shifting light touched the dark, linenfold panelled walls, the low, carved ceiling and the gilt-framed paintings, making them glitter and waver as if alive.

Clio paused to slip off her heeled shoes, peering closer at one of those paintings. It was a modern creation, an oil of the Minotaur in his labyrinth. A great, hulking, hairy beast with red, fiery eyes, lurking in a dark space much like this corridor. All around him were smoking torches, stone walls painted with strange, glowing symbols.

The duke must feel some affinity for this particular myth, Clio thought as she studied the scene. She had seen several depictions of it tonight, in stone as well as paint, and in that one odd costume in the ballroom. Well, she knew that everyone had within them a dark heart—a Minotaur. And that sometimes a person had to venture into the labyrinth to confront that side of themselves. To confront the truth.

Was that not what she was doing now?

Clio turned her back on the Minotaur and hurried on stocking feet to the end of the corridor where there was a small, winding staircase, a miniature of the grand one soaring up from the foyer. The duke was being very cagey about the Alabaster Goddess's whereabouts tonight. But his servants were not all so secretive. Clio was able to persuade a footman to tell her where Artemis waited.

At the top of the stairs ran a long gallery, almost the entire length of the front of the house. Its bank of windows, uncovered, looked out at the front garden and the street beyond, the open gates that still admitted latecomers to the ball.

The gallery was dotted with tall, heavy iron branches of candles, half of them unlit. No doubt waiting for the "grand reveal" after supper, when they would spring to life as if by magic. Right now the light was dim, falling only in shimmering bars on some of the treasures displayed there, leaving others in darkness.

Clio found herself holding her breath as she crept along the gallery, peering right and left at all the wonders jumbled together. Her father's friends were all great collectors and loved to show off their prizes, so she had grown up surrounded by beautiful antiquities. But this—this was something else entirely. A cabinet of curiosities such as she had never seen before.

The gallery almost resembled a warehouse, it was so thick with objects. Ancient stone kouros, stiff and precise, their empty eyes staring back at her. An Egyptian sarcophagus, with traces of bright paint still clinging to its surface. Bronze warriors; marble gods finer than any she had ever seen; cases full of gold Etruscan jewellery, lapis scarabs, tiny cat mummies in gold coffins, jewelled perfume bottles. Steles propped against the walls. Shelves of vases, kraters, and amphorae. All jumbled together, just to serve one man's vanity.

Clio frowned as she remembered the duke at the British Museum, pressing so close to her she was overcome by his spicy cologne. That strange light in his green eyes...

She shook her head, her satin snakes trembling. She couldn't think about him now. She didn't want to think about him *ever*.

At the end of the gallery, alone in a pool of candlelight, was an object covered in a drape of black satin. Only a bit of the separate coral-coloured marble stand was visible. Clio approached it carefully, half-expecting some sort of trap, some alarm. All was silent, except for the whining hum of the wind past the windows. She reached out and carefully lifted an edge of the drape, peering beneath.

"Oh," she sighed. It was really *her*. The Alabaster Goddess. Artemis in her solitary glory.

The statue was not large. It was easily dwarfed by many of the more elaborate creations in the gallery. But she was so perfectly beautiful, so graceful and elegant, that Clio could understand why she had become such a sensation.

Carved of an alabaster so white it seemed to glisten, almost silver, like a first snowfall, she stood poised with her bow raised, an arrow set to fly. Her pleated tunic flowed over the curves of her slender body as if caught in a breeze, ending at mid-thigh to reveal strong legs, tensed to run. Her sandals, the little, ribbon-laced shoes every lady had copied this Season, still bore bits of gold leaf, as did the bandeau that held back her curled hair. A crescent moon was attached to the band, proclaiming her to truly be the Goddess of the Moon. Her gaze was focused intently on her prey, not heeding mortal adulation.

Clio stared up at her, enthralled, as she imagined the Delian temple where this goddess once resided, where she once received her worship from true acolytes of the moon. Not just *ton* ladies with their "Artemis" coiffures.

"How beautiful you are," she whispered. "And how sad."

Clio reached out to gently touch Artemis' foot in a gesture of silent sympathy. As she did, she noticed that the goddess stood on a modern wooden base, a thick block of mahogany. A thin crack ran along its centre. She leaned closer, trying to see if that crack was a fault or deliberate. It seemed such a strange perch for a beautiful goddess.

"Ah, Miss Chase. Clio. I see you have discovered the whereabouts of my treasure," a voice said, quiet, gloating.

Clio ducked away from Artemis, spinning around to find the duke standing halfway along the gallery, watching her intently.

Even in the dim light, his eyes gleamed like the snakes in her headdress. He smiled at her gently, shrugging his leopard pelt back from his shoulders. Clio thought of that scene from the *Bacchae*, where Agave, under the evil influence of Dionysus, tore her son Pentheus to death, thinking him a lion. Then she carried his severed head back home, still delusional.

He moved closer, light and silent, as if he was a leopard himself. "She is beautiful, is she not?" he said, still so quiet. So soft. "I knew you would be drawn to her, as I was. She is quite—irresistible, in her mystery."

Clio edged back against the goddess. She had indeed

found Artemis irresistible. So much so that she let her guard down, and that was not like her. As the duke came closer, she reached behind her, her fingers just touching Artemis' cold sandal. She slid her touch down, finding that strange crack in the wooden base…

Calliope took her place in the set with Lord Westwood just as the music began, a quick, lively tune that made her toes tap in her sandals. She was not Terpsichore, the Muse of Dance, but she did love the movement, the rhythm of the music, the swirl of other dancers around her as they formed the patterns and picture of the dance. Usually, it could lift her out of herself for a few moments, send her into a world where there was only the music.

Tonight, though, the beat was not soothing, not transporting. There was so much in her mind—Clio's disappearance, the plan to protect the Alabaster Goddess. And, not least, the fact that her partner for this dance was Cameron de Vere.

Never would she have imagined they would be dancing together at a ball, quite as if they were—well, as if they were friends! No one was shouting or scowling or throwing things. He stood across from her in the line, smiling at her. Calliope smiled back, and all at once she felt the old magic of the dance come upon her once more. A new energy surged through her veins, lifting her up on to her toes as she stepped forward to meet him. Their hands touched, and they turned to move down the line, swirling among the other dancers in a quick, intricate rhythm.

He was a good dancer, light and graceful, but then she did not expect anything less after seeing him drive his phaeton. No jerky, ham-handed movements for him. He moved his horses—and his dance partners—with gentle persuasion, and made it all look easy. Calliope barely felt she had to move, so easily did he twirl her from step to step, spinning her until she vowed her feet left the floor and she was flying!

As they were separated by the design of the dance, Emmeline leaned close and quickly whispered, "Is he the thief, then, Calliope?"

As Calliope turned in a circle, she glanced towards Lord Westwood. Surely he had the fleetness to climb in a window, the strength to carry off the Alabaster Goddess. But… "I don't know. What of Mr Smithson?"

Emmeline shrugged, and was spun away into another circle. Westwood caught Calliope's hand again, drawing her near as they turned in allemande. "You are a fine dancer, Miss Chase," he said, not even out of breath.

Calliope, though, felt suddenly winded as she stared up into his eyes. "I could say the same about you," she answered. "Where did you learn such grace on your travels?"

"Oh, I am a man of *many* talents, Miss Chase," he said, catching her against him for a moment, so very close she could feel the damp heat of his body, the tense strength of him. Their bare arms brushed together, and his skin was so smooth and warm. "You have no idea."

No. But Calliope thought maybe she was beginning to have an inkling.

They slid back into their own places in line as the music ended, and Calliope ducked into a curtsy. Her heart fairly pounded, as if she had run a mile rather than just danced an easy reel. It was as if the earth shifted under her feet, an earth she had always been so certain of, and it had not yet re-formed. Perhaps it never would.

Westwood held out his hand to help her rise. She slid her fingers into his clasp, still warm from the exercise, and let him lead her from the dance floor. The ballroom was even more crowded than before, newcomers swelling the throng until it reached the very walls, spilled out on to the terrace and the grand staircase. Yet Calliope could hardly hear them for the humming in her head, could not feel their press, their clamour. She only felt his hand on hers.

"Did I tell you that you look quite lovely tonight, Miss Chase?" he said, so close to her ear that his breath stirred the loose curls at her temple.

Calliope shivered. "I—thank you, Lord Westwood. You did say I made a plausible Athena."

"I would not be surprised if you started a battle right here, leading us to victory over the Spartans."

Calliope laughed nervously. "I don't think I could, Lord Westwood. Even Athena could not find her way through this crush. And I can't find my sister. A poor goddess I would make."

"Perhaps she went to peek at Artemis," he suggested.

"But the Alabaster Goddess is hidden! The duke said she would only be revealed later."

"Ah, yes, you did speak to our notorious host. Or should I say inadequate host, for I have not seen the man since I arrived."

"Yes, I did see him, but not in quite a while. It was over there, by that Daphne…" Calliope paused, remembering the duke's caress on Daphne's cold cheek. "I would feel better if I could find Clio."

"I'll help you search," he said. "This is a big house, to be sure, but she has to be in it somewhere."

"Oh, would you? I don't want to take you away from the dancing. Or the cards."

"A mystery is always more fun than a game of loo, Miss Chase. And 'find the missing muse' should be more interesting than a dance—unless it's with Athena, of course." His tone was light, but Calliope thought she sensed disquiet in his eyes, in the tight line of his jaw. It made her own uncertainties stronger. She was very glad of his help, not at all sure she wouldn't get lost in this vast mausoleum on her own.

Plus, if he was with her he couldn't steal the Alabaster Goddess!

"Thank you, Lord Westwood," she said. "I appreciate your assistance."

"What!" he cried in mock astonishment. "Calliope Chase *appreciates* something about me? Never say so."

"I won't let it become a habit," she said. "And I will appreciate it even more if you actually find Clio."

"Then let us waste no time. I'm sure two instances of gratitude in one evening would be quite more than I could bear."

He steered her adroitly through the crowd, deftly side-stepping human barriers and looming statues until they found their way out the ballroom doors. There were also people in the small foyer at the head of the grand staircase, and in the card room and antechambers, but none of them were Medusa. Clio was also not in the ladies' withdrawing room, which Calliope checked without Westwood's assistance. Nor had anyone seen her.

Even more unsettling was the fact that no one had seen the duke for quite a while, despite the persistent buzz of gossip about him.

Calliope rejoined Westwood in the foyer, removing her helmet from her aching head. The headache forming behind her eyes was pounding and persistent, insisting that something was amiss.

"Did you say you know where the Alabaster Goddess is?" she asked Westwood.

"I've heard a rumour."

"I think we should look there, then. Unless you think Averton has a secret dungeon somewhere?"

He gave a humorless laugh. "I wouldn't put it past him. But we'll ask Artemis first."

He turned on his heel and set off from the foyer, finding a deserted narrow corridor. Calliope followed closely as they left the light and noise of the party behind. The duke's house was even more of a crypt than she had first thought, or perhaps more of a catacomb. An odd, twisting series of corridors and chambers. Unlike the Roman version, though, these catacombs held not human bones and ashes, but the bones of civilisations. A jumble of marble and basalt and mosaic, all piled together with no concern for the various cultures and time periods.

Calliope thought of her father's own collections, so carefully labelled and placed neatly in glass cases. How much each piece meant to him, and his daughters, so much more than a mere beautiful object. More than something to possess and show off, they meant knowledge, a link to lives long turned to dust. A way to understand the past, or at least begin to understand it.

It was obvious from this opulent clutter, this clash of Minoan, Archaic, Classical, Egyptian, Assyrian, Roman, Celtic, that the duke did not see them in this way. Their true value was lost to him.

As was surely the true value of her sister. Wherever Clio was.

At that unsettling thought, Calliope stumbled, reaching out to catch herself on a stone Egyptian lioness.

"Ouch!" she gasped.

Westwood spun around, and her hand landed not on the

cold statue but on warm, shifting flesh. His arm went about her waist, holding her steady.

Only she felt even dizzier now, pressed so close to him, than she had falling towards the ground.

"Are you all right?" he asked, his voice rough.

"Yes," Calliope answered slowly. "I must have stumbled on something."

"Easy enough to do in this warehouse."

Calliope eased herself away from him, leaning back against the kore until she could catch her breath. "I was just thinking it was a catacomb."

"A most apt description, Miss Chase. A pile of dead things, hidden away from the daylight."

Calliope studied the reclining Egyptian lioness, her muscles coiled and massive paws flexed, as if she would rise at any moment. How fierce she looked! How unhappy at being caged. Would she try to run away like Daphne? "Do you think they are dead?"

"Let us say sleeping, rather," he said. He ran his hand over the lioness's head, and Calliope felt as if she, too, could experience that touch. Rough and chipped, battered by the centuries, but still holding the imprint of her creator. "They can't breathe in such a gloomy place."

"Exactly. With no one to see their true worth." She paused, turning her gaze from the lion's obsidian stare to meet Westwood's. In this shadowed light his eyes were just as dark, just as mysterious. "But we don't agree on what their worth is."

"Do we not?" His hand tightened on the rippled stone. "I think we agree on far more than is first apparent, Miss Chase."

If only that were true! Calliope remembered her long-ago daydreams, that he could be the one man who under-stood her, who shared her dreams. Those hopes were shattered when she had found the Hermes statue gone. "How so, Lord Westwood?"

Instead of answering her, of telling her what she found she yearned to hear—how they could find common ground and be friends at long last—he just smiled. "Do you not think that sometimes you could call me Cameron? I still look around for my father when I hear 'Lord Westwood'. Everyone I met in Italy and Greece called me Cameron. Or Cam."

"I'm not sure." *Cameron.* How informal it sounded. How—inviting.

"Come, now! No one can hear us but our friend the lioness. And she won't tell. She loves to keep secrets."

Indeed, there did seem to be a satisfied gleam in those obsidian eyes, as if she relished having one more secret to add to the vast store she had collected in her long lifetime. Like the Aphrodite statue in the conservatory, and her remembered orgies. "Do you not think she holds enough secrets as it is? I'm sure this house has more than its share."

"No doubt you are right. Nasty secrets. But, while she is the duke's captive, she is *our* friend. She wants us to be in accord."

"Very well. I suppose I could call you Cameron, when only inanimate objects can hear us."

"Shh!" He put his hands over the carved ears. "She's not inanimate, remember? Only sleeping."

"When will she awaken? When she's taken from this place at last?"

"When she sees the sunlight again?"

Calliope remembered Lady Tenbray's Etruscan diadem, far from the sun of its homeland. "And will you be the one to liberate her—Cameron?"

He gave the lioness a considering glance. "Do you think

I'm strong enough, Miss Chase? Calliope?" he said teasingly, flexing his—admittedly impressive—arm muscles.

"Are you a hidden Herakles, then?"

"Ah, fair doubter! But as I am not Herakles, merely Hermes, I fear your doubts are justified. She would be much too heavy for me, winged sandals or not. One day, though, someone will free her from this place. Free all these things."

"Send them back where they came from?"

He shrugged. "Some place where they can be safe. I don't think anything can be safe here."

"Oh!" Calliope cried, sharply reminded of their errand. "Clio."

"Yes, we should move on. If you're quite recovered?"

"Of course."

He held out his arm and she accepted his support, letting him lead her down yet another corridor towards a narrow, winding staircase. She couldn't help but glance back at the lioness, so silent and stolid. Except for that gleam in her eye. That secret glint.

Had she seen Clio tonight?

"The Alabaster Goddess is up here," Cameron said, clambering up the steps.

Calliope looked up. She saw only a stout wooden door, somewhat ajar, and yet more shadows. More darkness. "How do you know?"

"Still so suspicious! And after I asked you to call me by my given name and everything."

"The duke said her location was a secret."

"I have my ways. Come, do you want to see or not, Athena?"

She glanced again towards that doorway. It could conceal anything at all. She half-expected a many-headed Hydra to leap out at them, snarling and slavering. "I want to see."

"Follow me, then. I may not be Herakles, but I promise I'll keep you safe."

He held out his hand, beckoning, and Calliope reached out and clasped it. Held fast to it, like a lifeline in a stormy sea. They climbed up the last of the stairs together, and slowly pushed open the silent door.

That entrance led not to Hades or a vast black river, but to a long, narrow gallery. Tall windows let in moonlight, which mingled with the glow of sputtering candles and cast a soft illumination on more antiquities, more statues and stele and sarcophaguses. Calliope blinked at the light, at first unable to see anything beyond the rich clutter.

Next to her, Cameron stiffened, and a curse escaped his lips in a soft, ominous explosion.

"What…?" Calliope began. Then she saw it.

The Alabaster Goddess, the pride of the Duke of Averton's collection, lay on her back on the floor, her bow aimed upward at the inlaid ceiling. Her gleaming alabaster body seemed intact, tangled with a length of black satin, but her wooden base was split and splintered.

And, at her feet, lay the duke himself.

Cameron dashed forward, Calliope close on his winged heels. The duke's bright hair was darkened with a spreading stain, his eyes closed, his skin as pale as Artemis's. His leopard skin was torn beneath him, and the coppery tang of blood was thick in the cool, dusty air.

"Is he dead?" Calliope whispered.

Cameron knelt down beside the prone duke, reaching out to touch the base of his bare neck. "Not yet. I can feel a pulse, but it's thin. See here," he said, gesturing to a gash along the duke's forehead. "It matches Artemis's elbow."

Calliope glanced at the goddess and saw that her arm was indeed stained, a dried smear of rust-coloured blood.

"He must have been here for quite a while, for it to dry like that. Do you think the statue fell on him?"

"Maybe her base broke as he was gloating over her. It would seem to be poetic justice of a sort."

"Or maybe…" Calliope leaned closer, pushing down her nausea. "No. It can't be."

"What?"

Shivering, Calliope gestured towards the duke's hand.

Clutched in his fist was a ripped swathe of green-and-gold silk. Half-hidden underneath his arm was a scattering of sparkling green beads.

"What is this?" Cameron asked tightly.

"Clio," Calliope groaned. "These are from her costume."

Cameron straightened, peering intently into the shadows. But Calliope could not be so cautious. She shot to her feet, dashing behind the marble plinth Artemis fell from. "Clio!" she cried. "Where are you? Clio!"

"Shh!" Cameron caught her hand, pulling her up short. "What if whoever did this is still lurking about? What if your sister…?"

"No! Clio couldn't do this, or if she did I'm certain she had a good reason. You were at the British Museum, you saw. We have to find her."

"And we will. But there are no other bloodstains on the floor, are there? She isn't hurt. We need to get help for the duke first. He's still alive."

Calliope looked at the man sprawled on the floor. He was still pale, yet she could see that he stirred. "You would help him? Even though you loathe him?"

He laughed wryly. "I may be tempted to leave him to die, done in by his famous Alabaster Goddess. But I would loathe *myself* even more than him if I did that. I will run back to the ballroom and fetch help, if you think you can stand guard for a few moments. I promise I won't be gone long."

Calliope sucked in a deep breath. "Yes. I can stay."

He studied her closely, as if to gauge her words. Finally, he nodded. "Of course you can, you're Athena. When you hear people approaching, hide behind that sarcophagus. It would never do for anyone to know that we were alone here!"

Calliope thought of the rumours Emmeline told her about, the gossip about Westwood and her, the bets. How upset she had been by that! Now it hardly seemed to matter. "Not at all," she said tartly. "Then you would be forced to offer for me."

"A dreadful fate." He caught her close in a swift, hard embrace, pressing a kiss to her brow. "I won't be gone long."

Calliope watched as he dashed back down the gallery and out the door, as fleet as any true Hermes. When he was gone, the silence gathered around her, thick and muffling, like a true London fog. The shadows also seemed to gather closer, creeping around as if they sensed doom, fed off it.

Calliope wrapped her arms tightly around herself to ward off the cold, to hold Cameron's embrace close. Some of her stout, Athena-ish courage was ebbing away without him to hold it up, but she knew she had to hold strong. Hold on to her composure. So much depended on it.

Steeling her nerves, she knelt by the duke and reached for his hand. Swallowing a sudden bitter rush of bile, she loosened his fingers to pull free the strip of telltale silk. His grip tightened, as if reluctant to relinquish his prize, but she tugged it loose. Then she set to gathering the green beads, the scattered snake eyes.

As she picked up the last one, she noticed the broken wooden base of the statue. Even though it was splintered, it appeared to not be broken so much as split along an opening. Calliope peered closer, and saw that a tiny, torn bit of paper protruded.

"How odd," she whispered. A secret compartment? To conceal—what?

Before she could investigate further, she heard the echo of voices and footsteps coming up the staircase. Gripping the silk and beads, she ducked back behind the sarcophagus, lying on her side. It was even darker, colder back there, the floor hard on her hip. She pressed herself tight against the carved, painted hieroglyphs, holding her breath as she listened to the shouts and exclamations.

She had never felt more alone in her life.

Chapter Nine

Calliope crept up the stairs of her own home, her steps weary and slow. The house was quiet; no one expected them back for hours yet, and the servants were tucked away in their own quarters. Her father and Thalia were still at the duke's, her father to observe all the excitement, and Thalia to look for Clio. Calliope had come home to see if Clio had returned, but she had also come for herself. For the comfort only her own surroundings, her own well-ordered space, could provide.

After such a long, bizarre night, there was something in her that craved the sight of *home*.

"Perhaps I will write my own horrid novel," she muttered, catching up a warm shawl draped over a chair and wrapping it tightly around her bare shoulders. Wouldn't Lotty enjoy *that*?

She would call it *The Duke's Revenge*. Or perhaps *Vengeance against the Duke*. Yes, that would be more fitting.

Calliope shuddered. It would be a very long time before she forgot the way Averton looked, so pale except for that crimson gash. The confused clamour when the crowd burst into the gallery and carried him away, while she huddled behind that sarcophagus.

"Oh, Clio," she whispered. "What has happened to you?"

And what had happened between Calliope and Westwood—or Cameron? For those brief moments it seemed they were allies, united in one cause. *That* was something she never thought to see happen. Never thought to be so affected by. But his humour, his kindness, the quick, cool way he dealt with the duke…

No. She couldn't think about that right now. It was too baffling, too dizzying. And she had to find her sister. Find out what had happened in that gallery.

There was a thin line of light beneath Clio's bedchamber door, flickering and shifting like flames. Calliope didn't even knock, just gently eased that door open, holding her breath as she paused on the threshold.

And Clio *was* there. After all the searching through the labyrinth of the duke's house, she was in her own chamber. The room was in darkness except for the blazing fire in the grate. Clio knelt beside the flames, wrapped in a white dressing gown, her auburn hair loose down her back. The red-orange glow reflected on her spectacles as she fed scraps of green silk into the fire. Her face was utterly expressionless.

"Clio," Calliope called softly.

Clio jumped, spinning around on her heels, crouched for battle. "Calliope!" she cried. "Don't creep up on me like that. I nearly had apoplexy."

"I'm sorry. I wasn't even sure you were here or just a mirage." Calliope slowly moved to Clio's side, hands held out as if in surrender. She knelt beside her sister, studying the torn remains of the Medusa costume.

"What happened tonight, Clio?" she said. She reached

out to touch the ragged edge of a gold sleeve. It was stiff
with smeared blood.

Clio stared straight ahead into the flames. "What do you
mean?"

"Lord Westwood and I found him. The duke. He held
a scrap of this very silk in his hand."

"Was he—dead?"

"No, not yet."

"And what did he say?"

"He was unconscious. Lord Westwood went for help,
and when they carried the duke away I came home. To find
you." Calliope couldn't hold herself back any longer. She
seized Clio, drawing her into a fierce hug. "Oh, Clio, I was
so frightened!"

Clio held herself stiff for a second, then she gave a
great shudder and fell against Calliope's shoulder, clutching at her. "Cal! It was—was horrible."

"My dear, you're safe now. We're all safe, I promise,"
Calliope said, struggling to convince herself as much as
Clio. "Why were you alone with him?"

"I was a fool." Clio drew away, wiping her cheeks
with her dressing gown sleeve. "I wanted to see the Alabaster Goddess without all the gawking crowds. I got one
of the footmen to tell me where she was, and I slipped
away for a peek. But he must have been watching me.
He followed me to that gallery, and just as I saw the
goddess, he…"

"He what?"

Clio shook her head fiercely. "I don't want to say. I
swear he did not get very far, though, Cal. He just kissed
me. Artemis saved me."

Calliope gave her a gentle smile. "You mean she leaped
off her pedestal and coshed him on the head?"

Clio laughed. It was a strained, choked sound, but very welcome none the less. "Well, she did need a bit of mortal help. I grabbed her by that wooden base and swung it towards him. I just wanted to scare him, make him back away. I thought for a moment he was dead, and I didn't mean to kill him! I wouldn't *mind* if he was dead, but I don't want his blood on my hands." She held out one trembling hand, palm up. "Of course, it's there anyway."

"No!" Calliope took that hand, holding it tightly. "He is alive, and will probably recover, more is the pity. Hopefully his wits will be scrambled enough, though, that he won't hurt anyone else."

"And so he won't talk of this to anyone?"

"Why would he? Being known as an attacker of women—and being so weak a woman could attack *him* and bring him low—could hardly be what he wants."

"For a normal man, perhaps. I don't have any idea what a man likc thc dukc could want."

They sat there for a long moment, clinging together, the only sound the snap of the fire. Outside the window the sky was beginning to lighten, a lark twittering in the trees. London coming to life again for one more day.

"There is something I want to show you, Cal," Clio said. She rose unsteadily to her feet and crossed the room to her bed. From under the mattress she drew a folded, rumpled sheet of paper, covered with a spidery black hand. One corner was ripped away.

"What is it?" Calliope asked, as Clio came back to the fireside.

"I'm not sure. When I—well, when Artemis made contact with the duke's head, the wooden base split and this paper came out."

"Oh, yes!" Calliope exclaimed, remembering that

broken base, the tiny scrap of parchment. "I saw that it was broken. But what is the paper?"

"A list of some sort." Clio smoothed it out on the hearth rug. "I can't quite figure it out, though."

Calliope leaned closer, peering at the tiny words. "Cicero. The Grey Dove. The Sicilian. The Purple Hyacinth. Nicknames?"

"Perhaps. There are ten of them in all, and they're each so strange. I wouldn't have thought the duke was one for secret societies, he seems so solitary, but after seeing his Gothic horror of a house I know anything is possible. What could they be nicknames for?"

Calliope ran her finger down the baffling list. "Charlemagne. The Golden Falcon. I have no idea. It must be very important, though, to hide it in the Alabaster Goddess like that."

"Important—and illegal, no doubt. Immoral goes without saying."

Illegal contacts? "Oh, Clio," Calliope breathed. "Do you suppose the duke is the Lily Thief?"

Cameron splashed cold water over his face, hoping the icy drops would finally wake him from the bizarre dream this whole evening had been. It didn't work, though. When he opened his eyes, slicking back the wet strands of his hair, his rumpled Hermes costume was still tossed over a chair. And he faced himself—eyes bloodshot, face strained—in the mirror.

In his travels to Greece, he and his companions were chased by bandits and rebels on occasion, running through the rocky hills with bullets zinging at their heels. That was surely dangerous, but also exhilarating. Life-affirming. After a narrow escape, they would drink and sing around campfires until dawn, when they would run again.

Why, then, did he feel so weary *now?* So—old, almost. Was it because bandits and bullets had a strange honesty to them? Unlike whatever it was that had happened at Averton's house tonight. *That* had a murky, corrupt air, a mystery he didn't care for.

Would he have left Averton to die, if Calliope Chase's solemn dark eyes weren't watching every move he made? He was surely tempted to, and the world would be better off. In the end he couldn't. He couldn't even let a man he detested die. Because of some weakness in himself? Because he didn't want to seem less than good, seem the flawed man he was, in front of Calliope?

Cameron shook his head, droplets flying, and reached for his dressing gown. He drew the warm brocade over his chilled nakedness, watching as the first light of day, grey-pink and fuzzy, peeked through the window. Now wasn't the time for agonised self-examination. He had never been good at that, anyway; he was no poet. Now was the time for action, for solving whatever it was that had happened last night. Someone had tried to kill the duke. Perhaps they had tried to steal the Alabaster Goddess.

The duke himself was always up to something. What did he want with Clio Chase? What did she have to do with last night's events? What was going on with the Chase sisters?

Cameron went to the window, staring down at the street coming to life for the day. Milkmaids and greengrocers hurried along on their errands; a maid scrubbed at the white steps next door. She yawned as she worked, but Cameron, despite his long night, was suddenly wide awake, his earlier weariness quite forgotten.

Something had happened between him and Calliope

Chase, as they made their way through those dark, moul-dering rooms. He had always thought her beautiful, of course. And sharply intelligent, sure of herself as only a truly clever person could be. But also stubborn and mad-dening!

Last night there was a new connection, a new spark that intrigued him, drew him in, even as his suspicions grew. He *would* find out what was going on with her, with his deep Athena who hid so much. It wouldn't be easy to gain her trust, her confidence. In fact, he had the feeling it would be the most difficult thing he would ever do. But something was afoot in the small world of antiquities col-lecting, in the world of the Chases, and he was determined to find out what that was.

Even if he had to spend time—lots of time—with Calliope Chase. Not that that would be a terrible hardship, he thought, remembering the way her Athena costume clung to her bare, white shoulders. But someone had to solve this riddle, before more artefacts like the Alabaster Goddess fell victim to its spell.

And he was just the person to do it.

Chapter Ten

Calliope tied the ribbons of her bonnet into a jaunty bow just under her left ear and examined herself in the mirror. Did it really look well on her? It was her favourite hat, chip straw trimmed with blue satin ribbons. But was it too—plain?

And why was she so very worried about hats, when there were so many other more important things to be concerned about? Clio and the duke, the Lily Thief, the Ladies Society.

She knew why the sudden preoccupation with fashion, though, and she didn't like it. She was worried because she was to wear the bonnet to go driving in the park with Lord Westwood.

Cameron.

With a frustrated sigh, Calliope pulled off the bonnet, completely disarranging Mary's careful construction of curls, and reached for the note that had arrived over breakfast.

"Miss Chase, would you do me the honour of driving with me in the park this afternoon? I think that there, sur-rounded by hundreds of people, would be the only place where we could really talk. If you are agreeable, I will call for you at half past three."

If she was agreeable. The gossips would certainly have a splendid time to see them together in Cameron's yellow phaeton. Calliope idly wondered what the betting books would say. She didn't *want* to be talked about, especially now, when she needed to move as unobtrusively as possible in society to discover the Lily Thief. Was it the duke? Westwood? The mysterious Minotaur from the ball? Or someone she had not yet even thought of? She could never find out if everyone was watching her, laughing behind their fans.

But she did need to talk to Westwood. He was the only one, besides Clio and the duke, who knew what really had happened in that dark gallery. Perhaps he could help her now, but she had to be careful. It was possible he was also her biggest obstacle.

Calliope pushed the bonnet aside and reached for the newspapers from that morning. The more disreputable ones were full of news from the masquerade ball, nearly all erroneous. One had the duke's head split completely open, blood and brains spilling forth on to the floor. It didn't mention how the man still lived after such carnage. One had jewels stolen from the house, ladies fainting, masked thieves brandishing pistols. Or swords. Or daggers.

None of the accounts were as bad as her own memories, though. Of the smell of coppery blood mingling with dust. Of that scrap of silk in the duke's hand.

Calliope shuddered and shoved the papers away. Under all those black headlines, under her own confused memories, there lurked the truth. And she intended to find it. Surely it was the only way to stop the Lily Thief, and keep Clio safe.

Yet she couldn't do it alone. She was no Athena. She

needed as many allies as she could find. Her sisters, the Ladies Society. Cameron de Vere?

Could she trust him? Last night he had been like a rock amid chaos and confusion. But that did not erase his old attitudes towards antiquities, their old quarrels.

There was only one way to find out. Talk to the man. Try to see beneath his light, charming façade to the truth beneath.

Calliope reached again for her bonnet and popped it on her head. She wished it had some flirtatious feathers or bright fruit and flowers, or that she herself possessed Thalia's blue eyes or Emmeline's fine figure. Brown eyes and skinny limbs, clad in classical white plainness, weren't likely to coax secrets out of any man, let alone one as admired by the ladies as Westwood.

It was no use worrying about it, though. She was who she was, and there was nothing to be done about it. And she was going to be late if she didn't hurry.

Calliope retied the bow under her car and reached for her blue spencer. Maybe she didn't have flirtatious azure eyes, but she did have one thing she shared with Cameron—a knowledge of history and antiquities. They could speak the same language, if they just tried.

As she pinned a tiny brooch, a golden owl of Athena, to her collar, a knock sounded at her chamber door.

"The Earl of Westwood is waiting for you in the morning room, Miss Chase," the footman announced.

"Thank you," Calliope called. "I will be down directly." She touched the owl and whispered, "Courage."

The fashionable hour was just beginning as Calliope and Cameron turned into the gates of Hyde Park, his dashing yellow-and-black phaeton rolling smoothly along the lane, joining in the bright parade. Calliope opened her parasol, turning it over her shoulder to block the afternoon sunlight—and some of the stares of the curious.

"Are you quite well today, Miss Chase?" Cameron asked, steering his horses down a slightly quieter pathway. She had been right about his driving skills. His gloved hands were featherlight on the reins, his horses perfectly responsive to his slightest touch. Just as she had been responsive when they danced.

"A good night's sleep and a strong pot of tea can do wonders," Calliope answered, nodding at Emmeline as they passed her and her mother in their carriage.

"Did you sleep well, then?"

Calliope laughed ruefully, and shook her head. "Hardly at all. I had such dreams!"

"Dreams of falling statues?"

"Of being chased by hairy Minotaurs down endless corridors."

He gave her a sympathetic smile. "That house would be quite enough to disturb anyone's dreams, even without other—events."

"Quite. I hope never to see Acropolis House again."

"Or its owner?"

"Him, too. Will he live, do you think?"

"The doctor who was summoned last night says his prognosis is quite good. Once his brain is set right. Whatever *right* might be for such a man."

Calliope swallowed hard, her throat suddenly dry. "And have you heard what the events of the night are supposed to be?"

"That the duke was examining his treasure, and she fell from her unsteady base. A tragic accident."

"At least until the duke awakens and tells the truth."

"Until then. How is your sister today?"

"Quiet, but well enough. Clio does not stay discomposed for long. But her account of events is much what you would think, I fear. The duke surprised her as she examined the Alabaster Goddess, and when he tried to do—something, she hit him with the statue."

"Well done for her."

Calliope laughed. "I think she is mostly disappointed she didn't finish the job."

"Well, I'm sure one day someone will—finish the job. The duke has many enemies."

"Like you, Lord Westwood?"

He glanced at her from the corner of his eye. "Perhaps. One can never predict what might happen in the future. And I thought I asked you to call me Cameron."

"When we are alone."

"Aren't we alone now?"

Calliope looked around at the crowd of carriages and equestrians. "Hardly."

"No one can hear us."

"All right, then—Cameron. I hope that, if something *does* one day happen to the duke, it won't be by your hand."

"You wouldn't like to see me in Newgate, then?"

Calliope had a vision of him locked behind stout bars, dishevelled, waiting for the noose or the ship to Botany Bay. Once it might have made her laugh; now it made her shiver. "Not for the likes of the Duke of Averton. I don't want to see you or my sister hurt because of him."

"I don't want to see such a thing, either, believe me."

"Then how can we prevent it?"

"We?"

Calliope examined the passing scenery, the neat rows of trees, feigning a carelessness she was far from feeling. "I think we worked together well last night, did we not?"

"Yes," he agreed slowly. "Certainly we prevented anyone knowing what really happened in that gallery, though I'm sure there is no power on earth that could stop speculation."

Calliope thought again of those rumours Emmeline told her about. The wagers on how soon she and Westwood would be betrothed—or would kill each other. "No, indeed. People do like their gossip."

"But not us," he said teasingly. "We are above all that. We care only for the benefit of *art*."

Calliope laughed. "I am not so high in the instep as all that, I hope! I confess I do indulge in a spot of, shall we say, speculative conversation now and then."

"Never! Not Miss Calliope Chase."

"Sad, I know, but I must be honest." Calliope sighed.

"And what do you speculate about?"

You, she almost said. She bit her lip, turning away again to peer at the passing pedestrians on the walkways. They were in a more sparsely populated part of the park now, most of the stylish gawkers behind them. Here were mostly serious strollers, nurses with their charges, footmen with dogs on leads. The phaeton rolled past them slowly, at a snail's pace. "Oh, this and that. Bonnets, of course. Parisian fashion papers. Fans and plumes. Don't ladies always interest themselves in the latest styles?"

Cameron shook his head. "Some ladies perhaps, Miss Chase. Not you, nor, I dare say, your sisters, or your friends in that Ladies Society of yours all the females of the *ton* are so anxious to join. You can't fool me."

She hoped she *could* fool him, at least some of the time. He couldn't know how much they really did talk about him at Ladies Society meetings, how most of her acquaintances were half in love with him, called him their "Greek god". He couldn't know why she needed his help so much now. Why she had to keep an eye on him.

And he *really* couldn't know that she was beginning to like him.

There. She said it, at least to herself. She was beginning to like him, to look forward to his conversation, his smiles. It surely wouldn't last, though. Such silliness rarely did. She knew this from watching ladies like Lotty, who were infatuated with a different gentleman every week.

It was like one of Lotty's beloved novels, turned farce rather than Gothic tragedy. *The Folly of Calliope*. At least it was folly with a purpose.

"Very well," she admitted. "Sometimes we *do* talk about hats, and sometimes suitors. Mostly we talk about art and history. And books." No need to mention that once in a while the books were things like *Lady Rosamund's Tragedy*.

"I knew it. Did I not say you cared only for the benefit of art?"

"You did. And that, Lord Westwood—Cameron—is why I need your help."

He glanced at her, his brow arched. "My help? Dear me, Miss Chase, I fear I shall swoon!"

Calliope lightly slapped his arm. "Don't tease! I'm serious."

"As am I. Who would have thought this day would come? I'm quite dizzy with surprise."

"Hmph." She snapped her parasol closed, just in case she was required to rap him over the head with it. "Do you want to hear what I have to say or not?"

"Always."

"Very well, then. I think we both agree the duke is an odious man, yes?"

His smile melted, the corners of his beautiful, Greek god-ish lips turning down. "Of course."

"You know that better than I, I'm sure. You went to university with him. I only have his behaviour towards my sister to judge by. And his rapacious collecting habits. Those are quite vile enough."

"Believe me, my dear Miss Chase, you don't want to see what the man is like outside of polite society," he said darkly.

My dear? Calliope peered closer at him, trying to read his face under the shadowed brim of his hat. It was as smooth as a statue, as Hermes. Only an obsidian glint in his eyes betrayed the depths of emotion roiling inside.

"No, I don't," she said softly. "But I will, if that's what it takes."

"If that is what *what* takes?"

"To protect my sister. And the Alabaster Goddess."

"The Alabaster Goddess?"

"Of course. It is too much to think I could protect all those objects in that dreadful house. The lioness, the sarcophagus, Daphne. But I think Artemis is in the most immediate danger. Both from the duke and from whoever might think to take her from him."

"The Lily Thief again?"

"Perhaps. He is not the only petty criminal about, you know. She could be in danger from any number of people."

"You think some pickpocket from Whitechapel is likely to break into Acropolis House and steal a Greek statue? Maybe some of those cat mummies while he's at it?"

Calliope sighed. "Put like that, it does sound silly. No, I don't think some cutpurse is going to haul the goddess away. There are plenty of criminals with more sophistication who could carry off such a crime, though. She is a prime target. Not too large, in beautiful condition…"

"Too famous to sell on the open market."

"That wouldn't stop a collector who wants only to gloat over her in private."

"As the duke has done?"

"Yes, just so."

He turned the phaeton on to yet another lane, this one more crowded. Their progress slowed even further, caught in a knot of vehicles. "Say the Lily Thief—or someone else—does steal the Alabaster Goddess. How is she worse off than she was in Averton's possession?"

"At least with him we know where she is. There is a chance she could pass to a museum or a respectable scholar one day. If she is stolen, she would likely never see the light again. Never be studied properly."

Cameron shook his head. "Calliope, she *has* been studied, as much as can be. Taken from her original context, most of her lessons are lost for ever anyway. The duke does not deserve her."

"I won't argue with you about that. He doesn't deserve any of those antiquities in his house! But he *does* own them, for good or ill, at least for now."

"And so you think that gives him the right…"

Calliope reached out and pressed her fingers to his tense arm, stilling his angry growl. This was that old quarrel of theirs, and there was just no time for it now. She needed him. "Please, Cameron. I need your help. Let's not argue."

He stared down at her intently, perfectly still under her touch. "My help with what exactly?"

"I told you—to keep Artemis safe. No matter what our disagreements are, we both want that, yes?"

"Yes, of course."

"Then can we declare a truce? A new alliance, to save the Alabaster Goddess?"

He was silent for a long moment, until Calliope half-feared he meant to reject her truce, to set her down here in the park and drive away, laughing at her folly. Finally, though, he pressed his hand atop hers. "Very well. A truce. Now, how do your propose we protect our divine charge? Put surveillance on the duke's house? Follow him around town—once he is conscious, of course."

Calliope laughed in sheer relief. "I'm afraid I haven't thought that far ahead. That is one reason why I need your help."

"I thought strategy was Athena's strong point."

"I fear I had to put my helmet and shield away and don this bonnet instead. But I am sure we will soon think of something. Come to my house tomorrow evening. My father is having a small card party, and we can talk more there."

"Strategise over a game of astralasi, eh?"

"Perhaps if the Trojans had done so rather than make war, things might have ended better for them." Calliope sat back in her seat, opening her parasol again. She felt a new, warm glow of satisfaction. The truce was begun; a new game was afoot. "Thank you, Cameron. You won't be sorry, I promise."

You won't be sorry.

Cameron laughed aloud as he bounded up the steps of his house. That was where Calliope Chase was wrong, for he was already beginning to be sorry. If he joined forces with her, allied with her to protect the Alabaster Goddess, he would have to spend time with her. And then how would he ever stop himself from kissing her?

When he looked at her today, the sun dusting her fair skin with glistening gold, her cheeks flushed with the excitement of her mission, her lips parted on a breath, it took everything in his power, every ounce of self-control, not to grab her. Not to pull her close and kiss those pink lips, feel their softness, their warm yielding. He was so hot to kiss her, embrace her—*her*, Calliope Chase of all women! A woman who always seemed to regard him with suspicion and disapproval. A woman who was beautiful, but oh so stubborn.

Until that blasted masquerade ball, anyway. The drama and danger, the strange nightmare quality of that evening, had changed something between them. The old distrust cracked and broke, but hadn't yet reformed into something he could identify.

Except lust. And he'd always had *that* for her.

Now they were to be allies in some scheme she had to "save" the Alabaster Goddess from the Lily Thief, the duke, and who knew what else.

Cameron opened the door to the library and found Athena's painted image, her solemn grey-eyed stare. Aside from the fact that Calliope's eyes were brown—a deep, melting chocolate brown that a person could drown in, happily unable to extricate himself—they were the mirror image of each other. He wondered if Athena had been a member of a Ladies Society, too.

They were certainly up to something, Calliope and her Ladies Society friends. He knew that even before they found the duke in his gallery, when they were dancing and she and Emmeline Saunders kept exchanging glances and whispers. Everyone thought they were some sort of harmless study group, a way for ladies to occupy themselves before they married, yet Cameron had always suspected otherwise. Any society with the Chase sisters as members could hardly be called "harmless". And now he was somehow a part of it all, God help him.

If he was truly wise, he would stay far away from Calliope and her plans, would pack his bags and retreat to the countryside. Retreat, though, was never his way. Nor was running away from an intriguing puzzle. His curiosity had always got the better of him, especially since life was so dull since he had returned from his travels.

Cameron remembered the way his father would look at him, puzzled, taken aback, as if this son wasn't what he bargained for. He would shake his head, and say, "You *are* Greek, aren't you?" And he was. That insatiable curiosity, that temper that so often got the better of him—that weakness for a pair of dark eyes.

He laughed ruefully, as the painted Athena gave him a scolding stare. He was her acolyte now, a soldier in her adventure. Perhaps it *was* foolish of him. The last thing he wanted was to be involved in the Duke of Averton's sphere again, in any way. Perhaps he *would* be sorry. It was obvious Calliope and her sisters trailed trouble in their beautiful wake.

But he very much looked forward to it. He had been rather bored lately, floundering in his new English life. Unsure of his place, even though he was brought up to it. He was far from bored now.

Yes. He would *not* be sorry.

Chapter Eleven

Calliope surveyed the tables set up in the drawing room for the card games. All seemed to be in tidy readiness: the neat white cloths, the new decks of cards, the tea table for refreshments. Through the half-closed doors of the dining room she could hear the servants setting the table for a late supper. The clink of silver and china, the soft murmur of voices.

Drawing her shawl over her shoulders, she stopped to straighten some of the teacups, twitch a crooked cloth into place. There was nothing left to do in here. She should go up and dress, get ready for the guests' arrival. She was too restless, though. She wanted to keep moving, keep adjusting cloths and fidgeting with cards, not sit down to have her hair dressed!

Calliope stopped at the window, peering down at the darkened street. It was quiet now, a calm lull between the bustle of the day and the flow of evening partygoers. She should feel calm, too. There was surely no need for nervousness. She had played hostess for her father since her mother died, and while they certainly did not entertain as much as they once did, she could manage a small card party.

Perhaps it was not the party itself, but the guest list. Or one guest in particular.

Cameron de Vere was coming to the party tonight. And, what was more, he was going to help her in her schemes to save the Alabaster Goddess. Of course, she didn't yet know what the scheme would be, but surely with his help things would soon be figured out. He disliked the duke as much as she did. He wanted to see Artemis safe.

A lone carriage rattled down the street, a phaeton hurrying homeward. It was not bright yellow, yet for a moment she remembered staring down from here to see Cameron's equipage in that very spot, his laughing face turned towards the sun, hair tossed in the breeze. Free. He was always so very free, so careless of what others thought of him. So secure in who he was.

How she envied that.

Calliope sighed, and drew the curtains closed. Free or not, she had a job to do and not much time to do it. She was wasting precious minutes, reflecting on Cameron's handsome face, his self-confident ways. She just couldn't seem to help it, though! Thoughts of him crept up on her at the oddest moments. Perhaps she was infected by Lotty's novel-reading habits, after all.

But then, maybe in a situation like this—stolen antiquities, wicked dukes, mysterious thieves—horrid novels could be more help than Plato or Aristotle. Too bad those novel heroines always seemed to be such fainting cabbage-heads.

"Calliope? Are you not dressed yet?" she heard her father say. She turned to find him in the doorway, leaning on the walking stick he seemed to employ more and more these days. He glanced around with a puzzled air, as if surprised to find himself in his own quiet drawing room, and not the bustling Athenian agora of his studies.

Calliope gazed at him with concern. How frail he looked since her mother died! How distracted and distant. As if he was not of this world, but living more and more in the ancient past. Who could blame him, really, with so many daughters to worry over? So many wild Muses. At least his distraction gave them lots of free time. Time to track down thieves.

"I just wanted to be sure everything is in readiness," she said. She hurried to his side, taking his arm to lead him to his favourite armchair. "We want our guests to be comfortable, do we not?"

"Ah, Calliope. So much like your mother," he said with a sigh, patting her cheek.

"Am I, Father?"

"Certainly. Oh, Clio looks the most like her, with that red hair, but you have her spirit. Always thinking of other people, always wanting things to be right for them." He chuckled. "Whatever *you* think right is. You and your mother—always so certain of everything. How I always relied on her sureness…"

Calliope gently took his hand in hers. "You miss her very much. Just as I do."

"Indeed. She was an excellent companion, your mother, so intelligent and steady. Practical, as you are. And beautiful, of course. I can't seem to find my way without her." He covered her hand with his, holding her close. "But she left me you and your sisters. I'll always have a part of her. I tell you, Calliope, my dearest wish for you, for all my Muses, is that you find such a partner in life."

"Oh, Father," Calliope said carefully, fearful she might start to cry, "you and Mother were so fortunate to find each other. I fear I've never met anyone I could be so compatible with. Could love that way."

"No one? What of young Westwood?"

Calliope stared at her father, startled. Had he, too, heard those rumours? She thought he noticed nothing that hadn't happened thousands of years ago! "Lord Westwood? Of course not him, Father. We argue too much."

"So did your mother and I, when we first met. It's a sign of passion, y'know."

"Father!" Calliope cried, feeling hot embarrassment flood her cheeks. She turned away to fuss with an arrangement of chairs.

Her father chuckled. "You don't want some milquetoast who would just agree with everything you say, would you? Not my Calliope. You would be bored within an hour. And Westwood appreciates the same things you do. Art, history."

"His father appreciated those things, too, and you two were great rivals."

"So we were. And enjoyed every moment of our rivalry. One wants to be opposed at times. Life is so dull otherwise."

"I don't think I would want a rival as a spouse, though," Calliope protested. "And Lord Westwood's views are so different from mine."

"I'm sure he would come round to a more correct way of thinking, with my Calliope's help. One more for our cause, eh? You always did enjoy a challenge, my dear."

Calliope had to laugh. "I do indeed. He might prove too great a challenge, though."

"For a Chase Muse? Never!" He gave her a sly wink. "Lady Rushworth tells me Lord Westwood is considered quite handsome among the ladies. An Apollo to adorn your side?"

"Father!" Calliope said, kissing his cheek amid helpless laughter. "You should not try to matchmake, you do it ill. I will find the right gentleman, never fear."

He patted her hand. "I just want to see you happy."

"I *am* happy. But I will be even happier once I dress, so I don't have to greet our guests in my round gown and shawl."

"You run along, then, Calliope. I will sit here and savour the anticipation of trouncing Mr Berryman at cards. He won ten shillings off me last time."

"Such shocking extravagance, Father," Calliope teased. "While you sit here, make sure the servants properly arrange the cakes for the tea table."

"I shall, my dear. You can always trust me with cakes."

Calliope left the drawing room and went up the stairs, past servants bustling with final preparations. She should be thinking about refreshments and the guest list, too, but instead she thought only about her father's words.

For a man with such a crowd of daughters, he seldom showed any concern for their matrimonial prospects. He lived in his own classical world, where dowries and betrothals had little place. Had he really been looking to Lord Westwood with an eye for an engagement? Scheming a match, along with his friend Lady Rushworth? Was *everyone* around her expecting her to marry Cameron, simply because they were prone to quarrels?

Calliope stepped into her bedchamber, watching as Mary prepared yet another white evening gown. Had she grown so predictable, then? She feared she had—white gowns, arguments with Lord Westwood, the evening was set. Too bad life couldn't follow such easy patterns. It always insisted on throwing obstacles in one's path. Things like thieves, and dukes obsessed with one's sister.

And handsome young earls.

Calliope pushed all that away, and discarded her shawl to begin her evening *toilette*. A card party was not the place to suddenly become *un*predictable. But if society thought they really knew Calliope Chase—well, soon, they would just have to think again.

The scene in the Chase drawing room was a distinct contrast to the one that happened in the duke's grand ballroom. There were no fantastical costumes, no gods and monsters and nymphs, just ordinary mortals in stylish, if subdued, evening dress. No wild dancing, no crowds packed to the walls, and much less artwork. But at least *their* statues, Calliope thought with satisfaction, were legally obtained and properly looked after.

But one thing was the same. Lord Westwood was there. He sat across from Calliope at the card table, no Hermes with bare arms and loose curls, yet still as mysteriously alluring in a fashionable blue coat and impeccably tied cravat. Calliope peeked at him over the edge of her cards. He was obviously better at this sleuthing-subterfuge business than she was. He was his usual self, smiling and joking, calmly examining his cards, while she had to restrain herself from staring boldly into people's faces, searching for any minute, hidden signs of villainy.

Thus far her surreptitious glances revealed nothing. No avaricious expressions when looking at her father's antiquities. No careless words or frowns. No flush of guilt when the duke was mentioned. No ancient bibelots dropped to the floor to give irrefutable proof.

Calliope sighed as she studied her cards. What a dreadful Bow Street Runner she would make! She had no idea how to look beyond the obvious, how to see into people's hearts. How to find the motives of the Lily Thief.

Cameron was her ally now, an ally of convenience. Could he also be the thief? And what of the duke and his strange list? Who were Charlemagne and the Grey Dove?

The Purple Hyacinth and Cicero? It was all very vexing, turning her well-ordered world topsy-turvy. What would set it right again? Could anything?

"Well, now," said Mr Smithson, who, with Emmeline, played against Calliope and Cameron. "Shall we play?"

"Have you discovered anything yet?" Calliope asked, as she and Emmeline lingered by the tea table during a lull in the play. They had a quiet moment, since Calliope's father was holding forth on the Punic Wars, and a debate threatened to ensue as Lady Rushworth heartily disagreed with his point. There was really nothing these people loved more than a good argument over ancient wars. Unless it was speaking of imaginary "courtship" between Calliope and Westwood.

Emmeline shook her head. "I have been spending a great deal of time with Mr Smithson. He is most amiable, but I doubt he is our thief."

Calliope glanced at Mr Smithson, his open, freckled face avid as he listened to her father. Obviously he did appreciate history. It would be so convenient if he *was* the thief, for she did not know him very well. "Why not?"

"Well, for one thing I doubt he would know a lock pick from a candlestick. He is not very mechanically inclined. He can scarce drive his own carriage. For another, he was at his estate in Devon when Lady Tenbray's diadem was stolen. He spends a great deal of time there, cataloguing his collection of Hellenistic silver."

"Oh…" Calliope sighed "…I'm sorry you wasted your time, Emmeline."

"Not at all! I quite like him." A delicate pink stain flooded Emmeline's cheeks. "In fact…"

"Emmeline! Never say he has become a real suitor."

"Perhaps. We'll see."

"But don't your parents want you to marry poor Freddie Mountbank, who is so loudly in love with you?"

"They do, but surely they will change their minds when Mr Smithson comes up to scratch. His income is twice Mr Mountbank's. Mr Smithson hasn't said anything yet, though, so don't breathe a word to the rest of the Ladies Society!"

"My lips are sealed," Calliope vowed. Well, well—perhaps something good could come of this wild goose chase after all. If only everyone didn't start thinking the Ladies Society was just a matchmaking operation!

"What of you, Calliope? Any progress?"

"Not yet. At least nothing I can decipher." Calliope thought of that list hidden in the Alabaster Goddess's base, of Clio, pale-faced, burning her blood-stained costume. Clio sat beside their father now, sipping her tea, her gaze very far away.

Calliope's stare moved to Cameron, who played a lively game of Pope Joan with Thalia. He slumped back in his seat, ostentatiously defeated, as Thalia merrily clapped her hands. Calliope wondered what he would make of that list, if she showed it to him.

"It is all very puzzling," Emmeline agreed. "The stolen items are all so very distinctive. If the thief sold them to a collector we know—and we all do seem to know each other—he could never display it. We would recognise it in an instant."

"True. And I can't imagine any of this lot keeping such a secret." Calliope gestured towards the noisy debaters.

"Then where are they going?"

Calliope shook her head. "I have no idea."

"Do you think it is Lord Westwood?"

"I don't know that, either." Calliope laughed bitterly. "I don't know very much, do I? But it does seem that Lord Westwood is a bit too open to be the thief."

"Wouldn't one of the characteristics of the thief be good acting skills?"

"Very true."

"Are there any new suspects on the horizon?"

Calliope remembered the duke's jumbled house, Daphne, the lioness, the great piles of precious objects. Anything could be hidden in there. "The Duke of Averton seems quite greedy," she whispered.

Emmeline's eyes widened. "Greedy, to say the very least. And whatever could have happened to him at the ball? It's all quite sinister."

"Quite. I can't help feeling that the Alabaster Goddess is somehow the key. Oh, Em! If only he wasn't going to take her away…"

Emmeline smiled. "I think I may have a solution to that."

"What? Are you going to kidnap Artemis yourself?"

"If only we could! I don't think even the whole Ladies Society could manage that. We are simply not quiet enough. No, I have a slightly more legitimate plan."

"Do tell me! We need all the help we can get right now."

"You know my father has an estate in Yorkshire, near the duke's mouldy old fortress? We seldom go there; too rustic for Mama."

"So, you're going to Yorkshire to watch the duke's house? In the middle of the Season?"

Emmeline laughed. "Better! We will all go. We'll take the Season with us, the part that matters, anyway. My father has a great scholar coming to visit from the university at Cologne, his name is Herr Mueller and he is an expert on all things Greek. Papa is going to invite us all to a house party in Yorkshire, to meet this scholar and wander about the moors discussing history and such."

"All of us?"

"The Ladies Society and their families, of course. And Mr Smithson, Lady Rushworth, Lord Westwood, everyone. And most of the other suspects, if I ask him to. So, we can watch them *and* the duke. Or the outside of his castle, anyway."

Calliope grinned. "We could pretend to be bird watching. Oh, Emmeline, it's a brilliant idea! It will be so much easier to observe everyone in the country than here in town."

Emmeline laughed. "Easier to get Mr Smithson to pop the question, too! The invitations go out tomorrow."

"Calliope!" Thalia called. "What are you and Emmeline talking of so secretly? Come here for a moment, see how much I won from Lord Westwood."

Calliope gave Emmeline a nod, and hurried over to Thalia's side. "You did indeed triumph, Thalia. What a poor gamester Lord Westwood must be."

"Ha!" Cameron said, all mock-contempt. "Did we not win at whist, Miss Chase? Thanks to my clever strategy."

"We did win," Calliope agreed. "But I think it was mostly due to the fact that Mr Smithson kept losing track of his cards."

"Staring all moon-eyed at Emmeline, no doubt," Thalia said. "But Lord Westwood here tells me that there is to be a most interesting lecture at the Antiquities Society tomorrow, Calliope. A discussion of the Panathenic Games with Herr Mueller, all the way from the university at Cologne."

"You enjoy hearing about Athena, do you not, Miss Chase?" Cameron asked quietly. "Is she not your patroness?"

Calliope stared at him, their gazes meeting, clinging. For a moment, it was as if all the rest of the room vanished, became a mere muted blur, and they were all alone. Just as they had been in the darkness of the duke's house, bound in some ancient spell. She couldn't breathe, couldn't turn away.

"I fear Athena's wisdom is not often mine," she murmured. "But I enjoy learning whatever I can from her."

"It is settled, then!" Thalia said, her voice the last, strongest tether to drag Calliope back down to earth. "We will ask Father to take us to the lecture. Perhaps it will lift Clio from whatever doldrums she has fallen into."

"I hope to see you there, then," Cameron said. He was shuffling the cards, the pasteboard squares flashing through his long fingers. Calliope shivered, certain she could feel that touch on her own skin.

"Oh, yes," she murmured. "I hope so, Lord Westwood. There is something I would like to ask your opinion about..."

Chapter Twelve

"We might just as well have stayed at home," Clio muttered.

"Hmm?" Calliope said, distracted. They stood in the foyer of the Antiquities Society, waiting to go into the lecture hall, and she occupied her time by observing the people around her. The chattering, laughing groups, all so polite and civilised. How could ideas of theft possibly lurk behind one of those smiling faces? "What do you mean, Clio?"

"I mean we always seem to encounter the same people, just like at Father's card party. The same people having the same conversations," Clio said, her tone so quiet, so impatient. "We should just have one continuous party, instead of always changing our clothes and moving about. If nothing different is ever to happen…"

Calliope peered closer at her sister, puzzled. Ever since the—occurrence in the duke's gallery, she had been so quiet. So serious. Calliope could not blame her, of course, but Clio always seemed so resilient. So strong. The strongest of all the Muses.

She was certainly as pretty as ever tonight, in her turquoise-coloured gown, her auburn hair pinned up in a loose, classical knot bound with gold ribbons. Yet her eyes behind the spectacles were dull, her skin pale.

"Are you ill?" Calliope asked, concerned. "Do you want to go home?"

Clio made an impatient noise, fiddling with her fan. "No, I'm not ill. I'm just—oh, I don't know!" With that most uninformative outburst she stomped off, moving across the room to examine one of the plaster statues of gods and dying Gauls that lined the red-papered walls.

The statues had been there for ever, ever since their parents started bringing them here when they were girls. One of the "unchanging" things Clio complained of tonight. Calliope could look around this room, this building, and remember her first visits here, listening to tales of ancient wars, politics, heroic deeds, doomed romances. Most of the people she remembered from then, too, though perhaps they were a bit greyer now.

When she was an old lady, would she be here, too, surrounded by her children and grandchildren? By Emmeline and Lotty and their children? She had never thought of such a thing before. This was just how the world was.

Calliope frowned, feeling a prickle of some strange unease. Was Clio right? Did nothing ever change?

She thought of Cameron de Vere, of how he seemed to trail the intriguing allure of exotic lands behind him wherever he went. Even in stuffy drawing rooms, dull assemblies, he emanated adventure, intrigue. Danger.

Intrigue and danger were the last things she needed. She *liked* her well-ordered world, her old friends and familiar patterns. Or at least she thought she did.

"You seem very thoughtful tonight, Miss Chase," she heard a voice say. A deep, rough-edged voice that made her shiver. She knew who it was even before she turned. She always knew.

Cameron. How was it she had only to think of him and he appeared?

She pasted a bright smile to her lips before she faced him. He looked so handsome tonight, of course. Yet also rather sombre, in a dark burgundy coat, his hair smoothed back.

"One *should* be thoughtful before a lecture," she answered.

"Thoughtful of questions you can pepper the speaker with, eh?" he said, with a glimmer of his old smile. "I would wager you know far more than this—what's his name?"

"Herr Mueller, from the university at Cologne. Lady Emmeline Saunders and her parents have invited him to their house party, you know," Calliope said. "And I hope he knows a great deal, since we will have to listen to him for several days."

"Ah, yes. The house party. Strange, isn't it, how their estate just happens to be so near that of Averton?"

Calliope shrugged. "It is a lovely, rural spot for some academic contemplation."

"And a bit of spying, maybe?"

Calliope laughed, smothering the sound behind her gloved hand. The Antiquities Society was always such a hushed, serious place, not one for loud laughter. "I understand there is some interesting bird watching in the area, too. That would require the use of opera glasses, I think."

He laughed, too, but not behind his hand. The joyful sound caused several heads to swivel in their direction. *Oh, dear*, Calliope thought. *Yet more gossip.* Somehow, though, his warm chuckles made her feel too giddy to even particularly care. At the moment.

"So, you are planning your rustic intrigues already?" he said.

"Not really. I am finding I don't truly have a gift for sleuthing. We must hope that events provide us with an opportunity once we are there." Calliope glanced at Clio, who stood across the foyer with their father, his friend Lady Rushworth, and the head of the Antiquities Society, Lord Knowleton. She was still so quiet and watchful. "My sister tells me our lives are dull and full of sameness, anyway. That nothing unusual can ever happen to us. So perhaps I should not hope for much in Yorkshire."

"What do *you* think? Do you find life to be dull, Miss Chase?"

Not when you are near, Calliope thought. Ever since he had come into her life she wasn't sure of anything. "How can it be, with a thief among us, and dukes being coshed on the head in their own homes? I fear perhaps the excitement may prove to be too much."

"Perhaps a spot of bird watching might be just what you need, then."

Before Calliope could answer, the doors to the lecture hall opened and everyone began to file inside, discreetly vying for the best seats. Her father, Clio and Lady Rushworth vanished in the crowd. "I should find my father," she said.

"Let us look for him together," Cameron suggested, offering his arm. "I would be honoured to sit with the Chases and benefit from their wisdom in historical matters."

"As long as you don't whisper satirical comments, trying to make us laugh," she said, accepting his arm. It had become almost a natural gesture.

"Would I do such a thing?" he said, all wounded innocence.

"I am just warning you…"

* * *

"…as you see here, the young ladies of the procession carry the vessels for pouring offerings to the gods, in this case Athena. The *oinochoai* and the *phialai*, and here is the incense burner, the *thymiaterion*. The purpose of the maidens on this side, however, is less clear. Perhaps they carried the peplos, newly woven for the goddess, or perhaps they were even the famed *Arrephoroi*…"

Calliope tried to listen to the learned Herr Mueller, to study the large sketches of the Parthenon friezes set up behind the podium. She watched as the small, bespectacled scholar pointed out each figure in the carved procession she knew so well from days at the British Museum. But she could not seem to focus her thoughts where they should be, on the worship of the gods. Couldn't seem to sit still. And it was all due to Cameron, sitting beside her.

He, too, stared straight ahead, yet every time Calliope glanced at him from the corner of her eye his lips quirked with a barely suppressed smile. Finally, he caught her looking at him and raised his brows.

Calliope snapped forward again. *Ridiculous man!* Herr Mueller's speech was not so comical as all that, merely a bit—dry. Nothing to laugh about. Why, then, did she want to burst into giggles all over again?

Clio, seated on her other side, whispered, "Must I play Miss Rogers now, Calliope?"

Miss Rogers had been a particularly stern governess of their childhood, prone to furious frowns and threats of the rod. She hadn't lasted long with the young Muses. Thalia quickly dispatched her with the aid of a bag of frogs. "Of course not."

"Then tell me what you are laughing at, before I perish of boredom!"

"I don't know what I'm laughing at," Calliope admitted.

"…and here we see the nine Archons of Athens, or so they are assumed to be," Herr Mueller went on.

"I sense you are getting restless, *fräulein*," Cameron whispered. "You are not paying attention to the lessons. However will you pass the examinations?"

"Be quiet, or I'll have to pinch you," Calliope hissed. Were they really to be trapped in Yorkshire with endless lectures? For the first time, the intrigues of the Lily Thief, the mystery surrounding his exploits, seemed truly exciting to her. A most welcome distraction.

If she could survive the days in Cameron's company without completely losing her senses.

Calliope folded her hands in her lap, facing sternly forward again. But her calm attention was not to last. As Herr Mueller turned to the figures of the gods watching the procession, the doors to the lecture hall swung open. Everyone swivelled around to see who dared intrude on the sacred hush of the Antiquities Society, and slowly, gathering speed like an approaching thunderstorm, a chorus of whispers swept over the crowd. Even Herr Mueller sputtered away into nothingness.

"Oh! It's an avenging spirit!" Lotty, who sat behind Calliope, moaned.

If only it was something so mundane, Calliope thought, but they were not so fortunate. It was the Duke of Averton. He stood there for a moment, perfectly still, framed by the open doors.

His brow was bound by a stark white bandage, the skin of his face nearly as pale, yet he stood there unaided, unwavering, wrapped in a black, fur-trimmed cloak. His burning gaze swept over the assembly, as if it was his own private domain. His little kingdom. The demon emperor.

Oh, dear, Calliope thought. She *was* turning into Lotty.

Beside her, Clio stiffened. Calliope laid a gentle hand on her arm, but it was as if her sister took no notice. She just stared straight ahead, listening to a lecture gone silent.

"So, he didn't die," Cameron muttered.

"Are you sure?" Calliope answered. "Lotty says he's a spirit, and I half imagine she might be right."

As they all watched, as mesmerised as if they observed Hamlet's ghost at Drury Lane, the duke made his slow, stately way down the aisle to an empty seat near the front. Like Clio, he looked neither right nor left. Once it became apparent he was not going to do anything fascinating, the whispers abated and Herr Mueller began again.

"Though the gods are shown seated, the proportions are quite unusual, as their heads are parallel to those of the approaching humans..."

"I need some fresh air," Clio muttered tightly. Before Calliope could question or stop her, she leaped up from her seat and hurried out of the room, a turquoise silk blur. As some of the other ladies also took that opportunity to escape to the withdrawing room, her exit was unremarked.

Calliope stared after her, worried. She remembered how still and brittle Clio looked after the masquerade ball, bent over her ruined costume, as if she would shatter at a touch. Calliope sat there for a moment, unsure of what to do, scared of breaking into Clio's careful reserve. Finally, though, she could bear it no longer.

"Excuse me," she murmured, and followed her sister up the aisle.

There were a few groups milling about in the foyer, whispering together, speculating on the duke's sudden appearance. Or perhaps they were just congratulating themselves on their happy escape from the boring lecture. Clio was not among them, nor was she in the ladies' withdrawing room or the library. The study rooms and storage attics abovestairs were mostly locked tonight, so Clio would not be there.

Her concern mounting, Calliope rushed out the doors that led to the street, peering frantically both ways. The night was quite dark and chilly, broken only by the clattering rush of passing carriages.

"Clio!" she called out, even as she knew there would be no answer.

"Miss Chase?" she heard Cameron say, and turned to find he had followed her outside. The chilly breeze ruffled his hair, tugged at the folds of his beautifully tied cravat, but he did not seem to notice. He watched her solemnly.

Calliope had never felt more helpless in her life. Her family, the thief, the duke—she understood none of it. Every bit of her control was slipping away, and all she could do was grab at it frantically. Watch in horror as it slipped ever further away.

She held out her trembling hands. "I can't find her," she said, hoarse with unshed tears.

"I know," he answered. He came down the steps to her side, taking her hand in his. How very warm he was, how strong. He tucked her fingers into the crook of his arm and led her back into the building. "Your sister is a sensible woman. I'm sure she wouldn't just go dashing off into the night."

"Then where could she be?"

"Well, at least we know the duke isn't with her, as he is still sitting in the lecture hall being subjected to Herr Mueller. Perhaps she went to one of the study rooms?"

Calliope shook her head. "They are locked in the evenings."

"All of them?"

"I don't know." She glanced up the darkened staircase. The twisting corridors up there seemed silent and deserted, but one never knew. The Chase Muses were nothing if not resourceful, even in the face of locked doors. "Will you look with me?"

Cameron arched his brow at her, in that satirical expression she was coming to hate—and to find much too attractive. "Why, Miss Chase. How shocking of you."

"Don't go missish on me!" Calliope snapped. "No one will see us. And I—well, it's dark up there. What if the duke does decide to leave the lecture?"

"Ah, so you need protection from your friend's 'avenging spirits'?" he said, looking about at the thinning crowd. No one paid them any attention; they were all still too busy clucking about the main story of the night, the Duke of Averton. "Well, I'm always happy to play protective knight. Lead on, Miss Chase."

Before she could lose her nerve, Calliope dashed up the stairs, her slippered footsteps muffled by the thick red carpet. She didn't know what had come over her. Usually she was not such a ninny as all that! Not as wildly fearless as Thalia, to be sure, but surely able to search deserted study rooms by herself.

Ever since the masquerade ball, though, it was as if something had shifted in her world. The safe, cosy environs of her life had taken on new shadows, new uncertainties. Dangers she didn't understand and had never expected. Even this dull lecture seemed ringed round with them. She was glad of Cameron's solid presence at her back.

As they crept down the corridor, she was reminded of their journey through the Duke of Averton's mad house. Not that the dark, stolid Antiquities Society was much like the jumble of Acropolis House, yet there were all the statues and paintings. Shifting bars of dark and light on the red-papered walls, a hushed murmur from below them. And she was alone with Cameron, acutely conscious of the sound of his breath, the scent of his soap and starch and skin that floated over the miasma of lemon polish, dust and old books.

The first few doors they came across were indeed locked, and when she pressed her ear to their stout wood panels she heard nothing. Not even a soft footfall or sigh.

"How could she just vanish like that?" Calliope murmured, twisting yet another unyielding doorknob.

"We can hardly blame her," Cameron answered. "For not wanting to stay in there with Averton."

"She could have told me where she was going."

"Perhaps she didn't know. Come, let's try this room down here."

The next door was unlocked. It swung open to reveal one of the small studies used during the day by members of the Antiquities Society, since their books could not be taken out of the building. There were two desks and a few armchairs, a bookshelf, large pieces hulking in the shadows. The one window let in the meagre moonlight.

Calliope peered through its thick glass at the street below. Still no Clio. She wrapped her arms tightly around herself, around her waist in its thin white muslin, watching the parade of passing carriages.

"You knew the duke at university," she said.

"Yes, sadly enough." He did not come to her side, staying just inside the door, yet still she was aware of him. His heat and presence. It assured her, even as it made her nervous.

"And he—mistreated women then?" she said. "Behaved dishonourably?"

He sighed. "Oh, Calliope. I'm sure in many people's eyes he did nothing 'dishonourable'. Nothing most other young men of his rank do every day."

"But you don't agree."

"Most of the women he, as you say, mistreated were tavern wenches or shopkeeper's daughters, milliners or housemaids. Not fine ladies to be protected. But he took them whether they agreed or not, sometimes hurt them. One girl drowned herself."

Calliope gasped, closing her eyes tightly against a sudden vision of Clio sinking beneath cold waves.

Cameron came to her side then, his hand gentle on her arm. "I'm sorry. I shouldn't have said that."

"No, you were right to tell me. I'm glad to know the truth. He's a terrible man. Those poor girls…"

"Yes, poor they were. Unprotected, alone. Yet they were human beings, the same as us, and he had no right to treat them that way."

Calliope could feel the anger simmering inside of him, the fury of his memories. Yet his touch was still soft on her arm.

"No, indeed," she said. 'What could he want with my sister? She is hardly poor and unprotected!"

"Perhaps he wants to marry her, sire an heir."

Calliope snorted in disbelief. "He had best look elsewhere, then. Clio would never marry a villain like him, and he must surely know that after she knocked him unconscious."

"It's probably the challenge he enjoys. You Chase Muses are full of prickles and nettles. It takes a brave man to try to get close to you."

Calliope turned towards him, studying his face in the

moonlight. How beautiful he truly was, she mused, a creature of the Greek sun and sea, so full of youth and freedom. She lightly traced the chiselled line of his jaw, feeling a muscle twitch beneath her fingers. "*You* are close to me."

"I must be brave, then. Or very foolish." His hands circled her waist, tugging her closer. She went unresisting, overcome by curiosity and some heady, overpowering emotion she didn't understand. It was intoxicating, dizzying, and she clutched at his shoulders to hold herself upright.

She had never been so close to a man. How giddy it was, like too much bubbling champagne! Or like lolling in the grass on a hot summer's day. All her senses tipped and whirled, and she knew only him. The feel of him under his hands, hard and alive, hot, the strength of him bearing her up.

"Which do you think it is?" she whispered.

"Foolish, definitely," he answered, his voice so rough it was almost unrecognisable.

As if in a hazy dream, far away, yet more immediate than anything she had ever known before, his head tipped towards her and he kissed her.

The touch of his lips was soft at first, velvety, warm, pressing teasingly once, twice. When she did not, *could* not, move away, when she instead edged closer to him, tightening her clasp, his kiss deepened. Became hotter, damper, more urgent.

Something inside her heart responded to that urgency, a rough excitement that expanded and expanded until she feared she would burst with it! She moaned, parting her lips until she felt the tip of his tongue seeking entrance. The world utterly vanished, and there was only *him*. Only this one moment, this one perfect instant.

A moment that was shattered all too soon. A shout from

the street below broke into Calliope's dream, dragging her back down to earth, leaden and heavy. She tore her mouth from Cameron's, tilting her head back to suck in a deep breath of chilly air.

He stepped away, breathing hard. "Calliope," he said hoarsely. "Calliope, I—"

"No," she managed to say, though her chest was tight, her throat aching. She longed to cry, to burst into silly tears, and she didn't know why! Because she had kissed him? Or because they had stopped? "Please don't say you're sorry."

"I'm not. How could I be? But—"

"No 'but', either. I can't—that is, I…" For once in her life, Calliope Chase had no words at all. She spun around and ran out of the room and along the corridor, dashing down the staircase and into the empty ladies' withdrawing room as if a demon was at her heels. And surely a demon was—the spectre of her own wretched emotions. Her weakness.

She stared into the mirror that greeted her as she slammed and locked the door behind her, hardly believing she saw herself in the glass. Her cheeks were a hectic red against white skin, her hair mussed, and her eyes fever-bright. She looked…

She looked like Clio, as her sister fled from the Duke of Averton.

Chapter Thirteen

Calliope leaned forward to peer out the carriage window, scarcely daring to breathe as she waited for some new wonder to appear. It had been such a long journey to Yorkshire, days in the carriage with Clio and Thalia, reading aloud or playing cards. Not talking about what was truly on their minds. But it all must be worth it now, she thought, to see such a strange and glorious landscape.

Calliope had never really been much for the current craze for "nature" and wild emotion, fed by the fashionable poets. Classical order was what she craved, and in town, hemmed in by houses and shops, the neatness of squares and gates and parks, it was easy to believe that such order was possible. Here she could imagine no such thing. Here, she could begin to think the poets had a point. Could remember that the Greeks were not just about order, either, but about insanity and blood and monsters.

This country was beautiful, to be sure, but it was not the white beauty of a marble statue. There was such a wildness to it, a feeling of remoteness and profound solitude, a sense of being alone at the end of the world. Even Thalia had fallen silent, staring over Calliope's shoulder as the land rolled past. Crooked stone walls climbed bare hillsides, dark grey on greenish-purple, rugged squares and rectangles that disappeared over the summits.

Those old walls, clotted with moss, were one of the few signs of human life since they had changed horses at the last village. Only the occasional farmhouse, a wandering band of woolly sheep, spoke of present life. *Past* life there was in abundance—Romans, Vikings, Saxons, Normans had all passed this way, leaving their mark on the land. Even pirates, not too far away in Robin Hood's Bay. And perhaps something earlier, something even from beyond time, hidden in the hilltop tumuli and barrows.

Calliope lowered the window, letting in the cool breeze, the heavy, peaty scent of the earth. In the distance, she saw a narrow trail, a pale scar on the grey earth, leading to a ruined church. Its empty windows stared back, beckoning. Yes, the past was certainly alive here in this country, not just cold, dead stone. She could just envision Cameron here, galloping his horse over the windswept landscape...

Calliope slumped back in her seat. Why was it that he kept springing into her mind at every moment, no matter what she was doing? Reading, walking in the park, planning menus with the cook, playing cards with her sisters—it didn't matter. There he was. Yet she had not seen him since that night at the Antiquities Society. She had heard he had fled town, gone to see to business at his country estate.

It was so hard to think of anything else but that kiss they had shared, to concentrate on the things that usually made up her days. She would begin to forget him as she read a book on, say, the Trojan War, but then a mention of Hermes brought him right back. The glow of his eyes in the moonlight, the soft, hot press of his lips on hers, the smell of his skin. She had listened to her married friends whisper of their physical passion for their husbands, of course, had even read some of Lotty's silly novels, but had always thought such things must be exaggerated. How could a man's mere touch make one forget everything else?

Now she knew it was not exaggerated, for she had surely become as silly as any of them. Sighing over a man's kiss; longing for him to kiss her again, yet fearing it at the same time. What if it swept her away entirely, and she was lost, drowned, in him? All over Cameron de Vere, of all people! It was ridiculous.

He didn't seem to feel the same way, though, leaving town like that. She didn't even know if he would be at this house party, and she dared not ask Emmeline. She couldn't let anyone else know of her absurdity. Not even her sisters.

Would Clio even hear her if she *did* tell? Clio had also been so distant since the lecture, as if she was always thinking of something else. Something no one else could even fathom.

And Calliope and the Ladies Society were no closer to finding the Lily Thief. There had been no more thefts, no clues. This party, so near the duke's lair and the Alabaster Goddess, seemed to be their best chance.

"We should be almost there," Thalia said. "Oh, I can't wait to go walking over these fields! Do you think we could even go swimming in the river we drove past earlier today?"

"If you want to freeze your blood in its veins, Thalia," Clio answered, peering out the window as they lumbered up a steep hill.

"Pooh! It's not as if this is January. I'm sure the water is fine. Invigorating."

"As long as no one sees you," Calliope said. The Chase sisters had surely courted enough scandal of late. They were just fortunate they hadn't yet been caught.

"I am the picture of discretion. Oh, look!" Thalia said, pointing indiscreetly. "I think we're here."

They turned through a pair of open gates and rolled along a gravel lane, lined with wind-bent trees. At the end of the long, straight sweep was Kenleigh Abbey, the home of Emmeline's parents, the Earl and Countess of Kenleigh.

It was just as Emmeline had described at the last meeting of the Ladies Society, a medieval abbey half-converted for domestic life and gifted to one of her ancestors by Henry VIII, along with the title. Built of the local grey stone, it was weathered and harsh, overlaid by ropes of greenish moss. The upper floors boasted modern glass windows, while the lower still consisted of antique arches and walkways. In the watery sun of the afternoon, the light of the pale blue sky, it was odd and charming. At night, though, would the ghosts of old monks peer out from those empty arches?

That is it, Calliope, she told herself sternly. *No more novels!* First Byronic heroes galloping over the moors, now ghostly monks. Whatever would she conjure up next?

Around the front of the house circled a modern drive with a covered entrance, sheltered from the wind. The coach rolled to a stop just as the doors opened and Emmeline appeared, wreathed in welcoming smiles.

"You're here at last!" she cried as Calliope alighted, closely followed by Clio and Thalia. "It has been so dull waiting for everyone these last few days."

"Dull? With Herr Mueller to listen to?" Calliope teased.

Emmeline laughed. "He is very knowledgeable, to be sure, but I will be glad when he has a larger audience on which to impart his wisdom. Where is your father, by the way? Papa is most anxious to show him a new funeral stele he just purchased."

"He stopped in the last village we passed to examine their little museum," Clio said. "Something about Saxon arrowheads."

"Ah, well, no matter—you are all here now! Come inside and have some tea, you must be exhausted by your journey," Emmeline said, leading them through the open doors. They had barely a glimpse of drafty stone corridors and arches before she led them up a narrow flight of steps to a modern, firelit sitting room. Lotty was already there with her family, watching as the maids laid out a tea service.

"I have to tell you of everything I have planned," Emmeline said, pouring out the tea, slicing cake. "So many ruins to see! We can even go to the seaside, if you like. Robin Hood's Bay is a bit of a journey, but not too far, and terribly exciting."

"Where the smugglers are?" Thalia cried. "Oh, yes, we must. I have never seen smugglers' caves before."

"You probably wouldn't this time, either," Clio said. "Aren't smugglers notoriously choosy about who they let into their tunnels?"

"Clio, you are simply determined to ruin all my fun," Thalia answered. "When have you become such a fussy old lady?"

As she spoke, there was the sound of footsteps on the stairs, a woman's voice and the click of dog's claws on the stone floor. "It's just Mama," Emmeline said. "Shh! Don't let her hear you talk of smugglers, or she'll never let us go to the bay."

As Lady Kenleigh, a warm, welcoming older version

of Emmeline, came into the room, the conversation turned
to town doings and the more genteel outings planned for
their party.

As they chatted and sipped their tea, Calliope realised
she had not thought of Cameron in fully twenty minutes.
And she had not even asked if he was to be among the
guests. Quite a feat, and surely it indicated that he was at
last fading from her mind.

It simply had to.

Cameron paused at the top of the summit, gazing out
over the grey-green landscape stretched out below. It was
as if he could see for miles, over the great sweep of moor-
lands beyond, the dark lumps of farms and cottages. The
roadway into the village wound below, a pinkish ribbon,
but the only living being he could see was his own tethered
horse, grazing at the bottom of the steep slope.

No wonder the Romans had built a fort nearby, now just
a tracery of walls, the cracked remnants of a mosaic floor.
They could see for ever from here, all the wild acres
spreading out, full of freedom and magic.

Cameron took off his hat, letting the wind catch at his
hair, buffet his skin. He had been stuck in town for too long,
trapped by streets and crowds and stale smells. Here the
wind carried only the scent of earth, of peat and heather,
the hint of woodsmoke. He was alone at last, alone with
the wind and the light, the old spirits of the fort.

Alone, except for the thought of Calliope Chase. She
followed him even up here, the memory of her solemn dark
eyes. The way her slender body felt under his touch, so
warm and pliant. The taste of her lips, the innocent, passionate wonder of her. The way his body hardened, quickened, at the merest breath of her scent.

The way she ran from him, never looking back.

How he had longed to chase after her, to hold her, kiss her again! He even ran to the doorway of that dark room, frantic as her racing footsteps faded to nothing. Frantic to hold on to her again, to hold on to whatever that rare feeling was that grew between them when they kissed.

Yet something held him back. The look in those eyes, maybe, so very confused. The memory of Averton, so brutal with women—so unlike the way Cameron wanted to be. Muses were not as other women. They dwelled in their own world above mortal men. They were rare and precious, not to be coerced. Pressured. Not to be pursued like prey, lest they turn their backs on the man entirely, withdrawing their grace and shining good fortune from him for ever.

So, he did not run after her, even as every fibre of his being screamed at him that he must. Once his heartbeat slowed, and his body was fit to be seen without causing a scandal, he made sure that she was safe in the ladies' withdrawing room. Then he went home. For one fleeting second, he considered visiting Mrs Parker's discreet, expensive little establishment on Half Moon Street, where he was sure to find an enthusiastic welcome from one of her very pretty girls. But even as the thought occurred to him, he dismissed it. None of them would be Calliope, and it was Calliope alone he wanted.

How had such a thing happened? How had he gone from being exasperated by their quarrels, to longing to make love to her on the Antiquities Society floor?

The desire hadn't vanished, either, even though he stayed away. Even left town for his own estate. There he tried to bury his turmoil in long gallops, even labouring in his own fields, much to his tenants' astonishment. He thought about not coming to this house party. Calliope was certain to be there.

But he couldn't stay away. Not any longer. He didn't want to frighten her, but his Greek blood burned too hot now to be denied. He had to admit it to himself—he wanted Calliope Chase.

And he intended to have her.

Chapter Fourteen

"Emmeline certainly has so much planned for this party," Lady Kenleigh said, pouring out more amber-coloured tea and passing around the porcelain cups. "Picnics by the river, nature walks, charades. There is even an assembly in a few days, in the village rooms. Not Almack's, to be sure, but amusing enough. You young people do need your music and dancing!"

"It sounds delightful," Calliope said, peering at Emmeline over the rim of her cup. Emmeline blushed. So, it was as Calliope suspected—her friend was using picnics and the like as a scheme for more time with Mr Smithson. "But will we have time, with Herr Mueller's lectures?"

Lady Kenleigh smiled knowingly. "You needn't worry, Miss Chase. There will be more than enough time for Herr Mueller. My husband thinks everyone should be able to live on Attic vase painting and the Punic Wars alone, but Emmeline and I know that is not always true. We want you to enjoy yourselves here. After all, you are away from the busy Season. We must make it worth your while, if we can."

Calliope smiled at her, but she was afraid she knew what Lady Kenleigh meant. After all, Emmeline's mother was one of the most notorious matchmakers in all England. Since she had seen her daughter almost settled—though not with poor Freddie Mountbank, her first choice!—she needed other objects for her attention. And who better than the motherless Chase sisters?

Calliope looked across the room to Clio, who was examining a book with Lotty. Clio was smiling as she listened to Lotty's chatter, yet there was still that shadow, that wisp of greyness that seemed to follow her about ever since that blasted masquerade ball. Calliope doubted Lady Kenleigh would have much success matching *her*. But maybe a distraction—like fending off "suitable" introductions—was just what Clio needed.

As for Thalia…

Calliope turned her gaze to her other sister, who was banging out a stormy Beethoven concerto at the pianoforte. The light from the windows touched her silver-gilt curls, the very picture of an English rose. But Calliope knew it would take a special, and strong, man indeed to match her inner Amazon.

And as for herself—she had no thoughts of marriage. She was too busy, with her father and sisters, the thief, the Alabaster Goddess. There was no man who could understand. None she had ever encountered, anyway.

Except…

Calliope had a sudden vision of the dark room at the Antiquities Society. The hot, rough feel of Cameron's touch on her skin, the press of his kiss. The undeniable rush of need, bubbling in her veins, curling her toes. *He* was not like any other man she had ever met.

But he was not for her. They were not for each other.

Calliope frowned. She felt suddenly sad, as if Clio's dark cloud spread its misty tentacles over her own head. She put her teacup down on the nearest table and drifted over to a window, the murmur of conversation and laughter trailing after her.

She found herself gazing down at a side garden, neat, narrow pathways leading out towards the dip of a ha-ha and beyond. On the edge of the manicured lawn, just before the careful landscape vanished into a stand of trees, she could see a pile of dark grey stones. At first it seemed haphazard, an odd structure rising up out of nowhere, yet she could see how closely the slabs fit together. Like the walls they drove past, bisecting the hillsides.

A barrow of some sort? They had seen such things on their journey, old structures on summits, built so sturdily by long-dead hands that they still stood, reminders of a vanished world. Lotty would surely be eager to explore this one, to build elaborate tales of ancient romance around the cold stone.

Emmeline came to her side, offering a fresh cup of tea. "I was thinking perhaps a walk to the falls would be interesting for tomorrow morning," she said. "It's quite picturesque. They even say there's a grotto hidden behind the water, though I don't expect any of us would care to look for it! Much too damp."

"Don't tell Thalia. I'm sure *she* would attempt it, given half a chance."

Emmeline laughed. "I won't, but I'm certain she'll hear of it from one of the tenants. They love to tell of local folktales."

"Is there one associated with that?" Calliope gestured towards the pile of stones.

"Those? I have no idea. They've just always been there.

Shall we go take a look?" Emmeline glanced back at her mother, who was talking quite intently with Lotty's mother. "She is determined to match Freddie Mountbank with *someone*, you see. Poor Lotty."

"A walk would be lovely," Calliope agreed hastily. Heaven forbid Lady Kenleigh turn Freddie Mountbank on to *her*.

With Emmeline's efficiency, it took only a few moments for everyone to gather hats and shawls and set off across the gardens towards the mysterious stones. Thalia dashed ahead, her hem quickly muddied, and leaned down to peer over the low wall.

"Emmeline!" she called, her voice echoing hollowly off the rocks. "How could you never have looked closely at this? It's quite fascinating."

"We just don't come here very often," Emmeline answered. "It's too remote and quiet for Mama. Why? What do you see?"

"It's very dark down there, but it appears to be stairs of some sort. Cut into the earth." Thalia would surely have leaped right down off the wall, if Calliope hadn't caught the sleeve of her spencer. "An ancient basement of some sort?"

"A Viking root cellar?" Calliope said doubtfully. She peered past Thalia's shoulder, but all she could see was dirt and blackness. Maybe those *were* stairs, but she couldn't tell.

"It must be a passage!" Lotty cried. "A secret tomb, where forbidden lovers lie cruelly murdered. I read about something just like it—"

"I'm sure," Calliope said hastily, before they were treated to a lengthy and detailed plot synopsis. "But if those *are* stairs, they appear to go nowhere. They must belong to a structure that's vanished. An old gardener's shed, maybe."

Lotty pouted. "It could be a tomb."

"Calliope is surely right," Clio said briskly. "These stairs just end, see? Blocked up. Thalia, come away from that, you'll get all muddy."

"I have to wash before dinner, anyway," Thalia protested. "A little dirt never killed anyone."

"But Mary would not appreciate having to clean your gloves yet again," Calliope said, suddenly impatient. Really, living with her sisters was like herding a particularly recalcitrant band of sheep! Or something more slippery, wilder. Foxes, maybe. A herd of arguing foxes.

Thalia muttered, but she did back away from the mysterious steps that led to nothing. She and the others wandered off towards the trees, and Calliope turned in the opposite direction, seeking just a moment of quiet.

She walked around to the front of the house, strolling down the tree-lined lane. In the far distance she could see the front gates, partly open, as if inviting her to dash for their promised freedom.

Her thin half-boots weren't up to dashing, though. Instead she walked along the gravel drive, wondering at her strange mood. Her sisters often squabbled; it usually didn't bother her at all. Probably it was just lack of sleep, worry over the Lily Thief and where he might strike next. It was making her impatient and snappish. This holiday was just what she needed. A few days to rest and regroup, to breathe fresh air, enjoy the picnics and waterfalls…

The gates at the end of the lane swung open, admitting a single galloping horse. The creature dashed towards her, and she saw her peaceful hopes vanish like chimney smoke into the sky.

Even from here she recognised the horse's rider. It was Cameron. He wore no hat, and his curls were even longer and more wild than usual, his greatcoat billowing behind him like wings. An English Perseus on his Pegasus. She glanced around her, and could see nowhere to hide. No place for concealment. She just stood there, frozen, watching as he drew ever nearer.

He reined in a few feet from where she stood, tossing up a plume of gravel dust. A faint sheen of sweat glistened on his brow, matching that of his horse's glossy coat. He had been riding hard, then. Trying to outrun this thoughts, perhaps, just as she was?

He stared down at her in silence, the only sound his rushed breath, the wind in the scrubby trees. Calliope half imagined he was a mirage, a dream figure, but then he swung down from the saddle and walked towards her, all too real.

Calliope took a step back, until she felt the rough bark of a tree trunk against her hips. He stopped several feet from her, just watching her as he stripped off his gloves.

Calliope swallowed hard. She didn't know what to do, what to say! Her mother's careful etiquette lessons had never addressed how to treat a man after one kisses him.

"Good afternoon, Miss Chase," he said.

"G-good afternoon, Lord Westwood," she answered. *This* she could do. Polite conversation. "How was your journey?"

"Most uneventful. I trust you are well? And your father and sisters? Especially Miss Clio."

"Quite well, thank you. Clio seems quite recovered. They are looking forward to hearing Herr Mueller."

The corner of his lips quirked. "Indeed? They did not benefit from his, er, great wisdom sufficiently in town?"

Calliope wanted to laugh, but she kept her face perfectly serious. She could not give in to hysterics now! "The country air will also be beneficial, I believe. We did hear that you have been taking advantage of the healthy qualities of the country of late. We missed seeing you at the Burke-Smythes' Venetian breakfast last week."

"I had business with my steward, so I went to my own estate on the way here."

"Indeed?" Calliope cast about for something safe to say. So, polite conversation was not so easy as all that after all. Not when she couldn't say what she longed to— why had he kissed her? And why had he left town so soon after?

Had she been so truly dreadful?

"I have heard that your estate is quite pleasant," she finally said.

"It is very pretty," he agreed. "But lonely since my mother died. The arrangements are sadly out of date and require a lady's touch."

A lady's touch? Calliope was suddenly back to not knowing what to say. She turned towards the house, walking quickly away. "You must be tired after your journey," she said. "Lady Kenleigh has tea in the drawing room. And Emmeline is planning many excursions. A walk to the waterfalls tomorrow."

Cameron caught up his horse's reins and followed behind her, catching up with her near the empty portecochère. The abbey's blank lower windows stared out at them, unblinking.

"Calliope," he said quietly. He stopped her flight with a gentle touch on her elbow. "I've been wanting to talk with you about that night at the Antiquities Society."

"Oh. Yes." Calliope couldn't quite meet his gaze. Instead, she stared past his shoulder at the quiet horse. He watched her with a large, liquid, completely indifferent gaze. Just like the house and all those ghost monks. "You must not feel you have to apologise. It was entirely my fault. I was so worried about my sister, about the Lily Thief, and I—well, I was not myself. I'm sorry. Think no more of it."

She hurried up the steps. "Tea in the drawing room, Lord Westwood," she called, not looking back.

His voice followed her, though. It was a quiet, rough mutter, but she could vow he said, "You can't run from me for ever, Calliope Chase."

Not for ever, perhaps. But she could surely run for now.

Chapter Fifteen

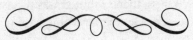

The excursion Emmeline organised for their first day was a nature walk, a trek to explore one of the area's many famous waterfalls. "You will love it," Emmeline said, as they strolled away from the house, bundled in cloaks against the morning mist. "It's so very mysterious. Like a place out of time."

A place out of time. Calliope could well believe it as she gazed around at the landscape, so different from anything she saw in her everyday life. The mist hung low to the ground, a net of silvery tulle over the dark green earth, clinging to the old stone walls. The silence was thick, broken only by the occasional bleat of a sheep or the hushed laughter of their group.

Cameron fell into step beside her, and she gave him a tentative smile. He, too, seemed different here, his fashionable town clothes and dashing yellow phaeton left behind in favour of plain scuffed boots and his blue greatcoat. His hair was carelessly brushed back, sparkling with a few bits of mist that clung to the dark strands like diamonds. Strangely, he seemed to belong here, just as he belonged at a society ball or on a Greek seashore. Wherever he went he was surely at ease.

Calliope did envy him that.

"We look like some ancient band of Norsemen, don't we?" she said. "Marching out with the dawn for some watery battle."

Cameron laughed, and as always the warm, champagne sound made her want to laugh along with him. "Do you know of the Vikings, then? I thought the Chases cared only for ancient Greece. Democracy, philosophy, the Olympic gods."

"Much like the de Veres, you mean?"

"Touché."

"It's true that Greece came first in our educations. But we read of the Vikings and Gauls, too. And once we had this governess who would tell us tales of longships and bloody raids. We did enjoy those stories."

"What happened to her? Your Viking nurse."

"She left, of course, and my mother found a new governess. One who taught us more *appropriately* bloodthirsty history of Greece and Rome."

Cameron held out a hand to help her over a low wall, and their gloved fingers clung together for a moment longer than was proper. Calliope felt quite unlike herself, for she longed for nothing more than to hold his hand tightly, to race recklessly with him across the fields.

"I hadn't thought of her tales in a long time," she said as they walked on, trailing behind the others. "This place just brings them back so vividly."

"It *is* different here," he agreed. "Mysterious."

"Do you think there were Vikings here?" she said. "Perhaps they lived among those stones up there, on the hilltop! Worshipping Thor and Odin and Freya."

Cameron laughed. "That was a Roman fort, but I fear that is the extent of my knowledge. The de Veres, much like the Chases, believe history ended some time around 300 BC."

Emmeline, strolling at the head of the group with Mr Smithson, turned back and called, "Catch up, you two! We're nearly there."

Calliope and Cameron hurried their steps, joining the others as they entered a small, gorge-like formation of rocks. The sun was beginning to peek between the clouds, burning off the mist, but not in here. Here shadows reigned, along with that ancient magic Calliope could not explain.

He took her hand as he had at the wall, holding her steady as they descended a steep, sandy path into the enchanted land. The soles of her half-boots slipped a bit, but she trusted he would not let her fall. The river, a quiet, silvery-blue stream, suddenly seemed to bubble and writhe, stirred to a wild froth by some invisible hand. It rushed down into the gorge and dropped, dozens of feet, into a pool, tumbling and arcing over rock slabs.

The smell of the earth was strong, dark green in Calliope's nostrils, wild garlic and moss, wildflowers that miraculously peeked out of the rocky bed.

Her steps paused, and she just stared and stared, captured by the otherworldly scene. She clung to Cameron's hand, and it was as if everything—her friends, her place in the world, even the Alabaster Goddess—disappeared. Everything she thought was important slipped away, and she had only this one moment.

"Calliope?" Cameron asked quietly, peering back at her. "Are you all right?"

"It's so beautiful," she whispered. "Have you ever seen anything more lovely?"

"Only once," he said, and one of his gloved fingertips

reached up to touch, ever so delicately, a curl that sprang free from her hood.

Flustered, her face hot, Calliope tugged away from him. Her moment of magic was gone, vanished in her old awkwardness, and she walked towards the group, as quickly as she could on the slick sand. How could he do that to her, every time she saw him? Make her forget herself, her task, her place in their oh-so-careful world.

He swept her up in his golden glow, all his freedom and beauty, and she forgot everything for that happy moment. She was as drawn to his spell as every other woman in London—"the Greek god", she remembered her friends sighing.

A god, one of light and merriment. And she was the most didactic of the Muses, full of practicality and lectures, the need for careful study and preservation. Not romance. Not wild paeans to nature and culture.

That was what she could not forget. She and Cameron were allies now, true, drawn together to save the Alabaster Goddess. But when Artemis was safe, they would still be themselves. Two very different people.

Once she reached Clio's side, she paused to gaze at the sky above them, a pale blue sliver that barely lit the dim grotto below. It was like her own mind—she almost grasped some truth, some hidden purpose, and it was like that bit of light. Far away and elusive, it slid away before she could grasp it.

She peered at Clio, who solemnly watched the tumbling falls. Somehow, her sister had become like this grotto, too. Dark and elusive, full of mysterious crevices where ghosts could hide. It frightened Calliope, because she would do anything to save Clio from whatever haunted her. Yet she couldn't save her, not if she didn't know what that was.

"I love it here," Clio said. "It's surely an ancient place. Older than human memory, than anything we can fathom."

"They say there's a cave back there, behind the falls," Emmeline said.

"I should swim over, then, to see!" Thalia said. She spoke teasingly, as if to recall their earlier quarrel. But Calliope closed her eyes in despair, for it was just the sort of thing Thalia really would do.

"You would catch your death," Clio said absently. "Do tell us more about these falls, Emmeline, for I'm sure there must be so many legends."

For the next hour, they all sat perched on the stone slabs by the water, listening to Emmeline's tales of ancient water spirits. Calliope was all too aware of Cameron's gaze on her, across the cold chasm of the magical river.

By the time they started for home, the sun appeared in earnest, breaking through the clouds to dispel the last of the morning mist. The land was no less beautiful, but it *was* less mystical, laid out for view in squares and rectangles divided by those ubiquitous walls. There were farmers in their fields, carts and hulking horses, white lumps of sheep meandering in search of fodder. Just daily life, free of magic.

Still, Calliope could not quite shake off the spell of the falls. That sense of being lost, even in her own mind. She didn't like these feelings, didn't like being confused.

There was only one way to break free. She had to concentrate on the Alabaster Goddess. She remembered the paper tucked secretly into her baggage, the list of names she had copied from the one Clio had found inside the Alabaster Goddess. Surely they meant something important? Perhaps they were that elusive clue that shimmered just out of her reach, and they would unlock all else.

She glanced back at Cameron, who strolled with Lotty, listening to her talk of her latest novel. He listened to her most seriously, nodding at all the appropriate moments, making polite comments. He betrayed not one jot of impatience. Maybe he was a reader of horrid novels himself.

There was really nothing else to do but show him the list soon. She couldn't decipher it herself, and perhaps he, knowing something of the duke and his world, would have some ideas. Or perhaps he would just indulge her whims, as he was doing with Lotty.

"Let's go this way," Emmeline said, breaking into Calliope's thoughts. "It's a quicker route back than the main road, and Papa said Herr Mueller wants to talk to us before luncheon. Something about Socrates, I think. Or Sophocles?"

"One can hardly wait," Clio muttered. "We'll be sitting there until after dinnertime, getting hungrier and hungrier. *Ja, fräulein...*"

Calliope laughed. "Shh! Herr Mueller is very distinguished. We're fortunate to benefit from his knowledge."

"If you say so," Clio said doubtfully. "Indeed, knowledge is never wasted. But I prefer the waterfall."

They followed Emmeline down a narrower path, between an arch of wind-bent branches that cast shifting shadows over the ground. It was quiet here, almost eerily silent, broken only by their own murmurs, the crackle of their footsteps on the underbrush.

"I believe Lotty would call this *The Lair of the Forest Witch*," Clio whispered. "Beware, o ye who enter here!"

Calliope laughed, but she had to suppress a shiver.

At last they left the wood, turning on to a wider, sunnier walkway, only to be faced with yet another enchanted scene. A castle, set high on a distant hilltop, framed by the vast sky.

It was not as old as the Vikings, but surely old enough. Fourteenth century, Calliope guessed, gazing at the rough stone walls, the crenellated battlements that needed only fluttering pennants to make them complete. Arrow slits stared out at them darkly, and no doubt a drawbridge and moat could be seen on closer inspection. It was silent, a solid hulk guarding the landscape. Beautiful, in its own way. Complete in a way other local castles, famous ruins like Bolton and Richmond, were not.

Permanent, and cold.

"That's Averton Castle," Emmeline said.

Somehow, Calliope was not surprised. The structure was so like the duke. Mysterious, beautiful, but in an off-putting way, strangely archaic.

The Alabaster Goddess was in that chilly fortress somewhere, locked away. Hidden.

Calliope reached for Clio's hand. Clio didn't turn her gaze from the castle, but neither did she pull away. Her fingers curled tightly around Calliope's. "Typical," was all she said. Then she drew away, and walked on.

Chapter Sixteen

"...In Oedipus, Sophocles shows us a man both cursed and blessed, vindicated through his many sufferings. He has lived out the themes of both freedom and destiny, as you see from this passage here..."

Calliope shifted slightly in her chair, watching Herr Mueller politely as he talked on about the Oedipus plays. Really, tonight she had no time for men killing their fathers, marrying their mothers, and ending up blind and wandering the countryside! She had concerns of her own.

Concerns that hopefully would end a bit better than tangling with "freedom and destiny".

She folded her hands over her beaded reticule, feeling the edges of the paper folded within. Across the room sat Cameron, also watching the professor. But his eyes seemed curiously blank, as if his true self had slipped off somewhere.

What was he thinking about? she mused. The Greek lands Oedipus wandered? She could almost see it—sun beating down on broken marble statues. Lizards skittering through dried thistle. A different place of old spells, of heat that never ended.

Maybe that was really what they were trying to recapture here, with their lectures, their endless discussions of old politics, old gods. Not freedom really, *or* destiny. Just that Greek sun, and the old creatures who reigned there. Gods and nymphs and naiads.

She glanced again at Cameron, who always seemed to embody those very dreams. Summer laziness that concealed a quicksilver changeability.

He shifted in his seat, catching her gaze. He smiled at her, and she nodded, tucking the reticule more securely in her clasp. After the lecture, she would have to find some way to speak to him alone, without incurring her friends' speculation—or Clio's questions. Somehow she wasn't yet ready to tell her sister she had enlisted Cameron's help.

Calliope turned her gaze to her sister, who sat on a chaise with Thalia and Lotty. She appeared to be listening to Herr Mueller, but her fingers kept plucking at her skirt, pleating the Turkey red muslin. Like Cameron, she seemed far away.

Soon enough, they would surely have all the answers. The thief would be caught, the goddess safe, and life would go back to normal.

Only Calliope feared that "normal", whatever that was, would be quite impossible after all this. After Cameron. He had turned "normal" topsy-turvy, and she wasn't sure she could ever right it again.

Or if she even wanted to.

Lady Kenleigh at last managed to bring Herr Mueller's lecture to a long-winded close, long after the light of sunset had vanished beyond the windows and night's chill set in. Calliope's father and a few of the others clustered around the professor with their questions, while Emmeline led the younger set into the dinning room, where a buffet supper was laid out.

"Hearing about Oedipus's travails certainly does work up an appetite!" Thalia said, reaching eagerly for her plate.

"I certainly feel that way after hearing about a good eye-gouging," Clio muttered. "Just tea for me, thank you."

Calliope strolled casually to Cameron's side, keeping an eye on her sisters to make sure they stayed together, too far away to overhear.

"And what do *you* think of poor Oedipus, Miss Chase?" he said, handing her a cup of tea from one of the footmen.

"Herr Mueller's views are most interesting," she answered.

"His views are most commonplace. They're what every scholar says these days. When will someone come out and say something shocking, such as that Oedipus's downfall was a Spartan plot? Or a Persian ploy?"

Calliope laughed. "Is that what you really believe?"

Cameron shrugged, but grinned at her laughter. "I have no strong feelings about Oedipus at all, I fear."

"Neither do I, I confess. I'm too fanciful. I prefer tales of gods and goddesses."

"'Fanciful', my dear Miss Chase, would be the last word I would think of to describe you."

Then what word *would* he use? Calliope ached to ask, yet truly she feared to know the answer. Would it be "dull"? "Annoying"? But all she said was, "I fear you may change your mind once I show you what is in my reticule."

A light glinted in his eyes. "I burn with curiosity, Miss Chase."

"I can't show it to you here. Emmeline is going to organise a game of charades later. I'll excuse myself to repair my hem or something, see if you can meet me in the small sitting room off the library. It won't take long."

She gave him a nod, and moved away to chat with Emmeline and Mr Smithson. Would this work?

Of course it would. It simply had to.

Calliope stood by the window of the little sitting room. The view was not of the terraced gardens as her own windows were, but of the sweep of the front drive, the long avenue of trees leading out the gates where she had watched Cameron come galloping in. The moon was bright tonight, the sky clear, and she fancied she could see the battlements of the duke's castle.

That was silly, of course, for that fortress was too far away. The duke's presence seemed to make itself felt all over the countryside, though. He lurked over all, like a great bird of prey.

Calliope took the list out of her reticule, smoothing it over the windowsill. What did those names mean? How did they fit together?

Behind her, the door clicked open softly. She looked back to see Cameron, outlined for an instant by the light from the corridor before he shut the door behind him. He stayed across the room, leaning back against the wall, but the space was small and she could feel his presence most acutely. Smell him, feel his warmth. She remembered the last time they were alone in the dark, in that study at the Antiquities Society. He kissed her then, and she had not been able to forget the way it felt.

Calliope tugged her shawl closer about her shoulders. "Did anyone see you leave?" she asked.

He shook his head, the movement distinct in the chalky moonlight. "Most of the gentlemen excused themselves for a quick brandy before being forced to play charades. I just slipped away at the same time—the ladies will think I went with the men, the men will think I stayed with the ladies. For a few minutes, anyway."

"Very clever."

"Of course. Is my cleverness not why you summoned me here? Or was it my handsome—eyes?"

"Both, as a matter of fact."

"Indeed? I'm intrigued." He came closer, standing with her by the window.

"I need your eyes to look at this, and your cleverness to tell me what it means," she said, firmly setting away memories of that kiss. Or trying to, anyway. She handed him the paper.

Cameron tilted it to the light, a frown touching his brow. "The Golden Falcon? The Purple Hyacinth? I fear my cleverness is not equal to this task. It seems like gibberish. Where did you get this?"

"Clio found it on the night of the duke's ball. Hidden in the base of the Alabaster Goddess."

He glanced at her in surprise. "This?"

"Well, this particular list is a copy. Clio has the original. I can't figure it out at all. Is it a code, do you think?"

"I have no idea." He read it over again. "At university, I remember Averton and his equally noxious friends had some ridiculous nicknames for each other. I don't think these are they, but it may be something similar."

"A list of his friends? Some kind of secret society?"

"Like your Ladies Society?" he said, smiling.

"Our Ladies Society is hardly secret," she huffed. "And we don't give each other silly monikers."

"Of course not. It's others who call you the Chase Muses."

"I didn't ask to be named Calliope, you know. I would have much preferred Elizabeth. Or Jane."

"Really? You don't strike me as a Jane."

"I'm much more a Jane than a Calliope. And we are off the subject! What do you think this list is? A criminal ring?"

His smile faded as he examined the list again. "I wouldn't put it past Averton. The man is capable of anything when he's bored, or determined. But I can't decide why. The days of smuggling French wines and silks are past, yet from here he does have access to the old tunnels at Robin Hood's Bay for whatever he has going on." Cameron stared out the window, as if he, too, imagined he could see those forbidding battlements. "I need to think about this, and you should get back to the drawing room. May I keep the list?"

Calliope nodded. Those odd names were surely burned into her brain by now. "Of course. But won't you come back, too?"

"Not yet." He smiled at her, reaching out to briefly, softly touch her hand. "Whatever would people say, if they saw us come into the room together?"

Calliope laughed. The gossip would increase, of course, and they would have to become engaged. And that would be terrible.

Wouldn't it?

Calliope opened her eyes to find herself lying not in the comfortable, curtained bed in her guest chamber, but on a cold stone floor. She blinked into the darkness around her, her mind as heavy and hazy as if it was wrapped in cotton wool. She slowly pushed herself upright, confused. She didn't remember leaving her bed! And certainly didn't remember seeing anything like this.

It was a grotto of some sort, a room all of rough stone, treacherous as daggers. The only light came from a mys-

*terious source high overhead, a pale, wavery yellow-green.
As if from far away, she heard a dull, rushing noise.*

Oh, *she thought.* I'm behind the waterfall.

And, in the same moment, I must be dreaming.

*Of course. A dream. But what could it mean? Why
would her dreams be of a spot she had never actually
seen? A cold, stony place full of chilly draughts and dank
smells.*

*Calliope pushed herself to her feet. She wore her
dressing gown and bedroom slippers, but was not cold at
all. Now that she knew it was only a dream, she had only
curiosity. What in her sleeping mind had brought her here?
She followed the source of the light.*

*It led out of the grotto room down a long, narrow
corridor. The ceiling was very low, the stone floor under
her thin shoes slippery. Strangest of all, the walls were
lined with objects she remembered from Acropolis House.
Daphne, the Egyptian lioness, Pan with his flute. Their
marble eyes followed her as she rushed past, their mute
stares accusing.* Why didn't you save us? *she could almost
hear them whisper.* Why did you leave us?

*Calliope's steps quickened until she was running,
dashing down the corridor as if she could leave them
behind. Their cold stares, their eerie voices. She ran until
she tripped, falling forward into rushing wind, into nothingness. Too terrified even to scream, she covered her eyes,
waiting for the crushing death she was sure awaited her.*

*It never came. Instead she landed on what felt like a
feather bed, soft and enveloping. Warm. Cautiously, slowly,
she lowered her hands, peering around her.*

*It was not a bed, but the sarcophagus she was laying
on. And in front of her was the Alabaster Goddess, bathed
in that murky green light, her bow held aloft. Like the*

statues in the narrow corridor, her eyes seemed alive, yet not accusing. She looked—compassionate. Concerned. That was odd, for Artemis was surely one of the least caring of the rather callous Pantheon! She had no compunction about turning men into deer and shooting them full of arrows if they displeased her.

Don't be foolish, *Calliope chided herself, sitting up on the sarcophagus.* This is only a dream. *A friendly Artemis made as much sense as a grotto full of antiquities.*

"What am I doing here?" *she asked.*

"I summoned you, of course," *Artemis answered. Her marble lips didn't move, yet her voice echoed all around. She sounded just as Calliope would have imagined— young but full of authority. Confidence. She seemed, in fact, much like Clio.*

"Why?" *Calliope dangled her feet off the sarcophagus's gilded edge, but dared not jump down. She could see only darkness below.*

"You and your friends have loved and served me well," *Artemis said.* "I must warn you, though. Your mission here holds many dangers."

"Dangers?" *Calliope thought of the duke lying on the floor bleeding. Of Clio's ruined costume. Cameron kissing her in the dark.* "Surely we have already faced dangers."

She fancied Artemis looked pitying. "Not like what is to come, my Muse. I have many hidden enemies, you know. Enemies that are yours now. You must stay strong. Stay your course—my course—and all will be well in the end. Remember that when you have doubts. Remember this when the enemies at last reveal themselves, and you find all is not as you thought."

"But…" *Calliope began, even as Artemis faded away into the shadows. She fell again, toppling from the sar-*

*cophagus into that waiting blackness below. When she
landed, it was not on a hard floor or jagged rocks. It was
a grassy summer meadow. She felt herself rolling, rolling,
down a slope scented with sunshine and wildflowers.*

*Her headlong trajectory was only halted when she
collided with a pair of polished boots. Stunned, breathless,
Calliope stared up to find Cameron peering down at her.
He was outlined in brilliant sunlight, dazzling after the dim
grotto, his curls tangled in the breeze.*

*"Calliope," he said, his tone coaxing. Alluring. He leaned
down, smiling at her. That merry, careless grin she loved so
much. What did it hide? "Please. Let me help you…"*

*He held out his hand, and she wanted to take it more than
she had ever wanted anything. To feel his skin on hers. But
she remembered Artemis's words.* Hidden enemies.

*She scrambled to her feet, backing away from him—
from what she felt. It was no use, though, for she found
herself all alone in that meadow. And a cloud was passing
over the sun…*

Calliope awoke with a gasp. She glanced around frantically, half-expecting to find herself back in the damp
grotto. She was in her bedchamber, though, the fire burnt
down to glowing embers and the bedclothes twisted and
kicked away. The canopy and half-drawn curtains, so dark
and heavy, red brocade so unlike her own blue-and-white
chintz at home, seemed suffocating. Engulfing. She
climbed out of bed, wrapping herself tightly in her dressing
gown as she went to the window.

The moon was still bright as it glimmered down on the
deserted gardens. Silvery-green, it turned the fountain and
statues below into shimmering, magical objects so different from their solid, daytime presence.

Calliope took a deep breath, still caught in that dream. How very vivid it was! Usually she didn't remember her dreams at all, or if she did they were terribly prosaic and dry. No hidden enemies or water-fall rooms. No Cameron.

She remembered those antiquities in her dream, their empty gazes that seemed so alive. Their eerie whispers. Such objects had never really seemed *alive* to her before. Important, of course. Beautiful, to be sure. Symbols of something that had once been alive, of lessons to be learned. But not living, vital objects in themselves, with their own desires. Their own wills.

Their own proper place in the world.

Calliope crossed her arms tightly against the late night chill. The disturbing shift of something inside herself. Was this, then, what Cameron meant when he spoke about art? When he sent his father's collections back to Greece? She had not understood then. Truth to tell, she did not understand now. Modern Greece was *not* the Greece that produced such objects. But still...

Her roiling thoughts were interrupted by a ripple in the shadows below her window. Calliope leaned closer to the cold glass, peering down. Was she still dreaming? Seeing things that weren't there? The next thing she glimpsed could be the Alabaster Goddess herself, marching down the walkway!

But the figures that appeared, detaching themselves from the shadows to step into the moonlight, were all too real. A tall, lean person in a greatcoat and wide-brimmed hat, and a smaller figure swathed in a cloak. They lingered next to the fountain, heads bent close together as they talked.

Slowly, Calliope opened her window, careful of squeaks and creaks as the old latch gave way. Surely it was just a couple out for a rendezvous. But it wouldn't hurt to eavesdrop, just a bit. Artemis had warned about hidden enemies.

There was little breeze to carry voices to her ears, unfortunately. All she could make out were soft, indistinct murmurs, unidentifiable. Just a few words carried—"...soon", "...tide", "...here."

Calliope frowned. Even she could make nothing of such meagre scraps! She still watched, listening closely to see if anything else would be revealed. After a few moments, the cloaked figure handed the other a letter, a pale square in the darkness. "Wait," Calliope heard. Then the hatted one hurried away, and the cloaked one turned back towards the house. For just an instant, the hood fell away and a silvery beam glinted on the glass of spectacles. A long braid of auburn hair.

Calliope gasped, drawing back to the concealment of the draperies. *Clio!* As she stared, disbelieving, her sister drew the hood back into place, rushing towards the house. She disappeared, and the night was silent once more.

Calliope pressed her hand to her mouth. What was Clio doing? Who was that person in the hat? Some sort of illicit romance? Yet the scene had not had a romantic quality. No furtive embraces, no passionate kisses. Clio surely had been behaving strangely of late. So solemn and short-tempered. Yet who could blame her, after what happened with the duke? Did this, then, have something to do with Averton?

Hidden enemies, Artemis had whispered. Calliope foolishly clapped her hands over her ears, but the words were still there. She feared they would never leave again.

Chapter Seventeen

The next day dawned bright and clear, as if in mockery of Calliope's late night. She opened the window of her bedchamber, leaning out to breathe deeply of the clear, misty air, the cold, clean tinge of earth. The cold breeze lashed at her cheeks, reviving her after the strange dreams of the night. The image, equally dreamlike now, of Clio in the garden.

She scowled as she watched the gardens come to life, workers hurrying out on their morning tasks, the distant bleats of sheep. Had she made a mistake last night, showing Cameron that list? Especially since Clio was now somehow involved. She remembered his unreadable eyes, his non-committal response. And yet he had asked to keep the list, so the names must mean something to him.

She rubbed hard at her itchy eyes, trying to stop her thoughts from spinning so endlessly, trying to erase the vestiges of her dreams. She almost wished she had never seen that list at all, never heard of the Lily Thief or his deeds!

Oh, but then she would never have gotten to know Cameron, a treacherous little voice whispered in her mind. Would never have seen what he was truly like. She would still be caught in her old notions of him. Her old impressions of carelessness and empty drama.

But what was it she thought of him now? What had she seen behind the charming façade that convinced her to ask for his help, to show him that list?

He was a puzzle, and one she didn't have time to decipher this morning. She had to get ready for today's picnic, for more of Herr Mueller's lectures—even when the ancient world was so far from her mind. For once, the here and now seemed far more important. More urgent.

She reached out to close the window, to block the morning wind, but paused as she heard a door below open. Clio again? She leaned back out, watching in surprise as Cameron came into view. After her dreams last night, she could almost believe her thoughts had summoned him.

He seemed so much a part of this wild place, with his dark greatcoat, his hair tumbling free, no hat or cravat to restrain him. She remembered hearing gossip, vague drawing-room whispers that he had run with bandits in the Greek hills. She could believe that now, as he strode across the lawn, his boots scattering the morning dew on the grass. There was something not of this world, the everyday English world, about him. Maybe that was why she trusted him with the list, trusted him to see what it all meant. A Greek bandit would never react as any other man of her acquaintance, men of convention, would.

He *was* different, and that was what had both scared her and drawn her in from the first moment she saw him. Yet what would a man like him see in a woman like her?

"Cameron," she called softly.

He spun around, and saw her there in the window. His expression, one of serious thought, did not alter, but he lifted his hand to wave to her. She gestured at him to stay where he was and shut the window. Catching up her cloak from where she left it after their walk to the falls, she swirled it over her shoulders as she hurried downstairs. No one else was about so early, except for the maids with their firewood and buckets of water, and no one questioned her as she slipped outside into the fresh morning air.

Cameron waited for her on the gravel walkway near the fountain, the same place where Clio had met her mystery man. "You're up early," he said. She could still read nothing in his countenance, in his cognac-coloured eyes, not surprise or pleasure—or irritation that she had interrupted whatever errand he was on.

"So are you," she answered. "I couldn't sleep for thinking about everything." She couldn't tell him about the dream. About his place in it.

"The list," he said. "Yes. It puzzled me, too."

"Have you been able to decipher it yet?"

He shook his head. "It does seem to be a code of some sort. Without the key…"

"A list of some criminal circle?"

"Led by the duke?"

"Well, it *was* found in his statue. Would it surprise you to learn he led some sort of illegal antiquities scheme? That he was up to criminal deeds?"

Cameron laughed ruefully. "Not at all. But, really, why would he? He can gain any piece of art he wants by more straightforward means."

Calliope remembered the glow in the duke's eyes as he gazed at his Daphne. As he stroked her cold marble cheek, comparing her to Clio. "The thrill of the chase, perhaps. The *frisson* from doing something forbidden, when so little is denied a duke."

Cameron smiled at her, that serious, flat look vanishing

like the mist. "Forbidden—like talking to me alone in the garden, before the rest of the house is even awake?"

Calliope laughed. He did have her there, and it was yet another sign of how things had changed between them. The old Calliope would never have done this! "It is hardly on a level with stealing art. But I do suppose I understand a bit better now the attraction of the—unconventional."

"I knew you would be converted eventually," he said, and reached out to touch one long curl of her loose hair. His touch was light, teasing, yet there was something in his gaze that made her breath catch. Her stomach lurched nervously.

Silly, she told herself. *It's because you haven't had breakfast.* She batted away his fingers and stepped back. "I haven't been 'converted' to the unconventional that thoroughly, sir," she said lightly.

Cameron shrugged, tucking his hands into his pockets as if to prevent them from touching her hair again. "It's only a matter of time, you know, Calliope. Freedom once tasted is addictive."

"Is that what you have found, Cameron?" she asked quietly. "Do you miss freedom?"

He smiled, yet she could see it was not his merry grin. It was a mere shadow. Like her dream. "Am I not free?"

"They say that in Greece you lived with bandits."

"So I did. For a time. They needed money for their causes, you see, and I paid them to take me to ancient sites most people never see. Temples and tombs, far from civilisation."

Calliope could almost see it—broken pillars, hidden gods in faraway caves, dusty, sun-drenched valleys, scrubby olive trees. "That is what I mean. It must be hard to go from that to—this."

"Being an English lord, you mean? We all do what we must. What we're born for. Is that not so, Calliope?"

Do what we must. Yes. For was that not what she always did? What was expected. What was her duty. "Do you never miss Greece? Want to go back?"

"Perhaps one day I will."

There was a noise behind them, a shutter opening, the splash of water pouring down the old abbey wall. The house beginning to stir in earnest.

"I should go in," she said reluctantly. She didn't want to go inside, she wanted to stay here and hear more about Greece. About sunshine and bandits.

"Yes," he said.

"But we do have to talk more about the list," she insisted. "At the picnic."

He nodded, and she spun around and dashed into the house. More servants were on the stairs now, carrying clothes to be pressed for the day, water for washing, breakfast trays. She hurried past them to her own chamber, chased by visions of those dashing bandits.

Cameron watched Calliope run away, watched even after she disappeared into the house, leaving only a whisper of rose perfume in the air.

He had never seen her hair down before. It was beautiful; long black curls spreading over her shoulders, down her back in untamed spirals and whorls. She didn't resemble Athena with that hair, but a wood nymph, running free, laughing with abandon among the primeval trees.

Primeval trees? Blast it all, he *was* in trouble now if he had resorted to such whimsy! Such cheap poetics. Calliope Chase was just a woman, a lady, and yet he was finding she was a woman like no other. A woman who wouldn't leave his thoughts, his fantasies.

New fantasies of walking with her, hand in hand, on a

Greek shore, the turquoise waves lapping at their bare feet. Of kissing her under the hot Mediterranean sun, tasting the salt and light on her lips.

Cameron turned away from the house, striding off down the pathway as if he could walk away just as easily from *her*. From the memory of that night at the Antiquities Society, and the soft press of her body against his in the darkness. She wouldn't be so easily abandoned, though, her pale ghost trailing beside him. *What about the list?* she whispered.

Ah, yes—that list. Those odd names, exactly like silly young men in a secret society would devise. Charlemagne, the Grey Dove, the Purple Hyacinth. It did seem rather like a gambit that would appeal to Averton, with his flair for the dramatic, the archaic. Yet to what purpose? Why write such a thing and then hide it in the Alabaster Goddess?

Cameron considered himself to be rather a straightforward person. Subterfuge was so very time-consuming. The duke surely had money and artwork aplenty. Why indulge in some kind of game of theft, unless it was just for the thrill of it? And what role did Clio Chase play in all of this?

He had to confess he couldn't understand it—yet. But he soon would. He was determined on it.

As the long afternoon advanced, the feast of their picnic put away, Calliope felt the lassitude of the day wash over her. The sun was warm on her head, her stomach happily full, and the sleepless night suddenly too much. She leaned back against the rough bark of a tree trunk in perfect laziness, closing her eyes as she listened to the murmur of the stream, the voices of the others as they strolled by the water. Their laughter rose and fell, an indistinct hum, soothing, familiar. How lovely this was, she thought, how easy, with dreams and worries far away for now. Just to *be* for a few minutes.

"'By the blue and shining lake, where the grasses trail, I hang my purple robes in golden rays of sunlight,'" she heard Cameron say.

She opened her eyes and smiled at him. He lounged at the edge of their picnic blanket, his face turned up to the light, hair falling back from his brow, his beautiful cheekbones. One finger reached out to touch the hem of her skirt, and she kicked at him playfully, not quite hard enough to dislodge him. He merely tightened his clasp, feigning to tug her down next to him.

Laughing, Calliope said, "I thought you were going walking with the others."

He shook his head, eyes still closed. "Not at all. I'm far too full of that excellent lemon tart to even think of moving. Besides, we should enjoy the sun while we have it. The sky will be grey again soon enough."

"Very true." Calliope tipped her head back against the tree, watching, mesmerised, as he stroked the fabric of her hem, smoothing it, caressing. "It's a splendid day. All blue and yellow."

"The ancient Greeks measured colours not as we do, in shades, but in light."

"'Violet-crowned Athens.'"

"Exactly. I never knew how true that was until I saw it. Such a strange luminosity."

Calliope lazily gazed at the others, who sat now by the side of the stream, singing, their shining hair and pastel muslins like flowers. She could believe that about colours and light today. The grey-green of the earth, the silver of the water. It glimmered in the sun, something so alive and vibrant. "Tell me more about Greece," she said, remembering the living statues. "I have studied it my whole life, yet I don't know it at all. Not as you do, not as a living thing. Full of bandits and such."

Cameron laughed. "Greece is *hot*. Dry, dusty. Yet there are bays of rugged coastline, which make the country seem half-land and half-sea. The sky and the sea are so brilliant a blue, sometimes turquoise, sometimes deep and mysterious, like a sapphire. The Greeks are attuned to nature, you know, in a way we aren't. Or at least haven't been since the days of that barrow up there. They people the mountains and woods and streams, the sky, even the salty breezes from the sea."

"Like the Muses in their groves, or Zeus from the peak of Olympus?"

"Just so. The land is truly alive to them."

"And did it come alive for you?"

He didn't answer right away. Instead he sat up, swinging around to stare at the stream, his knees drawn up to his chest. Calliope sensed he didn't see that satiny water, the cluster of their friends. Surely he was far from her, ensnared in hot, dusty Greece.

"One of my mother's favourite places was the island of Delos," he said. "Her father, who was a great scholar, used to take her then when she was a girl, and she would tell me tales of it when I was a child. Great sagas of how Apollo and his twin Artemis were born there, of how, long before the golden age of Athens, the rise of Delphi, Delos held all the great riches of the land in its marble sanctuary. Gold, silver, gems. The necklace of Eriphyle, the tiller of Agamemnon."

Calliope leaned forward, fascinated by this sudden glimpse of Cameron's soul, a solemn essence so often hidden behind his dazzling smile. "Did you go there?"

"Of course. It was not the place of my mother's tales, though. Like you, I grew up on stories of Greece as it was thousands of years ago. Marble pillars, great temples, the birth of freedom. It is not like that now, especially on Delos."

"Perhaps it is best I stay here, then! Preserve my illusions."

Cameron tossed her a grin. "I wondered that, too, when I first saw the dusty reality of modern Greece. And yet on Delos I found something I did not expect. Something—magical."

Calliope crept closer until she sat beside him, slowly, lest she break the spell the sunny day bestowed on them. "Tell me about it."

"You know the *Homeric Ode to Delian Apollo*?"

"A bit. 'How shall I receive the god, the proud one, the arrogant one who stands in the highest place, above all the gods and people of the teeming earth.'"

"Yes. From Delos Apollo became the protector of human reason. He may have ruled from Delphi, but he was born and raised on Delos. Yet it seems such an unpromising place for such youthful gods. Tiny, barely three miles long and one mile wide, barren, with marshes and crags. I first went there in the early morning; it was so grey and misty as the boat drew near. The place had the look of an abandoned quarry, littered with broken stone among the wild barley grass.

"Yet by noon the mist had cleared, the sun was out in full force. And I saw what my mother saw. The stones there are not the honey colour of the Parthenon, Calliope, but such a pure white it is almost silver. They glitter in the light, flashing off the water and marble. Never still. Alive in the hot silence where only lizards live."

Calliope could almost see it all. "Wasn't Apollo a scourge of lizards, among his many other talents?"

Cameron laughed. "So he was. He seems to have made peace with them, though. They dart among his sacred swans, as those stone birds peacefully circle their lost lake."

"The swans don't sound very careful of the island's treasures."

"They have no need to be. Artemis and her army of lionesses take care of that."

"Like our friend at the duke's house? Greek cousins, perhaps?"

"Indeed, I believe she must have been the ancestor of those Delian creatures. They are young, you see, hot for battle. Crouched and ready to spring. Once there were fourteen of them, they say; now there are only five, and one guards the Arsenal in Venice. But though they are fewer they are no less vicious. The swans happily circle their lake, while the lionesses guard."

"Yet they allowed *you* entrance."

"Perhaps they remembered my mother. Artemis was her favourite goddess."

Calliope remembered the Alabaster Goddess, poised with her bow, whispering of enemies. For an instant, she pictured her at the entrance to Delos, fierce and elegant, keeping intruders away from the circling swans sparkling silver-white in the intense sun. "How I would love to go there."

"One day you will, Calliope."

She shook her head. "I'm not fearless like you are. Not full of adventure."

He shot her an unfathomable glance. "No? I would think anyone who was determined to chase down a thief would have to possess a heart full of adventure."

"No. I just want to see justice done." If she even knew any longer what *justice* was.

Cameron just shrugged and reached for the picnic basket, rummaging about until he found the last of the lemon tarts. "I think you might surprise yourself, Calliope Chase."

He held out the tart, the bright yellow cream poised temptingly just beyond her lips. She bit into it, feeling the sharp burst of tart citrus on her tongue, echoing the sun overhead.

How she liked this day, Calliope thought as she swallowed the lemony morsel and smiled at Cameron. She liked the sun and sky, the whisper of the water, the nearness of her dearest friends. She liked the strange, ancient magic of this land. She felt free here, far from the prying eyes of town, the shackles of her own practicality. It seemed a time out of time, a short span where she didn't have to be herself. She could be whoever she wanted.

She could even be someone adventurous. And it was Cameron who made her feel that. Believe it. Because *he* was so free, she could be, too, as long as she was with him.

"What are you thinking?" he asked, reaching up with his thumb to wipe away a trace of lemon on her chin.

Calliope trembled at the brush of his skin, so rough on hers. "I was thinking what a very beautiful day it is."

He grinned at her, and leaned just a tiny bit closer. The dark glow of his eyes said he wanted to kiss her, and, despite the proximity of the others, she wanted him to. More than she had ever wanted anything in her life.

But before their lips could touch, a shadow descended over his face as his glance flashed over her shoulder. Suddenly cold with disappointment, Calliope looked back—and froze.

At the top of the slope that led down to their little sheltered valley was the Duke of Averton, mounted on a large black horse that snorted and pranced in place. With his long cloak and loose, bright hair, his expression intent as he stared down at their party, he reminded Calliope of an unhappy god. Hades, perhaps, breaking up a summer flower-picking party to snatch poor, unsuspecting Persephone.

Calliope turned frantically towards Clio, surely the prospective Persephone. She hadn't seen him, was examining a cluster of water plants with Thalia, laughing. It was surely the first time Calliope had heard her laugh for days, especially after her mysterious late night. Why did the duke have to come ruin things, as always?

Beside her, Cameron rose to his feet, all of his warm lassitude vanished. Calliope closed the basket where the cheese knives were—just in case.

In the end, though, there was no need to lock up weapons. The duke wheeled his horse around and galloped away, leaving only a ray of chalky sunlight in his place. Clio never even saw him.

Calliope sat back on the blanket, suddenly limp with relief. Cameron, though, still stood next to her, stiff and alert. Combative as any creature of Artemis.

"This can't go on," he muttered. "Not like this."

Clio *had* seen the duke. How could she avoid it, when the man insisted on appearing like some black wraith alighting on the hill? She didn't betray her notice, though, just went on talking as if a cloud hadn't just shadowed their lovely day.

Why did he have to plague her so? Why did he always have to appear wherever she happened to be, watching, reminding.

But she knew why. And she intended to be the victor in this particular game. There was simply no other way.

After a few moments, that icy sensation at the back of her neck vanished, leaving only the kiss of the sun, and she knew he was gone. She stood up, stretching her back as she gazed at the now-empty ridge. He wouldn't always be gone so easily, she knew that. And she wouldn't always have a stone statue within reach, either. She had to watch herself, be far more careful than she had ever been before.

Not just careful of the duke. She saw Calliope watching her, eyes narrowed in concern. Just as she had watched ever since the night of the masquerade ball. Not asking, not prying, for surely she knew Clio would never divulge all. Just watching. Had she been watching last night, too?

Clio sighed. How she hated deceiving Calliope, of all people! She loved her sister dearly, despite Calliope's managing tendencies, despite her need to make things *right*, even when that was clearly impossible. But it had to be done. Clio would never endanger Calliope, or any of her family.

She had chosen this path. She was willing to risk its dangers. Her sisters had not. In fact, Calliope was surely one of the very dangers she feared!

But no danger was greater than the Duke of Averton. He was like the hydra. Cut off one of his fearsome heads and another popped up in its place.

Clio waved to Calliope and shot her a bright smile. There was no fighting the hydra today. The sun was too warm, the air too sweet, rich with the scents of crystal water and mossy earth. A rare day of peace and accord. It shouldn't be squandered.

Chapter Eighteen

The village assembly rooms were surely not Almack's, just as Lady Kenleigh had said. But then, Calliope had always found Almack's vastly overrated—indifferent music, abysmal refreshments, and insipid conversation, not to mention arbitrary rules. Order was one thing; senseless silliness another.

This building was the largest in the village, long and low, sturdy local grey stone with high windows shining with welcoming light. She could hear the faint, lively strains of a reel as they alighted from the carriage. Music and laughter, brightly clad figures darting behind the old, wavy glass, beckoning her to join in the fun.

"At least we won't see any dukes here," Clio whispered, taking Calliope's arm as they climbed the shallow stone steps.

"We can always hope, anyway," Calliope answered.

"He does have the disconcerting habit of popping up wherever we are, lurking about behind trees and statues. I doubt he would want to bring such attention to himself by appearing at a village assembly, though." Clio handed her shawl to an attendant, pausing to smooth her upswept hair, the skirts of her apple-green gown. "Don't you think?"

Calliope straightened her own attire, pale blue on white embroidered muslin, and hoped that Clio was correct. It would indeed create a great stir for his Grace to show up here, but Averton never did shrink from attention.

And what of Clio's mysterious midnight visitor? Would *he* be here?

The main room was quite crowded, with the musicians, more enthusiastic than talented according to Thalia, playing away on a raised dais at one end. The dancers twirled and spun in the energetic reel, their feet tapping out a loud, staccato beat on the worn wooden floor. Refreshments were laid out on long tables under the windows, hearty sandwiches and pies, vast bowls of punch—very different from Almack's, indeed.

As they moved slowly through the thick crowd, Calliope carefully examined all the faces. A few of the men were tall, but not as much so as Clio's visitor. They were mostly large, red-faced country squires, as well as one elderly vicar and an extremely young curate.

She couldn't picture any of *them* donning hats and cloaks to go sneaking around at midnight! Nor did Clio react to any of them in any fashion other than distant politeness.

Calliope sighed as she took a seat near one of the windows. She was assuredly not cut out to be a sleuth! There was something below the surface, something just beyond reach, that she was missing.

"So very serious this evening, Miss Chase," Cameron commented lightly, dropping into the chair beside hers. "Do you not enjoy dancing?"

Calliope smiled at him, glad of the distraction from her labyrinthine thoughts. "Of course I enjoy dancing."

"Ah, yes, I remember. Athena was very light on her feet at the masquerade ball."

"And her dance with Hermes was surely the only bright spot of that dismal evening!"

"Well, we mustn't let this event turn sour, too. May I have the honour of the next dance?"

Calliope gazed out at the spinning dancers. They laughed and clapped, full of high spirits. "Perhaps later. Maybe we could walk for a bit? Take a turn about the room?"

"Whatever milady likes."

They made their way around the crowded room slowly, greeting people politely. Cameron leaned close to her as they skirted around the dance floor and murmured, "I think I may have found out something. Can you meet me tonight? In the garden, perhaps, near the ha-ha?"

Meet him? Calliope's stomach gave an excited lurch, and for a second she was actually frightened. Not of Cameron— of her own feelings. She longed to run away, back to her safe old practicality. But then she remembered the waterfall, the Greek bandits, and she knew she could not.

She just had to leap forward.

She only had time to nod as they came to a group of their own friends, Lady Kenleigh and Emmeline, Calliope's father and Lady Rushworth, and fell into conversation with them, an oasis of quiet familiarity. Cameron soon left them to procure glasses of punch, disappearing back into the crowd.

Calliope nibbled at a sandwich, feeling her own spirits rise to meet the lively music, the chatter and colour. How very excited she was—a midnight meeting! She was surely becoming just like the adventurous ladies of Lotty's books.

She laughed as Lady Kenleigh told a story about Emmeline's childhood, how she would play "antiquities hunting" with her brother by digging deep holes in the garden.

"…they were certain they would find a buried city, like Pompeii," she said. "The gardener was quite livid!"

"That sounds like something you and your sisters would have done, Calliope," Sir Walter said. "You were always so very—suggestible."

"I would prefer the word 'imaginative', Father," Calliope protested. "'Suggestible' makes us sound like little automatons. You always taught us to think for ourselves, to apply what we learned."

"And you girls always took that very much to heart!" Sir Walter said, chuckling. "Gave your dear mother fits. D'you remember when Thalia—?"

Sir Walter's tale was interrupted when the assembly room doors opened, as if brushed aside by a giant, invisible hand. Everyone turned to see who arrived so late; even the music seemed to slow. It could only be one person, of course.

"The Duke of Averton," Lady Kenleigh murmured. "Whatever would *he* be doing at a village assembly?"

Lady Rushworth lifted her lorgnette to peer at the new arrival. "And looking so positively restrained. For him, anyway. He always was such a peacock of a man."

"They say he keeps very much to himself at his castle," Emmeline said.

"Yet he deigns to come down among us peasants," Clio murmured. "How curious. Should we all bow and curtsy, do you think? Pretend we are being presented at Court? Too bad I forgot my plumes and train."

Indeed, it seemed that the crowd was quite unsure of what to do with such a personage in their midst. The press of revellers had grown so that there was hardly room to walk through the throng around the dance floor. Someone had opened the windows, but it was still warm and stuffy, heavy with the scents of perfumes and silks, woollens, wilting flowers. The music had grown more raucous, the dancing faster and less organised.

Now, it all seemed to slow, to grow muted and shadowed. The music did not cease—*that* would have been far too dramatic. But the focus of the room shifted, the lively conversation shading into whispers and murmurs.

Calliope turned towards the doorway, edging closer to Clio. The duke *was* looking rather restrained, just as Lady Rushworth said. No satin-lined cloaks or embroidered waistcoats, no leopard skins or chitons. He seemed a bit puritanical, even, in a black superfine coat and stark white cravat, simply tied and skewered with an antique cameo pin. His hair was tied back in an old-fashioned queue, and his face was serious but not haughty as he gazed out over the room.

Calliope glanced at Clio from the corner of her eye, to find that her sister gazed back at the duke with her own air of solemn serenity. The candlelight glinted on her spectacles, hiding her eyes.

Cameron was not yet back with their punch, and Calliope could not see him through the crowd.

"I do believe he's coming this way," Lady Kenleigh said, straightening the gauzy shawl over her shoulders.

Calliope's gaze snapped forward again to see that he really was "coming this way". The crowd parted for him, like an obedient little Red Sea. He nodded at the vicar and various other village worthies, but his progress was steady, his goal unmistakable.

Calliope caught a fold of Clio's green sash in her hand, as if *that* could hold her sister back if she really wanted to bolt or cause a scene. But it helped her feel connected to Clio in some way, anchored to the real world.

Scenes were never Clio's way, though. She watched the duke approach with a polite half-smile on her lips.

"Good evening, Lady Kenleigh. Lady Rushworth, Lady Emmeline. Sir Walter. Miss Chase. Miss Clio," he said, bowing his head to them. The shifting light caught on his brushed-back hair, turning it to burnished gold, like an antique mirror. "It is good to see you all. We have not met since Herr Mueller's talk at the Antiquities Society, I believe."

He was really quite handsome, Calliope thought with some surprise. Too bad he was also so very—strange.

"Good evening, your Grace," Lady Kenleigh replied, ever the gracious hostess even when taken by surprise. "What a pleasant surprise to see you here tonight."

"I am hoping to spend more time at Averton Castle in the future, Lady Kenleigh, so I thought I should get to know my neighbours better. I trust you are enjoying your holiday?" His inquiry was addressed to everyone, but his gaze was on Clio. As they watched each other, Calliope had a vision of two lions circling each other on the Delian shore.

Calliope tightened her grasp on Clio's sash, and said, "Indeed we are, your Grace. The landscape here is most intriguing. We took a walk to the falls a few days ago."

"And did you see the secret grotto?" the duke asked. "There are many fascinating tales of the water spirits who live there."

Water spirits like poor, trapped Daphne? Calliope wondered. Up close, she could see the red scar on his forehead, where his own fleeing Daphne had bashed him.

She also saw something else. The carving on his cameo pin was a tiny scroll. The symbol of Clio, Muse of History.

"Alas, most of us can't swim," Emmeline said brightly, cracking the tense mood. "We can only imagine the glories of the hidden grotto."

"Perhaps that is for the best, Lady Emmeline," the duke said. "It is probably just a cold, rocky cave."

"Or a place of hidden wonders," Clio said softly. "Which some fairy king wants to keep all to himself."

"Then it would be unfortunate for the fairy king that some of us mere mortals *do* know how to swim," the duke answered.

Lady Kenleigh, as if sensing the tension growing back, said quickly, "Have you had much time to explore the local landscape yourself, your Grace? The Roman fort, or some of the ancient barrows?"

"Not as of yet, Lady Kenleigh. I hope to remedy that very soon. And, in the service of getting to know my neighbours, I am having a small dinner party the day after tomorrow. I know it is shockingly short notice, but I hope you will all be able to attend. Your entire party, of course, Lady Kenleigh."

Lady Kenleigh and Lady Rushworth exchanged surprised glances. "Of course, your Grace," Lady Kenleigh said. "We have no fixed engagements. We would be honoured to attend."

"Excellent! I will see you then."

With one last bow, the duke strolled away, vanishing into the crowd.

"My goodness," Lady Kenleigh said weakly. "A dinner invitation to Averton Castle."

"Shall wonders never cease," Lady Rushworth answered. "Come, Sir Walter, I think I need to find some good, strong wine after such a shock to the system." She took his arm and they ambled off, chattering happily about the possible treasures to be seen at the duke's castle, and looking not in the least "shocked".

Clio, though, was rather pale. She tugged her sash free

of Calliope's clasp and snapped open her fan, ruffling her hair with a stiff breeze.

"I wonder if we'll see the Alabaster Goddess," Emmeline said. "They do say she is hidden away somewhere in those medieval passages!"

"It would not be worth going if we *didn't* see her," Clio said. "Along with whatever else he might have locked up in that fortress. Mummies, perhaps? Cursed jewels?"

Emmeline laughed. "Don't say that to Lotty! She will imagine mummies rising up out of their coffins at night and going lurching about in dark corridors, putting curses on all who dared invade their tombs."

"I wouldn't be surprised if they did resort to curses, finding themselves in the clutches of the duke," Clio said. "Ah, look, Emmeline, there is your handsome brother. I do believe I promised him the next dance."

Clio shut her fan and hurried over to Emmeline's brother, taking his arm to usher him into the forming set. Emmeline, too, set off to dance with Mr Smithson, leaving Calliope standing by herself.

Where on earth was Cameron?

Cameron made his slow way through the thick crowd, balancing delicate glasses of punch. The line at the refreshment tables had been quite lengthy, the punch and cakes growing sparse under the increasing demand. At last he claimed his prize and turned back to Calliope and their friends, only to be brought up short by the Duke of Averton.

So that was what the commotion at the door had been. Cameron should have guessed.

The duke stood directly in his path, a sombre statue in black and white. Those flat green eyes gave nothing away—no thoughts or memories, no anger or remorse.

Cameron felt himself go cold in response, an icy chill spreading to his very heart. His fists tightened on the glasses. It was a good thing he held them, solid impediments that prevented him from starting a brawl in the middle of a genteel assembly.

"Averton," he said coldly.

"Westwood," the duke answered quietly. "I am glad to see you here. I never had a chance to thank you."

"Thank me?"

"I was told you were the one who found me in my gallery, who summoned help."

Cameron nodded curtly. "I was."

"I'm grateful. You could have easily left me there."

"Abandoning wounded creatures is not my way."

A small, ironic smile touched the duke's serious expression. "What? The 'Greek god' is not given to careless cruelty?" He touched the side of his slightly crooked nose.

"Unlike some."

"Hmm. Well, whatever your motives, I'm grateful. My blasted carelessness! When I am near my antiquities I don't notice anything else."

"You needn't pretend, Averton. I know what happened. I know you were not alone in that gallery."

The duke's only reaction was a muscle that twitched along his jaw. His gaze shifted to the dance floor, where Clio promenaded with the Kenleighs' son. "Ah, yes. Our beauteous Muse of History, who has a temper to equal her loveliness."

"If you come near her again…" Cameron growled.

"So very protective, Westwood. But then they do say you cherish a *tendre* for the elder Muse. Perhaps you seek to impress her with your threats."

"It is no threat. Merely a warning."

"I remember your 'warnings' very well. In this case, they are quite unwarranted. I wish Miss Clio no harm; quite the contrary. You and I have no need to be enemies."

Averton gave him a nod and walked away. Cameron swallowed his cold anger, burying it deep in that ice, and went on his interrupted way.

No need to be enemies? Au contraire.

"What did the duke say to you?" Calliope asked when he reached her side, taking one of the glasses from him.

"Nothing of any consequence."

"Did he invite you to his dinner party?"

"No. Does the blasted man *have* parties? That seems far too normal a pastime."

"Very true. But you are invited to one. He has asked the whole house party. For some unfathomable reason, it seems he is newly determined to be sociable."

Cameron gave a derisive snort. "I doubt he'd want me in his precious castle."

"Perhaps not, but you have to come anyway. It may be our last chance to see the Alabaster Goddess."

"Or to corner a thief?"

Calliope frowned. "I'm not sure. Could the Lily Thief have followed us from town? Or be one of our own party after all?"

"Your friend Miss Price, perhaps."

"Lotty? She could assuredly think up such a dramatic scheme, but carrying it out would be something entirely different."

"The duke himself, then."

"I would like that. He is already a villain. Why not add one more black mark? But why would he? He has the Alabaster Goddess already."

Cameron shook his head. "I can't help but feel it has everything to do with that list. Why would he have it?"

"And hidden away like that." Calliope sipped at her punch. "Perhaps all will be revealed at the party!"

Chapter Nineteen

"**O**uch!" Calliope gasped, as her elbow connected with the wall. Cradling the throbbing arm close to her side, she hurried down the narrow back staircase, holding her breath lest anyone hear her. At last she tumbled out into the midnight air, drawing the hood of her cloak up over her head.

She was glad of the aching elbow, though. It distracted her from her nagging doubts.

"What am I doing here?" she muttered, as she hurried across the garden. Shivering in the wind, running off to meet Cameron, like…

Like Clio and her mysterious night-time visitor.

This was not much like her, throwing caution to the winds, running off to meet a man in secret. But maybe that was the point. She no longer really felt like herself, like sensible Calliope. Not since she came to this place, felt its strange magic. Something new and frightening possessed her, and she just wanted to see him. Be close to him.

And here she was, slipping out of the house all alone. She laughed aloud at the deliciousness of it all! No wonder Thalia was so addicted to wild behaviour. It was wonderful.

But she was early to her rendezvous. Cameron was nowhere to be seen yet, and she was alone with the ancient ghosts. With the pile of old stones that led to those non-existent stairs.

Calliope drifted towards them, as towards an anchor in the wide sea of the night. They were still an oddity, so out of place in the neat bit of garden. She wondered that no one had dismantled them and carried the stones away for a wall or cottage. Perhaps this spot had some mysterious significance and therefore none dared touch it? A curse or spell?

Calliope tiptoed closer, her nervousness about meeting Cameron concealed by sudden curiosity. Yes, the stones *were* different from before. She was sure none had been loose when she and her sisters examined them when they arrived at the Abbey. She cautiously nudged one with the toe of her half-boot, but couldn't shift it.

She glanced back, making sure Cameron wasn't near, before she leaned over the low wall, peering down into what had been only a shallow pit and a couple of steps cut into the dirt. Though it was dark, lit only by the bright silver moon, it didn't seem so shallow now. The shadows extended on and on, like a corridor stretching away into the earth itself. She remembered her dream, a strange new world.

Calliope took a deep breath of the cold, peaty air. What *was* all this? Someone had surely been here since she last saw the stones, someone who had uncovered and opened an old trapdoor. Clio and her visitor? But why?

The gardens of Kenleigh Abbey were an absurdly busy place.

Calliope edged closer, taking a tentative step down into the pit. The dirt was spongey under her feet, but firm enough. She took another step and another, deeper into the shadows, hardly daring even to breathe…

"Well, and there you are, Miss Chase! Running away from our appointment?"

"Ack!" Calliope shrieked, her heart flying into her throat at the sudden sound. She lost her balance, sliding down on her backside and slipping down another step.

Gasping, she stared up to see Cameron staring down at her, outlined and shadowed by the moonlight so that he seemed an apparition. "Blast it, Cameron!" she cried, frightened into cursing. "You scared me."

"I'm sorry, Calliope. I thought you were expecting me," he said, scrambling down to her side. His boots knocked some pebbles loose, sending them skittering down into the abyss. "Are you all right?"

"Everything but my dignity," she muttered. She took his proffered hand and let him lift her to her feet. Their heads barely reached the top of the stairwell, and they were pressed close. Calliope clung to him, sure they balanced alone on the edge of a cold precipice—just like her dream.

"No bruises?" he asked gently.

"Not yet."

"I'm fairly sure I asked you to meet me near the ha-ha, not in a giant's grave," he teased.

"A grave!" she yelped. She hadn't thought of *that*. Could there really be bones under their feet?

"Not literally, I think. Still, these steps must lead somewhere. They do appear to go down a long way."

"That's the odd thing," Calliope said. "When my sisters and I first saw it, there seemed to be only one or two steps. Then just dirt."

He peered up at the opening above their heads. "It must have been blocked up."

"Why open it now? What is it?" *If not a grave.*

"If we knew that, my dear Calliope, I'm sure all our

questions would be answered. But then, sadly, we would have no need for secret meetings!" His hand tightened on hers, and he led her back up into the night air. "We'll have to come back when there is more light."

Calliope held on to his hand, feeling the warm safety of him envelop her until all the ghosts vanished and they were all there was in the darkness. As he drew her closer to him, his hands around her waist, she felt that excitement grow and expand, tingling and irresistible, like life itself.

She didn't want to let it go, ever. She didn't want to lose this fragile, beautiful spell.

She smiled up at him, winding her arms tightly about his neck so he could not fly away from her. His hair, too long, too curling, was like warm satin against her skin, his body so warm and solid and delicious against hers. How she yearned to stay here in his embrace all night—for ever! To kiss him, *feel* him, and forget about thieves and ghosts and families and everything.

"How beautiful you are, Cameron," she whispered.

His eyes widened in surprise, but before he could answer, she went up on tiptoe to kiss him, pressing one swift caress to his lips, then another and another, teasing him until he groaned and pulled her even closer, until there was not even a breath between them. He groaned, deepening the kiss, his tongue seeking hers, and she was lost in him. Of her need to be just this close to him, always, taste him, smell him, draw all he was into her until he was *hers*.

It wasn't like their first kiss, soft and tentative as they learned the taste of each other. It was fast and hungry, filled with the yearnings of their time together, the drive to be close and know that this was real.

Calliope didn't question herself, for once in her life.

She didn't know what all this fury of emotion meant; she only knew she had to be close to him. The muse united with the god.

Cameron drew back slowly, pressing tiny, fleeting kisses to her cheek, her jaw, the sensitive spot behind her ear. She trembled at the warm rush of his breath.

Calliope laughed, shivering, clinging to him as if she would never let go.

"Oh, Calliope," he groaned, resting his forehead against her hair. "We can't go on like this!"

She nodded, pressing her face to the curve of his neck, inhaling deeply the salty, heady scent of his skin. Yes—she saw now. *This* was the true thing she always sought, the eternal beauty. And she knew what she had to do.

She had to let go of her old self entirely, of her old inhibitions and fears. She had to be reborn—with Cameron.

She had to be bold.

"Come with me," she whispered. She clasped his hand in hers, leading him across the darkened garden, beyond the secret stairs. Her steps were shaky, weak with the force of their kiss, with what she was about to do. She could feel his puzzlement, yet he followed her without a word. Trust was one of the things they would have to find together.

She led him into the stand of trees, along a narrow, overgrown pathway until she found a small clearing, a ragged, enclosed circle. In the centre was an old ash pit, pale grey in the moonlight. A magical fairy circle, the perfect spot.

"Calliope…" he began, his voice hoarse.

"Shh." She pressed her fingers to his lips. Words would only shatter the spell. She was done with words, with worry and thought and always being proper. "Just follow me."

She stepped back from him to unfasten her cloak, letting it pool around her feet. As he watched her, his eyes narrowed, she drew down the deep, low neckline of her gown, revealing the curve of her bosom, the line of her pale shoulders. Calliope swallowed past a dry lump in her throat. What if she was doing this wrong? What if she wasn't pretty enough? What if...

No! She shoved away the fear. This was right. This was what she needed to do, to free herself—free *them*.

She pulled the pins from her hair, shaking the black curls free over her bare shoulders.

"You see, Cameron," she said, cursing the girlish tremor in her voice. She was trying to be *seductive!* "Surely I can be Aphrodite as well as Athena." She reached out and took his hand, urging him closer.

"Calliope!" he moaned. She felt his muscles tense, resisting her. "What are you thinking?"

"Please, Cameron." She shook her head, her hair spilling down her back so he could see her breasts in the moonlight. If only they were bigger! "It has to be here, now, in this place." She pressed against him, kissing his cheek, his neck, his jawline. His breath sucked in on a hiss. *Ah-ha!* She was getting somewhere.

"I want you, Cam," she whispered. "Don't you want me?"

"Of course I do, my beautiful Calliope. But..." His words were swallowed in her kiss, her lips soft and open on his, not to be denied. With a deep moan, he gave in, his touch seeking the bare skin of her shoulders.

It was as if Aphrodite *did* take over her soul, Calliope thought as she boldly untied his cravat, dropping it to the ground at their feet. The goddess guided her hands as she pushed his shirt away from his muscled chest, her mouth as she kissed the damp hollow of his throat, the curve of his shoulder. How smooth his skin was, hot under her caress. The feverish warmth seeped into her own soul, and she knew only him.

This *was* right.

Twined together, they fell to her cloak, the trees whirling dizzily over her head. Calliope landed on top, tossing away his shirt. He was exquisite, she thought in breathless awe. More glorious than any ancient statue, for he was alive, his skin glowing, vibrant with breath and desire and strength. Her trembling touch traced the light, coarse hair of his chest, the thin line that led tantalisingly to the band of his breeches. His stomach muscles tightened, his breath uneven as her touch brushed the tight press of fabric just below that line.

"Calliope," he gasped. "Be careful. If you are not sure…"

"I am Aphrodite, remember? I wouldn't be here if I was not sure." Exhilarated, bold, scared, she awkwardly opened his breeches and tugged them down over his lean hips. "Oh!" she whispered.

Cameron went very still, lying back on the cloak as he watched her warily.

"It is not very much like a herm, is it?" she said musingly. Those ancient talismans, tall, straight pillars with a startlingly large organ below, had thus far been her only experience of the male private parts. The reality was ever so much better. "Can I touch it?"

Cameron laughed roughly. "Only if you want all this to be over before it begins. Come here, my Aphrodite, and kiss me again before I go utterly insane."

Calliope fell happily back into his arms, their lips meeting, heartbeats melding. There was nothing at all careful about this kiss, it was all sun-hot desperation, urgent need that burst free like fireworks into the night sky.

Calliope felt the slide of his hands on her back as he released the last tapes of her gown. The breeze was cold on her skin, but she was hardly aware of it. Clothes were only a prison now, a barrier between her and the touch of his own bare flesh. She shrugged her gown away, rising above him as a naked goddess.

"Calliope," he groaned, his hands on her hips, holding her still for his starving gaze. "You are truly glorious."

"Not as glorious as you," she whispered. "My beautiful Greek god."

Still holding her tightly, he rolled her beneath him, on to the softest part of the cloak. Calliope laughed as her hair spilled all around them. She did feel glorious as he looked at her, felt free at last, as she knew she would! The past was gone. There was only now, this one moment, where she was one with the man she loved. He kissed her, and all thought vanished into sheer, undiluted sensation.

She closed her eyes, revelling in his caress, the press of his mouth on her breast, the curve of her ribs. Her palms slid over his back, so strong and young, so alive under her touch. Her legs parted as she felt his weight lower between them, the press of that hot, heavy organ she marvelled at.

She knew what would happen; she and Clio had once secretly peeked at some of her father's ancient sketches of Dionysian rituals and Pompeii bawdy houses. But those images never hinted at how it *felt*. Of the heady, dizzy sensation of falling, falling, lost in another person. Another world entirely.

"I don't want to hurt you," he gasped.

Calliope smiled, feeling the press of the tip of his penis against her, the way her whole body ached for that final union that meant he was hers. "You never could."

She spread her legs wider, invitingly, and he drove inside her. It *did* hurt; how could it not? A burning pain, but it was nothing to the way he filled her, joined with her at last. She arched her back against the pain, wrapping her arms and legs around him so tightly he could never escape her.

"You see? You didn't hurt me," she whispered. "I feel completely perfect."

Cameron laughed tightly. "Not half as 'perfect' as I do. My beautiful, wonderful Calliope."

Slowly, so slowly, he moved again within her, drawing back, lunging forward, just a little deeper, a little more intimate every time. Calliope squeezed her eyes closed, feeling the ache ebb away until there was only the pleasure. A tingling delight that grew and expanded inside, spreading through her arms and legs, her fingertips, out the top of her head like flames. Pleasure unlike any she had ever known or imagined.

She cried out at the wonder of it all, at the bursts of light behind her closed eyes, blue and white and red, like spinning Catherine wheels. The heat and pressure were too much, too much! How could she survive it without being burned up, consumed?

Above her, around her, she felt Cameron tense, his back arch. "Calliope!" he shouted out.

And she exploded, consumed by those lights. She clung to him, falling down into the fire.

After long moments—hours or days?—Calliope slowly opened her eyes, sure she had tumbled into a volcano. But it was the same forest clearing, the looming trees and pale moonlight of everyday life.

A life with a new sparkle.

Beside her, collapsed on to the cloak, his arms tight

around her waist, was Cameron. His eyes were tightly closed, his limbs sprawled out in exhaustion.

Calliope smiled, feeling herself ever so slowly floating back to earth. She felt the crackle of twigs and leaves beneath the fabric, the press of a stone against her hip. The soreness of her limbs, of her most secret places. It didn't matter, though. Nothing mattered but this time out of time. She had become Aphrodite, at least for a moment. Or perhaps she had just become truly herself.

Calliope half-drowsed, warm where her skin pressed to Cameron's, the night breeze playing over her body until she shivered. She felt sore and tired—and lighter than she had ever been before! Surely she could soar right up into the trees.

Cameron's arm was heavy over her waist, and she curled herself tighter into the haven of his body, feeling his breath on her shoulder, the uncoiled strength of his muscles under her touch as she lightly ran her fingertips to his elbow and down again to his wrist.

"Oh, Calliope," he murmured into her hair. "I can't pretend to understand you. But I do know one thing."

Calliope smiled. "And what might that be?"

"That you are truly magnificent."

She laughed, and rolled over to face him. The moonlight outlined his beautiful features, casting sharp angles, mysterious shadows across his eyes and brow. She traced his face carefully, all those commonplace things—nose, lips, cheekbones—that made up the wonderful thing he was. Cameron.

"I would have thought you would call me *bossy*," she said. "And managing…"

"Those things, too," he teased. He caught her hand in his, pressing her fingers to his lips, one after another.

Calliope trembled. "My darling, managing Athena. What made you what you are?"

"I wondered the same thing about you," she said. "You are so unlike anyone else I know. Have ever known."

He laid back on their cloak, his arms stretched under his head as Calliope sat up, gazing down at him. His expression was blank. "Me? I am the simplest of creatures, as easy to read as a book."

Calliope snorted. "A book in Latin, mayhap. I seldom understand you at all."

Cameron laughed, reaching out to catch her around the waist and drew her close again. "You surely understood me very well tonight!"

"Don't tease." Calliope slapped him lightly on the shoulder. "I want to understand your *mind,* too."

"Perhaps I just seem a puzzle because I did not grow up here, as your other suitors did. I often don't feel *English* at all."

Fascinated by this glimpse of his past, Calliope rested her head on his shoulder. "Do you feel Greek, then?"

"Not that, either. Perhaps I don't really belong anywhere."

A cold sadness touched Calliope's heart. As vexing as her family could be, as maddening as their squabbles and disorderly ways were, she did know she belonged with them. That they were a part of her, whether she liked it or not. "What was your childhood like, Cameron?"

He shrugged, and she felt the smooth ripple of his muscles beneath her. His fingers moved gently in her hair. "Perfectly ordinary, I would have said. I knew nothing else. I thought everyone spent their lives moving from Florence to Naples, Lake Geneva to Rome to Vienna. I loved seeing new places, learning new ways of life."

New ways of life. And Calliope had only ever known

one. "Why did your parents choose such a nomadic existence? Your father's studies?"

"That, of course. He was always in search of new *objets*, new curiosities. Just as so many of our friends do. But also…"

"Also what?"

"My mother was not truly—comfortable in England."

Calliope realised she knew little about the late Lady Westwood, except that she had been Greek. And, from the one or two times Calliope had glimpsed her, very beautiful, with the same sculpted features and cognac-coloured eyes as her son. "She was homesick?"

"Probably. And she had a natural melancholy, too. She never showed that to me, of course. With me, she was always cheerful and smiling, always telling me tales of her own childhood or one of the Greek gods. Artemis was her favourite. But even as a child I could see the sadness in her eyes. The loneliness of having left her home for a place where she could never be fully accepted."

"But she was a countess!" Calliope cried, aching for the unhappiness of a woman she had never known.

"A countess who was the daughter of a Greek scholar. Oh, she was invited places, of course, and a few people—like your parents—were her friends. Yet I think she always missed the warmth of her homeland, the spirit of her own people. She especially missed the island of Delos, the birthplace of Artemis and Apollo, where her father often took her in his studies."

"Was she happy when your father took her to the Continent?"

"Happier, I think. It was sunnier there, the people more open. She never went back to Greece, though. She died in Naples when I was still very young, and I was sent back to England to school."

"So, you went to Greece for her."

Cameron laughed. "I suppose I did, though I never thought of it like that! I wanted to see if her tales were true."

"And were they?"

"Oh, yes. True—and more. It was her finest gift to me."

Calliope gazed up at him, at the wistful glint in his eyes. "She gave you your freedom."

"My freedom?"

"It's what I've always admired, and envied, in you. The way you care for no one's opinion—the way you follow your own path in life."

"It's not true that I care for no one's opinion, Calliope. I cannot really be a part of a society that treated my mother unkindly, so I do care little for their rules and strictures. But I very much care what some people think of me, like the Saunders. Like you."

"Me?"

"Especially you. Your disapproval has cut me to the quick in the past, Athena."

Calliope gave a startled laugh. "I would never have imagined my opinions would be taken in such a way! And anyway, I feel so very different now."

"You envy freedom? Care-for-nothingness?"

"Sometimes."

"And here I have always envied your family."

"My family? My wild, quarrelsome family?"

"Of course. The way you and your sisters are bonded so tightly together that no one could ever separate you. That is so alluring, you see, to someone with no family at all."

"I do love them very much. I could never do without them. But sometimes I just want…."

"What is it you want, Calliope?"

She propped herself up on her elbow, swallowing hard. Could she say it? Tell him? She had never spoken of it before, even to Clio. His face was so open as he gazed up at her.

"When my mother was dying," she said slowly, "I sat beside her and held her hand as the fever raged. And she made me promise to always take care of my father and sisters. She said I had always been so careful of them, so responsible, she could die in peace knowing that they were safe in my hands. That I would always see to their welfare. That I would be their new mother."

Cameron took her hand in his, twining his fingers with hers. "Such delicate hands for such a great task."

Calliope tried to shrug it away, as she always had. She was a dutiful daughter, or she tried to be. But how could she convey the heavy feeling that came over her then, like a loop of chains, binding her for ever? "I was the eldest, and I always did feel responsible for my sisters anyway. Ever since Clio was born."

Cameron wouldn't let her dismiss those chains so easily, though. His clasp tightened over her hand. "My dear, managing Athena. Of course you care about your family, you want them to be well and happy. But it doesn't have to be a burden only for your shoulders."

"What do you mean?"

"I mean—I have too much freedom, and you have too many charges. We should share what we have."

Calliope sat up straight, staring down at him in wary surprise. Did he mean… "What are you saying?"

He drew her down on to his chest, stroking the tangled length of her hair as one would soothe a startled bird. "We work well together, do we not?"

Calliope sucked in a shaky breath. "We argue. All the time."

"Not *all* the time. We didn't quarrel for, oh, at least two hours tonight, did we not?"

She had to laugh. "Our mouths were too busy."

"Ah, you see! You made a joke. You must feel freer already." He cradled her closer, as if he would not let her go. "Just rest now. We have a few hours until daybreak."

And a few hours to change her very life....

Chapter Twenty

"Since the ladies have gone into the village to do some shopping, I thought you gentlemen might like to peruse these," Lord Kenleigh said, unlocking a hidden safe in his library and drawing forth a silk-bound album. "Lady Kenleigh doesn't know I have them, of course. I bought them in Italy years ago, when I was on the Grand Tour."

Cameron was only half-attending to Lord Kenleigh and his album, predictably filled with erotic etchings of various goddesses and mythological figures. His mind kept turning on the night before, and Calliope and their burst of irresistible passion.

He was truly bewitched by her fathomless dark eyes. How else to explain why he got involved in her harebrained scheme to somehow find the Lily Thief? Anyone clever enough to snatch that diadem would easily elude their fumbling detective work. And Cameron could rather see the thief's point—Averton, Lady Tenbray and their ilk were hardly responsible stewards of ancient culture.

But he had come to see Calliope's view, too. Theft, no matter the artistic motives, was not a solution. This was not

Greece, where banditry ruled. Theft was quickly and sternly dealt with in England. And Cameron was beginning to fear that the thief was closer than Calliope thought. Perhaps even one of the members of her beloved Ladies Society.

He never wanted to see Calliope hurt, never wanted to see those beautiful eyes clouded with pain, that wonderful confidence falter. Especially after last night. Nothing was the same now.

"Ah, now, this one is delightful," Herr Mueller said. Cameron glanced up to see that the professor had abandoned the naughty etchings of Leda and the swan, Danae and the shower of gold, to examine the more conventional paintings displayed on the walls.

Cameron strolled over to peer closer at the canvas. It was "Cupid Blindfolding Youth", a tiny pink-and-white cherub laughing and tying a scarf over the eyes of a young woman. Glossy dark curls draped over her bare shoulders as her white silk gown slipped off, and she, too, was laughing, one hand outstretched as if reaching for the viewer.

She looked like Calliope, in those rare moments when she forgot herself in merriness. The curve of her lips, the faint rosy flush on her cheeks.

"Delightful, indeed," Cameron said.

"This one, too, is very fine," Herr Mueller said, pointing out a scene of Socrates lecturing to his followers in the marketplace. Unlike Calliope-Youth, it invoked no emotions in Cameron, but he had to admit that the details were beautifully wrought, the fallen ruins of Greece brought back to vivid life.

"Yes, the columns here and here, the steps Socrates sits on, the colours," Herr Mueller said. "It evokes what we love about the classical world, *ja*? Order and symmetry."

Cameron smiled. "Some would claim 'order and symmetry' are cold."

"But you and I know that is not true, Lord Westwood! The Greek forms can be rigorous and mathematical, yet also full of life."

Cameron looked back at the raven-haired Youth. "A harmony between passion and order?"

"Exactly so, Lord Westwood. They say you have travelled in Greece?"

"I have. My mother was Greek, I was raised on tales of the gods and goddesses who lived under its hot sky and sun."

"Then you must understand this dichotomy between rationality and emotion better than most Englishmen. And far better than us Germans! I have studied the order all my life. I cannot seem to grasp the passion. Perhaps I ought to travel to Greece myself, *ja*?"

"I would definitely recommend it," Cameron said. "I never really understood the stories myself, until I stood on the land where they originated."

In truth, he had never fully understood until he met Calliope. Never saw how cool order and hot passion could unite so perfectly.

"Then I will go. Just like all your English poets! How they flock across the Mediterranean. Ah, and here is a painting of the Muses at Helicon!" Herr Mueller pointed out a large scene of the nine Muses, gathered around their sacred spring with their various symbols and accoutrements. "Just like the young *fräuleins*, the Chases."

Cameron's gaze went to the figure in the middle, set slightly higher than the others. Calliope, eldest of the Muses, patron of epic poetry, holding her writing tablet. Unlike the real Calliope, she had golden blonde hair, but her expression was much the same. Steady and serious as she peered out at the viewer.

"Perhaps not *exactly* like the Misses Chase," he said.

"Ah, no! For you see, this Clio does not have the red hair. And this Thalia is, how do you say, not so *exuberant*."

Cameron glanced at the Thalia, her face half-hidden by the mask of comedy she held up. Beside her sat Clio, light brown hair braided into a neat coronet. She held a scroll and a pile of books. Beside her sandalled foot, springing from the dark green grass, was a single purple hyacinth.

"The artist has made fine use of symbolism," Herr Mueller said, gesturing to the flower.

"Indeed. For Clio was the mother of Hyacinth…" Cameron's voice trailed away as he remembered that blasted list. *The Grey Dove, the Golden Falcon, the Purple Hyacinth…*

The Purple Hyacinth. It couldn't be. And yet—it made a strange sense.

"…and here we see the Oracle at Delphi," Herr Mueller said, having moved on to the next painting as Cameron still stared at Clio and her purple flower. Her painted gaze seemed direct, mocking, as if she dared him to say it aloud. "Surely you have been to Delphi, Lord Westwood?"

Cameron shook away the cold sensation of surprise, or dawning realisation. Of the knowledge that he had been very, very foolish. There was no time for that now. He could hardly just run off and accuse her, the sister of the woman he loved! He wasn't even fully certain. He had little to go on besides a flower and his gut instincts. He had to move softly, carefully.

And how, blast it all, *how* was he to tell Calliope?

"Yes," he said, turning his back to the Muses. "Though Delphi is just a dusty little village called Kastri now. There is nothing of the Pythia to be found there, just some broken columns and overgrown thistle."

"Very sad. None the less, it must be exhilarating to stand exactly where such great prophecies arose!"

Cameron continued his conversation with Herr Mueller, examining the paintings, the artefacts displayed in Lord Kenleigh's glass cases. He must have made a credible job of it, too, for Herr Mueller seemed to find nothing amiss. But his thoughts were focused on that one little flower.

Calliope sat back on the carriage seat, peering out at the road as they bounced along on their way back to the Abbey. Thalia and Emmeline chatted happily about the new bonnets they had bought in the village, while Lotty buried herself in a volume acquired from the small bookshop, occasionally exclaiming over an especially dramatic passage. Only Calliope and Clio, seated next to each other, were quiet.

Calliope could not fathom her sister's thoughts, but she herself remembered only the night before. Her body joined with Cameron's, their kisses and moans in the darkness, the humid blurriness when they lost themselves completely. The confidences she had never shared with anyone

He was—well, he was wonderful. But what would happen now?

Calliope slumped back on the seat, having thoroughly confused herself. She had surely got no closer to answers of any sort since coming to Yorkshire! Not about the Lily Thief, about Cameron. About herself.

They turned down a different lane and the duke's castle came into view, pale grey and hulking against the blue sky. The first time Calliope saw it, she had thought it needed only pennants to make the picture complete, fabric snapping in the wind to welcome warriors to the joust. Those pennants were there today, bright rectangles of green, white and gold.

"Do you think it's meant to be a new Camelot, Cal?" Clio said.

Calliope turned to find her sister's gaze on the castle, opaque behind her spectacles. "Perhaps it's to welcome us to his party. A theme gathering."

"Medieval days? I must find my wimple and surcoat, then, and hope torture is not among the scheduled festivities."

"Hmm, yes. Shall he toss us in the dungeon, do you think?"

Clio smiled wryly. "*You* needn't fear such a fate, Cal. Lord Westwood would surely ride up on his white charger and rescue you from the beast."

Calliope took her sister's hand. "You needn't fear the duke, either, Clio. You needn't even go to the party at all! I don't understand why he invited us. I thought he came to his fortress to shut himself and the Alabaster Goddess away from the world."

Clio squeezed her hand. "I don't understand, either, yet I somehow feel I must go."

"To protect the goddess?"

"Yes, to protect the goddess. And…"

"And what?"

Clio shrugged. "What else is there?"

Chapter Twenty-One

Camelot, indeed, Calliope thought the next night, as their carriage turned through ornate iron gates and rolled up a steep incline towards the duke's castle. If it hadn't actually been built in the Middle Ages, it was a superb imitation, an impenetrable keep set atop a craggy hill, surrounded by a now-dry moat. The narrow windows were ablaze with light, a vivid glow that softened the harsh edges of the stonework. Those pennants snapped from the corner towers. Calliope half expected armoured knights to come galloping out to meet them as they entered the inner court-yard.

It was an austere, gravelled square of a space, with walls looming high all around, but torches flared in a straight line leading to the doors. An old well in the centre bubbled away, transformed into a modern fountain.

"I told you I should have worn my wimple," Clio said.

Calliope laughed. Even without a wimple, Clio had a vaguely antique look about her tonight, in a dark amber-coloured gown with long, draped sleeves and a wide sash embroidered with dragons and flowers. And her eyes seemed clear for the first time in days, her laughter unforced.

Calliope had her doubts about coming here tonight. Look what happened the last time they accepted an invitation from the duke! Strangely, though, it seemed to have done Clio some good.

"You would have ruined your coiffure with a wimple," she said, alighting from the carriage.

"Perhaps I would have felt less out of place." Clio stepped down beside Calliope, straightening her spectacles on her nose. "One almost expects William the Conqueror to come riding in. Do you think we will be served roast boar, to be eaten with our fingers?"

"Nothing so amusing as that, I fear," Thalia said, joining them as they went up the steps and through the open doors. "Just more lectures from Herr Mueller."

"Oh, I doubt his Grace will allow himself to be upstaged in his own house, especially by a mere scholar," Clio said. "But I don't think you need to be worried about being bored, Thalia."

"If I am, I'll just go and search for dungeons and secret passages," Thalia answered airily. "There are bound to be some. How else could one escape the siege?"

"How else, indeed?" Clio murmured. They followed the rest of the party out of the tiny, cold foyer into the drawing room.

If it could be called a "drawing room", Calliope thought. "Solar" was more like it. A long, rectangular space with fireplaces at each end, massive enough to roast oxen for the feast. Their great, crackling flames banished every bit of chill even from this room made of stone—stone floor, stone walls soaring up to timber rafters. The furnishings, too, seemed ancient, large, dark pieces carved with forest scenes and gargoyle faces. The chairs were strewn with gold velvet cushions; tapestries of knights and their ladies hung on the rough walls.

"His Grace will be with you shortly," the footman announced. Then he left them, closing the door behind him as if to shut them all up in this medieval prison. Laughter and conversation burst out as soon as the portal closed, exclamations over the house, over this chair or that painting.

"They do say Averton is a great eccentric, even worse than his grandfather. And they called *him* The Mad Duke!" Lady Kenleigh said, seating herself by one of the fires. "I certainly do believe it. Did you see his house in town? A veritable warehouse…"

Calliope watched as Thalia found an old set of virginals in the corner, and Clio wandered off to examine a tapestry. Her father was conversing with Lady Rushworth. Assured that her family was fully occupied, she looked around for Cameron.

They had not been able to talk alone since their tryst in the woods. It was probably just as well, since her cheeks turned hot every time she remembered how boldly she had lured him into lovemaking! Could she talk about such serious matters as thieves and codes without grabbing him, kissing him?

Yet she always seemed to know where he was in every room. Always sensed when he was near. Things just always seemed brighter when he walked in. As if he brought the Greek sun wherever he went.

Now he stood by a glass case near the other fireplace, far down the vast chamber, studying a cluster of Greek vases. With one more glance to be sure her family and friends were all busy, Calliope slipped to his side.

He didn't look at her, but he also seemed to know when

she was near. A smile touched the corner of his lips as the fringe of her shawl brushed his hand.

"Extraordinary, are they not?" he said, gesturing to the vases.

Calliope stared at them. They were a surprisingly small collection for a man as rapacious as the duke. No doubt the rest were stored elsewhere, and these were just the choice bits. And "choice" they were, glossy and perfect. She recognised a red-figure piece by the Andokides Painter, coppery red against velvety black. And an amphora depicting a party scene, drunken dancers turning and twisting in a way that suggested extraordinary mobility.

Calliope leaned closer to see an inscription in Greek, etched near the bottom of the amphora. "'Euphronios never did anything like it,'" she read aloud. "These pieces are incredible. They look like new! Wherever did the duke find them?"

"Straight from the ground in Greece, or maybe Italy," Cameron said tightly. "They must have been buried for centuries in their original homes to be in such condition."

Standing close to him, Calliope could feel the coiled tension of his muscles, the curl of his fists. She knew his body well now. That anger was there again, the white-hot glow she sensed when they saw the duke's gallery in London. When he spoke of the women Averton had taken cruel advantage of in his youth. She didn't think a fight here, tonight, would do any good. Not when they were so close to their goal of finding the thief, and yet still so far away! She laughed and tugged at his arm, turning him towards another krater.

"This one puts me in mind of you and the duke," she said teasingly. It was a scene of two men, Herakles and Antaios, wrestling, while two goddesses on either side watched dispassionately. The delineation of the musculature was extraordinary, two straining, powerful men locked in mortal combat. It was obvious Antaios was losing. His face was white with the pallor of impending death.

Hmm, Calliope thought. Perhaps this particular vase was not such a fine distraction after all.

Cameron did laugh, though. "Ah, Calliope," he said quietly. "If only."

"I hope you don't decide to recreate this scene tonight. This is meant to be a party, you know."

"A party with no host, it would seem."

"The duke does seem to enjoy being fashionably late, even to his own events," Calliope said. "I can't help but feel this is not just a simple dinner party, though."

"Not just a newfound sociability on his part? I fear you are probably right."

Calliope turned away from the vases, from white-faced Antaios, to look at a tapestry, a faded scene of a medieval harvest. The castle in the background was much like this one. "Have you thought more about the list?" she asked.

A shadow seemed to pass over his face, erasing that smile. He still examined the krater, not looking at her. "I have. In fact, Calliope, I may have discovered something."

"You have?" Calliope cried in fresh excitement. *At last!* "How clever you are. I can't decipher it at all, no matter how long I look at it."

"It was hardly cleverness. Just sheer luck."

"What is it? What did you discover?"

Cameron glanced over his shoulder at the group crowded around the fireplace, far from them. They were all there now, except Clio, who stood on tiptoe to peer out of one of the narrow windows, as if she would fly away. "We can't talk here."

"But they are so far away, surely they can't hear," Calliope began. Her protests faded as he shot her a sharp look. His smiles, his light humour, were all quite gone. He was as hard and unemotional as one of the duke's statues. Whatever he had found must be terribly serious, then.

Did she really, truly want to know?

Suddenly, Calliope realised that this search for the thief had, up until now, been something of a game. Oh, not the antiquities part—that she cared about deeply. But the thief himself had somehow been abstract, a symbol for the evils of illegal artwork being shuffled about, not cared for, not studied. It wasn't real people. Now it was, all too much.

But she had come too far to give up, no matter what.

"Do you know who it is?" she whispered.

"I might. Or at least know what is part of it all," he answered. "We can talk later. For now, I think we should join the others to wait for our host."

"Yes, of course," Calliope said, her stomach queasy.

"And, Calliope, I think you should keep a close eye on your Ladies Society tonight. Just to be sure."

"My friends?" Her stomach gave another sick lurch, and she pressed her hands tight to the pain. "Are they in some danger?"

"Please, Calliope, just stay near them."

Cameron walked away towards the fireplace. Calliope took one halting step after him, determined to make him tell her what he knew. Discretion to blazes, if her friends and sisters were in danger!

She halted suddenly as she felt a cool burst of air against her ankle. The rest of the room was so warm, so muffled; she couldn't believe a draught would dare invade the duke's domain. But a small breeze stirred the hem of her white muslin gown, and it seemed to come from beneath the tapestry.

Calliope turned back the edge of the cloth, just enough to see a small crack where a door was hidden. The breeze came from just below, where the door would end, leaving a half-inch gap. A secret entrance to the outside, then? How was that possible?

She remembered the earthen steps at the Abbey. This place was more crowded with hidden portals than any of Lotty's novels!

She reached out cautiously, touching the crack with her gloved fingertips. The wood fit very tightly with the wall, painted grey to match the stone, but she could feel the metallic bump of a hinge.

The drawing-room door—the legitimate one—opened, and Calliope jumped back, letting the tapestry fall back into place. Their host appeared at last, no Dionysus or Celtic king tonight, but a stylish gentleman in dark burgundy superfine, his hair tied back. His gaze, green as sea glass, was as penetrating as ever, though, sweeping over his gathered guests. Calliope folded her hands together tightly to still their trembling, feeling like a child caught pilfering sweets.

"Good evening, everyone," Averton said. "Forgive my lack of punctuality, there was business that could not wait."

"Not at all, your Grace," Lady Kenleigh answered. "We were just admiring your very unusual arrangements."

"Ah, yes, my medieval castle." The duke strolled into the room to stand beside the fireplace, resting one hand on the massive mantelpiece. The rings he wore, emeralds and rubies, gleamed in the flames. "A weakness, I fear, stemming from the King Arthur tales I relished as a boy. The round table, the tournaments, the holy quests…"

"The code of chivalry?" Clio said. "Knights paying gentle court to their ladies fair?"

The duke turned towards her, his face expressionless. Calliope edged closer, mindful of Cameron's request that she stay close to her friends. Averton just smiled. "You have been reading *The Romance of the Rose* in addition to Plato, Miss Chase?"

"I am not a medieval scholar," Clio said. "But surely every lady must know the benefits—and the drawbacks—of being the object of chivalrous intentions."

"Is *The Romance of the Rose* like *Lady Edwina's Destiny*?" Lotty interrupted. "There is this curse, you see, and it can only be broken by true love's gift. A magical rose, of course…"

"Miss Price is a true romantic," Clio said, giving Lotty a gentle smile.

"How fortunate you are, then, Miss Price," the duke said. "Most of us no longer have that luxury, and must balance the romance of Arthur with the pragmatism of Charlemagne." *Charlemagne.*

A bell rang in the distance, cutting through the tension that hung in the firelit air. "Dinner is ready. Lady Kenleigh, may I escort you into the dining room? I fear I go against the convention with no hostess tonight, but my cook has been hard at work all day preparing a fine repast. I seldom entertain, you see, and the servants feel their talents go to waste."

Calliope looked about for Cameron, only to find that he had quite vanished in the crowd.

They were not served boar to be eaten by hand, of course, but a sumptuous feast that would put any London house to shame. Vol-au-vents, mackeral *à la* Stewart, duck and chicken pie, stewed vegetables, raspberry Charlotte. All of it perfectly prepared and delicious.

The conversation naturally turned on the duke's collections, descriptions of his favourite pieces, questions from Herr Mueller, everyone's travel narratives.

Calliope listened to it with half an ear, nibbling at the delicacies on her plate as she watched Clio, seated across the table from Calliope and fortunately far from the duke. Clio's face showed no reaction as she listened to tales of statues rescued from crumbling temples, fished out of the sea. Calliope noticed, though, that Clio ate little and seemed to imbibe more wine than usual.

Cameron, too, behaved oddly, slipping into the dining room as the soup was being served. He shot Calliope a quick smile, but was quiet. Most unusual indeed.

Calliope sipped at her own wine, wondering if she had tumbled into another dream. A strange blend of ancient, medieval, and modern where familiar faces were suspect and she suddenly understood nothing at all. The names on that list could surely apply to all of them, for they were not themselves any more. They were falcons, flowers, doves. Cicero. Charlemagne.

Calliope finally set her wineglass back down on the table. She had surely had enough! The conversation, the laughter, was like a clamour in her ears, the delicious food tasteless. She longed to jump up from her velvet chair and run away! To run all the way home to London and pull the bedclothes up over her head. To turn the clock back before she ever heard of the Lily Thief. Ever made love with Cameron.

But that could never be. The Calliope of that time was gone, everything was different. Her family, her feelings for Cameron, her whole way of seeing the world. She couldn't go back. Did she even want to? No.

She looked down the table towards Cameron, who was chatting with Lotty as if he hadn't a care in the world. How beautiful he was, her reckless Greek god. How she longed for him, despite how easily he could shatter her world.

He was loathe to tell her whatever it was he had found, because he didn't seem to want to hurt her. She knew him quite well now, knew his real kindness and compassion, and she could see it in his eyes. She loved that, but feared it, too. If the duke was the Lily Thief, or some stranger, or someone like Mr Smithson or Freddie Mountbank, it would not hurt her. So, it must mean it was not one of them. It must mean…

"…do you not agree, Miss Chase?" Herr Mueller suddenly said.

Calliope glanced towards him, startled. Which Miss Chase did he mean? Hopefully not her, as she had not been attending the conversation at all! But he watched her expectantly. "Oh, yes, quite," she said, hoping she had not agreed to something idiotic.

"There you see, your Grace, the word of a Muse," Herr Mueller said.

The duke smiled. His sea-glass gaze went to Clio, who was busily cutting a piece of lamb into ridiculously tiny bites. "Muses are notoriously fickle, Herr Mueller, as you must know. They withdraw their favour in an instant, heartlessly leaving a man bereft."

"Not *my* Muses," Sir Walter said stoutly. "Perfect ladies, just like their mother."

"Certainly, Sir Walter," the duke answered. "I meant no disrespect to your daughters. They are a credit to their upbringing."

"Lady Chase and I certainly shared similar views on the education of daughters," Lady Kenleigh said. "When my Emmeline was a child…"

* * *

The rest of the meal passed in talk of education, of exposing children at a very young age to the glories of art and history. Calliope's reverie was not disturbed again until the ladies returned to the drawing room, leaving the men to their brandy and tales of ancient battles. Clio excused herself to retrieve her shawl from the footman.

"What a charming man the duke is," Lady Kenleigh commented, as she settled again by the fireplace. A servant brought in the tea tray. "I always thought him rather cold before."

"Are not most dukes rather cold, Mama?" Emmeline asked. "It seems to be something they inherit along with the title—ineffable haughtiness."

The others laughed, but Lady Kenleigh said, "Not at all! Your father was great friends with the Duke of Rothheil, and he was not cold at all. Averton, though, is something different."

Once some time had passed and everyone was very distracted by the conversation, Calliope excused herself to find the ladies' withdrawing room and wandered back to the hidden door, far at the other end of the room. It was still there; she had not imagined it. Slipping behind the tapestry, she groped along the stout wood until she found a handle. It shifted under her slight pressure, sliding inward.

A rush of cold air brushed over her face, making her gasp and fall back a step into the heavy tapestry. Behind her were the muffled, reassuring voices of her friends. Ahead of her—she had no idea. Chilliness. Darkness, broken only by a faint gleam far ahead.

Calliope was a sensible girl, or so she had always imagined. Surely the sensible thing would be to turn back, to shut the door and forget it existed. But had she not decided she was no longer the old Calliope? That she could not go back?

She couldn't burst into the dining room and insist Cameron come with her. If she wanted to see what was up there she had to go alone, while she had the chance.

Just one quick look, she decided. Then she could tell Cameron what she found, in exchange for his own news. Now resolute, Calliope stepped on to the first stone stair, drawing the door closed behind her.

The staircase was steep, leading up to that faint light she saw ahead. It was very cold. She drew her shawl close, hurrying upwards. She was beginning to have second thoughts, yet it was too late now. She had to go forward. She *was* a Muse, after all, and Muses might be fickle, but they were surely brave.

The light was a lantern, hung at the mouth of a corridor. She must be deep in the castle, she thought, for there were no windows here, no arrow slits. Just bare stone walls. The corridor was narrow and disappointingly empty.

Calliope sighed. What had she been expecting? Casks of jewels? A letter saying "I am really the Lily Thief, signed the Duke of Averton"? Feeling foolish, she started to turn back to the stairs, when a hollow clunking sound stopped her short.

She spun around, her stomach tight. "Who is there?" she called.

A figure emerged from the shadows at the entrance. "I should have known you would appear," a familiar voice said wryly.

"Cameron!" Calliope cried. She dashed back down the corridor, throwing her arms around his neck. He caught her close, lifting her from her feet. How warm he was, how solid and safe! "What are you doing here? Aren't you meant to be in the dining room?"

"I told them I had to, er, answer nature's call," he said. "What about you?"

"The same, of course. I just had to see what that door was."

"That's my Athena." He pressed a kiss to her hair and let her go, keeping her hand in his. "I should have known you couldn't stay away once you realised there was a hidden portal."

"It doesn't seem to go anywhere, though, does it?"

"There's another door at the end. Come, I'll show you." He unhooked the lantern, using its glow to lead them to the far corner of the empty corridor. Calliope held tightly to his hand. With him, these strange, cold halls were more an adventure than a fright. She peered eagerly over his shoulder as he opened that second door.

"More stairs?" she said.

"These go down."

"Into the bowels of the earth?"

"Just like those in the garden at Kenleigh Abbey. Do you want to turn back?"

Calliope stared doubtfully down those stairs. It was even colder here, darker, even more narrow. Of course she wanted to go back! She was no fool. Not usually, anyway.

But when would they have a chance to explore this place again? They would probably never even come back to Averton Castle. And she had vowed to finish this, no matter what it took.

Be Athena, she told herself sternly. No fear. "I want to go on. We have to take this chance while we have it."

He grinned at her. "Then on we go. Just don't step on any rats."

Rats! Calliope lifted the hem of her gown, tiptoeing down the steps behind Cameron. "Athena never faced rats," she muttered.

"Just Trojans," he answered.

"And Persians."

At the foot of the steps was yet another door. "We won't get lost?" she asked.

"And wander beneath the duke's castle for ever? Never fear, we'll remember the way back. See, another door."

This door led not to an empty corridor but to a small room. As Cameron lifted the lantern high, Calliope gasped. Surely *this* was what she had hoped for!

The room was a jumble of treasures. Some, like the sarcophagus, she remembered from Acropolis House, but many she had never seen before. A bare-breasted snake goddess and inlaid bronze dagger from Knossos. Golden Laconian goblets. A headless marble Aphrodite, and a bodyless warrior's head. A bronze, engraved mirror.

And, at the far end, like a queen reigning over her disorganised kingdom, was the Alabaster Goddess. Her stand now repaired, she stood proudly, her bow ever poised in defence.

She was not alone, though. Like worshipping acolytes, two people hovered at that base. They spun around, startled, when the light from Cameron's lantern touched them. The rays glinted on a pair of spectacles.

"Clio!" Calliope cried. "What are you doing here? And what…?" Her shocked gaze swept over the scene, over her sister and the man who was with her. He looked like a gypsy, with long, raven-black hair, a golden hoop glittering in one ear. He was tall and very lean, even slimmer without the greatcoat and hat he had worn in the garden. His black eyes watched Calliope warily, silently.

An open box of tools lay at Clio's feet, hammers and

slender chisels. Clio held a long metal bar in her hands, wedged beneath the goddess's repaired base.

"No," Calliope breathed. "It can't be."

Clio dropped the bar with a clang, holding out her hands. "Cal, I'm so sorry! I never meant that this—"

"Well, well. If it isn't the Purple Hyacinth," the Duke of Averton said from the doorway. "And let me guess. The Golden Falcon? At last we meet." He smiled at them all, a cold, tight grin that made Calliope shiver. "And Westwood, too. I shouldn't really be surprised. My, my. Such a very cosy scene."

The only sound was the rush of wind down the steps, the steady drip of water from somewhere above. Until Clio picked up the bar, its metallic scrape against the floor abnormally loud.

"Oh, no, my dear," Averton said, his voice sad. "That is not a good idea."

Chapter Twenty-Two

That bizarre dreamlike quality that had overlaid the whole evening intensified, closing in around Calliope like a fog. She pressed her fingers to her pounding temples, watching through the haze as Clio's companion edged closer to her protectively, silent, glowering.

Cameron took her arm gently, as if he feared she might crack like a piece of porcelain. She half-feared she might, for she felt as brittle and delicate as the framed papyrus hanging on the wall.

Calliope stared at that scene, at the shifting blues and reds of the paint. Thoth watching as souls were weighed, carefully recording on his scroll whether they were saved or damned.

The duke hovered in the doorway like a judgemental spirit himself, watching them with those flat green eyes, tense and unpredictable. Calliope was hardly aware of him, though, or of Cameron's touch on her arm. She could only think of one thing.

It was Clio all along. Clio, her sister, who was the Lily Thief, who snatched those antiquities away so they were never seen again. Clio, who had listened to Calliope's worries and plans, who showed her that list. Clio, who she had loved and trusted above all others, ever since the day she was led into the nursery and shown her new baby sister, red-haired and solemn in her beribboned cradle.

Clio, who had been scheming to steal the Alabaster Goddess all this time.

"How could you?" Calliope said, hating herself for the hurt and tears so thick in her voice. She didn't *want* to be hurt, to be vulnerable, ever again! "How could you do this, Clio?"

"Cal, please," Clio pleaded. She edged around her companion, her hand held out to Calliope, but she went still when Calliope gave her a freezing glance. "I never meant to hurt you, never wanted to lie to you. I would have told you everything, once it was all over."

"Once you had stolen every antiquity in England?"

Clio shook her head, her eyes diamond-bright. "It's not like that!"

"Is it not, Miss Chase?" the duke asked conversationally, as if they were sipping tea in a drawing room and he inquired about the weather. "How interesting. We see you here, prying my Artemis from her base, the trapdoor to the secret passage open. Tell us, then—how is it? And do be thorough. I told the others I was going to show all of you some special artefacts. They won't miss us for quite a while."

Clio swung towards him, her hands curled into tight fists. "I will tell *you* how it is, your Grace. Duke of Avarice. You took all these things from their rightful homes, the places where they belonged, and piled them up here to moulder away. To wither away to dust just to satisfy your pride and conceit. I know how you came by these items, how you yanked them from the dirt, from their altars. Or, no, you wouldn't soil your bejewelled hands! You paid lowly *tombaroli*, men who would do anything to feed their families, to snatch them for you. That is how it is."

The duke suddenly lunged forward, quick as a snake, to seize Clio's wrists and drag her close to him. Their gazes locked, and though only their hands touched, the air crackled with the tension of mortal combat. Combat Calliope was paralysed to stop.

"You think you know everything, don't you, Clio, the great Muse of History?" the duke said softly. "You think you are the champion of the ancient world, the storied heroine rescuing sacred treasures from the evil, rapacious dragon."

"I am not a heroine," Clio answered, staring up at him. "I am just a mortal woman who is trying to do what's right, to save what I can. You don't deserve the Alabaster Goddess. She is meant to…"

"To be yours?"

"To go home. She cannot be possessed by anyone, let alone you. A man so full of greed…"

"Careful, Clio." He drew her an inch closer, her hands tense in his clasp as she strained away. "You don't know everything."

"I know *you*! I know men like you. You think you can own things, own people, that you are entitled to imprison whatever you desire."

His gaze narrowed. "Is this because I kissed you in the gallery? Because you—"

"Let me go!" Clio cried, suddenly lashing out, kicking him in the leg. But her silk evening slippers were thin, and he didn't even wince.

Cameron let go of Calliope, pushing her towards the goddess as he tackled the duke. Averton, distracted by Clio, had obviously forgotten the rest of them were even in the room. He fell to the hard floor with a surprised shout, quickly strangled when Cameron's fists closed around his coat collar.

"I will not let you abuse another woman," Cameron growled, pinning the duke down.

Averton laughed breathlessly. "Are you going to break my nose again, Westwood?"

"No less than you deserve. I told you to stay far away from the Chases."

"True. And you are quite right—it's no less than I deserve. I *did* kiss her. Old habits and all that. I think you'll agree with me that the Chase Muses are quite irresistible. Why else would you follow Miss Calliope all over England on such a fruitless errand?"

Cameron's face went white with inexpressible anger, and he lifted the duke's head as if to bash it to the floor. Calliope, cold with fear, cried out, "No!" But she tripped and fell against the Alabaster Goddess, helpless to run to him—just like in a nightmare. Clio's gypsy companion helped her to her feet, saying, "Steady, *signorina*," as he held her upright. Perhaps, then, he was not a gypsy after all, for his accent was pure patrician Venetian.

"Oh, let him go," Clio said, burying her face in her hands. "Much as I would like to see his pretty nose bashed in, it would solve nothing. We're already caught. No doubt his exalted Grace will see Marco and me hanged."

Hanged? The vision of her sister mounting the scaffold was more than Calliope could bear. She pulled away from the patrician gypsy—Marco?—and stumbled to Clio's side, catching her sister's arm in a tight clasp.

Clio said nothing, but leaned into Calliope, boneless and exhausted.

"You see, Miss Chase, that is yet another thing you don't know," the duke said affably. Cameron had reluctantly stepped away at Clio's words, and now Averton rose stiffly to his feet, brushing the dust from his coat. "It's true that you must cease your Lily Thief activities at once, but I think means less than a rope would be sufficient."

"And you think *you* could be those means?" Clio said.

"Oh, I doubt that I personally—or any mere mortal man—could stop you from doing anything. But perhaps you could be persuaded." The duke reached inside his coat and withdrew a folded sheet of parchment.

"What is that?" Clio asked. "Some sort of arrest warrant?"

"Clio," Calliope murmured. She glanced towards the trapdoor Averton had mentioned earlier, a shadow of beckoning freedom in the dark corner. Could they run fast enough?

"Hardly a warrant. It is a letter from the director of the Antiquities Society, Lord Knowleton. I believe he is a friend of your father?"

"What could Lord Knowlcton have to say in this matter?" Calliope asked, puzzled.

"A great deal, as it happens. He and the other members of the Society, including Sir Walter, are deeply concerned about the theft of such precious objects as that sarcophagus over there. Or Artemis, who everyone seems so interested in right now. They knew of the tales of my rather reckless youth." The duke glanced at Cameron, who stood silently glowering next to Calliope, whip-tense and ready to pounce again at an instant's notice. "I sometimes consorted then with elements less than worthy of a duke's heir, and have a few connections still. They also knew I am rather interested in collecting."

Clio snorted. "*Rather?* Half of Greece and Egypt sits rotting in your house."

"You forget Assyria, my dear. I do have some rather fine lion figures, plus one or two steles."

"But what does this have to do with the Antiquities Society?" Clio interrupted. Clearly her shock was wearing off. Calliope held her hand tightly so she could not fly at the duke and scratch his eyes out.

"So impatient. But I will tell you. Knowing all this, Lord Knowleton and the Society came to me and asked me to use some of my old connections to discover who was carrying out these thefts. Those of the Lily Thief, and many others, less publicised. Not just here, you see, but in Italy and France. I track them down by whatever means possible, and eventually I see to it that the items return to their owners." Averton laid a gentle hand on the goddess's alabaster sandal. "So, you see, though these objects are exquisite, and I have loved having them for a time, they are not mine."

Clio drew away from Calliope, standing stiff and pale. "I don't believe you."

"Of course you don't." The duke handed her the letter. "Perhaps you recognise the signatures? Or the Antiquities Society seal? The document lays out my task. I insisted on such a thing in case an occasion for explanation arose, which of course it has."

Clio read the letter, her lips pressed together. Calliope peered over her shoulder, searching the neatly penned words until she came to the signatures at the bottom. "It appears to be legitimate," she said slowly.

"How did you find out it was me?" Clio asked, neatly refolding the paper.

"You should be very proud of yourself," the duke said. "You were quite evasive. It wasn't until luck sent me in the direction of your list of contacts that I was able to make the last connections. I knew the Alabaster Goddess was just the bait I needed to draw you out of hiding. She is exactly the sort of antiquity that you like, is she not? Beautiful, special, taken from a temple or sacred site."

"She was merely bait to you?"

"Not merely, my dear. Such a rare object could never be merely anything. My father bought her many years ago, but the selfish old monster never wanted to share her. I didn't even know she existed until I inherited the title."

Clio stared at Artemis. "So she…"

"Is the only thing in this room that is entirely mine." The duke's gaze lingered on the curve of Clio's cheek for a long moment before he turned away. "We should return to the party, I think. We have given them quite enough time to gossip about us."

"No hanging, then?" Clio said, her tone suspicious and tense.

The duke did not look back, as if he couldn't bear to see Clio's face again. "I think we've had quite enough drama for one night, don't you? It should be enough for thc Lily Thief to vanish from the scene. And be sure to take your tools when you leave. This place is cluttered enough as it is."

He departed, his footsteps echoing away up the stone steps. The silence in the room was thick, as muffling as wool batting. Calliope hardly knew what to say, what to do. For one of the few times in her life, her practicality, her precious good sense, was of absolutely no use. All she had believed she was working towards was gone.

"Do you hate me, Cal?" Clio said quietly.

Calliope shook her head, closing her eyes as if she could blot out the whole night. "Why would you steal those things, Clio? We don't need money! And we hardly need to add to our collection."

"Cal, surely you know me better than to think I could do this for money?"

"I thought I knew you. But how could I? You hid this from me. You knew how I hated the Lily Thief, how I hated the disappearance of these antiquities and how they were lost to scholars for ever. Yet you said nothing. You let me play the fool!"

"How could I say anything? For those very reasons I had to hide it all from you. But every moment of secrecy was agony. You're my sister, I longed to tell you! To confess everything."

"Then why didn't you?"

"Because the work was too important. I couldn't let my personal feelings get in the way." Clio's sharp, tear-filled gaze shifted over Calliope's shoulder, to Cameron. "*You* understand, don't you, Lord Westwood? After all, you sent your own father's collection back to Greece."

"I did," he said. "But they were mine to send."

Clio lifted her chin. "The people who held those objects were not their true owners. They stole them from their real homes."

"Clio, did you not think of—of *us*, of Father and the girls when you did this?" Calliope asked, suddenly so deeply sad and tired. Exhausted to her very bones. "What if you had been caught?"

"Caught by someone other than the enigmatic duke, you mean? Of course I thought about it. I left letters for you hidden in my room, explaining everything. But I was good at what I did, and I have—had—an excellent network of associates." She smiled at her gypsy aristocrat. "Is that not so, Marco?"

He grinned, and for the first time Calliope saw how very beautiful he was, her sister's silent accomplice. "*Sì, signorina.* Your sister, Signorina Calliope, she is the best smuggler in all England."

"Such a thing to boast of at Almack's," Calliope muttered.

"I am truly sorry I hurt you, Cal," Clio said. "Please, please believe me. But it had to be done." She turned away, going to help Marco pack up their tools.

"Come with me, Calliope," Cameron said gently, taking her arm. "It's cold here, and you look as if you could use a warm cup of strong tea."

"My mother always believed tea could cure anything," Calliope said, letting him lead her towards the door.

"Perhaps she was right, if the tea happens to have a measure of brandy stirred in."

They retraced their steps, climbing up the steps and turning back down the empty corridor. When they first traversed this path half an hour—or was it a hundred years?—ago, she had been full of tense, cold anticipation. Now she was just tired. Stunned.

"It was my own sister all along," she said. "How could I not have seen it? How could I have been so blind?"

"You probably did see it, but denied it. Even to yourself. It's hard to admit the faults of the ones we love. Almost as hard as admitting our own."

Calliope remembered her sister burning her Medusa costume, showing her the list of names. So quiet, so serious, so deeply wary of the duke. *Had* she seen? Had she simply refused to acknowledge the fact that the thief was right in front of her? "I don't know. I just don't understand. And I don't want to see her hurt."

"Of course not. She's your sister. She certainly went about things the wrong way."

"I should say so!"

"But she had reasons for what she did. She told you, she thought she was doing what was right."

Calliope paused, studying Cameron in the faint light. He

gazed back steadily, his cognac-coloured eyes full of concern, and—and pity. He pitied her, and thought Clio was right.

Suddenly, his very calmness, his compassion, infuriated her. She resisted the strange, primitive urge to hit him, to lash out and knock him down as he had the duke. "You don't seem very surprised by what has happened tonight," she said. "By Clio's confession."

His gaze turned wary. "Calliope, listen to me. I meant to tell you, later. Remember?"

"You did know, then? You knew about Clio?"

"Not for long. It was that name, the Purple Hyacinth."

"And that was what you said you had to tell me earlier?"

"Yes."

"So, why didn't you tell me *then*? You let me flounder around in my ignorance, until we were faced with that awful room, with Clio and her gypsy. You let me…" Let her have sex with him. Suddenly it was all far too much. The whole evening crashed down on her, and she wanted to cry, to wail, to beat her fists against the stone wall. To match childish actions to wild, childish emotions.

Everyone she loved the most, relied on the most, had lied to her. Hidden things from her for *her own good*.

"I want to go home," she said, spinning away from Cameron. "I'm tired. Tired of everything, everyone."

"Calliope, please, listen to me!" Cameron said urgently. But she hurried away from him, racing towards the light and noise of the party. If she could just be among people again, back in the real world, escape from cold caves full of anti-quities and lies, she could be herself again. Find her way.

But she knew, even as she ran, that nothing could be the same again.

Cameron watched Calliope flee, her white dress fading away like a ghost in the shadows. Every fibre of his being urged him to run after her, to catch her in his arms and hold her until she listened to him, until she heard him and understood. To *make* her understand.

But he knew Calliope well by now, too well to think that such tactics could ever work on her. He remembered the duke holding Clio, his stare burning into her as she resisted hearing him. The Chases were stubborn and wilful, set on their own course, and force would never change them. Only gentle, rational persuasion had even a chance. Something Averton couldn't understand, but Cameron was beginning to.

It was that very stubbornness, that strong will, that made him love Calliope so very much. That certainty, that passion for a cause, for *right*—even when her "right" wasn't his own. She had a fire she thought well hidden behind her cool good manners, her stylish white gowns, but which she could never extinguish from her eyes. Her laughter. He craved the blazing heat of that fire. He had been wandering in the cold world alone for too long.

He needed Calliope by his side for the rest of his life, to quarrel with, be exasperated by, to kiss and love. If only he could earn her love in return, to set that flame free once and for all!

But, blast it, that *stubbornness*! Cameron kicked at the wall, barely feeling the impact of the stone. She just wouldn't listen.

"Where is Calliope?" he heard Clio say. He glanced up to find her coming down the corridor towards him, holding a lantern. One would never guess she had just spent the evening trying to dislodge an alabaster statue from its base. Every auburn hair was in place, her amber-coloured gown impeccable. Cool and elegant.

And her very composure, oddly, gave him hope. For

another quality Muses possessed was changeability. Perhaps Calliope would not stay angry for long.

"She has returned to the party," he said.

"Without you?"

"She insisted rather, ah, forcefully that she wanted to be alone."

"Threw a bit of a tantrum, did she? That is not much like Cal. But then, who could blame her? It has been a trying evening, and all my fault."

"So it was, Purple Hyacinth. Lily Thief. Whoever you are tonight."

"Clio will do, since I am sure you will soon be my brother."

"If your sister can forgive me."

"Forgive *you*, Lord Westwood? Whatever for? You didn't try to steal the Alabaster Goddess. Is it because you defended my motives?"

"That, and the fact that I discovered your identity earlier and had not yet told her."

"Ah, I see," Clio said. "How did you guess?"

"I should have known even earlier, considering that we all live in such a classical world. I saw a painting of the Muses in Lord Kenleigh's library. Clio, the mother of Hyacinth."

"It was a mistake. I should have chosen a less obvious moniker. They're meant to be somewhat recognisable, though, at least by the people in the network."

"Like your friend Marco?"

"Marco. The Golden Falcon." She smiled. "He is so very dramatic. Most Venetians are, you know."

"Dramatic and gone, I hope."

"Of course. He left by the tunnel. It eventually comes out near Kenleigh Abbey."

"The steps in the garden."

"This house party was a godsend. Yorkshire is riddled with hidden tunnels and passages. Left over from smuggling days, of course."

"And the goddess?"

"Still here. I am not such a fool as to take her when I'm caught. I know when to admit defeat. For now."

As Cameron studied the hard glint in her green eyes, he could almost, *almost*, pity the duke. Desiring a Muse was never an easy thing.

"Come, Lord Westwood, you can escort me back to the party," Clio said, taking his arm. "And don't worry about Calliope. It is me she is truly angry with, not you. Her storms never last long." She paused. "Not usually, anyway."

It was that "not usually" that concerned him.

Chapter Twenty-Three

"Soon it will be time to return to town," Emmeline said, digging along the river's edge, looking for water flowers.

"Oh, yes," Calliope answered, distracted. Her sketch-book was open on her lap, but only a few rough lines began to denote the nearby bridge. "For your betrothal ball."

"Yes. At least one good thing came of this holiday, even if we didn't end up catching the Lily Thief. My parents quite gave up the idea of Freddie Mountbank as a good match!"

"Shall you be happy with Mr Smithson?"

"Oh, yes, I think so. He is very kind-hearted, you know, so I am sure of always getting my own way." Emmeline laid out her plants in a basket, brushing off her hands as she peered closely at Calliope. "Will we soon have news of your own engagement?"

"Mine?" Calliope ducked her head over her sketch-book, her face warm despite the cool, overcast day. "What would make you think that?"

Emmeline shrugged. "You were absent from the duke's party for quite a while last night."

"The duke was showing off his collection. Lord Westwood and I were with him and Clio, quite well chaperoned."

"I just thought you looked a bit pale and surprised when you came back to the drawing room. As if something had happened."

Pale and surprised? Calliope sighed. That was the very least of it. Those few moments in Averton's hidden room were the most surreal, the most difficult she had ever known. Even now, after a night of fitful sleep, she hardly knew what to think. What to feel. She had loathed the Lily Thief for so long, but she loved her sister.

She looked over at where Clio sat on a large, flat rock below the bridge with Thalia, the two of them dangling their booted feet above the rushing water. Clio was quiet today, and she had tried to catch Calliope's eye over breakfast and on the walk here. She wouldn't press, though, Calliope knew that. She would let Calliope talk to her in her own time.

If only Calliope knew what to say.

"I just think one person has no need of so many riches," Calliope said. "So selfishly hidden away."

Emmeline laughed. "What he puts on open display is quite astonishing enough. I can't imagine what he might hide."

Calliope hadn't imagined, either. "Averton is rather— surprising."

"To say the least." Mr Smithson called Emmeline's name and she turned towards him, leaving Calliope alone with her sketches.

She drew in a deep breath, closing her eyes. Despite everything that had happened here, she would miss this place. Its solitude, its quiet, silvery magic. Something about it had surely changed her, unlocked something deep inside so that, for a while at least, she felt lighter. Free.

Was it really this place? Or was it someone? Someone who had made her see things differently. See a new way.

Calliope saw a vision of Cameron's handsome face, his laughing eyes, as he held her close in the moonlight. As he kissed her until the whole world spun dizzily around them and she could hardly remember even her own name. She knew only him, wanted only him!

She also saw him as he had been last night, his face set in hard, angry stone, so white-hot with fury as he knocked the duke to the ground. All to protect Clio, to protect *them*. Yet he had known even then that she was the thief. Had known, and hadn't told Calliope.

Calliope pressed her hands to her aching temples. Nothing was what she had thought, nothing and no one— Cameron, Averton, Clio. She had built her whole life on a foundation of certainty as strong as granite. On beliefs she thought unshakeable. As fierce and permanent as the Alabaster Goddess herself, with her bow and her crescent moon.

That foundation proved to be ephemeral as sand. What would now replace it?

What could she be sure of?

"May I sit with you for a while?" she heard Clio say softly. She opened her eyes to find her sister standing next to her. Clio was as lovely as ever, every hair in place, her spectacles on her nose. But she looked worried, lightly poised as if to dash away at a sign of rebuff.

She had always been thus, Calliope thought, remembering when they were children running round the gardens. Calliope always the organiser of their games, Clio following, but as self-contained as a cat. As a goddess. Her thoughts and motives always her own.

"Of course," Calliope said. She slid over on her fallen log, making room for her sister.

Clio settled next to her, wrapped tightly in her cloak. They sat in silence for a moment, listening to the splash of the water, the distant laughter of their friends. Finally, Clio said, "I truly am sorry for deceiving you, Cal. I never wanted to hurt you."

Calliope bit her lip. "What if you had been caught? Did you think of that?"

Clio gave a humourless laugh. "Every day. I was quite terrified. Especially of you."

"Me?"

"You were so very determined to find the Lily Thief. I knew it was only a matter of time."

"You had nothing to fear. I wasn't clever enough to see what was right in front of me."

"You didn't *want* to see. And neither did I."

"What do you mean?"

"The duke, of course." Clio shook her head. "There was always something not right about that man. I thought he was just insane. And obsessed. Instead, he had a purpose I never even suspected. I was a fool."

Calliope remembered the duke's eyes as he watched Clio. "We were all fools."

"I had to do what I thought was right, Cal. To protect something precious and irreplaceable. I see I never should have concealed it from you, for we both want the same thing."

Calliope laughed. "I could never be brave enough to take up smuggling, like you! Or consort with people like that Marco. He seemed rather fearsome."

Clio laughed, too, a faint blush touching her pale cheeks. "Marco is all right. He has a soft heart under that impenetrable Venetian hide, and he loves art as we do. I don't mean that you would ever lose your good sense, as it appears I have. I mean we both wanted to protect the Alabaster Goddess and all she stands for."

"True." A silence fell over them again, but it was lighter, easier, touched with their old sisterly comfort. Eventually, Calliope held out her hand and Clio took it, holding it tightly. "You can tell me anything from now on, Clio. I have learned not to judge, not to make pronouncements. At least not until I've heard all explanations! Just promise me something."

"What?"

"That you will not take such risks in the future. We Muses have to stay together, all of us."

Clio didn't reply. Instead, her gaze narrowed as a large, glossy black carriage rolled into view. It dashed up over the bridge, and for one instant the window lowered to a glimpse of bright hair, a hand laden with emerald and ruby rings. Then it was gone, followed by a wagon filled with trunks and cases. In the centre, covered in heavy canvas and bound by thick ropes, was Artemis, her bow tightly swathed.

Clio watched the procession until even its dust was no longer seen. "I promise no more Lily Thief," she said quietly, reaching inside her cloak. She withdrew a white lily, wilted, brown at the edges of its satiny petals. No doubt it had been meant to be left in place of the goddess last night. She tossed it into the river.

Calliope had certainly noticed Clio hadn't promised to take no more chances. But the end of the Lily Thief was a place to start.

"What about Lord Westwood?" Clio said.

"I don't think he'll turn you in."

"That's not what I mean, Cal. I mean, what about *you* and Lord Westwood?"

Cameron and her? Before last night, she had begun to hope. To maybe think that her long-ago dreams of a man who could understand her were real. He did understand her, as she did him, for their hopes and ideals were much the same. With him, perhaps, she could at last be free. Free of being the eldest Muse, the one in control, the one who always knew the answers. With him, she could just be *Calliope*. Could begin to learn who Calliope was.

But then she had behaved so childishly last night. Refused to listen to him. And right when their quarrels at last seemed finished!

"Lord Westwood and me?" she said. "I don't think there is any such thing now."

Clio frowned. "Do you still argue with him, then?"

"No. Not like we used to, anyway. He is probably tired of me, of my silly schemes."

"Oh, Cal. What other man would have spent all this time helping you with your 'silly schemes'? Following you through secret tunnels? You just have to face facts, my dearest sister. He is meant for you, and you for him. There can be no one else for either of you, because you would make any other mate quite unhappy with your respective eccentricities." Clio gave a theatrical sigh. "It is the curse of being a Chase Muse. We're never happy with ordinary life. At least *you* have found someone who shares your oddity. The rest of us seem destined for solitude."

Thalia chose that moment to let out an Amazonian shout, standing up on her rock with her arms flung wide. She twirled around, her hair a golden flame.

"Especially Thalia, I think," Clio murmured. "Only Apollo himself could ever be *her* match."

Calliope laughed, suddenly feeling so light she could surely float away! Clio was right, and Calliope had been a fool to ever doubt it. She was fortunate to find her match, to find a man like Cameron—kind, funny, handsome, infused with the same love of history as the Muses. A man who could show her a new world.

Was it too late?

"I have to go," she said, jumping to her feet. Now, before one more minute was wasted, she had to find Cameron and tell him her feelings. Her yearnings.

"Yes, go, go," Clio urged, laughing as Calliope ran up the slippery riverbank.

Calliope soon left behind the voices of her friends, the river and the bank, as she dashed down the overcast lane. The wind was colder here, and she drew her cloak close, as if to shut away the outer chill—and her own inner doubts. When she was with her sisters, listening to Clio talk, it was easy to believe all would be well in the end. Now, alone, doubts always crept in. Old, plaguing doubts.

She remembered Cameron's face, the veiled hurt in his eyes, when she stormed away from him, refusing to listen to him. Was it all too late? Or, despite his kisses, had he really never cared for her at all?

She wished she could truly call on an ancient goddess, one who could banish all self-doubt, all fears. But all she truly had was herself, and that had to be enough.

"You have to tell him how you feel," she told herself as she turned through the gates of Kenleigh Abbey. "If you don't, you will surely regret it for the rest of your life."

And turn into a bitter old Muse, lecturing her bored nieces and nephews on the glories of the classical world.

She found him in the garden. He stood on the lower step of the terrace, staring out at the hidden passageway, now blocked up again. His hands were locked behind his back, his face expressionless, as if carved in marble. The wind curled his hair over his brow in that poetic tangle she loved so much. Her beautiful Greek god, staring into a world only he could see, a reality only he could know.

Would he share that world with her? Was it possible now?

"'How shall I receive the god, the proud one,'" she said softly, walking down the terrace steps to his side, "'the arrogant one who stands in the highest place, above all the gods and people of the teeming earth'?"

He glanced at her, his face unchanging. But she thought, hoped, she saw a gleam deep in his eyes.

"Are you back from your walk already?" he said.

"I am. The others are still at the river."

"Why did you return alone?"

"To find you, of course."

He brow arched in surprise. "To find me?" he said warily. Perhaps he thought she meant to berate him again.

"It was so very late when we returned to the Abbey last night, we never had another chance to talk."

"Ah, yes. Last night." He unclasped his hands, crossing his arms over his chest as he nudged at the grass with his boot. "Quite an adventure, was it not?"

"You could call it that. Who would have thought the duke could be on the side of good, for once? *Good* as he sees it, anyway. As for Clio…"

"I never meant to conceal the truth from you," Cameron said gently. "I just did not want to see you hurt."

"I know. If there is a god who is the protector of women, he is surely your patron! You would have told me, and in a far more gentle way than what happened last night."

"I only discovered the truth when I saw that painting in the library. Even then I wasn't sure. Not until we saw her with the Alabaster Goddess."

Calliope nodded. "I talked with Clio. She has vowed

there will be no more Lily Thief. But when I think of the danger she put herself in…!"

"That is just the way you Muses are. You care so deeply. Passionately."

Calliope laughed. "I never realised I had 'passion' at all! I just thought I had certainty. The knowledge of what is right and wrong. Until…"

"Until what?"

"Until you. Your passion, your daring—it ignited my own. You helped me discover things about myself, about the world, that I never imagined. *You* are the Muse, I think."

His mask finally cracked, and he turned to her with hope, fear, desire in his eyes. Emotions that matched her own. "Calliope, I never—"

"No." She pressed her finger to his lips, just as she had last time they stood on this terrace. "I have to say this before I lose my nerve. I was wrong not to stay and listen to you last night. Not to trust. It—well, it's not an easy thing for me to trust. But I know now I can always rely on you to tell me the truth, whether I want to hear it or not. I can rely on you to protect me and my family, to support me even when you think I'm wrong. Like when you agreed to help me find the Lily Thief in the first place."

He grinned at her, catching her hand in his. He kissed her fingers, sliding them down to press over his heart. Through the soft wool and linen, the trappings of civilisation, she felt the strong pulse of sheer, primitive life. "Calliope. I only agreed to help you catch the Lily Thief because I wanted to spend time with you."

Calliope laughed, thrilled at the admission. "You wanted to spend time with me? Even after I had argued with you, berated you?"

"It seemed the only way you would associate with me.

And you see the lengths I would go to in order to be close to you? Running down secret passages. Associating with thieves and false gypsies and even dukes. Horrid stuff."

"But why did you *want* to be close to me?"

"Because you are beautiful, of course," he teased. He caught her around the waist, twirling her off her feet in a heady whirl of laughter. "And because of that passion you deny possessing. I could sense it inside of you, like a flame burning in your eyes. It drew me in; I couldn't stay away. Surely you are more siren than muse."

"A stubborn siren?"

"I adore your stubbornness. I adore how you defend the ones you love, the ideas you hold so fiercely true."

Calliope laughed again, breathless, winding her arms tightly about his neck to hold him captive. "No one has ever loved my stubbornness before. And you think I'm beautiful? Really?"

"The most beautiful woman in all England."

"But not Greece? I'm sure you saw some *very* beautiful women there. Veritable goddesses."

"None to rival you, chief of the Muses. *You* are what I always sought. What I travelled the world seeking, and here you were all the time. My fierce Athena."

"I think we need to invoke another goddess right now," she whispered.

She felt the curl of his smile. "And who would that be?"

"Aphrodite. Did she not serve us well before?" Smiling, she took his hand in hers and led him again towards the trees. Only there, in their secret spot, could she truly show him what was in her heart.

He followed, unresisting but silent. Was this declaration going to be even harder than she feared?

She turned to him when they reached the clearing, her

heart in her throat. Balanced on her hand as she offered it to him. "Cam, I must say—"

But his lips swooped down on hers, swallowing her tentative words, catching her breath, her senses, her very balance, and sending them spinning away. She was surrounded entirely by *him*.

Her own fierce desire, awakened in this very spot, rose up to meet his, equal—no, surely greater! With a groan, she wrapped her arms tightly him as he lowered her to the ground. His weight was heavy and sweet, their bodies fitting perfectly as if always meant to be. How she had tried to push away her feelings for him, to deny what was in her heart! But those feelings were stubborn, and would not be banished. They burst free now, an explosion of sparks, bright colours, wild excitement.

She needed him, loved him, and that was all.

Calliope shoved his coat from his shoulders with impatient hands, fumbling with his cravat, his shirt and waistcoat, until she had what she wanted—his bare, warm skin under her touch. She scored her nails lightly along the long groove of his spine, almost to his taut buttocks, and then back up again to plunge into the satiny curls that tumbled over his neck. Her beautiful Greek god.

Cameron growled, low and rough, his tongue seeking hers in a kiss not practised and seductive, but blurry and needful. Calliope's skirts seemed too heavy, abrading her sensitive skin, and she reached down with one hand to pull at them. Not even breaking their kiss, he helped her, stripping away her cloak and gown until she lay beneath him in her chemise.

Calliope wrapped her legs around him, holding him so close he could never escape. Here, in their forest grove, entwined with him, she was finally free.

* * *

The grey-yellow light was hazy above them when Calliope opened her eyes. It grew late in the day, yet she could not shed her lazy, delicious heaviness. Couldn't bring herself to even move.

Their clothes were scattered about the clearing, little piles and tufts of wool and linen, stirring in the breeze. She kicked at a stray stocking, and Cameron's arms tightened around her. Calliope rolled over to find him with his eyes closed, a half smile on his lips. How lovely he was, so free of cares! So relaxed, like Apollo after his task of summoning the sun was finished. So irresistible.

Calliope arched into the curve of his body, pressing a soft kiss to his cheek. He smiled without opening his eyes, drawing her even closer.

"Thank you," she whispered.

"Shouldn't I be the one thanking you, Aphrodite?" he said hoarsely.

"Will you be thanking me when they read the banns and you cannot escape?"

"Or *you* can't escape. Muses are notoriously changeable. I think I should apply for a special licence. Less time for you to fly away."

"I shall never want to fly away. I'm going to follow you wherever you go, you know."

"Good. Then I'll always be aware of when you're chasing after thieves, putting yourself in danger."

Calliope ran her fingertips along his arm, feeling the tense strength of his muscles, his leashed power. He shivered under her touch. "My thief-chasing days are done. I don't always like what I find at the end of the chase, you see."

"I'm glad to hear it."

She propped herself up on her elbow, gazing down at his face, that lazy half smile she loved so much. "That doesn't mean I want our adventures to be over! I've just found that part of myself, after all. I'm not ready to go back to being staid and sedate."

He twined one of her long, black curls around his finger. "Were you ever staid and sedate? I must have missed it. But I am an old stay-at-home now. An old earl, soon to be an old, married earl. My gallivanting days are over."

"They had best not be over quite yet! For mine are just beginning. If I have to go adventuring by myself—"

"Never!" He stopped her words with a laughing kiss. "Very well, then, my Muse. What do you say to a wedding trip to Greece?"

"That will do—for a start."

"And when we return, we can start our own band of Muses. Of little goddesses and godlings."

Calliope laughed. "Do you really want that many daughters? It is no easy task, I can tell you. Especially when they possess the Chase wilfulness."

"Of course I do, if they all look like their mother. I would be the happiest man in the world."

"In that case…" Calliope pushed him on to his back, her hand lingering on his naked chest, trailing downward. "We had best get started."

Epilogue

As the boat drew nearer to the island of Delos, gliding leisurely through the azure water, Calliope saw it was just as her husband had described. Grey with morning mist, damp, shapeless, with no mountains or valleys to delineate it. A desert in the sea. How Apollo's mother Leto must have despaired when she was set down amid such barrenness to birth her sacred twins!

Calliope felt no despair, though, only a fluttering excitement as they drew closer, the mists parting. How long she had waited for this! Ever since the day she had sat by a Yorkshire stream and listened to Cameron tell her of this mystical place. Back then she could never have imagined she would see it for herself. That Cameron would be her husband.

She held tightly to his hand, watching the sun appear through the greyness, as if Apollo's chariot pierced the fog.

"Shall we see the gods today, then?" she whispered. "I fear the clouds will keep them away."

"Have patience, my love," Cameron said, smiling at her. "You should know the gods never appear on demand. They are as fickle as Muses. Almost."

She leaned closer, pressing a light, tickling kiss to his neck, bare without a cravat. "Was I so *fickle* last night?"

He laughed. "Not in the least."

Calliope smoothed back the tangle of hair from his brow. How very handsome her husband was, as if Apollo himself had alighted in their boat! Once she would have said he could not be more beautiful than he was on their wedding day, standing before a flower-bedecked altar in her father's drawing room and vowing to love her for the rest of their lives. But she would have been wrong, for he belonged *here*. In this ancient, wild, dangerous land, full of sunlight and sea air, he came completely alive.

And so did she. Never had she seen colours so vivid, heard laughter so clear and true. The sharp, briny taste of olives and new wine; the heat of the sun on her bare skin as she lay in bed with Cameron, lazy afternoons full of lovemaking; the cool, green smell of the night. The brilliant stars overhead. It was *life*, real life, as she had never even imagined it before.

"There was once a bridge between Delos and Rheneia," their boatman said, his oars sounding hollow in the waves as they entered shallower water. "Built by the rich and very vain Nicias. They say it was a golden creation, lined with fine tapestries and garlands. Worshippers could march right across with their offerings, no fussing with boats and such."

Cameron laughed. "No doubt Nicias was an orderly sort of man! My mother once told me a tale of earlier processions here. Everyone haphazardly leaping ashore in no particular order, singing, tossing garlands about. No order or ritual. Most shocking."

"I'm glad his 'orderly' bridge has vanished, then," Calliope said. "I like the idea of jumping ashore, singing and strewing flowers."

"Calliope de Vere! How shocking," Cameron said, his arm going around her waist to hold her close. "Where is my practical, orderly bride?"

"Left behind in London, of course."

Their boat at last touched the rocky beach, and Cameron leaped out, reaching back to swing her up into his arms.

Calliope protested, laughing. "I can walk, you know!"

"You don't want to get your shoes wet, do you? Besides, this is far more fun."

Once they left the narrow beach, he set her on her feet and they turned down a narrow, overgrown pathway, hand in hand. The landscape was thick with thistle and barley grass, blasted and brown. It appeared the only living beings besides themselves were lizards, brown and black, darting into the meagre shade of twisted trees and old boulders. The sun crawled up overhead, spreading white-hot rays until it seemed to come in pulsating waves, burning into the dusty earth.

Calliope shed her shawl, letting the light fall on her arms and shoulders, bared in a light muslin gown. This place, so barren and empty, hardly seemed a fit home for gods, not like better-preserved temples and theatres they had visited on the mainland and on Mykonos. Yet she could feel its magic. It was as real, as palpable, as that sun overhead. This was a place truly out of time. All her reading and study could never have prepared her for this reality.

If only her sisters could see it, too, she thought. How they would love it.

Finally, they emerged into a wide clearing, a ring guarded by the lionesses of Artemis. Weathered now, worn away by the centuries, diminished in their number, they still stood vigil. Ever young and fierce, poised to pounce on heretical intruders and tear them to bits.

Calliope was glad of her offering, then, a bouquet of bright flowers she laid at the feet of the first lioness.

"This was once the Sanctuary of Apollo," Cameron said.

Calliope gazed around at the littered ruins, the tumble of broken columns, steps leading to vanished portals, pieces of the colonnades that once guarded the sacred statue of Apollo, which was only a portion of torso now, but had once loomed tall. The marble, a silvery-white colour, sparkled in the heat.

"They say Apollo spent his summers here," Calliope said, adjusting the tilt of her straw hat. "One would have thought the winters would have been more practical."

He laughed. "You see, you *are* still my sensible bride. Come, I'll show you something else."

Calliope followed him to the far end of the sanctuary site, where the now-dry pool of Apollo stood, surrounded by the remains of his sacred swans. They were overlooked by a low, flat base of the same silver-coloured marble.

"This is where your Alabaster Goddess once stood," he said quietly. "Or so they say."

"Oh!" Calliope gasped. She knew that Artemis had originally come from Delos, long before she fell into the Duke of Averton's possession. Yet to see where she had once stood vigil, guarding the placid swans with her steady bow, was overwhelming. Calliope laid her hand on the base, feeling the heat baked into the stone rising up inside her like the power of the goddess herself.

And, for the first time, she understood what Clio must have really felt. Her despair at leaving the Alabaster Goddess in the clutches of the duke, when this was her home.

But Clio was on her own path now, gone on a tour of Italy with their father and Thalia. Perhaps one day she would come to this place, too, and would understand things that had been hidden for so long.

Calliope stared up at where the goddess once stood. All she saw was the clear turquoise blue of the sky, the dazzle of the light. In the distance, she thought she could hear music, young voices lifted to the Delian Apollo.

"I heard a tale once," she said. "Apollo and Calliope, chief of the Muses, once came to Delos together, and here they conceived Orpheus, the greatest of all musicians." She took one of Cameron's hands, pressing the palm flat to her stomach. "Will we be blessed with a new Orpheus, do you think, in about, oh, eight months' time?"

Cameron's gaze shot to hers, filled with doubt, wonder, and—and joy. Joy to rival the sun, to rival any god's greatest triumph.

And they kissed under the wide Greek sky, celebrating a new life blessed by the protection of the Alabaster Goddess.

* * * * *

Author's Note

The trade in illegal antiquities is nothing new, of course. It has probably been going on ever since one caveman envied another's wall art! But in recent years, with the rise of the internet and the development of more sophisticated equipment, it has become a huge global industry. Every day countries are stripped of their irreplaceable cultural heritage, and the study of the past is obstructed.

Two fascinating sources on this important subject are: *The Medici Conspiracy: The Illicit Journey of Looted Antiquities From Italy's Tomb Raiders to the World's Greatest Museums* by Peter Watson and Cecilia Todeschini; and *Stealing History: Tomb Raiders, Smugglers, and the Looting of the Ancient World* by Roger Atwood.

To Deceive a Duke

AMANDA McCABE

Prologue

Queen of fragrant Eleusis,
Giver of earth's good gifts,
Give me your grace, O Demeter.
You, too, Persephone, fairest,
Maiden of all lovely, I offer
Song for your favor.

Clio Chase glanced back over her shoulder as she tiptoed along the narrow corridor of Acropolis House, the labyrinthine London home of the Duke of Averton. No one followed her. Probably they did not even notice her absence from the ballroom, not in such a crush as the Duke's Grecian masked ball.

Perfect.

It was silent here, unlike the roar of music and shallow conversation. So quiet it was almost like a cave, lit only by a few lamps built to resemble flickering torches. The shifting light touched the dark panelled walls, the low, carved ceiling and the gilt-framed paintings, making them glitter and waver as if alive.

She paused to slip off her heeled green satin shoes,

hurrying on stocking feet to the end of the corridor where there was a small, winding staircase, a miniature of the grand one soaring up from the foyer. She held up the heavy green-and-gold silk skirts of her Medusa costume as she hurried up the steps. The Duke was being very cagey about the statue's whereabouts tonight. But his servants were not all so secretive. Clio had been able to persuade a footman to tell her where Artemis, the Alabaster Goddess, waited.

At the top of the stairs ran a gallery, almost the entire length of the front of the house. Its bank of windows, uncovered, looked out at the front garden and the street beyond, the open gates that still admitted latecomers to the ball.

The gallery was dotted with more lamps, most of them unlit. No doubt waiting for the 'grand reveal' of the statue after supper, when they would spring to life as if by magic. Right now the light was dim, falling only in shimmering, narrow bars on some of the treasures displayed there, leaving others in darkness.

Clio found herself holding her breath as she crept along the gallery, peering right and left at all the wonders jumbled together. Her father and his friends were all great collectors and loved to show off their prizes, so she had grown up surrounded by beautiful antiquities. But this—this was something else entirely. A cabinet of curiosities such as she had never seen before.

The gallery almost resembled a warehouse, it was so thick with objects. Ancient stone kouros, stiff and precise, their empty eyes staring back at her. Bronze warriors, marble gods; cases full of Etruscan gold jewellery, lapis scarabs, jewelled perfume bottles. Steles propped against the walls. Shelves of vases, kraters and amphorae. All jumbled together, just to serve one man's vanity, his lust for collecting.

Clio frowned as she thought of Averton. So handsome that half the women in town were in love with him—but so mysterious. That strange light in his green eyes when he looked at her…

She shook her head, the satin snakes of her headdress trembling. She couldn't think about *him* now. She had a task to do.

At the end of the gallery, alone in a pool of candlelight, was an object covered in a sheet of black satin. Only a bit of the separate coral-coloured marble base was visible. Clio approached it carefully, half-expecting some sort of trap, some alarm. All was silent, except for the whining hum of the wind past the windows. She reached out and carefully lifted the sheet, peering beneath.

'Oh.' She sighed. It was really her. The Alabaster Goddess. Artemis in all her solitary glory.

The statue was not large. It was easily dwarfed by many of the more elaborate creations in the gallery. But she was so perfectly beautiful, so graceful and elegant, that Clio could understand why she had become such a sensation. Why ladies wanted 'Artemis' coiffures and 'Artemis' sandals.

Why the Duke hid her away.

Carved of an alabaster so white it seemed to glisten, almost silver, like a first snowfall, she stood poised with her bow raised, a lost arrow set to fly. Her pleated tunic flowed over the curves of her slender body as if caught in a breeze, ending at mid-thigh to reveal strong legs, tensed to run. Her sandals, those ribbon-laced shoes every lady copied this Season, still bore bits of gold leaf, as did the bandeau that held back her curled hair. A crescent moon was attached to the band, proclaiming her to be truly the Goddess of the Moon. Her gaze was focused intently on her prey; she cared nothing for mortal adulation.

Clio stared up at her, enthralled, as she imagined the Delian temple where this goddess once resided, where she once received her worship from true acolytes. Not just *ton* ladies and their 'Artemis' shoes.

'How beautiful you are,' she whispered. 'And how sad.'

Much like the Duke himself.

She reached out to gently touch Artemis's foot in a gesture of silent sympathy. As she did, she noticed that the goddess stood on a wooden base, a thick block with a thin crack running along its centre. She leaned closer, trying to see if that crack was a fault or deliberate. It seemed such a strange perch for a beautiful goddess.

'Ah, Miss Chase. Clio. I see you have discovered the whereabouts of my treasure,' a voice said quietly.

Clio ducked away from Artemis, spinning around to find the Duke himself standing halfway along the gallery. Watching her intently.

Even in the dim light, his eyes gleamed like the snakes in her headdress. He smiled at her gently, deceptively, shrugging the leopard pelt of his Dionysus costume back from his shoulders. He moved closer, light and silent, as if he was a leopard himself.

'She is beautiful, is she not?' he said, still so quiet. 'I knew you would be drawn to her, as I was. She is quite—irresistible, in her mystery and solitude.'

Clio edged back against the goddess. She had indeed found Artemis irresistible. So much so that she had let her guard down, and that was not like her. As the Duke came closer, she reached behind her, her fingers just touching Artemis's cold sandal. She slid her touch down, finding that crack in the wooden base. She curled her hand around it, as if Artemis could protect her from Averton, from the dark confusion she always felt when he was near.

Just as it was now. He drew ever closer, slow but inescapable, like a leopard in the jungle. He watched her carefully, as if he expected her to bolt like a frightened gazelle. As if he could see all the secrets of her heart.

Clio stiffened her shoulders, tightening her fingers around the base. Suddenly, that silence she had craved in the crowded ballroom seemed oppressive. All the jumbled treasures of the room loomed higher, narrowing on just Artemis and her white glow.

It was like this whenever they met, she and Averton. He impeded her work as the Lily Thief, her mission. Yet they were bound together by invisible, unbreakable cords. They could not stay away from each other.

She would not give him the satisfaction of running now. Not yet.

He finally reached her side, and Clio held her breath. He touched the hem of Artemis's tunic, his jewelled fingers just inches from Clio's green silk sleeve. She could feel the warmth of his skin, the bright light of his gaze on her.

That tension between them grew, stretched taut until Clio thought she would scream with it.

'I cannot let you take her, Clio,' he said. So gentle. So implacable.

Clio tried to laugh. 'Oh? Do you think I could just tuck her under my skirt and spirit her out of here? Past all your guards?'

His gaze flickered almost imperceptibly over her green silk skirts. 'I would not be surprised at anything you did.'

'I *would* like to give her a finer home than this,' Clio said. 'But I am not such a fool as to try such a thing.'

'Not tonight, anyway.'

'As you say.'

His touch slid from Artemis's stone tunic to Clio's draped sleeve. Their skin did not even brush, but Clio felt the spark of his caress none the less. She swayed towards him as if spellbound. The crowded ball, the vast city outside—it all vanished. There was only him. Them, together.

And that scared her as nothing else ever had.

'I know what you're up to, Clio Chase,' he murmured, deep and seductive as a lover. 'And I cannot let you continue. For your own sake.'

Clio reared back from his sorcerer's caress, the lure of his voice. 'My sake? Oh, no, your Grace. Everything you do is surely for yourself alone.'

His hand tightened on her arm, not letting her go. 'There are things you do not know.'

'About you?'

'Me—and what is happening here. With the Alabaster Goddess.'

'I fear I know more about you than I wish to!' Clio cried. 'About your greed, your—'

'Clio!' He gave her a little shake, pulling her closer to him. So close there was not even a whisper between them.

He played the indolent, careless duke so well, but Clio could feel the iron strength of him next to her. The shift of his muscles. She wanted closer, ever closer.

And *that* frightened her even more.

'Why do you never listen to me?' he growled, his eyes like emerald embers burning into her.

'Because you never talk to me,' she whispered. 'Not really.'

'How can I talk to someone who so mistrusts me?' His touch convulsed on her arms, crushing the silk. 'Oh, Clio. What are you doing to me?'

His lips touched hers, a kiss that was utterly irresistible, like a summer thunderstorm. She tasted her own anger, her own frustration in that kiss, the desperate need of an impossible attraction.

Suddenly, the kiss, the nearness of him, her own heightened emotions—it was all too much. Something snapped inside her, and she had to escape. She pushed the Alabaster Goddess towards him, intending only to put a barrier between them. To remind them who, what, they really were.

Instead, Artemis's marble elbow connected sharply with his head. Both he and the statue crashed to the floor in a tangle of marble, leopard skin and drops of blood.

Clio gasped to see the red gash on his brow, his closed eyes. 'Edward!' she cried, dropping to her knees beside him.

She reached for his wrist, feeling the pulse beating there with a surge of absurd relief. She had not killed him.

Not yet.

'Stay here,' she whispered. 'I must fetch help!'

With that, she dashed away, past all the antiquities, the shadows, not sure what she ran toward—or away from.

She did not even notice the scrap of green silk caught in his hand…

Chapter One

Enna Province, Sicily—six months later

"'Thou grave, my bridal chamber! Dwelling-place hollowed in earth, the everlasting prison whither I bend my steps, to join the band of kindred, whose more numerous host already Persephone hath counted with the dead…'"

Clio Chase turned her spyglass toward the ruined amphitheatre, where her sister Thalia rehearsed the lines of *Antigone*. The crumbling stage was far from Clio's perch atop a rocky hill, yet she could glimpse Thalia's golden hair glinting in the morning sunlight, could hear the despairing words of Sophocles' princess as she was led to her death.

That eternal struggle of life and death, beauty and fate, seemed to belong to this bright day, this land. Ancient Sicily, where so many conquerors had overrun the rocky hills and dusty plains, yet none had ever fully possessed it. It belonged to old gods, far older than even the Greeks and Romans could have imagined. A wild place, slave to no master.

Clio turned her glass, purchased from their ship's captain on the voyage here from Naples, past her sister to the landscape beyond. No London stage director could have imagined such a glorious backdrop! Beyond the steps and stage of the amphitheatre were only mountains, a vast swathe of blue sky. The hills rolled on like a hazy sea, green and brown and purple, until they reached the flat, snow-dusted peak of Etna, cloaked in clouds.

Off in the other direction, just barely seen, were the calm, silvery waters of Lake Pergusa, where Hades had snatched Persephone away to his underworld kingdom.

Between were olive groves, orchards of lemons, limes and oranges, stands of wild fennel, the large prickly pears brought in by the Saracens. Carpets of flowers, yellow, white and dark purple, spread like bright blankets over the meadows, announcing that spring had truly arrived.

"'Enna—where Nature decks herself in all her varied hues, where the ground is beauteous, carpeted with flowers of many tints,'" Clio murmured, an Ovid quote she now truly understood. Enna had once been considered the heart of Sicily, the crossroads of the Trinacria, the three provinces, a sacred spot. The home of Demeter and her daughter.

And now it had been invaded by the Chase family, or part of the family anyway. Clio had come here with her father and two of her sisters, Thalia and Terpsichore, after they had seen their eldest sister Calliope off on her honeymoon. Sir Walter Chase had long heard of the archeological wonders to be found in Enna, just waiting to be discovered by a dedicated scholar like himself. His friend Lady Rushworth had followed, having equally heard of the excellent English society to be found in the town of Santa Lucia, high in the dramatic hills. Society of a most intellectual and stimulating sort, escapees from the endless shallow parties in Naples.

Clio lowered her glass, her eyes narrowed as she thought

of Santa Lucia. It was certainly a pretty enough town, with its baroque cathedral and old palazzos, with the ruined medieval castle guarding its town walls. But so often when she was there, except for their Sicilian servants and the shop-keepers of the town, it felt as if she had never left England at all. Receiving callers at their rented house, going to card parties at Lady Rushworth's or dances at Viscountess Riverton's and the Elliotts'—it was all so London-like.

And she did not want to think about England. About what had happened there, what she had left behind.

Clio drew her knees up to her chest, hugging them close, her old brown muslin work dress like a protective tent around her. The warm breeze, scented with scrubby pine trees and fading almond blossoms, ruffled the auburn hair pinned loosely atop her head. She heard the echo of Thalia's voice as she went down to her lingering death, felt the hot sun against her skin.

This was where she belonged, in this wild, ancient spot, alone. Not really in Santa Lucia, definitely not in London. Not the Duke of Averton's castle, so full of its dark, twisting corridors, where secrets and dangers lurked in every corner. Just like the unhappy shades of Hades' kingdom…

Averton. Clio hugged her legs tighter, pressing her forehead to her knees. Could there ever be one day when she did not think of that blasted man? Did not remember what it felt like when he touched her? When he looked at her with those golden-green eyes and whispered her name. *Clio…*

'He is miles away,' she muttered. 'Eons! You will probably never see him again.'

Yet even as she tried to reassure herself, she knew, deep down inside, that was not true. He might be far away, hidden in his castle, the famously reclusive yet always much sought-after Duke of 'Avarice', but he was never entirely apart from her. The way he looked at her, as if she was yet another Greek vase or marble statue he wanted, needed, to possess.

Well, he still had the Alabaster Goddess, that glorious figure of Artemis stolen from Delos, locked away in his castle. He would never do the same to *her*! Not even if she had to hide here in the wilds of Sicily for the rest of her days. The Duke was gone, he was past. Just like the Lily Thief.

For yes, once even she, Clio, had held her secrets. Had been the notorious Lily Thief for a few glorious months.

Clio unfolded her legs and stood up, stretching her limbs in the sunlight. How lovely it was to be alone, to be herself with no one to watch her, judge her. To just be Clio, not one of the 'Chase Muses'. Now that Calliope was wed, everyone looked to her to be next. To marry as well as her sister had— an earl!—and to start her own family, her own conventional life as chatelaine of a household, as a society hostess; to take her place in her family's scholarly, aristocratic world.

But Calliope loved her new husband, was happy in the life she had chosen. Clio had certainly never found anyone she could esteem as Cal did her earl. Clio did not belong in such a life. Maybe she didn't belong anywhere at all. Except here.

She lifted her spyglass again, training it on the valley below her rocky perch, the stretch of land between her and Thalia's theatre. It was really this valley that had brought them to Enna in the first place, an ancient Graeco-Roman site buried in a twelfth-century mudslide and only recently uncovered. Much of the site was still hidden beneath hazelnut orchards, but her father and his friends were working hard at exploring what was revealed: the theatre; part of the *agora*, or market place; some crumbling walls delineating shops and small houses; a great villa with almost intact mosaic floors in the atrium, which was Sir Walter's pet project; and a small, roofless temple, probably devoted to Demeter, with its *bothros*, or well-altar, still ready to accept sacrifices even if the grand silver altar set was long gone.

She could see them through the oval of her glass, her father sweeping off more of the mosaic floor as her fourteen-year-old sister Terpsichore—Cory—sketched the tile scenes of tritons and mermaids. Lady Rushworth, shielded by a giant straw hat, examined some newly found pottery fragments, sorting them into baskets. Other friends and servants scurried around like busy ants. They would not miss her when she crept away. They never did.

Clio snapped the glass shut and tucked it inside her knapsack. Slipping the strap over her shoulder, she turned and made her way up the steep stairs cut into the stony hillside.

When she reached a fork in the steps, with one way leading to Santa Lucia, she glanced up, raising her hand to shield her spectacles from the glare of the sun. The crumbling crenellations of the medieval castle's tower stood starkly against the bright sky, eternally vigilant as it stared out over the valley. She was again reminded of the Duke, of his Yorkshire castle that matched his strangely archaic, handsome appearance, his long red-gold hair, his strong hands that gripped her own so tightly, holding her prisoner to that intense light in his beautiful green eyes.

Clio frowned at the memory, unconsciously flexing her wrists. He could so easily have been one of the crusaders who had built that tower, standing between the crenellations, surveying his conquered land while his banners whipped in the wind behind him. Secure in the knowledge that his money, his exalted title, his fine looks would always gain him anything he wanted. The world was his.

But not her. Never her.

Clio turned away from the castle, from the safety of Santa Lucia and its old walls, and hurried up a second, even steeper set of stairs. They wound up and around the hill, and she soon left the noise and bustle of the valley behind. Even the sun grew dimmer here, the shadows longer, deeper, colder.

On the other side of the hill, the stairs suddenly switched back, taking her downwards again. Unlike the sunny valley where her family worked, this place still slumbered. It was a meadow, covered with a blanket of white clover, seemingly undisturbed except for the hum of bees, the distant tinkle of goats' bells in the hills.

She knew people must come here. There was rich fodder for those herds of goats, and wild fennel and oregano for the cooking pots. But she never saw anyone at all. The cook at their hired house, Rosa, had told her this was a sacred spot, a spot where once there had been an altar to Demeter. A crude sheaf of wheat carved into the trunk of a towering hawthorn tree, where offerings of flowers and fruit were often left at its base, seemed to confirm that. As did mysterious holes she found in the ground when she had first arrived, which seemed to indicate previous, illegal excavations.

Demeter never disturbed Clio when she was there. Nor did Persephone and her dark husband. They seemed to know Clio was one of them, that she did their work to bring them back to life.

She passed the tree, giving it a respectful nod. There were fresh lemons piled in a basket in its shade. There was a wide road nearby, a way for horses to get to the village, but she ignored it. Along another path, barely marked in the clover, she hurried her steps until she found what she sought. Her own perfect place.

While her father worked on the villa, once the dwelling place of rich men, and Thalia revived *Antigone* in the theatre, Clio looked for less exalted remains. Her explorations had brought her here, to this quiet little meadow, where she had found her farmhouse.

She paused at the edge of the site, as she always did when she arrived, drinking in the peaceful, quiet vision. It was not the ancient holiday house of a wealthy family, as the villa was. The people here had been prosperous, but they also worked for their coin. Lived off the fruit of their labour and their land. Once, this clover-covered valley had been fields of wheat and barley, with fruit orchards and groves of olives.

Until it all came to an end, one violent day in the second century BC. Now there were just some waist-high walls of small, uneven pieces of tan-coloured limestone, weather-beaten and crumbling, to mark where their house once stood. But Clio intended to find more. Much more.

She hurried to the walls, pulling out her stash of tools wrapped in oilcloth and tucked into a sheltered niche. The wooden handle of the small spade fit perfectly into her hand, as a soldier's sword hilt would in battle. Maybe she did *not* belong in London, not really, but she did belong here. When she worked, she forgot the world outside. She even forgot Averton—for a time.

All the passion she had once poured into the Lily Thief was now given to her farmhouse. To finding the voices of the people who once lived here.

She went to work.

Chapter Two

'Is it quite satisfactory, your Grace?' the agent asked, his voice quivering slightly. 'Truly, it is the finest palazzo to be had in all of Santa Lucia. The views are most exquisite, and it is quite near the cathedral and the village square. And there is a hunting cottage, too, in the hills, if you require it. The baroness is usually very reluctant to leave her furnishings for the tenants, but for you, of course, she is only *too* happy…'

Only too happy to have an English ducal arse touch her couches? Edward Radcliffe, the Duke of Averton, examined the flaking, worn gilt of the apricot velvet chairs with some amusement. They looked as if the slightest touch would reduce them to a pile of splinters and shredded upholstery. The baroque flourishes of the place, plaster cherubs peering down from the ceilings and faded apricot-coloured silk wallpaper, seemed no better. Chipped and crumbling away, like an abandoned wedding cake.

It could certainly use a thorough cleaning, as well, for the scuffed marble floor was covered with a fine layer of silvery dust. Cobwebs spun from the elaborate frames of old portraits, where the baroness's exalted Sicilian forebears gazed down at him in disapproval.

Well, they were not the only ones who *disapproved*, to be sure. Old Italian barons and their long-nosed wives had nothing on one Englishwoman's contempt-filled emerald eyes.

Edward turned away from them, away from that cool green gaze that haunted him everywhere he went. He leaned his palms on a chipped marble windowsill, peering down at the scene below. The baroness's palazzo perched at the edge of the hilltop where the village of Santa Lucia gazed out over the valley. The tall, narrow windows, curtained in dusty gold satin and tarnished tassels, stared right at Etna in the distance, to Lake Pergusa and eventually even to the sea.

The palazzo's small garden, wild and overgrown, seemed to drop off into sheer space. As if an eagle could launch itself into space and go wheeling out over the amphitheatre and into the mist beyond, right from this garden.

The front of the palazzo, on the other hand, sported a much more respectable-looking courtyard, paved and neatly planted with myrtle trees, with tall limestone walls and wrought-iron gates that opened to the narrow street beyond. Its cobblestone length was silent, and seemed rather little travelled, but it did lead right to the village square with its shops and cathedral, its view of the whole village and everyone in it.

Perfect.

'Tell me,' Edward said, not turning his gaze from the theatre, 'where is the house the Chase family rents?'

'The Chases?' the agent said, sounding a bit confused. His mind was obviously slow to turn from views and furnishings to the other inhabitants of Santa Lucia. 'Ah, yes, the family with the daughters! Their home is on the other side of the square, just beyond the cathedral. They are often seen on walks in the evenings.'

So, not far from here. Edward closed his eyes, and it was as if he felt her very presence beside him. The wilful Muse.

'I will take the palazzo,' he said, opening his eyes again to the dazzle of the Sicilian sunlight. 'It is perfect.'

By the next morning, Edward's battalions of servants had removed the baroness's dour-painted ancestors and the worst of the gilt furniture and replaced them with choice selections of the Averton antiquities collection. Graceful red-figure amphorae rested on stands under the shocked stares of the plaster angels. A few marble statues took up places in the newly dusted corners, touches of austere elegance amid all the wedding-cake flourishes.

Edward's own chamber overlooked the front courtyard and the street beyond. The largest bedroom, which was obviously the baroness's own to judge from the bedhangings draped from a huge family coat-of-arms, looked upon the grand view of garden and hills. But he preferred this smaller space, where he could watch the town and passers-by.

He examined the arrangements as the servants deposited the last of his trunks and crates. Gilded mouldings carved in the shape of roses, wheat sheaves and arrows garlanded the windows and doors, matching the white-and-gold bed and armoire. The blue-and-red carpet was faded and threadbare, as were the coverlets and bedhangings of blue watered silk. It all lacked the medieval grandeur of his Yorkshire castle, the Gothicism of Acropolis House in London. But the mattress was aired, the room spacious enough—and he could see almost the entire town from the window.

Including the edge of the Chase house.

'It will all do very well,' he murmured, watching closely as the footmen carried in the last of the antiquities so carefully shipped from London. A statue of Artemis with her bow raised. The famous 'Alabaster Goddess'. They placed her next to the fireplace, where she looked as if she was about to shoot down a row of simpering porcelain shepherds and shepherdesses on the mantel. Along her base, barely visible in the veined marble, was a scratch mark from a thief's lever.

Edward traced it lightly with his fingertip, the tiny groove that was the only reminder of that night in the gallery of his London house. Artemis's cool fierceness always reminded him of Clio. The goddess of the moon, of the hunt—she never let any mortal man stand in the way of what she wanted, what she believed to be right. She never shied away from any danger.

But Artemis was immortal, the favourite child of all-powerful Zeus, who would never let harm come to her. Clio, despite her daring, was all too human. One day her gallant recklessness would surely catch up with her, and she would tumble heedlessly into the danger. Foolish girl.

Edward turned away from Artemis and her bow, and found himself facing a full-length mirror. What a strange vision he was, framed in the gilt flourishes and ribbons of that rented glass! The shoulder-length fall of reddish-blond hair his valet so often hinted he should cut, for the sake of fashion, was tied back. As stark as his black wool coat and white cravat, skewered with a stickpin carved with a cameo head of Medusa. As stark as the sharp cheekbones and square jaw that was the legacy of all the Radcliffes, handed down from some distant Viking ancestor.

Yes, he *looked* like a true Radcliffe, the heir to the old dukedom, but he was flawed. His nose, thin and straight as a knife blade in the faces of his late father and older brother, was marred by a badly healed break across the bridge. The legacy of a boyish, long-ago brawl with the man who was now Clio's brother-in-law.

And, a gift from the Muse herself, a jagged scar on his forehead. Healed to a white line now, it was the exact shape of Artemis's stone elbow.

Edward laid his fingertips lightly on the mark, feeling its slight roughness. Feeling again the fire of her kiss.

Yet he did not let her go then. He could not. It was as if there was a devil inside him, a dark demon that dwelled there, hidden, from the time he was a boy. A part of him that desired Clio Chase no matter what she did—now matter what *he* did. But he could not let her stand in the way of his work in Santa Lucia.

Edward reached out and tilted the swinging mirror between its hinges until it faced the faded blue wallpaper, and he was hidden from himself. He took off his coat and tossed it over the foot of the bed, rolling up his shirtsleeves to reveal the glint of his ruby-and-emerald rings. His forearms were well muscled and sun-bronzed, the arms of a man who had been working on archeological sites under the southern sun for many of his years. The frilled sleeves hid those signs of un-ducal labour, just as the rings hid the white calluses at the base of his fingers.

It would never do for anyone to see what he was really up to. What the famously reclusive, famously louche 'Duke of Avarice' was truly like.

He unlocked the small, iron-bound box on the dressing table. Stacked in there were letters and papers, bags of coins, but beneath was a false bottom, which had stayed neatly in place ever since the box had left England. Edward levered it upwards and drew out two objects. A tiny silver bowl, Grecian to judge by its decorations, second century BC perhaps. It was exquisite, hammered with a pattern of acorns and beechnuts, etched with rough Greek letters spelling out 'This belongs to the gods'. A warning, and a promise.

Beside it was a scrap of green-and-gold silk, torn along a seam, edged with sparkling green glass beads.

He laid them both carefully aside, the bowl and the silk. They were the symbols of all that brought him to this place. All that brought him again to Clio's side—even as he fought against that desire.

But fate, it seemed, always had other plans when it came to him and Clio Chase.

Chapter Three

'Ah, another invitation from Lady Riverton!' Clio's father announced over the breakfast table. He waved the embossed card in the air before depositing it with the rest of the post.

'Again?' Clio said, only half-listening as she buttered her toast. Her head was still full of the farmhouse, of her plans for the day. It looked as if it might rain, as it so often did here in the mornings. The sky outside the windows was ominously grey, and she had to cover up yesterday's work before the house's cellar filled up with water. 'We were just at her palazzo last week. Weren't we?'

'But this is different,' Sir Walter said. 'An evening of amateur theatricals, it says. And her refreshments are usually quite good, you know. Those lobster tarts last time were lovely…'

Clio laughed. 'Father, I vow you begin to think only of your stomach! But we can attend, if you like.'

'Perhaps she would let me participate in the theatricals,' Thalia said, pouring herself more chocolate. 'I would like to try out some of my *Antigone* lines on an audience. I am not sure my delivery is quite correct. It all sounds very well in the amphitheatre, but then anything would be terribly dramatic there! I do want it to be right.'

'Have you yet found anyone for the role of Haemon?' Clio asked.

Thalia shook her head. 'All the Sicilians speak so little English, and all the Englishmen lack passion! I don't know what to do. Perform it all in Greek? Everyone seems to speak it around here.'

'Lady Riverton will be able to help, I'm sure, Thalia dear,' Sir Walter said. 'She does appear to know absolutely everyone.'

'And she's a terrible busybody,' Thalia answered. 'I don't want her taking over my play! But I will certainly call on her to ask about the theatricals. Will you come with me, Clio?'

Clio glanced again out the window, where the sky seemed even darker. She hurriedly gulped the last of her tea and said, 'If you go this afternoon, I can come with you. But I must run an errand this morning. If you will excuse me, Father?'

Sir Walter nodded distractedly as he read another invitation. He was quite accustomed to Clio dashing away at all hours now, which was how she liked it. Even the time she had gone off with the Darbys to see the temple at Agrigento with only a day's notice had not caused him to bat an eye.

As Clio hurried from the breakfast room, she heard her sister Cory say plaintively, 'May I go to Lady Riverton's, too? Please? I have been to no parties at all since we came here, and I am nearly fifteen.'

'That is because until October you are still only *fourteen*,' Thalia answered. 'You are not out yet, and you should feel lucky for that. You have no social obligations at all, and can do what you please!'

Clio paused at the front door to change to her sturdy boots.

If she ran, surely she could stay ahead of the rain and return in plenty of time to call on Lady Riverton. She dashed out the door and down the narrow lane that skirted past the cathedral and into the main square of Santa Lucia.

The village was just stirring to life for the day, fruit, vegetable and fish sellers setting up their booths, the bakery and patisserie opening their doors in a flood of sweet-sugar smells. Maids were fetching water from the fountain, gossiping and laughing. The great carved doors of the cathedral were still closed for morning mass, but soon they would open, letting out the prosperous matrons and pretty maidens of the town. The darkly dangerous-looking men were lounging in the shadows.

The day was still cool, but later the warm sun would bring out the smells of all this life, the salty fish and pungent herbs, the sweet cakes, the earthiness of the horses and dogs. The cathedral bells would ring out, crowds would flood forth to do their marketing, and the English tourists would dash away to view the ancient temples, and the day of Santa Lucia would begin in earnest. The wider politics of the world, King Ferdinand, the ruler of the Kingdom of Two Sicilies, far away in Naples with his young Sicilian bride, the collapse of the Sicilian feudal system after the withdrawal of the English forces—none of it mattered here. Not yet, not now. There was shopping and cooking to be done.

Marie, the baker's wife, leaned from the window to hand her a fresh roll as she dashed by. 'It will rain, *signorina*! You should stay inside this morning.'

Clio dashed past Lady Riverton's grand palazzo. The windows were still shuttered, but when they were opened Lady Riverton could spy on all that happened in Santa Lucia— which was surely just as the youngish widow wanted it.

Clio never really minded attending gatherings there. They were certainly dull enough, to be sure, especially when she had studies of her own to attend to and was forced instead to make polite conversation or listen to some young, talentless miss play at the pianoforte. But most of Lady Riverton's guests were also interested in antiquities, and the talk was usually lively. And, as her father had said, the food was quite good. If there was something rather *odd* about Lady Riverton, well, that was no different from dozens of other bored society matrons.

At the edge of town, also with a fine view of things and perched dramatically on the hillside, was the palazzo of the Baroness Picini. It had stood empty since the Chases had arrived at Santa Lucia, the baroness having taken herself off to Naples in the court of the new queen. Today, though, the vast old place was swarming with activity, servants hurrying in and out bearing trunks and crates and furniture. The court-yard gates stood wide open.

More guests for Lady Riverton, then, Clio thought. Despite her curiosity about who might dare to live in the mouldy old pile, she still had work to do, and turned down the steep pathway to the valley.

She reached the farmhouse site just as the first raindrops started to fall. The sunken cellar area where she had begun excavating, digging out clay amphorae and jars once used for oil and wine, smelled of the sweet, earthy rain, the sulphur of lightning and the imagined remnants of the old wine. Clio shook out a tarpaulin, dragging it up and over the cellar opening and tying it down to the limestone walls. She had done it several times before, so it was quick work.

It wasn't much, but at least it would keep the rain from filling up her excavation trenches before she had finished. So far she had found only the storage jars, a terracotta altar set and one battered silver goblet, but she hoped to discover coins, jewelled goblets and crockery, perhaps even some jewellery. Something to show her father and his friends, so they would not think she had wasted her time on an insignificant site!

She secured the tarpaulin as the rain began to fall in earnest, a soft, warm shower that pattered against the oiled canvas. Clio sat down on another square of canvas spread out on the packed dirt of the cellar, hugging her knees to her chest as she listened to the rain above her head.

It was a strangely soothing sound, cosy as she sat in her ancient house, imagining the blessing of the water falling on the crops in the fields, the flowering orchards. Surely the people who once lived here had done the same thing, thanking Demeter, goddess of the earth and all growing things, for her bounty, making offerings in hopes of a good harvest.

Clio had always loved envisioning the lives of the past. She could hardly get away from history, not with her family! There was her grandfather, who had written a famous treatise, *The Archeology of the Ancients*; her father, who had so richly inherited those scholarly sensibilities and had used them to co-found the Antiquities Society; her mother, the daughter of a French comte renowned for his collection of Hellenistic silver; her sisters, all the Muses. They had been fed on tales of the old gods, old battles and love affairs, glories that would never die, from the time they were in their cradles.

The classical world was as real to Clio as the everyday life of the London streets and squares—no, it was *more* real. More vital and true. She always took those stories far more to heart than even her sisters did, and it led her into trouble time and again—until it had all come to a terrible crescendo with the Lily Thief.

Clio closed her eyes tightly as the rain pounded louder above her, trying to block out the memory of Calliope's shocked eyes as she saw the truth—that Clio was the Lily Thief. *'How could you do this, Clio?'*

Clio never wanted to hurt her sister. She loved Cal so much, loved them all, her entire boisterous, noisy, eccentric family. But so often she felt alone, even when she stood in their midst. Even as the sound and passion broke all around her, just like the rain.

Things had changed since Cal had married and they had come to Sicily, though. Clio loved this island, loved its wind-swept whispers that seemed to speak only to her. She loved the roughness of the land and the people, the layers of history in the very earth itself. Just like this house, or what was left of it, where families had lived their daily lives, laughed together, made love, quarrelled and died, she felt herself slowly stirring back to warm, vivid life. She poured all her work, her secrets, into this place, and in return it gave her back herself.

Not that everything could be left behind, of course. At night, when she tumbled exhausted into bed, she had such dreams. Such vivid flashes of memory. The Duke of Averton, how his lips felt on hers, the cool brush of his breath on her skin, the heat and *life* of him, before she had driven him so violently away. The way he watched her, as if he could see into her very soul. See everything about her…

Thunder cracked overhead, loud as a cannon shot, and Clio reared back in surprise. She had almost forgotten where she was, lost in the haze of those memories. The dark gold-green of the duke's eyes, drawing her ever closer, so close she could almost drown in him.

She peered up to find her tarpaulin still securely bound, though bowed in the centre by the weight of the rain. Surely it would cease soon; these morning showers always passed, the thirsty land soaking up every drop until there was no sign of rain at all. Even now she could hear the thunder retreating back along the valley.

Clio took out her small spade again and went to work on her newest excavation, near the remains of the old stone staircase that once led to the upper floors of the house. She would probably have more luck if she worked faster, Clio thought as she carefully measured out a trench in the pockmarked earth. Tear up the floor and be done with it, as anyone else would. As those deceptively lazy men in Santa Lucia would. But then she couldn't come here alone, to her quiet sanctuary. Couldn't lose herself in work and dreams.

She had barely started digging when she noticed something odd, something that hadn't been there before. An indentation in the dirt, maybe. An old trench someone else had once dug. She pushed her spectacles atop her head, tangling them in her hair, and leaned in to peer closer...

Just then she heard a rumbling noise overhead, like the thunder except it persisted, growing ever louder. She froze, sitting back on her heels, tense, as she realised what it was.

Hoofbeats.

Her skin turned suddenly cold, the back of her neck prickling. The blood quickened in her veins, as it had not since she had left the Lily Thief behind for good. No one ever came out here; the old farm site was too isolated, too insignificant for tourists. She had been warned about bandits, of course, and thieves—Sicily could be a wild, dangerous place. But she had never seen any.

Was that about to change?

Clio carefully laid down the spade, and reached under her skirt for the sheath strapped to her leg just above the boot. In one smooth, silent movement, she drew out her dagger.

It was no dainty, ornamental little antique, but a well-honed, sturdy knife, forged to razor sharpness in the Santa Lucia smithy. Their Sicilian cook and her husband had given it to her when she kept insisting on wandering off by herself. At first they were utterly scandalised. Upper-class Sicilian girls were even *more* strictly chaperoned and protected than English girls! But when she had persisted, they had given her the dagger, certain that any lady as strangely independent as Clio would know how to use it.

Their kind confidence was not misplaced. Clio had once been the most famous thief in London. She could use a dagger if she had to. But she hoped she would not.

Surely the hoofbeats, which came ever closer, were only those of a traveller who would quickly pass by on the way to more elaborate sites. Still, she had to be careful. Clio silently crept up a few of the crumbling stone steps, poised on her toes, until she could ease back the corner of the tarpaulin and peer out on to the world.

The rain had finally ceased, leaving behind a damp, rich scent, a land that sparkled with waterdrops on flowers and treetops. The sky was still grey, but a few chalky sunbeams broke through. The horse was coming from behind the farmhouse, along the old, overgrown roadway.

Balancing the dagger hilt in one hand, Clio folded back the tarpaulin a bit more, until she could see past the canvas edge. 'Blast it all,' she muttered, wondering if she had fallen asleep on the dirt floor and was dreaming—or having a nightmare.

A glossy black horse, much like the ones that had probably drawn Hades' chariot as he had born down on hapless Persephone, galloped along the road where it skirted around the farm site. And riding it was the very man she believed, or hoped, to be hundreds of miles away. *Averton*. It could be no other. His bright, Viking hair was loose in the breeze, even longer than when she had last seen him in Yorkshire, falling to his shoulders. His black riding clothes and high leather boots stood in stark contrast to its glow, making him seem one with the horse.

A marauding centaur, then, as well as Hades. A dangerously handsome lord who took what he wanted, regardless of the consequences.

He drew up the horse just beyond the rim of the foundation, so near she could see the sheen of his bronzed skin, shining with rain and sweat. His face, all hard, sharp angles, was expressionless as he gazed around the site. She could feel the fire of his eyes, even across the distance.

White-hot anger burned away her icy poise, her calm wariness. How *dare* he come here, after all that had happened in England! How dare he invade her farmhouse, her one special place? All her old feelings—her fright, her fury, her fascination—boiled over, and she could be silent no longer.

She threw back the tarpaulin, rushing up the last of the old steps with her blade in hand, as if charging into battle.

'What are *you* doing here?' she demanded. 'You, Averton, are on private property, and I will thank you to depart immediately!'

He gazed down at her. His expression did not change—it so seldom did, remaining in its cool lines of ducal contempt even when he confronted thieves in his house. Only a very few times had she seen it alter, that veil of handsome privilege falling away to reveal seething passions and needs that were fearsome to behold.

But his eyes widened a bit as he saw her, the green as bright as sea glass, and she noticed the jagged white scar on his forehead.

'Oh, so you are suddenly the protector of private property, are you now, Clio Chase?' he said mockingly. 'That makes a fascinating change.'

'What do you want?' Clio said. She planted her booted feet solidly in the dirt, tightening her fingers on the dagger hilt even as she longed to flee back to her safe, hidden cellar. Back to an hour ago, when she thought him so far away.

'I want to talk to you,' he said, in a soft, steady voice. A coaxing voice. 'That is all, I swear.'

'So talk.'

His horse pawed at the ground, restless at standing still, and Averton's black-gloved hands tightened on the reins. 'If I dismount, will I be in danger of being disembowelled by that rather efficient-looking blade in your hand?'

Clio studied him carefully, eye to eye for one long, tense moment. She had seldom met anyone in her life quite as determined as she was herself. That stubbornness meant she usually got her own way, even in a big family. But she knew, just by looking at him now, just by remembering their past encounters, that here was someone of determination to match her own. He wouldn't go away easily, and if she tried to run he would just mow her down with his fearsome steed.

She gave a brusque nod. 'Very well. But stay over there. Don't come near my house.'

His brow arched sardonically. '*Your* house, is it?' But he followed her instructions, swinging down from his horse yet staying several feet away, holding loosely to the reins as his horse began to crop at the clover. 'Is this far enough?'

Clio nodded again. 'You said you wanted to talk, Averton.

It must be something important indeed to bring you all this way.'

'It is,' he answered. Yet then he fell silent, just watching her as if he had never seen her before in his life. As if she were some strange creature, a unicorn or phoenix, maybe, that he could not understand.

Clio shifted on her feet. 'Did someone snatch away your precious Alabaster Goddess? It was not me, I vow. I have been in Sicily for weeks. Or perhaps it was—'

'Clio,' he said, in a voice that was quiet, soft, but full of steely command. 'I have come here because you are in danger.'

Chapter Four

⚜

Clio could scarcely understand what she was hearing. *Could this just be a dream after all?* Every moment she had ever spent with Averton had been bizarre, to be sure, but this…

'Did you just say I am in danger?' she asked, studying his face for signs of—what? Joking? Subterfuge? It was not the Duke's way to make jests, nor hers.

There was no hint of humour or deception in his face, though. No change in those Viking-warrior features at all, except for a tiny tic in the muscle along his jaw as he stared at her.

Clio stared back, hardly daring to move, to breathe. The thunderstorm had left the air heavy and thick, the breeze practically crackling around her. Around *them*. It was as if snapping tendrils snaked out from the grey sky, wrapping ever tighter around her, binding her closer and closer to him.

It was like a myth, a tale of jealous gods and enchanted spells that bound mortals to them against their every sensible inclination. Every shred of sense.

Clio shook her head, trying to clear it of such dark fancies. It was just this place making her feel so, that web of myth and fantasy that had been woven around her ever since she was a child. And being faced with Averton, of all people, when she least expected him! Was least prepared for him, and the effect he always had on her.

As if she ever *could* be prepared for him. Every single time she saw him, it was like a lightning storm all over again. Beautiful, treacherous and so completely disorienting.

She took a step back. 'I know of no dangers here except you. You needn't have gone to all this trouble to warn me of *that*.'

His brow creased, as if in a flash of pain, yet that spasm was gone in an instant, banished under a mocking smile. 'Did I not prove to you in Yorkshire that you are never in danger from me? I sent you and your friend—Marco, was it?—on your merry way, with scarcely a scolding word. Even though you were in the midst of stealing from me. I am the last person you need fear, Clio.'

She swallowed hard, remembering another night, that gallery at Acropolis House. 'Indeed?'

'Indeed. I want to be your friend, if you will let me.'

'My friend, is it?' she said, nearly choking on a humourless laugh. 'So, that is why you are here? To offer friendship, along with cryptic warnings of danger? I think it more likely you are here to see what my father has found in his Greek villa. To see what you can snatch to add to your vaunted collections, hidden away in the darkness so no one else can ever see them.'

'Clio!' he growled, his icy calm cracking at last. He dropped the reins, his hands curling into fists.

And Clio felt a stirring of some strange satisfaction.

'You are the most obstinate woman I have ever met,' he muttered. 'Why can you not just listen to me for once in your life?'

'Just listen to you? Quietly do what you want, just as everyone does with the exalted duke? Well, I'm sorry, your Grace, but I am too busy to stand here arguing with you any longer.' She strode past him, not sure where she was going, only knowing that she had to get away. Had to escape from those crackling bonds before she exploded!

She gave Averton a wide berth, yet not quite wide enough. Before she had even seen him move, he had caught her by the wrists, pulling her close to him. Startled, she dropped her dagger. It landed mere inches from his booted foot, yet he did not glance at it at all. He only watched her.

As she stared up into his face, into the glow of his eyes, those bonds grew tighter and tighter. She could not breathe, could not move at all. She flexed her wrists in his grasp, the fingers of her right hand splayed out until she touched the very edge of his sleeve. The hot, smooth skin of his wrist. She felt the thrum of his pulse there, the tumbling rush of his life's blood, and his heartbeat seemed to meld with her own.

She heard the quick rush of his breath in her ear, smelled the clean, spicy scent of his skin. He was all around her, a part of her she could not escape, for truly he was not something outside, not a separate being she could run from, deny. He was inside her, part of her very breath and blood.

She arched in his grasp, her head thrown back like Persephone's as she tried to escape, tried to leap from the speeding chariot to safety. Escape, even as she longed to stay.

'Then tell me what it is you want here,' she whispered. 'Why you came here to find me.'

'Will you listen, then?' he said hoarsely. 'For once?'

'I...' she answered. 'It depends on what you say, I suppose.'

He gave a bark of laughter, his clasp loosening on her

wrists. 'Of course. Always conditions. Always wanting things your own way.'

'Muses are as spoiled as dukes when it comes to that,' she said. She raised her hand, still caught in that dream where she was not herself. She lightly touched the white scar with her fingertips, feeling the uneven ridge of it under her touch.

He tensed, as taut as a bowstring, but he did not move away. Perhaps he was as enchanted as she was. She trailed her touch over his temple, the pulse that thrummed there; over his sharp cheekbone, the crooked nose Cam de Vere had once broken in some unspecified brawl. A loose strand of his hair, bright silk, brushed against her hand, clinging. She traced its wave until she found the curve of his lips.

Her fingers hovered over them as they parted, and she felt his very life's breath. How close, how very close...

'Clio,' he groaned. His arms came around her waist, dragging her against him until there was not even a whisper between them. She was a tall woman, nearly as tall as he, but she felt fragile as his hot strength wrapped around her and she was surrounded by only him. She looped her arms about his neck, making him her captive just as she was his.

Their lips met, and there was nothing tentative or shy about the caress. It was quick, hot, desperate. A fervent need to be as one, to fall down into the dark myth and be lost for ever. That was what it was like when she kissed him—like being lost in the corridors of the underworld among all the shades, the misty illusions. She was a fool, an utter fool, to give in again. To reach for something that could only do her ill in the end.

But neither could she turn away, any more than she could tear her own soul out.

She dug her fingers into the fall of his hair, holding him

to her as she felt the smooth leather of his gloved caress slide across her shoulders, skimming along her bare skin until she shivered. She leaned deeper into him, losing herself, losing everything…

'Clio!' he said, tearing his lips from hers. His hands tightened on her shoulders, pressing her back from him. 'Clio, what am I doing? I did not come here to…'

And the spell was broken, like one of those invisible cords that bound her to him. She stumbled away, still intoxicated with the smell and taste of him. With the bizarre alchemy that happened whenever they were close.

She glanced away from him, covering her mouth with her trembling hands. She had to get away from him, now! 'No, you came here to *warn* me. Well, Averton, consider me warned.'

She snatched up her dagger from the dirt, in the process losing the spectacles she had pushed atop her head while she was digging. She scarcely noticed, though. She was too busy running away, dashing for the footpath along the hills that she knew his horse could not follow.

'Fool, fool,' she muttered, scrubbing at her aching eyes with the back of her hand. 'Bloody *fool*! How dare you?'

Yet she did not know if she talked to him—or herself.

'Damn it all!' Edward cursed, kicking violently at the dirt. This was not what he had planned!

He meant to gently alert Clio to his presence in Sicily, to be polite and calm, and make her see he meant her no harm before he revealed his true purpose. Or part of it, anyway. He had not even known she would be here today. The rain would have kept away any other would-be antiquities hunter. He should have known that it would take more than a bit of thunder to keep Clio Chase away! But he had wanted to see the site, do a bit of reconnaissance work while no one else was about. Get to know his opponent.

Then there she was, suddenly appearing before him, fierce as any Fury, her dagger in hand. Her eyes, usually a serene spring-green, sparkled with shock and anger. '*You!*' she had cried, as if a demon had landed in front of her.

And all his careful, measured plans, his resolve to not get close to her, exploded and disappeared like a cloud of smoke. That raw, passionate *need* that drew him to her whenever he saw her, that force that drove him to touch her, be close to her, was there. He could not resist it, any more than he could resist breathing. He forced himself, by sheer steely will, to stay where he was—until she hurried past him, ignoring his warnings with her maddening wilfulness.

Edward pounded his fist against a tree trunk, cursing, oblivious to the slivers that drove themselves through his glove. Oblivious to everything but the way he still smelled her white lily perfume on his skin.

Why, *why*, had he kissed her? Why had she kissed him? He had understood it far better when she had knocked him senseless with the Alabaster Goddess. He deserved no less. But now he wanted her to be safe, to listen to his warnings and stay out of his way.

Well, that was not *all* he wanted. Their little scene here, as well as what had happened at Acropolis House, clearly demonstrated that. He wanted Clio in his bed, in his arms, all her passion his at last. Her long legs wrapped around his hips, her head thrown back in a tangle of auburn hair as she cried out his name.

But their kisses could change nothing.

Edward strode toward his horse. As he caught up the reins, he saw the glint of sunlight on Clio's spectacles. They lay in the dirt, apparently lost when she had stormed away. He picked them up carefully, holding them up to the light. The lenses were strong, but not hugely so; the ground glass magnified the limestone walls only a bit, showing up the old cracks and pits. So, she did need them for the close, painstaking work she did, but she was not blind without them. Perhaps they were a sort of armour, as well. Something to hide behind.

He tucked them carefully inside his coat, and swung up into the saddle. Well, surely she would need them back again. Very soon.

Chapter Five

Earth with its wide roads gaped, and then over the Nysian field the lord and All-receiver, the many-named son of Kronos, sprang out upon her with his immortal horses...

Clio groaned, and slammed the book shut, pushing it away from her. Perhaps that particular one of the *Homeric Hymns*, the tale of Hades and Persephone, was not the best choice of reading material this afternoon.

She rubbed her hand over her aching head. In truth, she doubted she could concentrate on anything at all, even so much as a fashion paper. Her thoughts kept turning, leaping, back to the farmhouse, to Averton and his appearance there. As sudden and shocking as if he had 'sprung out upon her with his immortal horses'.

She had crept back to try to find her spectacles, peering from over the rocky ridge of the hills to be sure he was gone. And so he was, not a trace of him remaining at all. Perhaps she had just imagined him after all? Perhaps he, and his kisses, were the product of sunstroke. Of overwork and exhaustion.

Yet as she tiptoed closer, she saw the marks of horse's hoofs in the dirt. And her spectacles were gone.

She had hurriedly secured the site, putting away the tarpaulin and tools, and had run home for a quiet afternoon of study. Or so she'd hoped.

Clio could not fathom what had come over her. *Kissing* Averton? Touching him! Not wanting it all to end, even as every ounce of her good sense screamed at her to get away from him. The man who was rumoured to be a terrible libertine, who respected no wishes not his own, who took every shameful advantage of his exalted rank. Who was, worst of all, a hoarder of antiquities!

Yet she had kissed him. And wanted so much more.

Clio groaned, dropping her head to the hard, polished surface of the desk. If only she could leave this place, this island she loved with such fervour, which had been her refuge until today. She could go back to England, to see how her younger sisters fared at Chase Lodge. She could—

No. The Chase Muses were no cowards. She might not possess the reckless, headlong courage of Thalia, who swam icy lakes and scaled mountains without a care, or the rare grace of Calliope. But she had to be strong, to stand her ground. Even in the face of Averton. Who would work on the farmhouse if she left? Who would discover its secrets?

The Duke himself, probably. He had seemed rather interested in the site that morning, before he realised she was there. And that she could not allow.

Clio pushed herself up from her chair, walking over to the window as she stretched her aching shoulders. She gazed down at their little patch of garden, at the road that led around the cathedral and out to the square. It was quiet in Santa Lucia now, the shops closed for the afternoon siesta as a warm, sunny somnolence settled over the place. Her father sat beneath the shade of their almond tree, reading with Lady Rushworth and Cory, but they were the only living things to be seen.

Clio thought about going for a rest herself, crawling under the brocade blanket of the *chaise* in her chamber and forgetting the Duke in sleep. But she dismissed the notion. Afternoon sleep was always feverish for her, bringing strange dreams. He would surely appear *there*, and she didn't want to see what would happen.

Yet neither could she read and study. She was too restless, too scattered.

There was a knock at the library door, and Clio turned toward it, eager for fresh distraction. 'Come in!'

It was Thalia who peeped around the threshold. She had changed her classical Antigone robes and veil for a stylish blue-dotted white muslin dress and blue spencer, a chip-straw bonnet with pink ribbons tucked under her arm. With her golden curls swept up and bound with more pink ribbons, her wide blue eyes and creamy skin, she looked the perfect porcelain shepherdess. The angelic beauty.

Many men had been fooled by her pretty, innocent façade—and had been sorry when they discovered the warrior-woman beneath. She often declared she was far too busy to marry, and Clio was inclined to believe her. Where could she find her match, a man with the power *and* the trickery of Zeus, the golden looks of Apollo, the strength of Hercules?

Thalia, with all her adventurous 'projects', was endlessly diverting, always entertaining, and sometimes exhausting. Today, though, Clio was entirely glad of her company.

'Are you working?' Thalia asked. She hurried over to the desk, rifling curiously through the books and papers.

'I was,' Clio answered. She leaned back against the windowsill, her arms crossed at her waist, watching as Thalia examined first one title, then another. 'But I can't seem to concentrate for some reason.'

'Me, neither. I think it's the heat. Rosa says summer is coming on, and soon the sun will burn everything brown.'

'I hope not yet! I need to finish the farmhouse cellar first.'

'And I'll have to perform my play. If it is too hot, no one will want to sit on those stone seats and watch.'

'Except for every young swain in town! They would happily sit and watch you for hours. They're all achingly in love with you, you know.'

Thalia made a dismissive wave of her hand, tossing the book she held back to the desk. 'A whole village full of men, English and Italian both, and not one with a jot of interesting conversation in him! They just want to sit and stare like a pack of half-wits.'

Clio laughed. 'And send flowers, and serenade outside your window.'

'I haven't time for such things.'

'One day you will have to make time. So shall we all, I expect.'

'What do you mean?'

'Now that Calliope is married, everyone will expect you and me to be next.'

Thalia shook her head. 'Father doesn't care if we marry or not! He's too busy with his villa and mosaics to worry about such trifles.'

Clio glanced back to the garden below, to their father and Lady Rushworth reading together so companionably. He smiled as Lady Rushworth pointed to something in their book, catching her hand to press a quick kiss to her gloved fingers. Lady Rushworth, a widow herself with two grown sons and grandchildren, blushed. Clio had not seen her father so happy since her mother had died.

'Then again, perhaps the next Chase to wed won't be a Muse at all,' she said.

Thalia hurried to her side, gazing down at the scene. 'You don't mean—Father will marry Lady Rushworth?'

'Perhaps.'

'But they are just friends!'

'Maybe. But if they *do* wed, Father won't want so many Muses underfoot for a while. And, since you are the most beautiful of all of us, you will probably be next.'

Thalia frowned, turning away from the window. 'Me? I look like a bonbon, whereas *you* look like a goddess. You are sure to attract someone interesting, someone strong and clever and…' Her voice trailed away, and Clio saw her golden head bow.

Clio was suddenly worried. Thalia was seldom anything less than running at top speed, charging ahead with her glorious confidence. She reached out and caught Thalia's hand, drawing her sister back to her side. 'What's wrong, Thalia dear? Has something happened?'

Thalia tilted her chin up, smiling, but her china-blue eyes still held a strange glitter. 'Of course not, Clio. What could possibly have happened? I just don't care for all this marriage talk, that's all! Not when I am in danger of being stuck with one of my horrid suitors.'

'Thalia, there is no danger of being "stuck"! If you really don't want to marry…'

'I will marry—when I meet someone who suits me as Cameron does Calliope.' Thalia gave Clio's hand a reassuring squeeze before letting go to stroll back to the desk. She reached for a fat letter, holding it up. 'And I see you've heard from Calliope, the new Lady Westwood, today!'

'Yes, I thought we could all read Calliope's news together after dinner,' Clio answered.

Thalia turned the missive over in her hand. 'Where are they now, do you think? Capri? Tuscany? Venice?'

'On their way back to England, I expect. Hopefully, they'll be waiting for us when we return ourselves.'

'With a new little Chase-de Vere infant on the way.' Thalia put down the letter. 'Do you miss her terribly?'

'Calliope?' Clio remembered sitting by a Yorkshire stream with Cal. *"You can tell me anything from now on, Clio."* Clio had promised she would keep no more secrets, that she was done with the Lily Thief. And she had truly tried to keep that promise. Tried to live up to her older sister's confidence. It had gone well, until that very morning, when Averton had appeared. 'Of course. None of us have ever been parted for long before. Don't you miss her?'

'Very much. I just thought it must be worse for you. You and Cal were always so close.'

'Yes. But I still have you! And I always will, if we're going to be spinster Muses together.'

Thalia laughed, and the merry sound seemed to help her shrug off whatever hint of melancholy she was suffering. She twirled around and caught Clio's hand in hers. 'Cal's children will be sorry to have such formidable old aunts! I will teach them music and drama, and how to shoot a bow and arrow. You will teach them how to swim for miles, just like you, and how to read history from just a shard of pottery.'

Clio laughed, too, going along with her. 'How to sew very, very badly?'

'That, too. But as the child is not here yet we shall have to—oh!'

'What?'

'I forgot why I came in here in the first place. I am going to call on Lady Riverton, and you promised to come with me.'

Clio felt a sinking in the pit of her stomach at the mention of Lady Riverton. The widow was the self-styled 'social leader' of the small band of English travellers in Santa Lucia. People who, like the Chases, were deeply interested in history and antiquities. Everyone else was sensible, and stayed near the cool delights of the shore, the relative culture of Palermo.

Viscount Riverton had possessed a considerable collection himself, especially of Greek coins. His widow, while she claimed to be carrying on his work, seemed to be only really interested in parties, gossip and hats. She had lots and lots of hats. Clio often thought it was a pity she didn't also have a many-headed Cerberus to guard her door; then it could wear all of them at once.

But Clio *had* promised Thalia. 'I'll have to change my clothes,' Clio said, gesturing to her garb. She had left off her heavy boots, but still wore her old brown muslin with its dusty hem. Her hair fell down her back in an untidy auburn plait.

'Just plop on a fancy bonnet!' Thalia said. 'She'll never notice the rest.' She 'plopped' her own hat on to Clio's head, tugging at the pink ribbons and singing, 'Oh la la, aren't the Chase sisters so terribly *à la mode*!'

Clio laughed helplessly, trying to spin away from her sister. Thalia wouldn't let go. 'Brown and pink, Clio, all the rage from Paris! You must be—oh, I say. Where are your spectacles?'

Chapter Six

Lady Riverton's palazzo was the grandest in town, if not as dramatically situated as the Baroness Picini's rambling manse. Lady Riverton's abode had been refurbished before she took possession, freshly stuccoed and painted so that it gleamed a bright, artificial white in the sun. There were no gaps in the tiles of the roof, no overgrown ivy, no slats missing from the shutters, no chips in her garden fountain, which splashed and gurgled as Clio and Thalia turned in through her polished black gates.

'We won't stay long,' Clio said, waiting for their knock to be answered.

'Of course not,' Thalia answered, smoothing her pink kid gloves. 'I don't think we could take more than an hour without screaming, do you?'

The butler opened the doors, and Clio thought, as she always did when coming to visit Lady Riverton, that it was like stepping back into England. Unlike the Chases' own rented house, furnished with comfortable, slightly shabby pieces, Lady Riverton had filled her space with dark, gleaming tables and cabinets. Chairs, couches and hassocks upholstered in blue-striped satin, interspersed with displays of her collections: vases, coffers, fragments of statues, cases showing off her husband's ancient coins.

Lady Riverton herself sat on a throne-like chair and presided over an elaborate tea table, set with silver, porcelain, platters of tiny sandwiches and pink-iced cakes. Her light brown hair, untouched by any hint of grey, was crowned with a dainty lace cap matching the filmy fichu tucked into her pale green muslin gown. A pair of antique cameos dangled from her ears.

Once, in a different life, those earrings had been just the sort of thing to tempt Clio to 'liberate' them. But she had made promises, so all she said as she greeted Lady Riverton was, 'Such charming earrings.'

Lady Riverton trilled a light laugh, reaching up to toy with one of the fragile cameos. 'A gift from my dear late husband. He had such excellent taste! I am honoured you have decided to grace my tea table this afternoon, Miss Chase, Miss Thalia. We see so little of you lately, you always seem to be trailing around the fields with your father.'

Clio nodded at the other guests, Lady Elliott—whose husband helped her father at the villa site—and her daughters, Mrs Darby and *her* daughter—who had taken Clio on their impromptu Agrigento tour—as she and Thalia took their seats. Lady Riverton's friend, her 'cicisbeo' as Thalia called him, Ronald Frobisher, was not present, which was most unusual. 'There is certainly a great deal to see in Sicily,' Clio said, accepting a cup of tea. 'Much work to be done.'

Lady Riverton laughed again. 'Oh, certainly I know *all* about that! Viscount Riverton was one of the first to see the vast potential of this site. It was just a dusty valley when he came here with Nelson! I'm most gratified to see his work being carried on so admirably. But I also know that young ladies must have their share of amusement. Before I married, I had far too much energy and natural merriment to live by digging alone!'

'That is so true!' cried Miss Darby. 'I am always telling Mama—'

Mrs Darby laid a gentle hand on her daughter's arm, stilling the excited flow of words. 'And we are very gratified you provide such—amusements, Lady Riverton.'

'Not at all. I so vastly enjoy entertaining, and my dear husband always said my parties were so very elegant.' She gave another little laugh. 'He was so indulgent. But I do hope you will all be at my next gathering! An evening of amateur theatricals, very diverting. You all received your invitations?'

Clio calmly sipped at her tea, silently willing Thalia not to have an excited outburst *à la* Miss Darby. Lady Riverton hardly needed any fodder for her 'Gracious Hostess' act. 'Indeed we did, Lady Riverton. We will be most happy to attend.'

'So kind of you to ask us,' Thalia said coolly. Clio was proud of her. 'That is one thing I miss so much about London, the theatre.'

'As do I, Miss Thalia,' Lady Riverton answered. 'We are both cultured souls, I see! While I cannot procure the likes of Mrs Siddons, I fear, I do hope to show off some of our local talent, which I suspect is quite great. The Manning-Smythes have agreed to stage a scene from *Romeo and Juliet*. So appropriate, is it not, since they are on their honeymoon? And Miss Darby here will do Ophelia's mad scene. It is so important to include Shakespeare! His more *appropriate* bits, at least.'

'Oh, yes,' Clio said. 'The Bard is always welcome. But,

as this is Sicily, would it not be a fine thing to include some classical playwrights? For is this not where Ovid and Aeschylus worked?'

'But the Greeks and Romans are so very violent, aren't they?' Lady Riverton murmured, her lace cap quivering. 'So much blood and vengeance!'

Unlike Shakespeare, of course, Clio thought wryly. No blood or vengeance there.

'But always so vastly exciting,' Lady Elliott said over her sandwiches. 'You have been working yourself on some Sophocles, have you not, Miss Thalia?'

'Indeed,' Thalia answered. '*Antigone*. The amphitheatre here is so wondrous, with superb acoustics, it just seemed to call out to be brought to life again! To be used for its true purpose. Yet I fear *Antigone* features no blood at all.'

'Yes. All the death is offstage, is it not?' Mrs Darby said. 'Still, very dramatic.'

'No blood, you say?' Lady Riverton said. 'How interesting. Perhaps, Miss Thalia, you might grace us with a monologue at my little theatricals? Add some *appropriate* classicism to the proceedings.'

Thalia gave her a gracious smile. 'If you think your guests would enjoy it, Lady Riverton.'

The purpose of their visit now so neatly achieved, Thalia went on to chat with their hostess about the newest fashions in bonnets—feathers or fruit?—while Clio turned to Mrs Darby. They had become friends on that tour of the 'valley of the temples' at Agrigento, but did not see each other as often now that Mr Darby had turned his activities from excavating to writing. A novel, everyone heard, about the original destruction of the old Greek town during the Punic Wars.

'And how is Mr Darby's book progressing?' Clio asked.

Mrs Darby laughed. 'Well enough, I suppose. He hides himself away in his library after breakfast and does not emerge all day, so *something* is being worked on.'

'What do you do yourself, then, while he is scribbling away?'

'Pay calls, as you see. Go on excursions. I fear it's becoming rather dull for poor Susan.' Mrs Darby glanced at her daughter, who was nibbling at a cake with a very dreamy look in her eyes. 'We have been thinking of hiring a yacht to take us out to some of the other islands. Motya, for the Phoenician sites, perhaps. Maybe you would care to join us?'

Clio thought again of the Duke, of their kiss. Now that he was here, he was not likely to go away again any time soon. It was terribly tempting to run away, to sail off and put the endless blue sea between them! But she could not leave her work. Not just yet. 'That is very kind of you, Mrs Darby. I have heard such enticing things about the necropolis there. But I am not sure I can leave my family just now.'

'Yes. We have heard you are hard at work on a more remote site while your father explores that villa of his. It is very brave of you, I must say!'

'Brave? Not at all. *Dull* is what most people would call it. The site is just an old ruined farmhouse, but I am enjoying finding clues to everyday life here.'

'Yet it is so remote! I would fear for Susan out there. And, of course, there is the curse.'

Clio felt a tiny cold shiver along her spine. 'Curse, Mrs Darby? Is your husband by some chance writing a horrid novel?'

Mrs Darby smiled and shook her head. 'Oh, Miss Clio. I myself do not believe in such nonsense. I simply happened to overhear your cook gossiping with our housemaid, who I think is her daughter. They didn't seem to know I speak

Italian. They were saying how courageous you are to brave the curse.'

Clio laughed, though she still felt inexplicably cold. As if a goose had walked over her grave. 'How very amusing. I wonder who placed this curse?'

Mrs Darby shrugged. 'It seems something terribly violent happened at your farmhouse before it was destroyed. Something that deeply angered the gods. Now it is said that anyone unworthy who dares disturb the ground will be terribly punished. That's why the site has been so undisturbed all these years.'

'Perhaps the curse has a time limit,' Clio suggested, 'for I am still here.'

'Or maybe you are considered worthy. Oh, Miss Clio, Sicily is ever fascinating, is it not?'

'Indeed it is,' Clio murmured. Well, at least this little tale explained why she had trouble hiring assistants. If only ancient curses could keep Averton away, too.

The drawing room opened amid the quiet buzz of conversation, and the butler announced, 'The Count di Fabrizzi, my lady.'

Clio's teacup clattered in its saucer at the sudden announcement. *No!* Perhaps there were two Fabrizzis in Italy? There simply had to be. She couldn't take another sudden reappearance, not in one day.

She carefully put the cup and saucer down, schooling her expression into cool lines of casual interest before she looked toward the door.

There were not, after all, two Count Fabrizzis. Only the one she already knew—Marco, who had been one of the Lily Thief's cohorts, a man deeply concerned with the lost heritage of his homeland. And there he stood, raising Lady Riverton's lace-mittened hand to his lips for a polite salute as she giggled and blushed.

When she had known him in England, she had been quite aware that he was a titled nobleman from an old Florentine family. Yet he had been disguised as a gypsy, his long black hair tied back with a red bandanna, dressed in plain white shirts and scuffed boots. Now his hair was expertly trimmed into a glossy dark cap that emphasised his chocolate-brown eyes and high Italian cheekbones. He was dressed simply but expensively in a well-cut bottle-green coat, buckskin breeches and a gold-striped silk waistcoat.

Clio folded her hands in her lap, watching the scene warily. She did not feel that lightning shock that went all through her when Averton appeared, that hot fear and excitement. She knew very well Marco would never give away her secrets. But his arrival in Lady Riverton's drawing room *was* an unexpected wrinkle in her plans. What was he doing here? What did he hope to gain in Sicily?

If he looked to reincarnate the Lily Thief…

'Good heavens,' Mrs Darby murmured. 'What a beauty.'

Her daughter just giggled, hiding the giddy sound behind her fan.

'Indeed,' Clio said, glancing at her sister. Thalia had a frighteningly speculative gleam in her eye. She couldn't be thinking of recruiting Marco for her play! Could she?

Lady Riverton stood and took Marco's arm, turning him toward their eager little group. 'This is the Count di Fabrizzi, who has come all the way from Florence to grace our little society here! He and my dear Lord Riverton were such good friends, you see.'

'He would never forgive me if I did not pay my deepest respects to his lovely widow,' Marco said in his liquid accent, giving her a charming smile that made her plump, pretty cheeks turn bright pink. 'But I fear I will only be in Santa Lucia for a very few days. I have business in Palermo.'

'Oh, no!' Lady Riverton cried. 'Surely your business *here* cannot be concluded so quickly. And Santa Lucia is so diverting this spring, as I'm sure my friends can tell you. Let me introduce you. Lady Elliott and the Misses Elliott, Mrs Darby and Miss Darby. And the Misses Chase, Clio and Thalia, whom you must have heard of. They are the famous Chase Muses. Ladies, you must join me in urging the Count to stay a little longer.'

'Oh, yes!' Lady Elliott declared. 'If you were a friend of Lord Riverton, you must enjoy antiquities. There are so many around here.'

Lady Riverton urged Marco to sit down in the chair next to hers, pressing a cup of tea and some sandwiches on him. 'Yes, quite,' he answered. 'Ancient history is one of the great passions of my life.'

Miss Darby giggled again behind that fan, until her mother shot her a stern glance.

'Then you should stay and meet our husbands,' Lady Elliott went on. 'As well as Mr Frobisher and the Manning-Smythes. Most of them are working on the site of an ancient Greek town, and have already found many exquisite objects. We expect more great things. I'm sure they would welcome your expertise.'

'Welcome the free labour,' Thalia muttered to Clio.

'You must at least stay for my theatrical evening,' Lady Riverton said.

'It sounds most—diverting,' Marco answered. He gave their hostess another smile, displaying a deep-set dimple in his olive-complected cheek that made even Mrs Darby sigh.

'You enjoy the theatre, Count?' Thalia said.

'When I have the chance to attend,' Marco answered. He turned his smile on to Thalia, but it turned to a frown of puzzlement when he met her frank, speculative blue eyes.

Well, Clio thought, she could not save Marco if Thalia had decided he would act in her play. Anyone caught in Thalia's crosshairs was doomed. But she still could not decipher what he was doing here. Marco and the Duke in one place? So strange.

The conversation went along most politely, turning to the social events of Santa Lucia, the *objets* that had been found thus far in the Greek town. Clio sipped at a fresh cup of tea, studying Marco over the painted china rim. They exchanged only one meaningful glance, a long look that promised much conversation later, but other than that he gave no sign at all that he had ever seen her before. Perhaps Thalia was right about his potential acting skills.

And Clio had to keep up her own, too. Luckily, deception had become second nature to her in her Lily Thief days. But this afternoon, smiling and chatting as if she hadn't a care, she felt as if a bar of cold iron was pressing down on her. Making her want to scream.

Her cheeks hurt from all that smiling, too.

At last, the half-hour deemed polite for a social call passed, giving Clio and Thalia the excuse they needed to escape. As they collected their shawls and gloves and thanked Lady Riverton, the footman appeared again with a note on a silver tray. Lady Riverton scanned it quickly, and suddenly broke into a triumphant laugh.

Curious, Clio paused in drawing on her gloves. Surely there was little in Santa Lucia correspondence that could be *that* exciting. Not very much changed here from day to day. Until now.

'Oh, Count di Fabrizzi, now you really must come to my theatricals!' Lady Riverton said, carefully refolding the note. 'It would be quite the triumph to have in attendance both an Italian count *and* an English duke. Two handsome young noblemen to grace my drawing room!'

'A *duke*?' exclaimed Lady Elliott. 'I was not aware there were any such personages in the neighborhood.'

'There is now. He has just accepted my invitation, which I sent round as soon as I heard who had taken the Picini palazzo.' Lady Riverton gave them a supremely satisfied smile. 'And you will never guess who it is.'

'Devonshire!' guessed Miss Darby.

'Clarence,' suggested Thalia. 'Oh, no. He would be too fat to get up the hill.'

'Better,' Lady Riverton said. 'It is *the* Duke of Averton. So handsome and delightful! And he will actually be here for my theatrical evening. Won't it be glorious?'

Thalia glanced at Clio, her eyes wide. 'But how could…?'

Clio grabbed her hand, holding it tightly. 'Glorious, indeed. We do look forward to it, Lady Riverton, but now we really must go before our father misses us. It was lovely to make your acquaintance, Count di Fabrizzi.'

'Oh, no, Miss Chase,' Marco said, giving her an elaborate bow. Only the merest shadow in his dark eyes reflected a certain dismay at the mention of the name 'Averton'. He, too, remembered the Yorkshire dungeon. 'The pleasure was entirely mine.'

Clio left Lady Riverton's house, still holding on to Thalia's hand until they were at a safe distance on the street. When she let go, it was like releasing a tidal wave.

'Averton!' Thalia exploded. 'What is *he* doing here? How dare he show his face where we are, how dare he come as near us as—as Rome! Handsome he may be, but he is naught but a freebooter, a—'

'A freebooter?' Clio said, laughing despite herself. 'Thalia, he is hardly Drake on the *Golden Hind*.'

'No, he is worse. I would wager he only comes here to steal whatever Father finds in his villa. And to harass *you* some more.'

'And don't forget, to attend Lady Riverton's party. He has definitely come for that.' Clio spoke with a lightness she was far from feeling, hurrying her steps towards home. She longed for the quiet of her own room. The safe haven she had always found in Santa Lucia felt torn now, reshaped with the arrivals of Averton and Marco. Something was definitely afoot, something she could not see or understand. Not yet, anyway. 'Danger,' the Duke had said. How right he was.

Thalia hurried after her. 'Well, then, I *won't* go to that party. I have no wish to see that spoiled, arrogant—'

'Freebooter? Oh, Thalia, we have to go. We told Lady Riverton we would, and you were looking forward to it. Everyone will need your wonderful Antigone to save them from drowning in sugary faux-Shakespeareness. There will be lots of people there, we won't even notice Averton. Handsome or not.'

'Perhaps not,' Thalia said reluctantly. She was silent for a moment, then added, 'But we will be sure to notice Count Adonis! And *he* will notice *you*.'

Clio was careful not to look at her sister, just walking a bit faster on their way home. 'Don't be silly. Why would a gorgeous Italian count notice me, when your golden beauty or Miss Darby's conspicuous giggles will be near?'

'He kept looking at you just now,' Thalia said. Not for the first time, Clio cursed Thalia's powers of observation. 'If I was a reader of horrid novels, like our friend Lotty, I would call them "speaking glances".'

'You are just imagining things. I think all the theatricality is getting to you.'

'I think not.' Thalia opened their own garden gate, and went prancing up to the front door, chanting, 'Clio has a new admirer!'

'What?' cried Cory, who came into the foyer just in time to hear this bit of news. 'Clio has an admirer? Who is it? Oh! Not that silly Peter Elliott? I thought he was in love with *you*, Thalia.'

'Far better,' Thalia said. 'A dark Italian count! He kept staring at her over Lady Riverton's tea table. And he is *beautiful*.'

'Perhaps Clio will soon be a contessa!' Cory said, pretending to swoon. 'And we will all live with her in Italy for ever. In her grand palazzo, with her hundreds of servants and vast marble halls.'

Clio fled their merry laughter, taking the stairs two at a time until she could slam her chamber door behind her and be alone, in silence, at last. Heaven deliver her from *sisters*!

And from English Viking dukes and 'dark Italian counts'. They all knew far too many of her secrets already.

Chapter Seven

Edward watched the sun set from his overgrown back garden, seated on the edge of the old fountain, a Turkish cigarillo in hand. The vast sky was a swirling blend of orange and blood-red, streaked with shimmering gold dust, smoky lavender at the edges. Etna dominated the horizon like a silent queen, swathed in silver mists like a torn bridal veil. The breeze that swept up from the valley was cool, carrying away the heat of the afternoon.

It was unlike anything he had ever seen in all his travels—silent, eternal, dramatic. Every instant the sky shifted and changed. The vestiges of modern Sicily, the bustle of the village streets, the vast tides of tourists, receded and there was only the land itself.

It was like Clio. Changeable, mysterious, remote. Beautiful.

Not that she had been so very *remote* when they had met that morning. He exhaled a grey plume of smoke, remembering the feel of her in his arms, the taste of her mouth. She was intoxicating, worse than the brandy he had given up years ago. Every time he was near her, he wanted more and more of her! He wanted everything.

Her kisses took him out of himself, until there was only her. Only the two of them, floating high above the dark world, lost in a passion that promised everything. But the problem with soaring above the earth, touching the glory of the sun, was that he always fell, Icarus-like, to the rocks below. He had no heart left to offer her.

Edward took another long drag of the cigarillo, drawing the sour smoke deep inside, feeling it burn its way down his throat as he looked down to the marble ledge beside him. Clio's spectacles lay there, the vivid sunset glowing on the lenses, reflecting the light back to him. 'Remember why you're here,' he muttered. To finish his task. To make sure no one else got hurt. Not to kiss Clio Chase.

He ground the last of the cigarillo out beneath his boot. Maybe one day she might understand. Clio saw things even *he* could not fathom; so much was hidden in her eyes. Even if she never understood, never saw, he would take care of her. He thought about his first invitation here in Santa Lucia, to Lady Riverton's 'theatrical evening'. It was just the first step in his plan.

Edward turned and strode into the palazzo, wrapping the spectacles up in his silk handkerchief. He shoved the make-shift package at one of the footmen, and said, 'Deliver this to Miss Chase immediately.'

After dinner, when her father, Thalia and Cory were settled to reading in the drawing room, Clio crept down the back staircase to the kitchens. Lady Riverton thought she knew everything that happened in Santa Lucia, but Clio was sure her ladyship saw only the merest surface. Only the polite *English* side of things. Clio knew that if she wanted the whole truth, she needed to go to Rosa, their cook.

Rosa had a vast family, sons and daughters, nieces and nephews, who worked in every corner of Santa Lucia, the hills and the valleys, both in legitimate venues and those that were less so. Especially her strange younger son, Giacomo, who appeared to have no profession at all, one of the seemingly indolent men in the piazza. If anyone had heard anything of the English duke, it would be Rosa.

The cook was sitting by the kitchen fire, shelling fresh peas and chatting with her husband, Paolo, who ran the stables. A lamb lay on the table, ready to be dressed for tomorrow's dinner, which meant her butcher son must have been by. Or perhaps the shepherd son.

Clio sat down with them, enjoying the cosy crackle of the flames against the cool evening. Rosa and Paolo just smiled at her, used to her strange ways by now. Paolo held up a bottle of clear liquid.

'Grappa, *signorina*?' he asked.

'Yes, *grazie*,' Clio answered, watching as he poured out a generous glassful and passed it to her. One of their other sons distilled it himself, and it was rough and strong as she sipped at it. She laughed, wiping at her stinging eyes. 'It's, er, very good.'

Rosa laughed. 'Oh, Signorina Clio! You are an odd one.'

'Yes, I know. I've often been told that.' If they only knew just *how* odd. But no one knew, really. No one but Averton. And he was an odd one himself. 'Rosa, what do you know about the farmhouse site being cursed?'

Rosa made a quick gesture to deflect evil before going on with her pea-shelling, not looking at Clio. 'Cursed?'

'Yes. I heard something about it today, and I was surprised you hadn't warned me.'

'Pah! You are *Inglese*, it can't hurt you.'

Clio took another drink of the grappa. It was really quite nice once she got used to it. So, she took yet another. 'A strange curse, to respect national boundaries like that.'

'What Rosa means,' Paolo said, 'is that you have to believe in a curse for it to work.'

'How do you know I don't?'

Rosa gave a sharp laugh. 'You're still here, aren't you, *signorina*?'

'Are you saying there are some who are not still here? Victims of this curse?'

Paolo shrugged. 'That house was destroyed in a time of great violence. Bloodshed, battles, much fear. The last family who lived there, a Greek family, fled as the Romans drew near. But they were acolytes of Demeter, they called on their goddess to avenge them for the loss of their home as they left. Since that long-ago day, anyone who tries to live there, grow crops there, they fail. They die horrible deaths.'

'They see the ghosts,' Rosa added. 'It drives them mad.'

'Hmm,' Clio said thoughtfully. 'Maybe the ghosts leave me alone because I don't try to live there. Because my work is meant to help those people who fled, to tell their story.'

'Perhaps,' Rosa said. 'But if anyone comes there with evil intentions…'

Like Averton? Were his intentions 'evil'? 'What have you heard about the Englishman who has taken the Picini palazzo?'

Rosa and Paolo exchanged a long glance. 'Not a great deal yet,' Rosa said. 'Our youngest son got a place as footman there. He says this man is very great in your country. A prince of some sort.'

Clio laughed to envision Averton with a crown perched crookedly on his golden head. That grappa was certainly doing its work! She felt all warm and content. Even curses and dukes couldn't affect her, not now. 'Not a prince exactly. But very important, yes. I'm surprised to see him here.'

'You knew him before, *signorina*?'

'Yes, in England.'

'Ah. Our son says this prince seems to have come here for the antiquities, as so many do. He has many objects he moved into the palazzo. He keeps them in his very bedchamber!'

'Really?' Clio leaned forward, her interest sharpening. 'What sort of objects?'

'Vases, statues.'

'A statue of Artemis, perhaps? About as tall as me? Alabaster?'

'I don't know,' Rosa said. 'I will ask Lorenzo. Is this statue important?'

'It could be.' Clio sat back, sipping the last of her grappa. 'If you hear anything else interesting from Lorenzo, will you tell me? I'd like to know what he's doing here.'

'Of course, *signorina*. Is he a bad man, this prince of yours?'

Clio considered this, thought about their kiss, his touch. The madness that came over her every time she saw him. 'I don't know yet.'

She thanked Rosa and Paolo for the drink and the information, and left them to their own gossip. At the top of the stairs, she could hear the low murmur of voices from the drawing room, the sound of Thalia playing old English madrigals at the pianoforte. She should rejoin them, but her head was spinning with the grappa, curses, ghosts and thoroughly baffling princes. Instead, she turned toward the second flight of stairs leading to the bedchambers.

Her own room was silent and dark. No one had come yet to light the candles or turn back the bed. Clio walked unsteadily to the window, opening it to lean out and take a deep breath. The vast sky was indigo blue, with only one tiny star and a crescent of moon to light the inky expanse. It was still early; soon, the pearly stars would blink on one by one. Distant Etna was just a blur without her spectacles.

It would be a good night for the Lily Thief, Clio thought idly. Dark enough to avoid detection. But Santa Lucia was quiet, with nothing to distract people from their purloined ancient treasures. Maybe later, when everyone was cosy in bed…

She perched on the wide windowsill, tucking the Turkey-red muslin skirts of her evening gown around her. Those thieving days were behind her now, which was a pity considering the Alabaster Goddess might be so near. Clio peered out over the roofs, past the bulk of the cathedral, to the edge of the Duke's palazzo. It, too, was a bit blurry, but some of the windows were lit up, glowing bright squares. Someone was home.

What was he doing in there right now? she wondered. Did he gloat over his treasures? Plan how best to drive her even more insane? Did he consider whatever it was that had brought him to Santa Lucia in the first place?

Rosa said it was the hunt for antiquities, like almost everyone else here. But Clio had learned the hard way that Averton never did things as 'everyone else' did, and never for the expected reasons. He was a world unto himself, completely indecipherable.

Clio doubted his appearance here in sleepy Santa Lucia, so far from his ducal empire, could be a mere coincidence. So, what was it?

'I will just have to find out,' she murmured. She had gained many skills in her Lily Thief days. Maybe it was time to put them to use again. And, with Marco in town, she had a potential accomplice.

If *he* wasn't up to mischief himself. Marco was always up to mischief. The question was, what sort was it? What was happening behind the sleepy façades of Santa Lucia?

A knock sounded at her chamber door, and Clio stood up, shaking out her skirts. 'Yes?'

'A delivery for you, Miss Chase,' a maid said.

'Come in.' It was a strange package, a lump of white silk tied with a bit of string. Clio quickly unrolled it, catching her spectacles in her hand. There was no note, no message. Just the scarlet letters embroidered on a corner of the silk.

ER.

'Edward Radcliffe,' she whispered.

It seemed so strange that he even possessed a given name.

'Edward,' she whispered again, crumpling the handkerchief in her palm. 'I promise I will find out what you're doing. You can't escape from me. Prince or not.'

It was definitely not one of the finer streets of Santa Lucia.

Edward nudged aside a pile of rubbish with the toe of his boot. The cobblestones were old and cracked, streaked with refuse; the lane itself was narrow and dark, close-packed with ancient buildings that faced the world with barred doors and broken, shuttered windows, with walls of peeling, grimy stucco. From behind those walls he could hear the shriek of drunken laughter, the crash of quarrels, the two barely distinguishable from each other. The smell of rotting vegetables, sour grappa and old chamber pots hung heavy in the still night air. It was after midnight, but he knew it would be little different at midday.

This street was far from the Picini palazzo, or even from

the smaller, respectable abodes of shopkeepers and servants. This was another world entirely, one kept far from the tourists, the wealthy. Yet this was the only place where he could find what he sought.

There were surely answers behind those barred doors, answers that would never be easily given up. So, he would have to take them.

He paused, his black clothes and dark cap blending with the shadows as he studied the dwelling opposite. It appeared to be deserted, a dilapidated structure, yet it had to be the one he sought. He settled in to wait, his arms crossed over his chest. In his work, cool, predatory patience was a necessity, and he had learned it at long last after all his wildly impulsive years.

Like the impulse that led him to kiss Clio Chase at her farmhouse—despite what had happened in London.

He reached up to rub at the scar on his brow, that rough reminder of where 'impulse' had got him. He had a task here, one that included keeping Clio far away from it all. Far from places like this, and from him.

He was not doing a very good job of it so far. Kissing her; agreeing to meet her father. But that would change.

Right now, it seemed. A small, flickering light appeared in one of the broken upper windows. Someone was home.

Edward crept across the lane, drawing a dagger from its sheath beneath his sleeve. Holding it balanced on his leather-gloved palm, he made his way around the house to its back door. It faced on to an alleyway even narrower than the front street, barely wide enough for one man to walk down. More refuse was piled in the doorway, but, as he had suspected, it was not barred. The tip of his knife made quick work of the flimsy lock.

The corridor inside was dark and dank, smelling of dusty disuse. Surely no one lived here but the mice; it was perfect for nefarious plots. Everyone in Santa Lucia surely knew what went on here, but no one would ever speak of it. Tomb-raiding was the pastime of centuries here, the key to ill-gotten prosperity.

But that was also about to change.

Moving silently on the balls of his booted feet, Edward made his way up a narrow staircase. He did not stop at the lighted room, but kept going ever upwards until he found a narrow space under the eaves, just as his informant had said. There was a gap in the floorboards there, where he could hear and see everything that went on in that room below. But *they* could not see *him*, and would thus blithely go on with their plans.

Oh, yes. Things were about to change indeed.

Chapter Eight

The next day Clio did not go to her farmhouse, but to the villa with her father and sisters. She was tired from the sleepless night, the grappa, and was not sure if she should be alone in the secluded meadow until she knew more about the enemy's plans. She might have been a thief, but never an impulsive one. It didn't pay to act rashly, if a person wanted to achieve their goals and come out of the fray unscathed.

She had made the mistake of jumping in without the proper preparation in Yorkshire. She would not do that again.

She sat at the edge of the partially uncovered banquet hall of the villa, sketching the elaborate mosaic floor, carefully noting measurements. The people who once lived here were rather different from her prosperous but hard-working farmers. These had been the rulers of this distant outpost, this luxurious little colony built up from nothing to be the breadbasket of a kingdom. And their villa reflected that status, full of sumptuous touches like a thermal bath and elaborate courtyard gardens.

Here, in the banquet hall, the borders of the floor were inlaid with grapes, figs and pomegranates, common Greek fertility symbols, the purple and red colours still lush and glistening after all these years. They framed scenes of parties such as the ones that must have gone on long into the night here. Diners clad in purple, blue and white robes, lounging on low couches as they gorged themselves on delicacies such as fishcakes, white breads, honeyed sweets and copious vats of wine.

Clio smiled as she drew their laughing, satisfied faces, imagining their drunken conversations. The gossip about the sexual orgies of powerful officials, the talents of actors seen recently at the amphitheatre, favourite poets, onerous new taxes. The peccadilloes of their neighbors. Surely not much had changed over the centuries. Very similar talk could be heard at Lady Riverton's house, too.

Except for the orgies, of course. No one would even *say* such a word in the presence of an unmarried English lady! Clio laughed aloud. If only they knew how she had augmented her already surprisingly frank classical education with information from Rosa and the other Sicilians. If she had to, she now knew the best ways to breed strong goats. The best sexual positions for a human woman, too, if she wanted to conceive a boy child. The best herbal potions to use if she didn't want to conceive a child at all. That would surely some day be useful.

'Shocking,' she murmured. Yes, if they all knew, Lady Riverton, the Darbys and Elliotts, the Manning-Smythes, she would be cast out of 'good' society.

Would that be a terrible thing? Not for herself, maybe, but for her father and sisters. They were what kept her tethered to reality.

'What is shocking, Clio dear?' her father asked, coming up beside her to sit down at the edge of the floor.

'The colours of the tiles,' Clio answered, gesturing to a pomegranate bursting with ruby-coloured seeds. 'They could have been laid yesterday.'

'It's the soil, of course,' Sir Walter said. 'Perfect conditions for preservation, just the right level of acidity. We are quite fortunate.'

'Indeed we are. Travelling here was a very good idea.' Clio examined her father over the edge of her sketchbook. He seemed rather tired today, his face reddened from the southern sun, his eyes lined with purplish shadows. He appeared thinner, too, despite Rosa's excellent cooking.

This kind of work had been his life for so long, but he was not as young as he used to be. Perhaps if he *did* marry Lady Rushworth, it would be a good thing. She would take care of him, as Clio's mother once had.

He took the book from her hands, examining the drawings. 'Such careful measurements and proportions, Clio. You were always good at such things.'

'But not nearly as artistic as Cory! Her sketches grow more accomplished every day.' Clio gestured toward her sister, working with her watercolour box under the canvas pavilion.

'So she does. Her works bring this place back to life.' Sir Walter laughed. 'She talks of joining an expedition to Egypt when she is older! Painting the pyramids and hieroglyphs.'

'She would be excellent at that, I'm sure.'

'My dearest girls. You all were always so fanciful.'

Were? 'That is because of you and Mother. You always gave us much to be fanciful about.'

'Indeed we did. Yet I sometimes wonder…' His voice trailed away, and he stared out into the distance, to the ever-vigilant, ever-patient hulk of Etna.

'Wonder what, Father?'

'If we raised all of you the wrong way. We wanted you to love what we loved, to see the great importance of history and art. To think for yourselves.'

Clio laughed. 'We most assuredly do *that*!'

'Perhaps we should have been more realistic, though. Should have taught you more of the things young ladies of your position ought to know, and lived less in our own world with our own friends. I begin to fear we did not prepare you well for life.'

'Oh, no!' Clio cried. 'We all love you and Mother so very much. We love the life you've given us. None of us could bear the usual missish sort of existence, needlework and idle gossip…'

'Husband hunting?' he said teasingly, a glint in his eye.

'Especially that.'

'Oh, well, that is another way I have failed you. If your mother were here, she would know how to find suitable matches. I have been shockingly remiss, just drifting along, year after year, selfishly keeping you with me.'

'Not at all! Isn't Calliope well married? She's a countess now. And Cameron is a good man. He loves her very much.'

'Yes. Love. We never thought of that sort of thing when I was young. But I suppose you modern young Muses won't do without it.'

'You suppose correctly! But weren't you and Mother in love? Despite—' Clio snapped her mouth shut before she could let out those dreadful words. The secret knowledge she had held all these years, would hold for ever. 'Despite being so young when you married.'

He smiled sadly. 'Of course I loved your mother. Who could not? She was so beautiful, so—temperamental. Full of fire. Just like you, Clio.'

'Like me?'

'Of all my girls, you are the most like my Celeste. You have her hair, her eyes. Her passion.'

Clio reached out and gently touched his hand. 'Then I must wait for my perfect match, as she did.'

He laughed. 'I could never *match* Celeste! No one could. You must simply find someone who can keep up with you, a Herculean task in itself.' He stood up, prodding at a mosaic flute girl with his walking stick. 'Oh, I almost forgot! I have invited someone to take a look at the villa this morning. He'll probably stay and share our picnic luncheon, too.'

Clio slowly closed her sketchbook. Guests at the villa were certainly nothing new. All the English tourists who visited Santa Lucia were avid to see ruins. And they often stayed to eat, too, discussing antiquities far into the siesta hours. But something in her father's tone, in the way he refused to meet her gaze, aroused her suspicions.

'What sort of visitors?' she asked. 'Not one of those odd men from Palermo who are always offering to be a "security guard"? I don't trust them!'

'Certainly not. They only want to steal what they can dig up and sell, destroying everything else in the process. We have our own "security". No, my dear, it is—well, it is the Duke of Averton.'

'Averton?' Clio muttered. She knew she should not be surprised. The man had such a knack for insinuating himself into her life. A duke was always welcome everywhere. But now her own *father*? She had thought he did not much like Averton, or indeed any of the Radcliffes.

But then, Sir Walter knew nothing of what had happened between her and Averton last year. If Clio had her way, he never would.

'Yes,' he said, his voice far too cheerful. 'Thalia told me Lady Riverton said he was in Santa Lucia, and I thought he might be interested to see what we're doing here.'

'But, Father! He is so…'

He held up his hand. 'I know he is a bit more *avid* in his collecting habits than you would like. Yet he is not so bad as you seem to think, Clio. He is a great scholar, particularly knowledgeable about the Punic Wars, which would be very helpful to us at this site.'

He leaned down, laying a gentle touch on her arm, much as one would with a skittish horse. 'He did make many mistakes when he was a young man, that is true. But, my dear, I have heard that he is trying to make a new start. To live up to his title, his family and responsibilities. Look at the work he has done for the Antiquities Society! I feel we should give him a chance.'

'Then of course I will welcome him politely, Father. You and Mother *did* raise me to have proper manners, no matter what your doubts on that score.' And they were surrounded by people here. That would definitely limit the trouble she and Averton could get into. 'Do we have enough food and wine?'

Her father gave her a relieved smile. Apparently, being so much like her French mother made her unpredictable, too. 'Lady Rushworth has gone back to Santa Lucia to fetch more provisions, plus some footmen to set up more tables under the pavilion. Silver and china, linens and such.'

Clio laughed. 'What, is he bringing an army with him? An entourage of retainers?'

'One never knows with dukes, my dear. Lady Rushworth just thought we should be prepared.' He paused. 'But then, Averton has never been like most dukes, has he?'

No, indeed, Clio thought wryly. Averton had never been like anyone else at all. 'I will go and help Cory to clear up her paints, then. If I had known we were to have such exalted company, I would have worn my silks and feathers!'

Her father kissed her cheek. 'You look beautiful no matter what you wear, Clio. I have the suspicion that his Grace thinks so, as well.'

Before Clio could even begin to argue with him, Sir Walter strolled quickly away, whistling as he swung his walking stick. Exactly how much did her father know? And how much did he know that *she* knew?

Along with her worries about Marco's appearance, and about what Averton knew that she did not, it made her head spin more than any amount of grappa.

Clio helped Cory pack her paintboxes away in her baskets, hanging up finished watercolours to dry along a line specially hung for that purpose. They were really wonderful, Clio thought, examining a scene that was a reconstruction of the villa as it would have been in its prime. The frescoes on the walls were perfectly detailed, the water in the fountain sparkling. Far better than anything Denon had done in Egypt.

'These are truly wonderful, Cory,' Clio said.

'They're all right,' Cory answered. 'I'm having some trouble with the perspective in the thermal baths. If I could just work on it some more today, instead of having to pack it all up! Just to give luncheon to a stupid old duke.'

Clio smothered a laugh at her sister's petulant irreverence. It would never do to encourage her! Yet it was still quite funny. *Stupid duke*, indeed.

Cory was quite serious, though. 'I wouldn't think *you* would care to see him, Clio,' she said, taking off her paint-splattered apron and smoothing her pink muslin dress. Like Calliope, she had black hair and fair skin that glowed in pink. The colour just made Clio look like a demented strawberry. Not that her grey work frock was any better.

'Why is that?' Clio asked. 'I don't mind Father's guests.'

Cory glanced at her from the corner of her eye. 'Well, after that quarrel you had with the Duke at the British Museum last year…'

Clio froze. *Oh, blast.* How could she have forgotten that? Cory had been right there in the Elgin room when Averton had cornered Clio and tried to talk to her about the Lily Thief. When she had nearly stabbed him with her hatpin before Cameron de Vere had separated them. She had foolishly thought Cory had not noticed, being so preoccupied with her sketching, but she should have known better. Cory was a Chase, after all. Observation—some might unkindly call it snooping—was their *raison d'être*.

'That was just a misunderstanding,' Clio said.

'Was it?' Cory answered. 'You and the Duke seem to *misunderstand* each other a lot. Like that time at Herr Mueller's lecture at the Antiquities Society…'

'Well, we're not going to have any such misunderstandings today,' Clio said firmly. 'We're all going to be perfectly polite and have a pleasant luncheon. Correct?'

Cory gave a most impolite snort. 'I wouldn't count on that if Thalia comes back from the theatre. She doesn't like him, either, and you know Thalia is likely to say anything.'

Clio sighed. She *did* know that. Calliope, the most sensible and organised of them, had once likened managing her sisters to herding a pack of feral cats. Not flattering, but probably true. Maybe her father was right about their upbringing.

'Thalia will be polite, too,' Clio said sternly, trying to

sound like Calliope. 'We are *all* going to be polite. Yes, Terpsichore?'

'I will if you won't call me that.' Cory hated her full name.

There was no time to remonstrate further. The Duke himself came into the valley on his gleaming black horse, gazing around him with an air of wary interest. He had no entourage at all, no army of hangers-on. Not even a groom. Just himself, yet he alone seemed to fill up every corner with his vast presence.

He had left off his black garb in the afternoon heat, wearing instead a wheat-coloured linen coat over his buckskin breeches and high boots. His bright hair fell to his shoulders, under the shadowing brim of his hat.

Sir Walter hurried forward to greet him, and even Cory followed, dragging her feet only a bit before making a proper, pretty curtsy. But Clio found she was quite frozen to the spot, unable to move even one step on seeing him again. Seeing, feeling, the reality of his presence.

It was one thing to think about him, to ponder his mysterious motives and try to push away her own tangled feelings for him. But it was always something else entirely to be face to face with him in the stark light of day.

He swung down from his horse, shaking hands with Sir Walter, bowing to Cory. He slowly drew off his riding gloves, watching thoughtfully as her father gestured to the villa, the cracked steps leading to the agora. She saw that he did not wear his rings today. There was no gaudy sparkle of emeralds or rubies, no antique stickpin in his simply tied neckcloth. No satin waistcoat, either. Nothing to distract from his austere beauty. His simple clothes, his solemn mien, it all spoke of a seriousness of purpose here.

A purpose she still could not get to the bottom of.

Her father and Averton turned toward the pavilion where Clio stood, making their way slowly as Sir Walter talked and gestured avidly. Averton nodded, listening intently.

Edward, she thought suddenly. He was not the Duke today. He was Edward.

And she was shocked to realise she wanted to run forwards and throw her arms around *Edward*'s neck. To feel the press of his lips on hers as he lifted her from her feet, twirling her around and around as the world blurred and crumbled around them. No Duke, no Lily Thief, just Clio and Edward, free to feel and do whatever they chose. To forget the past.

As if such a thing was even possible. Clio was too much a realist to believe *that*.

She smoothed her skirt as they drew closer, folding her hands tightly to still their trembling. To keep them from reaching out for him.

'…should be here soon with our meal,' Sir Walter was saying. 'In the meantime, perhaps you'd care to see the mosaics of the villa. They are extraordinarily well-preserved.'

'I would like that very much, Sir Walter,' Averton answered. 'Everyone speaks of their beauty. Good day, Miss Clio. It is most pleasant to see you again.'

Clio swallowed past the dry knot in her throat. Where was that grappa when she really needed it? 'And you, your Grace. Father is always so happy to have someone new to Santa Lucia to show off his villa.'

'I'm honoured to be allowed to see it. I haven't yet had time to see any of the sites of Enna properly.'

'I think there are too many to see "properly" in a decade,' Clio said, surprised to find that she *could* chat politely with him. 'We have been here many weeks now, and my family have not even been to the castle. We've just seen it from a distance.'

'It isn't *Greek*, of course,' her father said dismissively. 'Just thirteenth century. Far too new for me.'

'But lovely, or so Rosa says,' Clio answered. Rosa also said it was haunted, just like Clio's 'cursed' farmhouse, but she didn't mention that.

'Rosa?' Averton asked.

'Our cook,' said Clio. 'Her family has lived in Santa Lucia for generations. She seems to know every inch of the land.'

'Then if she says the castle is worth seeing, she must be right.' Averton glanced at Clio, his expression unreadable under the shadow of his hat. 'Perhaps you would care to accompany me there after luncheon, Miss Clio? We could discover it together. And you, too, of course, Sir Walter.'

Her father laughed. 'Oh, no, not me! I have work to do on things that are truly old. But you two must go. Clio has been wanting to see it, have you not, my dear?'

'Well, yes, but…' she began.

'Then it is settled. Now, you really must let me show you the mosaics, Averton. Especially the mermaid in the baths. So extraordinarily well preserved.'

Clio watched helplessly as her father led Averton away. It seemed she was now committed to an outing with the Duke. Or was it with Edward?

Either way, she would have to watch her step very carefully. Any unwary move in this slippery game they played would send her tumbling right down into a new abyss.

'Just don't push him off the battlements, Clio,' Cory whispered. 'That would surely not be polite.'

Edward nodded as Sir Walter pointed out the sections of his villa, the old peristyle hall, the long space where the women had their weaving looms, the walled gardens. He listened closely, yet his attention was not on the ancient past. It was on the all-too-near present.

Clio sat with her younger sister in a pavilion, her dark red hair cast in shadow, her face unreadable. Servants scurried around them, setting up their luncheon, yet she was an island of stillness.

She had agreed to show him the medieval castle, but how did she feel about that? About spending yet more time with him? How did *he* feel about that?

Edward frowned, nudging at a bright mosaic tile with his boot. Self-examination was not what was needed now; action was. He thought of the dark house on its poor street, of what he had learned in his secret space there. Santa Lucia was not safe for Clio, not if she kept wandering off on her own in the hills. He could warn her again, but would she ever listen?

Truly, Clio Chase was maddening! Every time he determined to stay away from her, from the complications of her fierce intelligence and lithe body, of her tangled past, something pulled him back to her. Pulled them together.

Just like this castle outing. Perhaps it was one last chance, a chance for him to persuade her at last to leave things alone. Persuade *himself* to leave *her* alone! If talking did not work…

Then more drastic measures were called for.

Chapter Nine

Clio led the way up the steep stairs carved in the rocky hillside, the only access to the castle, conscious at every moment of the Duke's footsteps close behind her. Despite the fact that he was a tall man, he walked softly, gracefully, an ever-present ghost. His movements were light, stealthy, as unpredictable as the clouds overhead, and as always when he was near her senses were poised and alert. He had taken her by surprise more than once in the past—he would not do so again.

She glanced back at him as they climbed ever higher, to find him watching her with solemn wariness, his face half-shadowed by the brim of his hat. When she had come to Sicily, she had been so sure she had left him and his all-seeing gaze far behind. Perhaps she had thought she would never even have to face him again! Face the truth of her own feelings. What folly that had been. Even when he was not in the same country, he was always with her.

In her distraction, her boot sole slipped on a loose pebble, and she slid backwards. Caught off guard, her stomach lurching in a sudden jolt of panic, she reached out to steady herself, but clutched only insubstantial air. Before she could tumble off the narrow walkway to the valley far below, a strong arm came around her waist, stopping her in mid-fall.

Breathless, Clio found herself caught against the Duke's warm, muscled chest, his embrace surrounding her, holding her safe above the chasm.

'You should watch your step, Clio,' he whispered. 'These paths are treacherous.'

'The entire world is treacherous, to those who are unwary,' she said hoarsely. She disentangled herself from his arms, pressing close to the rock-cut hillside. She could not leave him entirely, though. He held on to her hand, their bare fingers a lonely connection in that treacherous world. 'Thank you for catching me.'

'Oh, Clio,' he answered, an undertone of sadness in his voice, 'don't you know that I will always catch you?'

Before she could reply, he slipped past her on the narrow path, holding her hand as they finished the climb to the castle. They didn't speak as they walked through the broken archway into the old keep itself. It was not much of a castle any longer; a year-long siege in the twelve hundreds had broken down the sturdy grey stone walls, reducing the twenty towers to ten, then three, and now only one.

But Clio loved the tumbling piles of stones, overgrown with vines and twisted almond trees, the cracked floors and ruined arches, more than she could have loved any intact fortress. There were stories here, thousands of them, tales of heroism and death and passion that whole walls could never hold. The wind whipped through the fissures, bending the overgrown tree limbs, and bright green lizards skittered over the chipped rocks.

The rest of the island seemed so far away, insignificant. And even the Duke seemed to belong here. In London, he was bigger than life, an awe-inspiring figure of brilliant light among the drabness of the grey city. A person of gossip and speculation, of envy for his title, his money, his fine looks. Here, among old scenes of battles and tragedy, of power won and lost, he was no less impressive or unique. But he *belonged*. Belonged in a way he never really did in England.

Which was exactly how Clio herself often felt. Calliope was so good at playing the lady, at being respectable and admirable. Whereas Clio always seemed to find herself floundering, fighting. Endlessly seeking for something, some beacon of meaning that would never be found.

Here, in the silence and the ancient memories, she only had to *be*. Even the Duke—Edward—could not mar that. Indeed, he, too, seemed to find a rare stillness. He played no role of extravagant overlord. He merely stood there, holding her hand, and just *was* in this moment.

If only all time could be like this! But Clio knew well it never could. He would always be a duke. She would always be a thief. And the world would always be waiting, besieging these walls as surely as it had hundreds of years ago.

She gently disentangled her fingers from his, hurrying through the three interconnected courtyards that had once held together the castle towers. She raised the hem of her skirt, stepping carefully over rocks and birds' nests. 'It was built in 1082,' she said, her voice echoing off the walls. 'The Bourbons once used it as a prison, since those stairs on the hillside were the only access and were easily blocked. There used to be twenty towers; now there is only this one still intact.'

'And is it always so deserted?' he asked. 'So—haunted.'

'Not at all. My family haven't been here yet because it always seems so crowded with English tourists. And too many Sicilian guides trying to part them from their coins.

They are very good at that!' She threw him a wry smile over her shoulder. 'Everyone must have heard you were coming and obligingly cleared the way.'

'You see, there *are* advantages to a lofty title,' he said. 'Even an unwanted one.'

'I have never heard of a ducal title being unwanted.'

'Well, my dear, there is much about me—and about being a duke—you don't know. Fortunately for us both.' With those puzzling words, he strolled past her to the base of the tower, entering its tall, empty doorway.

The tower, constructed of weathered local grey stone like all the castle and most of the village, rose up three stories in clean, flat straight lines, covered in ropes of emerald-green ivy. A narrow, winding staircase gave the only access to the top, lit by old arrow slits.

Edward waited for her at the foot of the stairs. Without a word, without even looking at her, he held out his hand. *I will always catch you.* Clio slid her fingers into his, and they climbed upwards into the sky itself.

The steep stairs were covered not just with loose pebbles and windblown dirt, but by the detritus of the tourists: torn, trodden handkerchiefs; empty wine bottles; an abandoned phrasebook. Edward nudged all those out of her path with his boot, holding her steady as they moved through the pale, chalky light. She could hear only the scuff of their boots, the distant cooing of birds hidden high in the old beams. The rush of breath, the pounding of her own heart in her ears.

Even during her Lily Thief exploits, she had never been as anxious as she was in his presence. To be alone with him was a dangerous, unpredictable thing. She never knew what he would do; what *she* would do! Kiss him, hit him. Their meetings always ended in one disaster or another.

They emerged into the daylight at the very top of the old battlements. The wind was quick and chilly there, whistling past in swift currents that pulled at her hair and skirts. But the view between the crenellations was glorious. Rolling waves of Sicilian hills, glowing gold and purple all the way to Etna. And, in the other direction, the silvery expanse of Lake Pergusa, where Hades had snatched away Persephone as she gathered flowers.

Yet another unwary female, Clio thought. She herself should learn from Persephone's example. Never take your gaze from the horizon.

Edward leaned his elbows on the wall, his gaze narrowed on the lake. He had taken off his hat, and the wind tangled his hair, tossing it over his shoulders as the sun caught on those beautiful red-gold strands. He looked so alone.

Clio knew what it was to be alone. But even as she felt drawn to his side, she could not give in to sympathy or understanding. When she was weak, that was when she fell. She leaned against the wall beside him, staring out over the rugged landscape.

'I have never seen anything so beautiful,' he said.

'Nor have I,' Clio answered. 'But surely you have seen far more of the world than I have! Are you not a member of the Travellers' Club?'

He gave a half-smile, not looking at her but at the lake, as if he thought to see Persephone herself strolling its banks, flowers falling around her. 'I am.'

'Which means you have travelled to at least four countries. Seen all the loveliest, most exotic parts of the world. Places far more sophisticated and elegant than this rustic place.'

'For sophistication and elegance, Clio, one need not leave London. For real truth and beauty, though, I think a person must come *here*. Why would so many—the Greeks, the Romans, the Byzantines, the Saracens—fight to possess it?'

'And why do *we* come here, struggling to find our own corner of it?'

'Because we, too, belong here, of course.' He turned to her suddenly, his gaze so steady and piercing. As if he could see right to her heart, her most secret desires.

Clio slowly nodded. 'Edward,' she said. The sound of his name was so strange, so delicious, on her tongue. His eyes widened at her word—Edward. 'Why do you and my brother-in-law hate each other?'

His half-smile faded, until it was only a bitter little quirk at the corner of his lips. 'Ah, yes, the esteemed Lord Westwood. I dare say you *have* noticed something of our old—mistrust.'

'I dare say I have. Especially when it came to fisticuffs in Yorkshire.' Clio remembered all too well Cameron's anger that night.

Edward rubbed at his crooked nose, the only flaw in his handsome, Celtic-god face. 'When I first knew your brother-in-law, we were both young and foolish. Though I admit I was far more foolish than he ever was. He cannot forget what I was in those days.'

Clio studied him carefully in silence. His expression, that mocking smile, did not alter. But it was as if an opaque veil had fallen over his eyes, shielding his deepest thoughts and feelings from her. It was always thus with him, a dark core of truth hidden away. Obscured by the glitter of his position, the sheer strangeness and charisma of his personality.

'How very quizzical you look,' he said.

'I merely try to make out your character,' she answered.

He laughed. 'Such a useless occupation for such an intelligent mind as yours. And how do you make out in such an endeavour?'

'Not well at all. I have never been able to understand you. Even when I think I am close, you change on me.'

'How ironic that *I* puzzle *you*. For you, my dear Miss Chase, are as ungraspable as the sea itself.'

Clio smiled to think of the Mediterranean waves breaking endlessly on the rugged Sicilian shore, blue, green, grey, white, never tamed. There were storms and tides that could kill, hidden glories under the surface, a dangerously beautiful place. One that most people feared, but for a few hardy mariners it was home.

She was not like the sea. She was shore-bound by her family, by expectations. Yet he—he was like the waves. Unpredictable, irresistible. She could not resist moving nearer and nearer, that dangerous undertow catching her skirts and drawing her down for ever.

'What foolish things did you get up to when you were young, then?' she asked.

He shook his head, turning away from her to stare out over the landscape again. The wind tossed his hair over his brow, hiding his face from her. 'You don't really want to know. Young noblemen are a terrible breed.'

'Hmm. It is true that I have no brothers, but I am not entirely a sheltered, delicate miss. I know the sort of japes young men get into at university, or on their Grand Tours. You were probably no worse than dozens of others.'

'I was more spoiled than most,' he said. 'And more angry, too.'

'Angry?' Clio well knew *that* emotion. The burning helplessness of it. She stepped closer to him, then closer still. They did not touch, not even the brush of his sleeve on her hand, but she felt the heat of his skin, the clean, spicy scent of him, reach out to wrap all around her. Binding them together.

'What were you angry about?' she whispered, longing to know, to understand.

'You are thinking that I, a rich duke's son, had nothing to be angry about?' he said lightly. He gazed down at her with those veiled, jewel-like eyes. 'And you would be right.'

'Everyone has something to be angry about. Something to fight against.'

'Well, I fought against myself. Or, I suppose, against expectations of myself. Until my older brother died, of course.'

Clio stared at him, startled by his words, by the hint of pain that lay under them. Like sharks circling under the blue sea surface. Before she could answer, a party of tourists appeared in the courtyard far below them, their laughter echoing off the old walls. Their prosaic reality seemed to pierce the quiet, tense web around her and the Duke, tearing their isolation.

She moved away from him, pressing her back to the wall.

'I beg you, Clio, do not try to make out my character,' he muttered. 'I could not bear for you, of all people, to discover the truth of what I hide there.'

'Discover what?' Clio asked, her throat dry. She felt as if she were teetering on a crumbling precipice, staring down at the rocky shoals of truth. One sharp push would send her tumbling down and down, falling into that whirlpool that was *him*. She was surely closer to discovering the essence of him than ever. Yet did she really, truly want that?

Maybe she *was* one of those eccentric souls who were drawn to the mysteries of the dangerous sea.

'I am many things, Edward, but coward is not one of them,' she said. 'I am not afraid of you, even if your soul is as fearsomely black as this castle's dungeon. There must be a reason we keep meeting. Why our lives keep colliding. Perhaps I am meant to discover it now.'

He studied her for a moment, the air tense between them as the visitors' voices grew closer, louder. Finally, he nodded. 'I know very well you are no coward, Clio. But consider that you are warned. I am no fit company for a young lady.'

'Perhaps you are not. But Muses are contrary beings, are they not? Seldom sensible, and never wanting what is good for them. And I have told you before, I can't bear a mystery.'

'So, I am like one of your antiquary sites, am I?' he said, a thread of shimmering amusement in his voice. 'Just like your farmhouse.'

'Oh, no. You are beyond my poor excavation skills.'

He did not answer, but he held out his hand to her as they turned back towards the stairs. She took it, letting him lead her down the steep, dim tower as if he led her into the puzzles and perils of Hades itself.

Something had changed between them there on that windswept tower; she felt the crack and shift of it deep in her heart. What that change could be—if it would destroy her in the end, keep her as captive as poor Persephone—she did not know. But she realised there was no turning back now.

Edward followed Clio as she led him back down the winding path to the valley where her family waited. Here, in the shadow cast by the castle, the wind ceased its cold moan, sunlight lay in warm, golden ribbons on the dusty earth. Here the world was solid again, they were firmly linked to the elements of growing, living things, of the present and future. Yet the silence was just as profound, just as rich, as it was high up in their fairy-tale tower.

Clio's tall figure moved lightly through the glow of the sun, her skirts catching on the scrubby clusters of lavender and goldenrod. The wind had loosened her hair, long auburn tendrils that escaped their pins and lay against her long neck like silk. She carelessly brushed them back, leaving one dusty smudge on her cheekbone. She did not even seem to notice; her gaze, shielded behind her restored spectacles, was far away, full of inward thought. She didn't even seem to notice his close regard.

But that yearning, that burning desire he felt for her, became ever larger, a palpable, pulsating thing that overcame all else when she was near, when they were together. The touch and taste of her were intoxicating, all-drowning, far more than the alcohol he had craved when he had been young and wild. Clio wrapped around all his senses until she was all he knew, all he wanted. He forgot everything else, and that was dangerous. He needed to be alert here in Sicily, at all times.

She glanced back at him as they made their slow progress down the narrow hillside, her expression serious. 'I have heard many tales of this island since we came here,' she said.

'Magical tales, I'm sure,' he said. 'For Sicily is surely a land of rare enchantment.'

'Indeed it is. I've never been anywhere I loved more.' She paused in her steps, gesturing to the distant mountains, the sea beyond. 'Do you know the story of Erice?'

'Tell me,' he answered, captured by the soft intensity of her voice. The wild timelessness of the land that matched the woman.

'Mount Erice, which guards the port of Trapani, belonged to the Elymians, and is one of the most sacred spots in all the Mediterranean,' she said. 'Its founding stretches back to the very beginning of creation, when the Titans revolted against their father, Uranus. Kronos castrated his father with a great sickle, and threw his, er, organs into the sea off Trapani. And then, to mark the spot where her ancestor had died, Aphrodite, the goddess of love, rose from the sea on her shell and created Erice, making it her home.'

'And it was there she lured Butes, the Argonaut, with the sirens' song. She gave him a son, Eryx…'

'Who gave the mountain its name.' Clio smiled at him. 'You do know the tale.'

'I'm always keenly interested in the doings of Aphrodite.'

'So I've heard. You should know, then, that her feast day is coming soon, according to our cook, Rosa. She says they used to release a flock of white doves from the slopes of Erice, but she doesn't think they do it any longer.'

'And can one steal Daedalus's golden honeycomb there?'

Clio laughed. 'I don't know. It's one of the many mysteries of the island I have yet to discover.'

'Ah, yes. So many mysteries…' And surely the greatest of all was standing before him.

Her laughter faded. 'Indeed. But Demeter's feast day comes before Aphrodite's, far more useful, I think. We should get back to the villa now. My father will be looking for us.'

'Of course.' They continued on their way, the path still too narrow for them to walk side by side. Edward followed her, not holding hands as they had at the castle, yet still bound in some unseen way.

'You are to attend Lady Riverton's theatrical evening?' she asked.

'Yes,' he answered. 'She was the first to send me an invitation here. I must go where I'm invited, or I would be too desolate.'

She laughed. 'I can't imagine *you*, a rich, handsome duke,

would ever be left desolate. I would think rather you would have an excess of invitations, and would have to turn most of them down. Not that there is much grand society in Santa Lucia.'

'You think me handsome, then?' he asked lightly.

She looked back at him, one brow raised. 'You know you are.'

'I know no such thing,' he said. 'My mother used to call me her "barbarian", her marauding Viking.'

'Truly? My own mother sometimes said I was an Amazon, taller and wilder than my sisters, and I should have been named Hippolyta. But, of course, after Calliope my father was set on his Muses theme. And my mother obliged by giving him so many daughters.'

'Then perhaps we should forsake Sicily for a colder shore, where our warrior tendencies will be properly appreciated.'

'Is there such a place?' They came around a bend in the path, into sight of the valley. Sir Walter and his younger daughter were seated under the canvas pavilion where they had lunched earlier, their heads bent over a pile of books. Lady Rushworth supervised the servants in packing the used plates and platters.

Clio paused, her head tilted to one side as she watched them. 'I sometimes think I would love to travel for the rest of my life, finding what is beyond each new horizon. Discovering different lives, new stories. Yet even when I do sail seas and climb mountains, it is always the same.' She gave him a sad smile. 'I always just find myself there, going to parties and sipping tea.'

Edward knew how she felt. He found he could never run away from himself, either, no matter where he went. His ducal life was always there, along with the piles of invitations, the clamouring obligations. When all he really wanted right now was to stand for ever on a windswept tower with Clio Chase. How very strange was *that*?

Chapter Ten

Lady Riverton's palazzo was lit up like a Chinese lantern, glowing a hot orange in the dusty-black Sicilian night. Clio gazed up at the windows as she stepped from the carriage, watching as figures already inside strolled past the glass like puppets in a pantomime. They talked and laughed, silent behind the panes, raising glasses of wine, examining proffered trays of delicacies. A liveried footman held the door open for the Chases as they made their way through the manicured courtyard.

How terribly civilised it all was, Clio thought, stepping into that light and noise. As if it were a million miles from the windswept medieval tower, the grey stones that whispered of battles and death and old, old gods.

She remembered what Edward had told her when he had first appeared at her farmhouse, that there was danger here. Well, at *this* house danger surely dared not show its face. The only real peril was in possibly finding oneself cornered and talked at by Lady Riverton's voluble friend, Ronald Frobisher. All in all, Clio preferred curses and spirits.

She surrendered her cloak to another footman, examining

herself in one of the gilt-framed mirrors hung on the marble foyer walls. She had left off her brown-and-grey work dresses for a gown in jade-green silk, trimmed on the bodice and cap sleeves with finely spun gold lace. Her hair was smoothed and pinned up, bound by a scarf of more gold lace. She wore a pair of antique Mycenaean gold bracelets over her gloves, pieces that had once been part of her mother's vast jewellery collection. The silk and lace, the gold, it was all an armour of sorts, a disguise carefully constructed to make her appear a fashionable lady, a part of this glittering throng, while her true thoughts were always hidden.

Thalia hurried into the drawing room, her blue eyes glowing with purpose, her pink-and-white muslin skirts whispering softly around her. In her gloved hands she held her rolled *Antigone* script. Clio followed slowly, staying to the back of the room until she had gauged the lay of the land.

Lady Riverton held court by the ornate plaster fireplace, clad in eye-catching red-and-bronze brocade, an elaborate plumed turban atop her curls. Next to her stood Ronald Frobisher, her 'special friend'—or lapdog, as Clio sometimes thought him—a man of delicately slender stature, lovely brown eyes and soft, dark curls. He claimed to be descended from the great Elizabethan mariner, but his life seemed to consist of naught but fetching and fawning. The two of them chatted happily away as they greeted guests, but Lady Riverton kept a sharp eye on the trays of wineglasses and lobster tarts, the new arrivals at the door.

And a great many arrivals there were. Clio slid into a corner near the stage, behind a pair of large comedy/tragedy statues. All the English families were there, the Darbys and Elliotts, the young Manning-Smythes, and also the noble Sicilian families who had not yet decamped to Naples. They stayed mostly in their own tribal clusters at the other end of the room, deigning to grace the foreign proceedings with their dignified presence.

Did they come for the food, then, as her father did? Clio watched as one black-silk-clad matron slid a tart into her reticule. Or perhaps they came to keep an eye on their local antiquities.

Well, whatever their reasons, they certainly added an *ancien régime* dignity to Lady Riverton's proceedings, and filled out her vast rooms quite nicely.

Thalia was making her own progress around the drawing room, trailed by the puppyishly devoted Peter Elliott. She seemed not to notice him, but he now carried her script for her. No doubt he would bear her shawl and reticule, too, if she would let him. Clio's father had found Lady Rushworth, and they were examining one of the cases of the late viscount's coins.

So, Clio thought, everyone was accounted for. Except for the most important piece of all, the Duke. He was nowhere to be seen, and surely if he was there she would sense it. He filled every room he entered; everyone always watched him.

As the moments ticked by, Lady Riverton's smiles became just a tad more brittle, her glances at the door more frequent. She, too, missed her most prominent guest. She took Mr Frobisher's arm, whispering fiercely in his ear until he scurried away on a new errand.

Someone slid up next to Clio in her corner, but she knew it was not Edward. She could sense it.

'Ah, *cara*,' Marco whispered. 'Such an amusing little fête! You English are always so endlessly diverting. I have missed it since I left your shores.'

Clio turned to smile at her old friend, her old partner in crime. He *was* handsome, she had to admit. Probably the most handsome man she had ever seen, a young Roman god with his dark eyes and broad shoulders, with those cut-glass cheekbones and smooth olive skin. He had surely broken hearts in a sad trail from Florence to London and back, hearts he scarcely noticed for he was devoted only to his studies. His burning Florentine patriotism.

But when Clio was near him, she never felt that still, hot *awareness* that came over her when she saw Edward. Marco never made her breath catch, her heart pound. They were friends, that was all; they understood each other, helped each other. It was a great pity, really. Forming an attachment to Marco would be less complicated than carrying a torch for Edward! A lot safer, too.

'So, you did not go on to Palermo after all,' she said.

'And miss this fine party? Never! Especially once I found you were here. It has been far too long, *cara.*' He gave her a melting glance from his chocolate-brown eyes, a woeful, lovelorn gaze that had made many a maiden melt into a puddle on the floor.

It made Clio laugh. 'Shameless, Marco!'

He laughed, too, a rueful sound as he reached for two fresh glasses of wine from a passing footman. He handed her one. 'Ah, Clio, my charms never did work on you. Am I getting old? Losing my romantic touch?'

'Never fear. I just know you far too well. But you are still the loveliest man I have ever met, and you are sure to garner many new hearts here in Santa Lucia. Susan Darby is already in love with you, I think.'

Marco gazed over the gilded rim of his glass toward Thalia, who was laughing with the Elliotts, her blonde hair a luminous halo in the candlelight. 'What of your pretty sister? Is she in love with me?'

Clio snorted. 'Thalia? I wouldn't count on *that*, my friend. She might look like an angel, but she has the soul of a demon. Be careful, or you'll find yourself galloping around the amphitheatre doing her every bidding. She has that effect on men, you see.'

Marco frowned. 'I never do a lady's bidding. Except yours, of course.'

'Only because *my* bidding helped you achieve *your* goals—bringing antiquities back to Italy.'

'Very true. You do know me too well.'

'So, what are your goals here in little Santa Lucia?'

He glanced quickly around the bright, crowded room, and shook his head. 'We shouldn't talk about it here.'

'Of course not.' Despite herself, despite her promises of reform, Clio felt the old excitement flutter deep inside, wakening from its long, respectable sleep. The excitement of secrecy and mischief, of righting old wrongs.

She tightened her clasp on the stem of her glass, until the heavy crystal bit through her glove. *No.* No matter what Marco was up to, she could not be a part of it. She had promised Calliope.

But surely it would not hurt just to *hear* what was afoot…

'Send me a message later,' she whispered.

Marco gave her a solemn glance, quite unlike his usual teasing flirtation. 'Be careful, Clio. There are things going on here, things that could be very dangerous.'

You are in danger—she remembered the Duke's words. Remembered Rosa's ghosts and curses, the deceptively lazy men in the piazza. 'Dangerous? Here in this sleepy town?'

'Surely you know, better than most people, how appearances can be ever so deceiving.' He placed his empty glass on Comedy's pedestal and folded his hands behind his back. 'Just be cautious in your work. Promise me, my friend?'

'I am always cautious.' Almost always, anyway. Just not when she found herself kissing Edward, unable to stop. She gulped down the last of her wine, even though the alcoholic bite of it could not erase the remembered taste of *him.*

Almost as if her thoughts had conjuring powers, the drawing room doors opened and the Duke himself stepped inside. And he *was* the Duke tonight, not Edward, not the man who had stood with her atop the tower and stared down into the whirling maelstrom of something they could not understand. Could not control.

His evening coat was of a glistening sapphire-coloured velvet, with diamond buttons and blue satin trim, over a fine gold brocade waistcoat. He wore his rings again, heavy, archaic gemstones that glittered distractingly on his long, elegant fingers, concealing their true strength.

She recalled the rough grace of those hands on her bare skin, the sparkling magic of them that seemed to flow from his very essence into hers, binding them together more than mere touch, mere sex.

Clio shook her head, trying to drive out those memories, those needs. Lady Riverton's crowded drawing room was no place for her lustful feelings. No place to start any new whispers circulating.

She watched, feigning only casual interest, as Lady Riverton's brittle smile lightened into radiant welcome. Trailed by Mr Frobisher, she hurried across the room to greet this long-awaited guest of honour.

The rest of the company also seemed to turn as one towards the door, once they realised who had arrived. A soft web of awed hush fell over all the loud chatter, the clink of crystal and china. A duke—and not just *any* duke, but the elusive, handsome Duke of Averton!—had joined them. A new kind of glamour-glitter fell over their little party.

And, if she was honest, over Clio, too. When he stepped into the room, even if they did not look at each other, she felt overcome by a flushed, giddy awareness that was not at all like her. He *did* bring a sort of magic with him, something that everyone felt. But it was the deceptive magic of the underworld, and she could not give in to its alluring, pomegranate-laden trap.

'What is *he* doing here?' Marco muttered roughly.

Clio glanced at her friend to find a dark glower on his face, his shoulders tensed under his elegant dark green coat as if he would rush forwards and attack the Duke, right in front of everyone. Rush forwards to avenge what had happened in Yorkshire all those months ago, when they had lost the Alabaster Goddess. Marco and Cameron both had this violent reaction to Edward, then.

Clio laid a gentle, restraining hand on his arm, holding him at her side. Every muscle in his body was taut with anger, yet he stayed with her. For the moment.

What would he do if he learned that the Alabaster Goddess, Artemis, was possibly here in Santa Lucia? Or did he already know? Perhaps that was his reason for being here in the first place. To finish what had begun in Yorkshire.

But there was genuine surprise in his aspect, in those fireworks in his eyes. So, if it was not for Artemis, why was he here?

Why had they all converged at this one moment, in this place?

Clio's head suddenly ached, and not from the wine.

'I don't know why he is here,' she said quietly. 'Probably just sightseeing, like the rest of us.'

'Sightseeing? Dear Clio, surely you do not believe that. He is here to make mischief.'

Unlike you, of course, Clio thought wryly. She watched as Edward raised Lady Riverton's gloved hand to his lips, as that lady laughed, blushing a glowing pink. Mischief just followed them—all of them, Marco, Edward, herself, even Thalia—wherever they went.

'Well, he will have to escape Lady Riverton's clutches before he can hope to make any trouble for us,' she said. 'And that won't happen any time soon. Shall we sample some of those stuffed mushrooms? All this confusion makes me quite famished.'

Marco still did not look at all happy, but he went along as she led him across the room to the trays of refreshments. She held firmly to his arm, talking resolutely of the superficial charms of lobster and white soup. Thalia joined them, and, as usual, her fairy-like beauty distracted male attention from more martial concerns. Once Marco was focused on charming Thalia, Clio glanced surreptitiously at Edward, who was being seated by their hostess near the front row of gilded chairs set up before the stage.

Even as he smiled politely at the viscountess's flutterings, Clio could tell he watched *her.* Her and Marco. His green-gold gaze beamed across the room, and it was as if they were alone in the very midst of the noisy crowd.

She still remembered the gallery at Acropolis House in London, the Alabaster Goddess and her steady bow. The crackle of the air, so heavy with fury and passion and raw need as he grasped her arms in her green silk sleeves. As he dragged her closer, closer, until she could not breathe…

Clio choked on a bite of mushroom, gasping as Thalia thumped her on the back. 'Clio! Are you quite well?'

'Signorina Chase, have some wine!' Marco cried, thrusting a full glass of Marsala into her hand.

'Thank you, I'm quite well,' Clio gasped. If she drank any more wine, she would have to be carried home. At least it was not Paolo's grappa. *That* stuff would send the night spinning completely out of control. 'Just too greedy for the mushrooms.'

'Well, there is no time for that now. The theatricals are about to begin,' said Thalia. She frowned up at Clio, as if she suspected her sister would be taken ill again at any moment. Felled by those pernicious mushrooms. 'Are you sure you are well?'

Clio gave her a reassuring smile. 'Very sure.' The rest of the guests were indeed taking their seats, and the young Manning-Smythe couple were preparing their *Romeo and Juliet* tableau. A papier-mâché balcony, twined with artificial ivy and roses, simulated Renaissance Verona.

'We should find some empty chairs, then,' Clio said. 'Some that are quite close. But aren't you meant to be changing into your costume, Thalia?'

Thalia shrugged carelessly, but Clio noticed her fingers nervously plucked at a fold in her pink satin sash. 'Oh, no, I'm the last performance. Besides, I'm not going to wear my costume. The drama will have to come from the *words*, you see.'

'No fear of that, Signorina Thalia,' Marco said gallantly. '*Antigone* is highly dramatic, and you, I can tell, will be perfect for the role of the doomed princess.'

Thalia tossed him a suspicious glance. 'How can you tell that, Count di Fabrizzi?'

'Because I have made a study of ancient theatre, and you have Antigone's great passion, her great capacity to do what is right—even when it is not easy.' He looked at Clio. 'Your whole family is like that, yes?'

Thalia peered between Clio and Marco, her lips pursed as she nodded. 'I suppose we are, in a way. Complete nuisances, the lot of us. But you say you are a student of theatre, Count? How very fascinating, and useful…'

Thalia took Marco's arm in a light clasp, turning with him towards the chairs with a most determined look on her face. Clio followed, sure of one thing now—she would soon see Marco on the amphitheatre stage, Haemon to her sister's Antigone.

But that was really the only thing she knew. The rest was still obscured by shreds of silvery mist, a disguising shroud that only allowed her fleeting glimpses. Like Etna on a stormy day. Soon, though, like the clouds parting, she would discover all.

'"O City of Theba! O my country! Gods, the fathers of my race! I am led hence, I linger now no more. Behold me, lords, the last of your kings' house—what doom is mine, and at whose hands, and for what cause—that I duly performed the dues of piety."'

Edward watched as Thalia Chase finished her dramatic scene, her arms folded and gaze cast forwards towards eternity. She was really quite good, he thought. Despite the fact that she wore a stylish pink-and-white muslin gown and jewels of pink pearls and diamonds, he had forgotten where they were for a moment. Forgot the modern world outside, transported by her simply spoken words, her solemn, dignified mien to ancient Greece. To a land of warring principles, of strict gods, high-minded maidens, unbending kings, and love destroyed by it all.

And he was not the only one so moved, either, to judge by the taut silence in the room. The breathless pause before everyone broke into effusive applause. Thalia made her curtsy, her eyes shining. It was really too bad she was a Chase, a baronet's daughter, he reflected as his applause blended with the others'. If not for her position, she would reign supreme on the London stage.

He watched as Clio turned to say something to her father, clapping madly. Her face glowed with pride for her sister, and for an instant Edward felt a strange, wistful pang. How must it feel to know you belonged with someone, with a family? That you were part of something larger than your own solitary self, that no matter where you went or what you did someone cared about it. Supported it. Loved it.

It sounded like a dream to him, a bright fantasy-world he had never actually seen except in Clio and her sisters. Nothing could break their loyalty and love for each other. He could only admire it, protect it, from afar.

He glanced toward the man who stood along the wall, alone. The dark, far-too-handsome Italian Count who had been Clio's cohort in Yorkshire. He was a gypsy-thief no longer, but a polished, well-dressed gentleman who had all the ladies sighing. He and Clio had seemed to take no notice of each other during the performances, but Edward had seen them talking quite cosily together when he had arrived. As if they made secret plans.

Blast the man, anyway! Blast him for his easy charm, that comfort and understanding between him and Clio. The Count's appearance in Santa Lucia was yet another shadowy fold in a mystery.

Edward had known when he set out for Sicily that his task would not be an easy one. Too little was known of the treasure. But the secrecy of the local townspeople, the determined sociability of the English visitors, and especially Clio's involvement, made it all that much harder. Matters were seldom simple where she was concerned.

So, progress was slow, but it was early days yet. And he was a very determined man.

Lady Riverton took the stage as Thalia exited. 'My dear friends!' Lady Riverton said. 'Miss Thalia's performance was, alas, the last of this evening's theatrical scenes. Yet I think you can agree we have a wealth of rare talent here in our little community.' There was more applause, and Lady Riverton made a pretty curtsy, as if she alone was responsible for that 'wealth of talent'.

But then, poor old Viscount Riverton, though an excellent judge of ancient coins, had been no keen judge of females. A pair of pretty eyes had quite blinded him to a certain lack of good sense.

Not that Edward was in any position to judge someone else's choice of love!

'There is, however, a supper waiting for us in the dining room,' Lady Riverton continued. 'If you would all care to join me?'

A great rustle and commotion arose as everyone made their way out of the drawing room, gilded chairs pushed back, the stage abandoned. Edward kept to the edges of the crowd, hoping to evade their hostess's attention for a moment. She soon gave up looking for him in the press, and took the Italian Count/gypsy's arm instead.

The Chases, he noticed, also lagged behind, lingering among the chairs.

'Lady Rushworth has a headache, and I said I would see her home,' Sir Walter was saying, as Edward listened in the sudden quiet. From the open double doors of the dining room could be heard the clink of china, the rise and fall of laughter. But the Chases were an island to themselves.

'And,' Sir Walter added, 'I must admit I am quite tired myself. These social evenings are quite fatiguing. I don't know why I come.'

'Are you ill, Father?' Thalia asked in concern.

'Not at all, my dear. Merely tired. I would like to get an early start at the villa tomorrow, also.'

'We will go with you, then,' Clio said.

'No, no! Thalia must stay and enjoy her theatrical triumph. I will send the carriage back for you…'

'Forgive me, Sir Walter,' Edward said, stepping forwards. 'I could not help but overhear. If Miss Chase and Miss Thalia would care to stay longer, I can see them home after supper. My house is not far from yours, and it is the least I can do to repay Miss Chase's kindness in showing me the castle.'

'Ah, Averton!' Sir Walter said happily. 'Very good of you, I'm sure. It would certainly make me feel more at ease to know they were with you. So late to be out and about.'

'Father,' Clio said, shooting Edward an unreadable look, 'we really should go home with you, I think.'

'Yes, indeed,' Thalia agreed, but her glance towards the noisy dining room was wistful.

'Nonsense, Clio,' Sir Walter said. 'You young people should have your amusements. Averton will see you home later, and I will no doubt be tucked up safe and sound long before then. Goodnight, my dears! Enjoy your supper.'

With no further to-do, Sir Walter took Lady Rushworth's arm and strolled out of the drawing room. Thalia, with a mischievous smile at her sister, hurried off to supper, no doubt to 'enjoy her triumph'.

For an instant, Clio seemed uncharacteristically non-plussed. She turned one way, then the other, as if seeking some recourse from his company. Finding none, finding indeed that they were quite alone for the moment, she turned back to him, her arms crossed.

'What did you do that for?' she asked quietly.

'Did you not want to stay for supper?' he asked, mock-innocent. At the castle, it had seemed as if they had come to a new understanding. Now, it was as if they had moved back two steps. Maybe a drawing-room party was not the right place for them. They belonged on that tower, or in a clover-dappled meadow, where there were no boundaries. No expectations.

'I would rather go home and finish some reading,' she said.

'I doubt your sister would agree,' he answered. 'And going home to read would be such a waste of your beautiful gown.' He offered her his arm, and she slowly slid her gloved fingertips into the crook of his elbow, letting him lead her towards the dining room. 'Also, I wished to take advantage of the time to ask you a few questions.'

'Questions about what?' she asked warily.

'Oh, this and that. Most particularly about your friend. The Count di Fabrizzi, is it?'

Clio stiffened, but did not pull away. Neither did she look at him, as a slight pink flush stained her cheeks. 'I hardly know him. Indeed, I did not know he was in Sicily at all until we met at Lady Riverton's tea.'

'Hardly know him? Ah, yes, I suppose you know only a gypsy nomad named Marco. A fellow most adept with a crowbar and lockpick.'

'I don't know why he's here,' she said stubbornly. 'But I do know he has given up his former ways.'

'Like you?'

'Yes. In fact, your Grace, his motives in coming here are as unknown to me as yours are.' She looked directly at him, a bright green stare that burned away secrets and lies, laying them both bare. 'Unless he is part of the "danger" of which you spoke. But you seem to be the only one who would know about all that.'

She broke away from him, making her way to an empty seat at the end of the long, food-laden dining table. Edward followed her slowly, reflecting that it had probably been a mistake to give her even the merest hint of why he was here. They were too much alike, curious and determined. They were like an inferno when they were together, burning all before them.

He would have to be far more careful in the future.

Chapter Eleven

Clio wandered the length of Lady Riverton's terrace, her sandalled heels slapping on the old white marble. Behind her, the tall glass doors were half-open, releasing patches of amber light, the hum of voices as the others gathered for an after-supper hand of cards. Before her was a row of terracotta pots, blooming with fragrant flowers and herbs that blended their bright colours with the darkness, the silvery glow of the waxing moon. Beyond the well-manicured garden was the village, quiet and peaceful—outwardly, anyway.

But, as Clio knew, quiet façades often concealed the greatest tumult.

She leaned her gloved palms on the cold stone balustrade, peering out into the night, the dim concealment and silence that had always seemed her friend. In only a few days, according to Rosa, the night would be torn by the music and illuminations of the springtime *feste*. A time to celebrate that fattening moon and the end of winter's chill, to hope for a good harvest and prosperous year to come. Once, it had been a feast of Demeter and her daughter. Now it was an excuse for a party.

What would *she* celebrate, hope for? What would the rest of the year hold for her?

Clio sensed she was at a crossroads of sorts, a turning of what had been and what was to come. She couldn't go on as she had, yet she could not go forwards, either. The Lily Thief was done, but not the ideals that drove her to such an extreme in the first place. What was she to do?

Clio heard the squeak of one of the glass doors opening, the soft sound of a footstep on marble. She knew who it was even before she turned, could smell his spicy-clean scent on the evening breeze, feel his beckoning warmth.

Edward placed a glass of ruby-dark wine on the balustrade by her hand. 'I thought you might be thirsty,' he said.

'Thank you,' she answered. She sipped at the sweet brew, half-turning to study him in the moonlight. His blue coat was dark as the sky itself, but his bright hair shimmered like a beacon, luring unwary ships on to deadly rocky shores. 'You don't have any yourself?'

He shrugged. 'I don't care for wine any longer.'

'Nor cards, either, it would seem,' Clio said, gesturing toward the doors, beyond which piquet and loo went on.

'I got my fill of such things when I was young.'

'Yes. I suppose we all have to give up that which is bad for us eventually.'

'Or be killed by it.'

Clio took another fortifying sip of the wine. 'I did give up my bad habit, you know. I promised my sister I would, and my work with antiquities has been strictly aboveboard ever since.'

She did not know why she felt such a need to assure him of that, but she did. She needed him to know that, why ever he had come to Santa Lucia, whatever he was trying to discover, she had nothing to do with it. She wanted only to work on her farmhouse, to be with her family.

'I know,' he said simply. 'I also gave up the bad habits of my youth. Yet sometimes our actions follow us far into the future, have consequences we cannot foresee.'

Clio studied him in silence, turning the glass in her hand. She ached to know what he meant, what had happened to him when he was young. She certainly knew he had got into the usual trouble of rich, titled young men—drinking too much, gaming. Frequenting women of dubious morals, no doubt. But for all the things about him that angered her now, common vices were not among them.

What she wouldn't give to find out the whole truth, why Cal's husband hated him. But Edward was not a person to give up his inner self so easily. And neither was she. Thus they circled each other, not entirely trusting, not certain, but attracted beyond all sanity.

'I really don't know why Marco is here,' she said. 'Any more than I know why you are here. I don't understand anything at all, it seems.'

Edward laughed. 'Then we have something in common, for I am as perplexed as you are. Perhaps your friend has come for the *feste*, eh? An acolyte of Demeter?'

'As you are the acolyte of Hades?'

'Indeed, my dear, you wound me. I have long sought to serve Athena, to absorb some of her cool wisdom. Yet she eludes me.'

'Was it Athena who sent you here? Or someone, something, more prosaic? The Antiquities Society, maybe.'

'Clio, I am a seeker, just like you. I travel here in search of scholarship. New sites, new works of art.'

'New ways of thinking?'

'That, too, my dear. And with you I find that every day.'

Clio finished the last of her wine, placing the empty glass back on the balustrade. 'You are not going to tell me why you are here, are you? Not beyond vague warnings of "danger", like infuriating Delphic riddles.'

'I have told you all I can, all I know. But you would be wise to take others with you to your farmhouse.'

Take others with her? When her quiet hours at the farmhouse were the only things that belonged only to her? 'Oh, Edward. Surely *you* are all I have to fear there.'

He gave her a strange smile. 'Clio. Have I not shown you that you have nothing at all to fear from me?'

From beyond the open door came the sound of chairs being pushed back. The voices and laughter were louder. The card games must be ending, which meant someone would soon come looking for her.

Clio glanced toward the doors, and when she turned back that smile was gone from Edward's lips. He was the Duke again, all calm arrogance. How many other masks did he possess?

'Shall we go in?' he said, gesturing to the palazzo. The jewelled rings on his fingers glittered.

Clio nodded, hurrying past him before she could do something truly foolish—like kiss him again. Clasp him so tightly he could never escape her, never hide from her, and she could lose herself in the essence of him for ever.

The drawing room was filled with clusters of people, conversing, studying Lady Riverton's collections as the servants set up tea. The chatter was quieter than earlier in the evening, but everyone was still clearly reluctant to disperse, to yet give up the amiable company of their own countrymen. Clio saw Thalia by the pianoforte with her swain Peter Elliott and some of the other young people, and she made her way towards them. Perhaps she could persuade Thalia it was time to return home. *Without* the Duke's escort, if it could be arranged.

Behind her, she heard Lady Riverton hail the Duke, latching on to him again. 'Oh, Averton, there you are! You are just the one to help me lead everyone in a new game.'

'Lady Riverton, I fear I am a hopeless fool at party games,' he protested lightly. 'My friends all quite refuse to have me on their teams for charades.'

'I vow this is *not* charades!' Lady Riverton answered. 'It is far more amusing. A little pastime I hear is all the rage in Paris. Gather around, everyone!'

Clio took Thalia's arm. 'Thalia, dear, should we depart? It grows rather late.'

'Oh, no!' Thalia protested, still obviously flushed with her thespian success. 'Not yet, Clio, please. Let's just see what this new game is. If it's not amusing, we can go.'

Clio found she could not disappoint her sister, not when Thalia was having such a good time. She nodded reluctantly. 'Very well. Just one game, though. An old lady like me needs her rest.'

Thalia laughed, and drew Clio with her into the crowd gathered around the fireplace, where Lady Riverton presided from her great velvet armchair. Clio and Thalia sat together on a couch, with Peter Elliott still staying close to Thalia. Edward stood beside Lady Riverton, his jewelled hands on his hips. His face was set in lines of cynical amusement, yet Clio saw tense suspicion in the set of his broad shoulders.

She, too, was suspicious. Party games were such a vast waste of time.

'Now, the title of this game is "Truth",' Lady Riverton announced. 'And it is perfectly simple. Everyone will surely be able to grasp it,' she added, with a glance at the giggling Susan Darby. 'Dear Mr Frobisher told me about it after his recent voyage to France.'

Mr Frobisher, seated on Lady Riverton's other side on a measurably lower chair, laughed. 'Yes, and it is *vastly* amusing! One discovers the most shocking things about one's friends.'

'*That* doesn't sound boring, Clio,' Thalia whispered.

No, not boring. Just potentially hazardous. Clio was certainly glad she had not overly indulged in the wine tonight, as it was clear that others had. Flushed faces and overly loud laughter flooded the drawing room.

Not with Edward, though. He folded his arms across his chest, looking quite as wary as she herself felt.

'Now, as I said, it is a simple game,' Lady Riverton said. 'We will go around the circle, and each of us will tell one truth we have never before revealed. The best truth of all, the most shocking, will receive a prize.'

'Oh, how delicious!' Susan Darby cried, clapping her hands even as her mother tried to restrain her. 'May I go first?'

'Of course, my dear Miss Darby,' Lady Riverton said, exchanging amused smiles with Mr Frobisher.

'I bought *two* ribbons at Signora Cernelli's shop yesterday, instead of only one. It was *red*,' Miss Darby said in a hushed voice. 'I hid it in my dressing-table drawer.'

Mrs Darby rolled her eyes, and Clio bit her lip to keep from laughing. It was a good thing her father had left early; his intellectual heart would cry out in fury at such twaddle! Ribbons had never interested him in the least, despite all his female offspring.

'I hardly think that will win the prize,' Thalia murmured

in Clio's ear. 'Perhaps everyone would like to know how we used to swim in the pond at Chase Lodge, wearing only our old chemises…'

'Don't you dare!' Clio whispered back. 'Though I'm sure the tale would liven up the proceedings considerably.'

As the circle moved outwards from Miss Darby, the 'truths' followed much the same vein. Pilfered teacakes, items lost and lied about, the time Peter Elliott told his parents he was going to Bognor Regis but instead went to Weymouth.

Clio suspected it would be a far more interesting game if only the older, married people were present without their offspring, with the wine and brandy flowing. But there were young ladies here, supposedly including herself and Thalia, and things could not get too out of hand. Though Clio was fairly sure Thalia had a whopper or two up her sleeve.

And Clio's own 'truth', of course, was a very great one. The Lily Thief, after all, had once made off with the Elliotts' own red-figure krater depicting the labours of Hercules, and sent it back where it came from in Tuscany in the care of Marco di Fabrizzi.

Marco's 'truth' was a romantic one. The girl he loved madly as a teenager had been forced to marry another, leaving him brokenhearted and sure he could never love anyone else. All the ladies in the room were left sighing.

Their hostess followed with yet another romantic 'truth', one that could have been easily predicted. 'I have had only one love, as well,' she declared, more dramatic than Thalia's doomed Antigone. 'One great, great love, my Viscount Riverton. Quite astonishing in these libertine days, I know, yet truly no one could ever compare to him.'

After her sniffles subsided, it was the Duke's turn. Clio watched him with great interest. Surely he, too, had a wealth of secrets he could share! His entire being was one hidden truth.

But his wry smile never wavered. The veil never lifted from his eyes. 'My truth is much like yours, Lady Riverton. I, too, have had only one love. Yet it was not to be.'

'Oh, Averton!' Lady Riverton cried, her hand pressed to her heart. 'How terribly sad.'

'Did she die?' Lady Elliott asked in a hushed voice, awed by the tale of the so-romantic duke.

'No, but she is far too good for me. Now, Lady Elliott, you must tell us your own secret.'

By the time the circle came to Clio, she had some faradiddle about how once, when she was a girl, instead of attending to her Latin lessons, she read one of her friend Lotty's horrid novels. *The Tragedy of Madame Marguerite*, she believed. And she enjoyed it. Very much.

But all the time she did not stop thinking about Edward and his 'one true love'. The perfect angel who was too good for him. Clio did not know the lady, of course, did not even know her name. But she was fairly certain she did not like her.

'Too good', after all, was a prickling reminder of how far she herself had fallen short of feminine perfection, in all ways.

Chapter Twelve

The next few days were quite busy, and Clio could not make it to the farmhouse site as the Chases were in an uproar preparing for the Santa Lucia *feste*. Sir Walter, at Lady Rushworth's urging, had agreed to host a small dinner party, and Thalia was occupied in planning for the costume ball that would occur in the town piazza.

She spent much time with visiting modistes, often calling for Clio's opinion, so Clio found herself running from kitchen to drawing room and back again, overseeing menus, examining fabrics and sketching seating charts. Not to mention answering invitations, as it seemed everyone in town insisted on holding some kind of event. The small local *feste*, celebrating favourite saints and the old worship of Demeter and her daughter, was overflowing its bounds.

But all the domestic commotion did serve one purpose. It kept her from brooding over the Duke. From wondering at every minute what he was doing. Most of the time, anyway. Well, *some* of the time.

On the morning of the first day of the *feste*, which would open with the masked ball that night, Clio went out early to buy fresh vegetables at the market. Usually the kitchen maid, a niece of Rosa's, went, but Clio longed for a breath of fresh air. A moment of quiet, for the bustling market *was* quiet compared to Thalia and her last-minute costume alterations. When she returned with her basket of provisions, she avoided the tumult of silks and tulles altogether and crept down the backstairs to the kitchen.

Rosa was working at twisting long strands of bread dough into ornate plaited loaves, painting them with olive oil until they gleamed. Over the fire, the kitchen maid slowly stirred a pot of something delicious-smelling, all herbs and preserved tomatoes. All along the walls were piled baskets and crates, containing delicacies for tomorrow's dinner party.

'I thought it was meant to be a small gathering,' Clio teased, hoisting her basket on to a work table. 'Not a Florentine delegation.'

'When a person eats at *my* table, they eat only the very best,' Rosa said, clearly pleased she would finally get to properly use her culinary skills in the Chase kitchen. 'Paolo has gone to find the right fish for my *tonno alla siciliana*. And for dessert, there will be *cassata*.'

'Cassata?'

Rosa shook her head at English ignorance of good food. 'Ricotta cheese with orange peelings and chocolate shavings on sponge cake. If Signorina Thalia does not drink up all the chocolate first.'

'She is too busy trying on her new finery, I think. She does so love a disguise, almost as much as she loves chocolate.' Clio gestured toward a brace of fresh rabbits, hanging from the beamed ceiling. 'I see Giacomo has been here.'

Giacomo was the only one of Rosa and Paolo's children who seemed not to have a vocation, beyond hunting—or poaching—Clio never asked. But he sometimes popped up with offerings, often chatting with Clio about antiquities and local mythology. He had a great knowledge of such things. She didn't ask where he had got *that*, either, for fear of discovering he was one of that dread breed of *tombaroli*. Men who raided undiscovered sites for antiquities to sell, and were not above murder and rape.

Rosa just grunted, not looking up from her bread. 'I will braise the rabbit with a marsala sauce for tomorrow's dinner.'

Clio nodded, sensing Rosa had no desire to chat at the moment. Not about Giacomo, anyway. She never wanted to talk about him. Clio went back upstairs to check on Thalia's couture progress.

The drawing room was scattered with lengths of silks, velvets and muslins, spools of lace and ribbon. Clio looked around, but could not see her father or Cory. They had probably taken refuge at the villa.

Thalia stood on the dressmaker's stool, undergoing final alterations on her costume. She had finally chosen the garb of a Venetian Renaissance lady, Clio saw, a high-waisted gown of gleaming ivory-coloured satin shot through with shimmering gold thread. Gold ribbons trimmed the tight sleeves and crisscrossed the bodice. Her blonde hair fell over her shoulders, crowned with a small gold satin cap trimmed with pearls.

'What do you think, Clio?' Thalia asked, fidgeting with the ribbons.

'You look like an angel,' Clio answered truthfully. '*You* should have been Juliet at Lady Riverton's theatricals, not Mrs Manning-Smythe.'

Thalia laughed. 'I have enough trouble being Antigone! Or even just trying to be Thalia.'

What if a person didn't know who they were at all? Clio wondered, as she sorted through a basket full of masks.

The dressmaker put the final touches on Thalia's hem. 'There you are, *signorina*! I think you are quite finished. Do you like?'

'I love, *signora*!' Thalia cried, hopping off the stool to spin around in an exuberant circle, a blur of white satin and floating ribbons.

'Now, Signorina Chase, shall we try yours?' the dressmaker asked Clio. She reached for another basket, drawing out a spool of black thread. 'There is much work to be done if the gown will be ready for tonight.'

'Oh, yes, do, Clio,' Thalia urged, slowing in her spins. 'I haven't yet seen your costume at all.'

'That is because I don't have time for fripperies like my beautiful little sister,' Clio teased. But the truth was she did love a disguise, just as much as Thalia did. Probably more. Was that not what life was, a series of disguises?

She slipped behind a screen set up in the corner, and quickly changed from her simple muslin morning gown to the basted-together costume. Her dress was the opposite of Thalia's, a creation of glossy black satin and cobweb-fine black lace that turned her into a Dark Queen. An empress of the night. With a jet-beaded black mask covering her face, and her hair drawn back under a tulle veil, surely no one would ever recognise her.

She would melt into the night itself, and discover the truth of all the puzzles that plagued her here in Santa Lucia. Even Edward could not hide from her tonight.

The town square was quite transformed after the sun set, with all the shops and booths shuttered, their façades draped with spring garlands and wreaths, all tied with fluttering streamers in green and white and gold. The full moon, amber-gold in the dusty purplish sky, shone down on the revellers, who spun and twirled over the cobblestones to old country-dance tunes. Tables of refreshments and wine were laid out under a portal, while on the cathedral steps presided the painted ivory statue of Saint Lucia. She was not usually brought out until her own feast day in December, but tonight she watched the celebrations with bright blue glass eyes, hands outstretched to receive offerings. At her feet were heaped fruits and flowers.

Around the perimeter of the 'dance floor' were set flickering torches, reflecting in the waters of the fountain, the closed shop windows, the eyes revealed behind beaded and feathered masks. Dancers wove in and out of the light, fantastic wraiths in black dominoes, rustling satin gowns, antique doublets, creations of brilliant fantasy. Saints and devils, Greek gods, dragons, princesses, butterflies.

Thalia clutched at Clio's hand in excitement, and Clio felt her own heart beat faster with anticipation. This was not like London masked balls, where everyone was meant to be incognito, but the world there was so small that each person was clearly identified. Here, it really was a great unknown. Behind that mask could be Mr Frobisher, or Peter Elliott or the Sicilian baker. Or someone else entirely. An exotic stranger. Or one of the deceptively lazy men who lounged about the piazza, watching, always watching.

'Oh, Clio, it is so beautiful,' Thalia whispered.

'Indeed it is,' Clio agreed. 'Most beautiful.'

Thalia was swept into the dance by a young man dressed as Harlequin in black and white silks. And Clio saw her father, dressed as Socrates, strolling toward the refreshment tables with Lady Rushworth in an elaborate Elizabethan gown. They would surely find friends aplenty, and talk about the work at the villa all night, just as Thalia would dance until dawn, as she was utterly inexhaustible. They wouldn't look for Clio for hours.

Clio turned and made her way toward the cathedral steps, keeping to the edges of the rowdy crowd. The music was intoxicating, spiralling higher and higher, carrying the noise and happiness on a great wave to the sky. She laughed as an Apollo tried to coax her into the dance, shaking her head until he whirled away.

She did want to dance, she realised with surprise. Dancing was not often her favourite pastime, and she was not graceful at it as Thalia was. But tonight the music, the torchlight, the beautiful masks, even the night itself, so very deep and dark and full of great possibilities, conspired to fill her with restless excitement. She wanted to whirl and whirl, until she was giddy, until everything blurred and faded.

But she only really wanted to dance in *one* man's arms. To find that mad passion only one man evoked in her.

Clio rubbed at her eyes through the mask, suddenly dizzy. Why had Edward come here at all, to remind her? When she was away from him, he haunted her thoughts, yet she could slowly find her balance again, come back to some sensible semblance of herself. Pretend. When they were together, nothing else seemed to matter. She was pushed off that precipice into a world where nothing at all made sense.

Clio hurried past the cathedral, the steps heaped with harvest offerings, and she could vow Saint Lucia's blue glass eyes followed her, seeing all. Knowing her every sinful thought. She fended off more invitations to dance, taking refuge behind the church.

The narrow street that ran along there was quieter, hidden from the party. She could still hear the music, the thunder of dancing feet and wild laughter, could see the torchlight flickering on the slick cobblestones under her feet. There was no one near, though, just a stray cat on a low wall and the flaking white stucco of the cathedral at her back. The glow of stained glass high above her head.

And, just a little further along the lane, the gates of Averton's palazzo. Clio peered closer at that arched shadow, the wrought iron slightly ajar in invitation to the garden beyond. One window was lit. Was that the room where the Alabaster Goddess resided?

Clio remembered that other masked ball, that other evening of champagne-fuelled revelry and strange disguises. She remembered taking refuge in the silent gallery, with Artemis. Remembered his hands reaching for her, and the longing, the terror she felt. Would it always be thus with her?

She shrugged her black tulle veil back over her shoulder, dragging in a deep breath of the smoke-tinged night air. This night was not that one; she was not the same person now. Edward wasn't the same, either, yet she could not say if it was he himself who had changed, or only her perceptions of him. But she would never go back to *that*.

She heard a slight sound in the shadows behind her, and spun around to find a cloaked figure standing by the wall. Despite the enveloping midnight-blue cloak, the chalk-white leather mask, she knew it was Edward. She faced him in silence, waiting with her breath caught in her throat to see what would happen.

'Does the Queen of the Night not care to dance?' he asked lightly.

Clio swallowed hard. 'I fear she lacks the grace for it.'

'And no doubt she is far too busy to practise. She has stars to rearrange, dreams to invade…'

Clio stepped closer, one tiptoe movement then another, her heavy black skirts and veils trailing behind her. She couldn't help herself, she had to be near him. He drew her, like a dark magician, that underworld god, luring her with shadowy promises of passion and freedom. 'Does she invade *your* dreams?' she whispered, suddenly bold. For she did know one thing now—she was not alone in this spell.

He reached out to touch the edge of her veil. 'Every night.'

Clio trailed her fingertips along the corner of his mask, down a loose lock of bright hair. His skin was warm and golden as sunlight, so alive—just like him. She could almost feel that powerful force of life, that flaming passion, flowing into her, coaxing her frozen heart to beat again. To want to know every part of life, every burning, fleeting, perfect moment.

She went up on tiptoe as he kissed her, twining her arms around his neck to hold him to her. She felt his own touch at her waist, drawing her even closer.

They fit so perfectly together now, their mouths, their hands, their bodies, as if made for this moment. Clio parted her lips, feeling the tip of his tongue touch hers. Their kiss was frantic, full of need, full of the hot desire to forget all the past and know only *now*. To fall into each other and be lost for ever, to be as one.

Edward pressed her back against the wall, his hands hard and hungry as they slid over her shoulders, tracing the curve of her breasts in her tight satin bodice. Clio moaned at the delicious friction, the sensations that shivered through her, fire and ice in the same instant. She forgot herself, her place in the world, her reputation, everything but the way he made her feel.

The way he always made her feel when they were together like this.

Vaguely, through the silvery haze of desire and need, she felt his fingertips trace the line of her bodice, drawing the thick fabric down to caress the bare curve of her breast. She twined her legs around his hips, holding him to her, not letting him escape until he gave her what she craved. She did not know what that was, only that she needed him more than air or water. He was like the warm flood of grappa in her blood, drugging, delightful.

Her head fell back against the wall, her hands tightening on his shoulders as she urged him ever closer. Her eyes drifted shut, blotting out everything but his touch on her naked skin. The warm, callused fingertips, the cold brush of his rings, the feel of his breath against her, mingling with hers.

He pressed a hot kiss to her neck, the sensitive spot just below her ear. She shuddered as his lips trailed along her collarbone, the curve of her bare shoulder, like a silky ribbon of fire, of molten Etna lava. Finally, finally, he placed a single soft, longed-for kiss on the upper curve of her breast.

The tip of his tongue lightly traced a circle on that soft, trembling skin, closer, ever closer, to her hardened nipple, just barely covered by her gauzy chemise.

Clio groaned again, tightening her grasp on his hips, drawing him deeper into the arc of her body. Through his velvet breeches, she felt the heavy length of his manhood, hard as iron with a desire that echoed her own.

She buried her fingers in his hair, holding him to her as his mouth finally touched her nipple, drawing it in deep to his kiss. She sobbed at the intense feelings, at the connection that was still not quite enough for her. At the desire that burned higher and higher.

As if she were indeed in a dream, a vision conjured by some goddess of the night to torment her. To drive her mad with crazy desire.

Through that haze of passion, she felt him draw back. Felt his kiss slide from her breast, leaving the skin cold as ice, felt him ease away from her until she stood on her own feet again. But he did not leave her entirely; his hands were still at her waist, tense, his forehead braced on her bare shoulder. Their rough, uneven breath mingled, their heartbeats pounding together until surely all the world could hear it.

Clio caressed his tumbled hair, her hand trembling. Oh, when, *when*, would this end? This terrible weakness, this painful yearning. She was not happy with him or without him.

'Oh, Clio,' he muttered. 'What you do to me…'

What *she* did to *him*? Clio almost laughed aloud. But then she just pressed one lingering kiss to his temple, to the life-pulse that beat there, clinging to him for as long as she dared before she let him go. She half-turned from him, adjusting her gown, drawing her veil forward to hide her flushed face. She sucked in one deep breath, then another, until she felt her trembling slow and stop.

'Clio,' he growled. 'I—'

'No,' Clio interrupted. Truly, she could not bear it if he apologised! If he made this all into something conventional and sordid. 'Masquerade balls do seem to cast some strange spell on us, don't they? Maybe we should avoid them in future.'

'Not *just* masquerade balls,' he answered wryly.

True. There were also castles, and ruins, and drawing rooms and meadows. Clio dared not look at him for fear she would jump on him again. So, she just laughed, and hurried on her unsteady feet back to the well-lit, welcoming noise of the piazza, and of real life.

Chapter Thirteen

Edward braced his palms against the rough wall, his eyes closed as he forced himself to breathe in deeply, slowly, trying to calm the fiery riot inside him. But he could still smell the fragrance of Clio's lily perfume in the air, still feel the warmth of her lingering on the cold wall. She was all around him, part of him.

His hands curled into tight fists as he thought of her, of all the times they met and clashed—and kissed. Her passion ignited needs he thought long buried; it inflamed his own lust until they were both consumed in the bonfire. He so longed for her that every part of his body ached from it—his heart, his flesh, his very soul.

It distracted him from his purpose here, blinded him to all but her, all but what they were when they came together. Something so strange and elemental, something that refused to be constrained.

The man he used to be would not have let himself be restrained. He would have taken what he wanted long ago, would never have denied himself. He was not that spoiled youth any longer. His heedless, impulsive actions had hurt others terribly. His family, his discarded mistresses, people who had tried to be his friend—and one sad-eyed young woman who haunted him still, a maidservant whose unwise love for that insufferable boy had led to her downfall.

He could not be that person now. Not with Clio. Even if the ache of it, of all that desire, killed him in the end.

Edward laughed ruefully at himself. Who would have imagined, ten or even five years ago, that he would be so constrained by honour? By his own version of courtly love? How astonished his parents and his long-lost brother would be to see it! They thought he would be a useless wastrel all his life.

He rubbed at the small, jagged white scar on his brow, the stark reminder of what happened when he forgot his resolve. He would not forget it again.

Clio made her way shakily back to the *feste*, strolling slowly around the edges of the dance. She watched the twirling, kaleidoscopic patterns through her veil, feeling far removed from all the music, the drunken laughter, as if she saw it all in a dream, a play.

Which was so very odd. This party should be the real life, so full of light and noise, and those frantic caresses in the shadows the dream. A tangle of emotions half-understood in the snare of darkness, but lost when daybreak came. Dispersed like so much smoke and fog.

Yet, more and more, the fleeting moments she spent with him *were* the reality.

Something would have to happen soon. Something would have to change. She could not stumble on like this for ever, wanting him with such a furious desire and yet so afraid of that wanting at the same time. Afraid of losing herself for ever.

Yes, she would have to take action. But what? She had never so longed for Calliope's sensible presence, her calm advice! She had never felt quite so alone.

Clio took a goblet of wine from one of the tables, sipping at it beneath her veil as she watched the crowd. Her father and Lady Rushworth sat with some of their friends under the shelter of a portal, conversing animatedly as they passed a platter of cheese and olives. Unlike at Lady Riverton's theatricals, he would have to be dragged away at the break of dawn. 'Old and tired', indeed!

Clio scanned the rainbow of brilliant colours, the masks and feathers and ribbons, searching for Thalia. At last she glimpsed her white gown, the gleam of torchlight on her pale hair. She was not dancing, but sat on the cathedral steps, laughing with a man in a red-striped cloak. They leaned together as they talked, and the man pushed his mask atop his head in one graceful, absentminded gesture, his gaze close on Thalia's face as she spoke.

Clio was startled to see it was Marco. He leaned one elbow on the step above them, gazing up at Thalia as if she was the only person there. The only one whose voice he heard, whose smiles he saw. And Thalia laughed again, her cheeks a pretty apple-pink under the edge of her gilded mask.

Clio frowned. Marco charmed dozens of other women just so, from gypsy camps to Lady Riverton's drawing room. She had watched him like this before. Thalia was not easily charmed, never easily fooled. Yet she *was* young, and she had the Chase quality of being headstrong and curious. And Marco was handsome, as handsome as Thalia was beautiful. If he hurt her sister…

He would certainly live to regret it. Clio would see to that, if Thalia did not unman him first!

Clio turned away as Thalia and Marco rose and moved back into the dance, hand in hand. Edward had not reappeared, and Clio was finally able to breathe again. She eased her veil aside a bit, strolling around the party, trying to guess who the various masks concealed. The shepherdess in bright pink brocade and diamonds was surely Lady Riverton, and the gentleman in the white fur cloak and painted sheep mask could be Mr Frobisher. The angel was Susan Darby, giggling with the Harlequin who had danced with Thalia when they first arrived. Was he Peter Elliott? For shame, to be transferring his affections from Thalia to Miss Darby so quickly!

Clio laughed, and took another sip of her wine. As she lowered the cup, she noticed a furtive movement just at the edge of the bakery building. A tall, muscular man in a rough brown cloak and white skull mask glanced back over his shoulder, his head swivelling quickly one way and then another before he ducked into the alleyway between the bakery and a shuttered vegetable stall.

It was only a flash of movement, unnoticed by any passer-by, but Clio knew all too well what an air of illicit activity looked like. Felt like. She could practically smell trouble in the breeze, more pungent than any perfume.

She set down her goblet and drew her veil back into place, creeping to the mouth of the alleyway. It was very dark here, darker than even the lane where she had met Edward. Yet her vision, filtered by the black tulle, grew accustomed to the dimness, and she saw a small patch of light at the end, emanating from one of the bakery's back windows. The man in the skull mask stood just at the edge of its glow, talking quietly with someone else, someone shorter and muffled in a hooded black cloak.

Clio felt her pulse quicken in excitement, with the tingle

of danger and secrecy. Holding her skirts close to still their satin rustle, she backed away before turning and dashing back around the vegetable stall. Hidden behind it, behind a pile of abandoned crates and the stench of rotting produce, she could barely make out their voices.

'But where can the objects be found?' one of them said, in a low, hoarse voice, muffled by a hood or mask. Clio could not tell if it was a man or woman, but the desperation was palpable.

'I told you, we don't know yet,' the skull mask said, rough with impatience. He spoke in English, but with a heavy Sicilian accent. Clio frowned in concentration, almost sure she had heard it before.

'But we have the bowl! Surely the rest must be near where it was found.'

'That piece must have been separated from the rest of the collection,' the impatient Sicilian said. 'We'll find the rest soon. We're digging whenever we can. It's close, I can feel it!'

'It had better be. This English customer was most pleased with the bowl, and is willing to pay a great deal of money for the rest. The silver is a rare find. It will set us up for life. Why can you not work faster?'

'You know why!' the Sicilian said angrily. Clio heard a rustle, as of a hood or mask being pushed back. Clio peered cautiously around the corner, and found that she had indeed recognised that voice. It was Giacomo, Rosa's rabbit-poaching son.

She felt a startled, sad pang for Rosa and Paolo, for the bitter realization that he *was* up to no good, and not just poaching. That he was one of the great plague of *tombaroli*. How dare he hurt his kind-hearted parents in such a way! How dare he destroy his own family's heritage? As Lily Thief, she had fought so hard against such terrible ills. She didn't want to fight again, not here.

'Those tomb frescoes last year were much larger and more complicated, and yet you delivered them in half the time,' the other person said querulously.

'No one was lurking around that tomb every day,' Giacomo answered, sullen. 'And the ghosts keep workers away.'

'That has never stopped you in the past. Take care of it. The English wants the silver, or nothing. If *you* want the money…'

'Of course I want the money!'

'Then do as I say. Take care of the site, and find the rest of the silver. No matter what you have to do. It must be there somewhere! All the indications say so.'

There was a snap of papers being unfolded, and the cloaked person said, 'This is what the English wants, the pieces in these sketches. Find it all within a fortnight, and there will be a fat bonus in your purse. Fail, and the consequences could be dire—for all of us.'

Clio stretched up on tiptoe, peering closer as the person hurried away, leaving Giacomo alone. He lowered his skull mask back into place, staring down at the sheaf of papers in his hand. Strangely, that hand trembled. She heard him mutter in Italian, something more about 'ghosts'. In her eagerness to hear him, she leaned too far forwards, accidentally nudging a crate with her toe. Startled by that scraping sound, she drew deeper into the shadows, not daring to breathe.

Giacomo spun around, scanning the alleyway, as nervous as a cat. She could smell his acrid fear. *Tombarolo* he might be, but perhaps not a very good one. Thievery required nerves of steel.

'*Chi è là?*' he called, glaring frantically one way then another. A slip of paper fell from his shaking hand.

'Ghosts,' he muttered, rubbing at his face with a shaking hand. He hurried out of the alleyway, tugging his cloak around him as if to ward off those ghosts everyone here seemed so afraid of.

Clio waited, perfectly still, until she was sure he was really gone. Then she tiptoed forwards, scooping up the lost paper.

As she peered down at it in the dim light, she saw it was a sketch of a small incense burner, the drawing carefully detailed and measured. It was carved with an elaborate relief of Demeter. An exquisite piece, even in the pencil sketch, and Clio had never seen anything like it except in the British Museum, which held the remnants of a Greek altar set.

She frowned as she tucked the paper into her sleeve. Giacomo had spoken of a bowl, a part of a great hoard of silver. Also temple pieces, probably, to judge by the fine style of the incense burner. It was a piece a collector, this *English* Giacomo and his cohort spoke of, would indeed pay a great deal for. Where were they digging for these pieces?

And who was the 'English'?

Clio had a sickening feeling that all the puzzles of the past few days were coming together, and they were centred on this silver. Was it the reason Edward had suddenly showed up in Santa Lucia? Was *he* the English who was after the stolen temple hoard?

She felt dizzy, remembering the long gallery at Acropolis House, packed with antiquities of every description—Greek vases, Roman statues, an Egyptian sarcophagus, Minoan snake goddesses, all jumbled together. She remembered the Alabaster Goddess, reigning over it all. He had vowed then that he had reformed his ways, that he worked for the Antiquities Society, that his task was to stop the Lily Thief and others of that ilk.

But perhaps the silver was too much of a temptation. Perhaps he had fought against his old ways and lost.

Clio shivered, suddenly icy cold and deeply sad. She crept back around the stall the way she had arrived, slipping back into the party. The moon was lower in the sky now; soon the night would give way to dawn. Yet she sensed that *her* darkness was only just beginning.

She sat down on the steps where she had glimpsed Thalia and Marco earlier, suddenly feeling so very old and tired. The music was louder than ever, but she seemed to be wrapped in silence.

From the crowd emerged a tall figure swathed in dark blue velvet, red-gold hair loose on his shoulders, like an angel. Everyone else moved in drunken, haphazard patterns, yet he was all predatory grace. She watched, still feeling that cold, dream-like distance, as he sat down on the step below hers.

Silently, silently, he leaned back against her legs, his head resting on her knees, heavy and sweet and reassuring through her skirts. She laid one hand lightly on his tousled hair, feeling the rough silk of it under her touch, the familiar rush of his pulse with hers. They sat there, wrapped in quiet, in that deep gulf between them, as the night spun on around them.

Oh, Edward, she thought sadly. *How can you be a villain?*

Or was it merely her heart who was the great betrayer?

Chapter Fourteen

The dinner party seemed to be going quite well.

Clio gazed out over the company from her place at the foot of the table. 'Hostess' was not her favourite role to play, but since Calliope's marriage it had fallen on her. Only until her father wed Lady Rushworth, of course. Luckily, Sir Walter did not often like to entertain in a formal way, and her domestic duties were not onerous.

And, she had to admit, there was something quite satisfying when a gathering came together so neatly. The conversation hummed along, assisted by the cosy number of guests, all with similar interests. Rosa's delicious food was much complimented, even though Lady Riverton threatened to steal her away for her own kitchen. The flowers, artful displays of local wildflowers designed by Thalia, were most lovely. And her father seemed happy, with the attentions of Lady Rushworth on his right and Mrs Darby on his left, both avid to hear about his newest discoveries at the villa.

Yes, it was all going very well indeed. The servants, relatives of Rosa and Paolo, hired for the evening, moved smoothly and quietly around the table. They made sure no one's plate or glass was empty, and left Clio with very little to do.

Except think. Which she had done ceaselessly since the *feste*. Her mind whirled until she thought she would scream with it all, and still she could make no sense of anything. The silver hoard that might or might not be real. The *tombaroli* and the 'English' who was going to pay them untold riches for their loot. The Duke—how did he fit in? It could be no coincidence he was in Santa Lucia just now, with a vast stash of illicit antiquities in the offing. Was he on another errand for the Antiquities Society, or had he fallen back into his old, unscrupulous collecting ways?

Did anyone, *could* anyone, ever really change? Or was the temptation sometimes just too great?

That was a conundrum she found herself wrestling with, far too often of late.

She nibbled at the cassata, studying the occupants of the table carefully. They were almost all 'English', all interested in antiquities and collecting. Which of them, behind their smiles and fine clothes, their polite chatter, would deal with thieves? Would steal and hide away what did not belong to them, but to the people of this island? To history?

Marco would surely know. He must have heard *something* about a discovery as rich and rare as a stash of temple silver. Yet they had had no chance of private consultation since he had come to Santa Lucia, and he had kept up his guise of light-hearted, flirtatious nobleman beautifully. Quite the actor, Marco was.

He sat next to Thalia, the two of them talking quietly over the dessert. Clio wondered what they spoke of after their little scene at the *feste*, their dances together. But their voices were too soft for her to overhear more than scattered words and laughter.

Edward was across the table from them, listening to Susan Darby's awed prattle with a polite smile on his lips. He had not touched the wine, Clio noticed, and barely eaten, though his compliments on the cooking seemed most sincere. He had not glanced at Clio since bowing over her hand at arrival.

She could tell nothing from his expression, his eyes, his oh-so-polite conversation. Even if they were alone, she knew she could not ask him about the silver. Could not confront him outright, as someone like Thalia surely would, an Amazon with no fear of attacking from the front. She would learn nothing, and the outcome of any battle would be uncertain indeed.

Despite their desperate intimacy, their kisses and caresses in the dark of the night, there was still a gulf between them of doubt and suspicion. A gulf she didn't know how to bridge, not with her own caution and reserve.

'I still have hopes, too, that Miss Chase will join us,' Mrs Darby said. The sound of her name shook Clio from her brooding, and she looked down the table to where Mrs Darby chatted with her father.

'I beg your pardon, Mrs Darby?' Clio said.

'I was just telling Sir Walter of our planned tour to Motya. The Phoenician sites, they say, are really quite worth seeing, especially the necropolis. The excursion would be so much more delightful if *you* were with us!'

'That is very kind of you, Mrs Darby,' answered Clio. 'I enjoyed accompanying you to Agrigento so much. But I fear I am too taken up here with work.'

'You should go, my dear,' her father urged. 'Mrs Darby tells me it is only an excursion of a few days, and the change of scenery would do you good. You have been working too hard of late.'

'Miss Thalia and I would be sure to take good care of your father while you're gone,' Lady Rushworth added. 'They do say the sea air is most bracing and reviving.'

Sea air? Did she look so much the pale invalid, then, that they all wanted to bundle her off for a salt-water cure? Clio felt the weight of Edward's gaze on her.

'I will certainly consider your kind offer, Mrs Darby,' Clio said.

'Excellent! We will not leave for a couple of days yet, plenty of time to make arrangements,' Mrs Darby answered. 'We plan to head home to England directly after the tour, so it will be the last time we can spend time with you until you yourself return to London.'

'You must come!' Susan Darby cried. 'Or I will be the only young person on the tour.'

'A great inducement indeed,' Clio said with a smile. 'We will be sorry to lose your society here in Santa Lucia.'

'And we shall be sorry to go,' said Mrs Darby. 'But my husband wants to seek a London publisher for his book. Is that not so, my dear?'

The conversation turned to Mr Darby's manuscript, and Clio sat back in her chair, gesturing to the servants to begin clearing. The Motya excursion *was* tempting, she had to admit. To run away from the confusion Santa Lucia had become, to just be a simple tourist for a few days, with her guidebook and the pleasant, undemanding company of the Darbys.

To be away from Edward.

Yet surely even miles of land, the vast sea itself, could not erase the way his kiss felt on her naked skin. The desire that trembled through her whenever he touched her.

No, she had to stay, to face whatever this was between

them. To discover what was happening here in sleepy, suddenly sinister Santa Lucia.

The ladies soon departed the dining room, leaving the men to their brandy and no doubt more talk about Sir Walter's villa. Clio made certain the tea tray was laid out in the drawing room before sitting down next to Thalia.

'You were having quite the coze with Count di Fabrizzi,' Clio whispered teasingly.

Thalia's eyes gave a quick lightning flash, veiled by her long lashes as she took a sip of tea. 'I have merely been attempting to persuade him to take part in my play.'

'Oh, indeed? So, it is merely for the sake of theatre that you spend time with him?'

'Of course.'

'It has nothing to do with his handsome eyes?'

'Clio!'

Clio laughed. 'You teased me about him before. It is my turn now.'

Thalia bit her lip, but Clio could see a smile threatening to break through. 'True. Very well, I admit he does have— handsome eyes. But I think his affections are already engaged.'

'Indeed?' Clio asked in dawning curiosity. She studied the ladies in the room: silly but pretty Susan Darby; her still-lovely mother; Lady Elliott with her bright red ringlets; and Lady Riverton, who was chatting loudly about some new jewellery she had just purchased. Who could it be? Or maybe it was a dark-eyed *signorina* back in Florence! Marco had broken so many hearts, surely turn-about was only fair. 'Has he confided in you? Who is it?'

Thalia shook her head. 'Oh, Clio. Do you not know?'

Before Clio could answer, Thalia rose and strolled over to

the pianoforte. Soon the tempestuous notes of Beethoven filled the room, and the other ladies gathered around the instrument. Lured, as people always were, by the siren song of Thalia's music.

Clio put down her own teacup and went to the window, gazing out at the garden beyond their little terrace. Thalia meant, presumably, that Marco was in love with her, Clio, but that was simply absurd. They were friends, allies, that was all. Despite his unearthly good looks, despite the ideals they shared, there had never been the spark of passion between them. Never a physical awareness, such as that which flowed between her and Edward whenever they saw each other.

No, if Marco was falling for anyone, it was surely Thalia. Clio saw the way he looked at her sister, so fascinated despite himself. She could not say she liked it. She knew what Marco was like, knew his hidden life, and she also knew that her beautiful, impulsive sister needed someone steady and calm. Not a wildly patriotic Italian count.

Likely it would come to naught, just like Clio's own passion for Edward. Clio was going to keep an eye on the situation, though. Starting, apparently, right now. Marco had appeared on the terrace, his chiselled features illuminated for an instant by the flare of a match as he lit a cigar. He seemed to be alone, having escaped from the dining room by one of the tall windows leading outside.

Clio glanced over her shoulder. The ladies were still gathered around Thalia as she moved into a Mozart sonata. Thalia loved an audience, and would thus surely keep everyone entertained for quite a while. Clio wouldn't be missed for a few minutes.

She slipped quietly out the door to the terrace, joining Marco where he stood by the steps leading into the garden.

'*Cara!*' he said with a wide smile. 'How very scandalous of you to join me out here, all alone.'

Clio grinned. 'Save your charm, Marco. It does not work on me, you know.'

He gave a dramatic sigh. 'Alas, I know it only too well.'

'Nor do my charms, such as they are, work on *you*. My sister suspects you are in love.'

Marco took a long draw on his cigar, wreathed in a disguising cloud of silvery smoke. 'Ah, yes, the beautiful Thalia, Muse of Comedy. She is indeed delightful. But also quite imaginative. I do not know why she would think such a thing.'

'Perhaps I am also overly imaginative. For I have been hearing such wild tales of late. Ghosts, curses, looted pieces of ancient temple silver.'

Marco smiled wryly through the smoke. 'That does sound like a novel, *cara*. Are you a writer now, like Mr Darby?'

'Are *you*? Otherwise I cannot quite account for your presence here. I am sure it cannot be on "business".'

'Your doubts wound me. Of course it is business, of the most vital kind.'

'Antiquities business?'

Marco nodded. 'I think so. What do you know of this silver?'

'Not very much. I know our cook's son is involved, I overheard him talking with someone at the *feste*. They spoke of a bowl, of finding the rest of the hoard to sell to some "English" collector. This buyer has apparently offered a great deal of money, if the pieces can be found soon.'

'So, they have not yet found them all,' Marco murmured. 'They must be getting desperate.'

Just like her! Clio felt quite *desperate* to know what was happening. She clutched at Marco's coat sleeve. 'So you *do* know! Tell me, I can help.'

Marco covered her hand with his. 'I know you can. There was none better than the Lily Thief. Yet I fear at present I know little more than you do. There have been some rather unusual pieces appearing on the market recently, and some of my— friends have traced them here. Enna is full of sites, both discovered and still buried.'

'What sort of pieces?'

'Coins, jewellery, finely carved grave steles. Silver.'

'Libation bowls, maybe? Incense burners?'

'Bowls, yes, but not yet anything like an incense holder. Have you seen one?'

'Just a sketch. Giacomo, our cook's son, dropped it at his meeting. Where—?'

She was interrupted by a sudden burst of fireworks, a shower of red and green and white that lit up the night sky in a crack of noise and fire. More celebrations in the village.

Surely the illuminations would quickly draw the other guests to the windows. She didn't have much time left. She squeezed Marco's arm and said, 'Send me a message saying where we can meet. I want to hear more about this.'

He grinned at her. 'And would you bring your lovely sister to our meeting? I have seldom seen such beauty *and* such spirit in one lady.'

Clio smacked his arm with the flat of her hand. 'Don't you dare turn your Florentine charm on Thalia! I don't want her involved in anything at all dangerous.'

'Oh, *cara*, I doubt you could stop her getting involved in anything she chose. She seems quite as stubborn as her sister. Perhaps more so.'

'That is all too true. And all the more reason for me to protect her. Promise me you will not embroil her in any of this!'

Marco sighed. 'I promise. And we will meet very soon. Perhaps I will have more to tell you then.'

Clio impulsively kissed his cheek, and spun around to hurry away. Another burst of sparkling light showed her they were not entirely unobserved. Edward stood at the dining room window, watching her. His expression was like a Roman marble statue, perfectly still and calm.

They stared at each other for one long, frozen moment before Edward turned away. Suddenly freezing cold, Clio dashed into the house. She drew her Indian shawl closer about her bare shoulders, but even its warmth could not ward off the chill that had invaded her world.

Clio paced the length of her bedchamber floor, first one way then back again. Books on the Punic War era were open on her desk, along with a new volume on late Hellenistic silver, but she could not concentrate on studies. Her mind was racing, her pulse thrumming with the need to *do* something. To move to action.

She stopped at her window, staring out over the rooftops of Santa Lucia. All seemed quiet enough now; even Etna was muffled in sleepy clouds. What seethed beneath such a surface?

The Picini palazzo was also silent, except for one lighted window beckoning in the gloom. Was the Duke awake, too?

Clio took in a deep breath. She had to think now, to be calm, not go off on a shower of emotions as brilliant as tonight's fireworks. That was what always happened when she was with Edward, and it would not help her now. Where was the silver, if it was indeed real? Where had it come from? And who sought it with such intensity? What meaning did it have?

She stared at that distant lighted window. There were many 'English' in Sicily, most of them collectors who vied to outdo each other. Surely any one of them would love to find a rare collection of temple silver.

Yet none of them cared about the art itself, about the history it represented, quite as passionately as the Duke of Averton. Once she had thought him the most rapacious of collectors. His holdings of antiquities were vast, and he did not seem to care from where he obtained them. The Duke of 'Avarice', some called him, and she had assumed it to be the truth.

Then she had found out that his guise of insatiable collector was a ruse. He actually worked for the highly respectable Antiquities Society, a group his revered scholar father helped found. And his task was to stop the Lily Thief, which he did—with the unwitting help of her sister Calliope.

What was his game now? Was he the thief-hunter, or the thief? If the silver was real, it could be a great temptation to anyone. But then, Edward was not just *anyone*.

Clio frowned in thought. Giacomo and his cohort had mentioned a bowl. If she could just find that one piece…

She shivered in her thin muslin nightdress, trying to calmly list her options. She could confront Giacomo, of course, lecture him about his loyalty to his parents, to his homeland. If she could find him, and if he didn't stab her through with his rabbit-poaching knife. Men like Giacomo, lower-level *tombarolo*, were usually desperate and unpredictable. She was good with a dagger and a pistol herself, but no match for such desperation. She might be a fool in truth, but hopefully not as big a fool as all that.

She could ask Rosa what she and Paolo knew. Yet Clio could see they would not tell the truth about their son's activities. They liked her, but that was nothing to the iron strength of their family loyalty. Not only would they tell her naught, they would warn Giacomo. That was the code of their village.

She could also confront Edward directly. No one was a better actor than he was, though, not even Marco or Thalia. He played the spoiled, eccentric duke and collector to perfection, fooling everyone, even herself.

No, she had to find that bowl. If it was in Edward's house, she would make her move. If not, then she would need yet another plan.

The Lily Thief would have to rise again, just this one last time. Clio felt a bitter pang at the thought. She had promised Calliope she would not do that any longer, but surely this was different. She would take nothing but the bowl, if it was found, and that only for evidence.

Even as she justified her plan, she shivered again in trepidation. Something *was* happening out there in the quiet town, something that sizzled and bubbled deep inside the tranquil surface. And she intended to discover exactly what it was.

Chapter Fifteen

'Shall we go the Manning-Smythes' waltzing party tonight?' Thalia asked over the breakfast table, as she shuffled through the stack of new invitations.

'Hmm?' Clio said, distracted. She had a book open beside her plate, but had not read more than two words together. Dances were as far from her thoughts as a subject could be.

'It is last minute, I know, but Mrs Manning-Smythe says in her note it will all be quite informal,' Thalia said. 'Just some dancing, a few hands of cards. You would enjoy the cards, Father, even if Lady Rushworth could not persuade you to waltz!'

Their father chuckled. 'Perhaps she could not get me to waltz, yet she will no doubt insist I be there. She says I need to get out in society more often. Live in the present sometimes, not always in the ancient past.'

'That is excellent advice, Father,' Thalia said.

'If only the present didn't move so very fast.' Sir Walter sighed. 'Always changes, changes. You can't rely on it, like you can the past. It won't stand still to be studied.'

Just like certain people, Clio thought. Just as she imagined she had a grasp on them, on their essence and motives, they changed on her.

'A waltzing party is not a mathematical equation, Father,' Thalia said. 'It will be most diverting. Everyone will be there, I'm sure.'

Everyone? Clio took a thoughtful bite of her toast. Surely that included the Duke. And while he was dancing at the Manning-Smythes', his palazzo would be empty.

'I think I must cry off,' Clio said. 'All these parties of late have made me neglect my studies.'

'Quite right, my dear. We cannot forget why we are here,' Sir Walter replied, his tone wistful.

'But *you* must come, Father,' Thalia reminded him. 'I need your escort.'

'Of course. It will be an early evening, though?'

'We shall see,' Thalia teased. 'I have so many people I must speak to.'

'People you must dance with,' said Clio, pushing her chair back. 'Excuse me, Father, Thalia. I'm off to work at the farm-house today.'

'Do be careful, Clio,' her father said.

'I'm always careful, Father, I promise.' Clio quickly collected her shawl and knapsack, changing her slippers for her work boots before leaving the house.

The village was quiet so early in the morning, just a few shops and stalls opening their doors, a few merchants sweeping out their doorways as they yawned. The tattered remains of the *feste* littered the square, bits of faded confetti and torn ribbon, empty and abandoned bottles. The smell of smoke from the fireworks still clung to the breeze, but there was no one lurking in the shadows today.

Clio hurried along the path to the valley, following the

well-known trail only by memory as her thoughts were far away. She had not planned to make her move so soon, but the Manning-Smythes' party was too good an opportunity to miss. She would find out if the Duke was attending, and if he was she would do what she had to do. A swift raid, a search for only the one item, and then she would be gone. She wouldn't be distracted by the Alabaster Goddess again.

Edward would never know she had been there.

The only problem was, what would she do if she *did* find the bowl? How could she fight against him?

She glimpsed the farmhouse walls with relief. *This* she understood. This was rational, open to study. It was knowable, if she just worked hard enough. She climbed the steps down to the old cellar and took her spade out of the knapsack. Work was all she had right now.

Another blasted party.

Edward tossed the Manning-Smythes' invitation on to the desk along with all the others, rubbing his hand over his scarred brow. It was almost as bad as London. Everyone wanted to lure a duke to their gathering, to write to their friends of his presence there. Everyone wanted *something* from him.

Except for Clio. She seemed to want nothing at all from him, except in the dark of a masked ball. Yet she was becoming the only one whose presence he craved. Whose opinion he cared about.

He glanced at the card. He would go, of course. His task would never be completed if he followed his own inclination and stayed home by the fire. An alluring vision suddenly flashed across his mind—he and Clio sitting by the fire in his chamber, laughing companionably over their books. Her smile warm as she reached for his hand. *You see,* she said. *Staying home together is so much better than any party...*

Edward laughed wryly at his own daydream. Erotic visions of Clio naked were one thing; dreams of domestic bliss with her were even more impossible. More insidiously attractive.

Even if Clio would care to sit with him by the fire, there was no time for such things now. The robbers who gathered at the secret house were growing more desperate, which meant their foreign customers were, too. The only way to find out who those customers were was to mingle in society. If they all thought him just an indolent, extravagant duke, they might be careless around him. They might even infer that he, too, was looking for stolen antiquities to buy.

And if he had the chance to waltz with Clio Chase in the moonlight—well, that would be a perk indeed.

Chapter Sixteen

It was a perfect night. Completely black, with just the waning moon for light, covered and then revealed by the drift of lacy clouds. Any passer-by would attribute a flicker of movement to those shifting shadows.

Everyone was dancing at the Manning-Smythes', but Clio knew she did not have much time. Soirées in Santa Lucia did not spin on until dawn, as they sometimes did in London, and the Duke was not the unobservant looby some of the Lily Thief's previous 'victims' had been. They had not missed their treasures for days, in a few cases. He would know something was missing immediately, and who was responsible.

But then, she didn't really intend to steal anything, unless it proved necessary. She just wanted to *know*.

Clio crouched low in the hedges outside Edward's palazzo, clad in black breeches and shirt, her hair covered by a black cap. She stared up at the façade, studying the windows, their narrow ledges, the loops of old ivy. Where would he stash a piece of ancient silver? Where would he hide something so valuable and dangerous?

Many of his antiquities were held in his own bedchamber,

according to Rosa via her son Lorenzo, who was a footman here. Clio would have to start there, and hope she found quick success.

She crept around the side of the house to the back garden, which sloped down to a dramatic cliff and soared out to the sea far beyond. Her soft boots were silent on the overgrown lawn, and she saw to her relief a tall old tree near the house. Its gnarled limbs spread to balconies and darkened windows. No light or noise disturbed the silence, so hopefully that meant the servants were congregated belowstairs with their supper and gossip.

With a master like Edward, gossip and speculation would surely keep them busy for hours.

Clio caught hold of a low-hanging limb and swung herself up into the tree, climbing lightly, higher and higher, concealed by the fresh spring leaves. Despite the danger, and her own trepidation, she felt a new exhilaration as she left the earth far behind. It was like a cool, crisp wind after being locked in a stuffy room too long.

She hadn't realised until this moment that she had been chafing so at her respectable, polite life. She felt like the eagles who sometimes flew out over the valley, her wings spread as she leaped into freedom.

She knew it could not last long. When she found what she sought and climbed back down again, this freedom would be lost and for ever. She had to make the most of this fleeting moment, this one last breath of air.

And, strangely, the one person she wanted to share this rare joy with, the one who would understand its intoxicating transcendence, was Edward. For was he, too, not bound with plush ducal chains? Being subversive was sometimes the only way to break them.

Yet that understanding, that bizarre kinship, was also what made him her enemy tonight.

Clio finally reached a balcony she could catch on to from the tree, and she leaped over its wrought-iron railing, landing softly on the tiled floor. Once she caught her breath, she tried the latch on the tall, narrow door. It was unlocked, of course. Who would bother with security so high up, in such a quiet town? But Edward of all people should know better.

The room was indeed a bedchamber, probably the grandest one in the palazzo. It was dark, but Clio could make out a vast bed, swathed in elaborate draperies, the looming hulks of oversize dressing tables and chairs. An elaborate fireplace gleamed pale as ice. Yet as her vision adjusted to the gloom, she saw the room was not inhabited, for most of the furniture was still draped in holland covers. There were no trunks or cases, no personal objects.

She hurried out of the chamber, opening the door a crack to peer cautiously into the corridor. A few branches of candles flickered there, but no servants bustled about on their errands. Not even a mouse stirred. Clio slipped out, keeping to the edges of the carpet runner as she tiptoed from room to room. She listened at each door before looking inside. Every chamber was cold and musty with disuse, either empty or swathed in more ghostly covers.

Not a man for houseguests, obviously, Clio thought. In London, that was part of what made him so talked about, so sought after in his elusiveness.

But it was one of the things that utterly maddened her.

At last she found what she sought, a chamber that was inhabited. A colza lamp burned on the dressing table, as if waiting to welcome someone home, and it illuminated a room that was luxurious but small. The satin bedhangings were tied back, the bedclothes turned down invitingly, while a brocade dressing gown and slippers were arranged at its foot.

And the small space was full of breathtaking treasures. Some of the loveliest things she remembered from Acropolis House—vases and kraters, carved caskets, obsidian cats, jewelled goblets. The Alabaster Goddess.

Artemis stood by the fireplace, pale and serene, her bow calmly levelled on some unseen foe. Clio stared at her, entranced. She remembered too well the last time she had seen her, in Yorkshire, as she and Marco had tried to lever her from her base. She remembered, too, the masquerade ball at Acropolis House, when everything came, quite literally, crashing down.

Clio shook her head. This was no time to get lost in the past! She had no moments to lose. She quickly turned her back on Artemis and set to work.

The armoire held only clothes, rows and rows of the finest-cut coats and rich waistcoats, stacks of soft linen shirts, perfectly white starched neckcloths. They all smelled of Edward, of that clean, crisp spiciness that was only him. She sifted through it all as fast as she could, shutting the carved doors firmly, as if she shut them on *him*.

He would never be so easily dismissed, though. She knew that well.

Drawers and crates also yielded nothing. Just antiquities she knew were already his, piles of history books, notes written in some odd shorthand she could not decipher. Letters from his stewards in England.

Clio sat back on her heels after examining a valise found under the bed, sighing in frustration. Now she would have to try to find a safe, and there was no time for that! A clock on the mantel loudly ticked away the moments, reminding her of that frantic fact. Why did Edward have to be so blasted cautious about this, when he left his balcony doors unlocked?

She scanned the room one last time, and her gaze alighted on the dressing table. She had not yet examined it, for the piece had no drawers, just a surface arrayed with brushes and bottles, a leather shaving kit. And a small, carved wooden box with a most intriguing lock.

Clio made her way to the table, drawing a thin wire lockpick from the pouch at her waist. The lock was more intricately made than most; it took her several minutes to find the mechanism with the tip of the wire and pop it free. But when she did she was rewarded.

There were more papers written in that baffling shorthand, heavy bags of coins. But the box was too small for its outside measurements. She found the false bottom and lifted it out, revealing one tiny silver bowl. It was a thing of rare beauty indeed, intricately decorated with hammered patterns of acorns and beechnuts. Clio turned it over in her hand, feeling the old metal turn warm against her skin as if it were alive.

On the bottom were crudely etched Greek letters spelling out 'This belongs to the gods'. Just like the sketch of the incense burner.

Still clutching the bowl in her gloved hand, Clio peered into the depths of the box. She half-hoped, feared, to see more silver. A hoard, as Giacomo had put it. What she found was even more disquieting.

A scrap of emerald green, ripped at one end, sewn with green glass beads. Torn from the sleeve of her Medusa costume from the Acropolis House masquerade.

She lifted it out, holding it to the light of the lamp. Along the very edge she could see tiny, rust-coloured stains. Blood and silk, binding her and Edward together. Why would he keep such a reminder of that night, locking it away so carefully?

Clio forced herself to put it back in its place, forced herself not to think of what had happened. After all, she had found what she came for, proof that Edward was somehow involved with the silver. If only she had not found so much more as well.

So absorbed was she by the bowl and the silk, she forgot her own first rule, always be cautious. Always be aware. She did not hear the soft click of the door until it was too late.

She spun around, the bowl still in hand, pressed back against the edge of the table as she faced Edward. Though her heart pounded, her palms turning cold in their gloves, she was somehow not surprised. It was as if the whole night had been spinning to this one moment, their gazes meeting across the room.

Edward leaned lazily against the door frame, his arms crossed over his chest. He still wore his evening clothes, a cloak shrugged back from the shoulders of his black satin coat.

He gave her a bitter smile. 'Well, my dear,' he said, his tone one of affable sociability, 'if you wanted an invitation to my bedchamber, you had only to ask.'

Chapter Seventeen

Clio backed away until she felt the hard edge of the dressing table against her hips, trapping her in place. She tightened her fingers over the bowl, staring at Edward, unable to look away. She was truly caught, like a helpless fly covered over in sticky, irresistibly beautiful amber.

Somehow, she was not even surprised to see him there. The whole hazy, unreal scene had the cold air of inevitability about it. The feeling that the two of them had played this through before and would again, on and on into eternity.

'Where did you get this?' she whispered, holding up the bowl.

'I think a more pertinent question for the moment, my dear, is why do *you* have it?' he answered. He moved slowly toward her, graceful and intent as a predatory tiger. He reached out and clasped her wrist in a lover-like caress, yet Clio found she could not move. His touch was like a velvet-lined iron manacle.

He plucked the bowl from her numb fingers, holding it up to the lamplight. The flickering golden-red flames shimmered on the old silver. 'Have you gone back to your old ways, perhaps?' he said. He did not watch her, his veiled gaze never leaving the bowl, yet Clio could not turn her stare away from him.

What was his intention? What would he do? Clio swallowed hard against the sudden cold wave of uncertain fear and growing excitement. The very unreadable quality she hated about him was also one of the things that made her feel so very *alive* when she was with him.

The infuriating man!

'I have not resurrected the Lily Thief,' she said, her voice tight.

His glance flickered over her black garb. 'Indeed? Just out for a lark, then?'

Clio flexed her fingers and twisted her wrist hard, breaking free of his grasp. She edged away from him until she stood with her back to the wall. She knew she could never escape from this room, not until he chose to let her go, but at least when they were not touching she could think more clearly.

Could remember why she was here. To find out the truth about the silver. To find out if he was the 'English' collector who would pay any price to possess it. The fact that he had the bowl at all pointed to 'yes'.

The question was, what was she going to do about it? What *could* she do, caught here as she was?

'I heard a rumour in town,' she said. 'Strange tales of a cache of fabulous Hellenistic silver, lost for hundreds of years. About people who would pay vast sums to keep that silver to themselves, no matter where it rightfully belongs. No matter who they hurt.'

'If such a treasure exists, I would say its "rightful" owners are long dead,' Edward said calmly. He laid the bowl back into the box with the silk, closing the lid over it. 'But I have heard such tales myself. Santa Lucia—indeed, all of Sicily—is rife with such things.'

'Is that why you came here, then? To follow Sicilian tales of treasure?'

'Why have any of us come here, Clio?' He turned to face her, his back to the box. His expression was still that veiled, blank look. Calm and faintly contemptuous as any classical statue hewn in marble. 'I am not the villain in this scene.'

'Then why do you have that bowl? Where did you come by it? Where is the rest of the silver?'

'So many questions, my dear. But I do not feel inclined to indulge someone who has broken into my home and rifled through my possessions—again. And after all your assurances that your life of crime was over. Tsk. What would your sister, the oh-so-proper Lady Westwood, say?'

Clio felt a lava flow of bubbling, sparkling anger rise up inside her, red-black and irresistible. She flew toward him, beating at his shoulders and chest with her fists, furious at his calm, at that little half-smile on his beautiful lips that hinted he just might be enjoying this little confrontation.

That smile vanished at the fury of her onslaught. He caught her shoulders in his iron clasp, holding her immobilised, a tiny, angry vein throbbing in his hard-set jaw. A ragged sob escaped Clio's lips, born of fear and frustration, of not seeing, not understanding. Not being in control.

'Tell me why you have that bowl!' she cried. 'Why are you here?'

Edward gave her a small shake, as if to awaken her, awaken them both, from the enveloping spell of their mutual anger and need. 'I have told you why I'm here,' he said hoarsely. 'I can help you, if you will let me. But, blast it, Clio! You make it hard indeed. Creeping around at night, climbing in windows…'

'How are you helping me? I *have* to climb in windows, to discover for myself what is happening when no one will tell me.'

'I cannot tell you, Clio.'

'Cannot, or will not? Because you think I am a mere weak female, who must be protected for her own good?'

'You are hardly a "mere weak" anything, Clio Chase. You are the most fearsomely courageous person I have ever seen, not to mention the most stubborn.'

Clio swallowed back the bitter knot of tears, more confused than ever. 'Then you know I am stubborn enough to not give up, to discover what is going on here on my own. Why won't you just make things easier for us both, and tell me?'

'Because, my dear, I do not yet know myself. You have been a terrible distraction.'

A distraction from buying the silver? '*I* have been a distraction? What of you? I have not been able to see to my work since you arrived here. My studies, the farmhouse, all neglected.'

'Perhaps that is all for the best,' he muttered.

Clio unclenched her fists, her palms flat against his chest. She felt the rich silkiness of satin, the crisp linen of his evening clothes, the strong, primitive beat of his heart beneath. The pounding of his life's blood, mingled with the fevered rhythm of her own. 'What do you mean?'

His touch gentled on her shoulders, sliding around her back. 'I mean that your precious farmhouse has something to do with the silver.'

'How can that be? The people who lived there were prosperous enough, but they could never have afforded pieces like the silver. I have seen nothing like it at the site. Besides, the *tombaroli* would have looted anything of value long ago.'

'Despite the curse of the angry spirits?'

'I don't understand,' Clio said. She didn't know if she meant the silver, or the strange, crackling energy pulsing between them. The invisible power that bound her to him wherever she went.

'Just please listen to me for once in your life, Clio,' he said, his touch tightening along her back, drawing her closer to him. 'Give up the Lily Thief, stay away from the farmhouse, and watch your back wherever you go. Forget about the blasted silver. It might not even exist.'

Clio shook her head. 'I *do* watch my back, Edward. But if that silver exists, if it is indeed a cache of lost temple pieces, it's too precious and sacred to let disappear. To see it vanish into some greedy collector's vault.'

She glanced over at the Alabaster Goddess, still poised in her eternal vigilance. Clio had let *her* down, had lost her to Edward. She couldn't lose the silver, too. How could she trust him when he hid the bowl away?

She turned from Artemis, staring up at Edward as if she could read the truth in his eyes. His face was half in gloomy darkness, lit by the flickering caress of the low-burning lamp. It was all sharply sculpted angles, smooth, sun-touched skin, the map of some undiscovered country.

He watched her, too, with a wary hunger to match her own.

'What will you do to me, then?' she whispered. 'You have no dungeon here, as you do in your Yorkshire castle.'

'I'm sure there must be one somewhere,' he muttered roughly. She felt his caress move up the arc of her spine, felt him remove her cap. Her hair, loosely pinned up, tumbled down over her shoulders. His fingers twined lightly in the strands, holding her his prisoner as surely as any dungeon.

'All those Normans and Bourbons,' he continued. 'They had to hold their captives somewhere.'

'Not to mention the Romans and Saracens,' Clio said. 'The Spanish mercenaries…'

'Perhaps there is a nice, quiet little oubliette somewhere in the castle,' he said, pulling her closer and closer until there was not even a ray of light between them. Clio slid her arms around his neck, closing her eyes to breathe deeply of his warm scent, to let herself be surrounded by him. To forget, for just a moment.

'An oubliette?' she murmured.

'Oh, yes,' he answered softly, his breath stirring her loose curls, moving over her aching skin like a cool breeze. 'A nice, quiet, dark hole, just big enough for two people to fall into and hide there for ever.'

Clio was sure she *was* falling, tumbling end over end into him and how he made her feel, leaving all else behind. Sense, practicality, even identity—they were all as nothing when she was with him. 'So, there are two prisoners, then?'

'Oh, Clio,' he said, his voice so rough and sad. 'Of course there are.'

And he kissed her, a kiss full of all the need and longing Clio could not express, could not even understand. Her fingers tightened on the nape of his neck, holding him to her, leaning into him. He tasted of lemons, of the night, of ancient mysteries, of all she had ever wanted and yet was forbidden. He was all she fought against, yet he felt like her only haven in a stormy world. She couldn't stay away from him.

Their lips slid away from each other, from the desperate melding of their kiss. He leaned his forehead to hers, and they stood there in heated silence, wrapped in a longing that could not be broken. They could not move forwards, yet neither could they snap that bond and move away.

'What will you do with me?' she asked, her words like a

whipcrack in the quiet. A lash that tore at their tenuous control.

Edward laughed harshly. 'Right now, I am going to take you home, before I forget who we are and carry you to that bed over there. Tomorrow, the day after? I have not yet decided. But I want you to stay away from your farmhouse, at least for a while.' He drew back, cradling her face between his hands as he studied her closely. As if he could read all her secrets in her eyes. 'Listen to me, Clio. Stay away.'

'So, I must still watch my back, eh?' she said. She reached up and closed her fingers around one of his wrists, holding him to her.

'Did you not say you always do that anyway?'

'I do, and my vigilance is usually rewarded. No one has ever caught me, except you.'

'I could say the same about *you.*' Edward scooped her cap up from the floor, handing it to her before he turned away. Their touch was broken, yet Clio still felt him wrapped tightly around all her senses. Like a beautiful, drugging dream that made her forget all else, made her want to bask in its glow for ever.

She, too, turned away, toward the dressing-table mirror. She looped up her hair, tucking it into the cap again. In the unforgiving glass she saw that her cheeks glowed a brilliant pink. Her eyes were fever-bright, glittering with desires and fears she dared not yet name. Even to herself.

The closed box lid was before her, concealing the silver and the scrap of green silk, hiding all that they meant. For a while, a moment, she could pretend they did not exist. That there was only her and Edward, and their kiss in the night.

But soon the sun would come up, and shine its mercilessly revealing rays on the world, on reality. She would still have to find the truth about the silver, try to save it, because it was in her nature to do so. Just as it was Edward's nature to stop her however he could, for reasons known only to him.

She would truly have to watch her back, as she did not know which would prove more dangerous, the *tombaroli* or Edward. Or even if they were one and the same.

She tucked the last wayward strand of auburn hair into her cap, and spun around to find Edward holding out his own black velvet cloak to her.

'It has a hood,' he said, draping the soft folds over her shoulders. His hands lingered there for a long, sweet moment, as if he would not, could not, let her go. 'In case we should pass anyone on the street.'

Clio gave a ragged laugh, drawing the cloak closer around her. The fabric smelled of him, still held his lingering warmth. 'Which would be worse, to be thought a thief, or to be thought your paramour?'

'Why not both?' he said roughly.

'Why not indeed?' Clio drew up the hood, retreating into its satin-lined concealment. It made her feel rather like a ghost herself, able to flit around ruins dispensing curses.

'Well, shall we go the way you came?' Edward said, gesturing to the windows. 'Or shall we be dull and take the door?'

'The door, I think,' Clio answered. 'I am not so young as I once was, and clambering in windows is harder than I remembered.'

'The door it is, then.' Edward took her arm firmly through the enveloping layers of wool and velvet, leading her out into the silent corridor. 'Just out of curiosity, my dear, how *did* you manage to gain entry to my house?'

'I am not sure I ought to give away all my secrets,' Clio

said, as they hurried out of the door and into the hush of the sleeping town. They were alone for a few minutes more. 'But you will no doubt discover it anyway. I climbed the tree in your back garden and found an unlocked window to one of the bedchambers.'

'Very clever of you,' he said. 'You are a veritable Artemis of athletic prowess.'

She glanced at him suspiciously from under the hood. 'Are you making jest of me?'

'Not at all, my dear. Your ingenuity never fails to astonish me. You find your way into places that seem quite impregnable.'

Clio laughed quietly. 'Indeed, I rather pride myself on that. But you are lucky I am not Artemis in truth.'

'And why is that?'

'Surely you remember Actaeon? He committed the unpardonable sin of watching the goddess while she bathed. Then she turned him into a stag and shot him full of arrows.' Clio saw her house just ahead, dark and dreaming in the night. It appeared no one had yet missed her. She hurried towards it, turning back at the gate to find him watching her.

'Goodnight, Edward,' she called softly. 'I will watch my back, I promise.'

And guard against *him*, above all. As always.

Edward stood outside the Chases' gate, observing the house intently until at last he saw the glow of a candle in one of the windows. For the merest moment, Clio appeared behind the glass like an apparition, clad in a white dressing gown, her hair loose over her shoulders. He wondered if she saw him, if she even looked for him there, staring up at her window like a love-struck supplicant. If she would fly down and land in his arms once more, so fleeting and precious.

But she merely drew the curtains, leaving him with just the reflection of light through silk, the diffusion of brightness and warmth that was all their relationship could ever really be.

Assured that she was safe in her chamber, that her street was quiet, he turned back toward home. A chilly wind had blown up from the valley, stirring the leaves over the walkway in rustling fits. Edward raised the satin collar of his coat to deflect the cold, or perhaps to hide from the world. From what he knew he had to do.

Edward had realised from the moment he arrived in Santa Lucia that keeping Clio away from the silver would not be easy. The Chases were famous for their strong wills, their free-spirited natures, no doubt inherited from their bluestocking French mother. And Clio was by far the worst of all the Chase Muses. Who else would have devised the whole Lily Thief scheme?

It was all only because she cared so very deeply, he knew that. Cared about history and knowledge and art, about doing what she thought was right and damn the consequences. It was one of the things he admired about her, that shining, warrior spirit. She was a passionate woman, and passionate people were seldom malleable. But his stubborn streak was surely at least as wide as hers, and he would not see her hurt.

Edward paused at the turning of the street, glancing back at Clio's house. The light still glowed in her window, but all else was dark and silent. Santa Lucia slept under the blanket of the cloudy night sky, a picturesque ancient village. Yet he knew that under all the beauty, under the peaceful visage, lurked something quite menacing. A shadow just beginning to form its shape.

Yet Clio was not alone. No matter how she pushed him away, how she fought against him, he would keep her safe. No matter what.

Chapter Eighteen

Clio stabbed at the dusty earth with her spade, anger and frustration in every furious dig. It was a warm day, the sun a merciless hard yellow orb overhead, and even the birds and insects were silent in the heat. Clio was all alone at the farmhouse, surrounded by the vibrating silence, the rich, organic smell of the dirt and the clover. She didn't mind, though, for she was unfit for human company that afternoon. The only remedy was to roll up her sleeves and *work*.

She wiped at her damp forehead with her wrist, staring down at the deep trench she was digging along the perimeter of the crumbling wall. She didn't know what she was looking for. Something, anything, to confirm or deny what Edward had said about this site, that it had something to do with the silver and she should stay away. But she found nothing, not even the pottery shards and coins she had come across before. The trench was empty.

Clio took off her spectacles, rubbing at the bridge of her nose. She hadn't slept at all the night before, lying in her bed until dawn going over and over her escapade at Edward's house. The hidden bowl, Artemis—their kiss. Why was it that whenever they met, no matter what the strange circumstances, she could not keep from touching him? From falling into his arms?

She tossed her spade down, relishing the loud 'thunk' it made as it landed point down in the dirt. If only she could throw it at Edward's handsome head! At least that would be one way to end the emotional storms they constantly battled. She didn't seem to have the willpower to end it herself. She couldn't even stay away from him.

Clio sat down under the meagre shade of a tall cypress tree, reaching into her knapsack for a bottle of water. There wasn't much left, and she sipped at the last warm drops, thinking back over all she had learned last night. It wasn't a great deal. Only that the silver existed, or at least some of it, the offering bowls. Supposedly it had something to do with her beloved farm-house. And Edward was trying to tell her what to do—again.

Why did he want her out of here? Because he saw her as a weak damsel to be protected? Or because he wanted the silver himself?

Clio sighed as she tucked the empty bottle away. Life here in Santa Lucia had certainly been far less complicated before Edward had showed up. But not nearly as interesting.

She laughed aloud. Yes, she must truly be insane to prefer theft, curses and stolen kisses to quiet study, but there it was! She could never be the fine, proper lady Calliope was, and she needed mysteries and causes in her life. But she *didn't* need Edward to make her feel so frustrated!

Clio stretched her legs out before her as she leaned her head back against the rough bark of the tree, gazing out over the remains of the house, her new series of trenches and pits. Lack of sleep made everything shimmer and shift, until the present ruins seemed to fall away, revealing the place as it had once been. Bustling and full of life. Full of happiness and joy, sadness and grief, the flow of daily living.

Until it was all destroyed in a moment. A victim of senseless war.

'You have been in Sicily too long,' Clio muttered. She was becoming too affected by the sun, by the talk of curses and spirits. She needed to go back to grey, sensible London.

Except she knew that even in England she wouldn't be safe from magic. It followed her everywhere, in the form of Edward—whether he was with her or not.

'Maybe I should go to Russia, then,' she mused. 'It is cold and icy there, no room for sunstruck dreams.'

Though surely the fact that she was talking to herself meant the madness was permanent.

And she knew she *was* mad, for she saw Edward himself coming into the valley, riding his black horse along the narrow pathway. He had shed his coat in the heat, and wore only his white shirtsleeves and plain black waistcoat with his buckskin riding breeches and high boots. His hair fell to his shoulders, the same colour as the sun.

Had she thought him a dark, brooding Hades? Well, she was wrong. He was surely Apollo, one with the sky and the light. But Apollo, like Hades, also had a tendency to grab what he wanted and damn the consequences.

Was he really here, then, or was he a figment of her imagination? Clio climbed to her feet, watching guardedly as he dismounted from his horse. He also seemed to watch her closely, as if unsure what she would do.

Not that she could blame him. In the past she had done everything from hit him with a statue to jumping into his arms for a passionate kiss. She wasn't sure herself what she would do any more.

Edward walked slowly toward her. 'Hard at work, I see,' he said.

'Yes,' she answered. 'And I have not yet encountered any vengeful spirits.'

'Perhaps they are very tiny, like pixies, and hide in crevices. Ready to jump out when least expected.'

'It doesn't take a tiny pixie to do that. Large dukes are equally adept at taking people by surprise.'

He laughed. 'I did try very hard not to sneak up on you today. I asked Zeus here to be as loud as possible on the trail.'

And yet, in her dreaming, she had not heard him until he was right upon her. So much for 'watching her back'. 'Will you sit with me in the shade for a while, then, as long as you insist on being here?' she said. 'Though I fear I have no refreshment to offer.'

'No matter. I brought my own,' he said, turning back to draw a flagon and two goblets from his saddlebag. 'A sort of peace offering, if you will.'

'A peace offering? It should be *me* giving that, considering I was the one to break into your house,' Clio said.

They sat down together by the tree, and Edward poured out the deep red wine. 'But I was the one who provoked you to it. I should have known you would not be content with vague warnings.'

'True. We Chases are not known for patient docility.' She sipped at the wine. It was cool and sweet, welcome refreshment on a warm day no matter who offered it.

'No, indeed. You are women of action, and I should have planned for that.'

'You have a plan, then?'

'Not yet. But one is forming.'

And would he let her be part of that plan? She could be of

help, she knew it, if he would only trust her. She knew how to catch villains, knew how they thought and acted. Unless Edward *was* the villain. Then she would have no idea what to do.

He didn't seem a villain today, lounging beside her in the shade. They sat together in companionable silence, letting the sunny Sicilian afternoon wash over them.

Clio finished her wine, turning the goblet around in her hand. Suddenly, the heavy glass vessel felt like iron, weighty, her wrist and fingers weak with numbness. As she stared down at her hand, bright spots danced before her eyes. Her limbs also turned heavy, her thoughts scattering as soon as she formed them.

What was happening to her? Frightened, she forced herself to her feet, clinging to the tree for support. The world tilted around her.

She sensed Edward standing up beside her, felt his hand on her arm. When she tried to focus her gaze on him, the sun behind his bright hair dazzled her. He seemed surrounded by shimmering heat.

As she tried to back away from him, her booted foot kicked at the fallen goblet. She stared down at it, one thought suddenly fearsomely solid.

'The wine,' she gasped. 'You poisoned me!'

'No, Clio,' he said insistently. His hands reached for her again, holding her upright, and this time she could not even try to fight him. 'Not poison. Just an herbal tincture to help you sleep. You will wake in a few hours with no adverse affects, I promise.'

Clio couldn't quite believe him. She struggled with all her might to stay awake, to move, to get away. But she felt bound with iron shackles. 'Why would you do that?' she said, her words slurred. Her vision was turning dark.

'To protect you,' he answered. He sounded so very far away. 'You wouldn't stay away from this place, so I had to do it. I'm sorry, Clio.'

Her knees buckled beneath her, and she felt him catch her up in his arms. He held her easily, as if she weighed no more than a feather, yet she felt weighty as a boulder. As she slipped into unconsciousness, she heard him say again, 'I am so sorry it had to be this way.'

Not half as sorry as he was going to be when she woke up…

Edward laid Clio gently on the waiting bed, his heart troubled. The horrified accusation in her eyes as she realised what was happening, the way she believed he could poison her—it wounded him.

But this was the only way he could think to keep her safe. She would not heed his warnings, would persist in breaking into houses and going alone to isolated valleys until she found what she sought. Or until trouble found *her*.

Keeping her out of the way for a few days was the only way. One day she would understand. Or, knowing Clio, she would never understand, but she would be alive.

He gently removed her spectacles and her boots, tucking the soft linen sheets and velvet counterpane around her. The potion was strong; she would probably sleep until morning. And when she awoke…

'It is only for a few days,' he whispered, smoothing her tangled hair back from her brow. In sleep, she was so peaceful, so lovely, a gentle smile on her lips. If only she could always be like this—but then she would not be *Clio*, the fiery, stubborn Clio he had come to care about so.

'Just a few days,' he repeated. 'You will be safe here. And then you can hate me for ever if you like.'

He turned the lamp on the bedside table down to a faint glow before he left the chamber, locking the door behind him. It was dark when he stepped out into the fresh air, the heat of the day banished by cool mountain breezes, by a cloudless blue-black sky.

When he had found this place on such short notice, it had seemed a godsend. A small stone cottage high in the hills, miles from Santa Lucia along bad roads, hidden from everyone. Old Baron Picini, who had been dead many years, had used it for his romantic liaisons, far from the wrath of his wife. It was almost windowless, quiet and solitary, perfect. He had brought in comfortable furniture, books, a quantity of firewood and food.

Surely a few days would see the resolution of the matter of the silver, and then he could let Clio go. Release her back into the world, like a fierce goshawk.

Edward rubbed hard at his eyes, pushing the loose strands of his hair back from his brow. It was a terrible plan, he knew that. But he had no time to come up with a better one, no way to persuade Clio to do as he said. Kidnapping was all he could think of.

He went back into the cottage, and settled by the fire to watch and wait. It was silent now behind the bedroom door, the silence of sleep, dreams, peace. That would not last long.

Not long at all.

Chapter Nineteen

Clio felt as if she were swimming, fighting her way upwards through a thick, warm liquid, like when she used to dive into the pond with her sisters as a girl. Something dragged at her feet, pulling her back down into waiting darkness. She wanted to go back, wanted to fall into the waiting snare of silent unknowing, but something urged her to fight. She kept struggling upwards, battling against the bonds until finally she burst free into the light.

And into pain. Her head throbbed, as if she had been drinking too much champagne or reading without her spectacles. Or both, like that silly evening she and Thalia stole a bottle of brandy from her father's cellar and then tried to act out all the roles in *Electra*.

Had they done such a thing again? Clio was sure they had not, but she couldn't quite remember. She forced her gritty eyes open, blinking against the sudden cold rush of reality. Where was she? Not in her own chamber, either in Santa Lucia or in London, she knew that.

She pushed back the bedclothes that were tugged up around her chin, and she saw that the counterpane was of soft, rich dark red velvet. The sheets were lace-trimmed linen, thick and luxurious. Her own sheets were nice, but not *that* nice.

As she sat up against a pile of bolsters and cushions, she noticed red brocade bedcurtains looped back from a carved bedstead, like a medieval bower. The only light, a fuzzy ray of chalky white sun that pierced her aching head, fell from one tiny window set high in a whitewashed wall. She squinted against its glare, studying her new and strange surroundings.

The room was small but very well appointed, with dark red-and-green Turkish rugs on the polished wooden floors and several paintings on the walls. There was a mirrored dressing table, laden with brushes, boxes and jars, and a large desk. It was piled with more books than she had ever seen outside a library, their fine leather bindings glowing jewel-like in the faint light. A wardrobe with carved doors lurked in one corner next to a small fireplace.

It was like a chamber in some old fairy story, a bower in a thicket where the princess could hide from the witch. But she was surely no princess! Was she dreaming this place? Had she really been drinking too much wine with Thalia again?

Then it hit her, like a rock tumbled from a hillside to land right on her head. Edward had drugged her! He had drugged her, and snatched her away from the farmhouse, and now she was here. In an enchanted castle.

Clio groaned, falling back onto the pillows. That horrid *fiend*! And to think she had begun to like him. Well, perhaps not *like* exactly, but definitely to think better of him. And she had kissed him! Let him see her naked breasts. Given in to her lust for him like a love-struck fool. Like the silly, romantic females she always prided herself on not being.

And just look what disasters had ensued! She ended up kidnapped.

Well, not for long. Clio rolled out of bed, her limbs aching and weak, and assessed the situation. Her spectacles rested on a bedside table next to a burned-out lamp. Her boots were lined up neatly by the bed, and she still wore her loose brown muslin work dress, now sadly crumpled.

The door was stout wood, bound with thick iron hinges and pierced by one tiny, barred window, a perfect prison door. It was, as she had suspected, firmly locked. But this seemed to be an old place, and old places often hid such things as trapdoors and secret passages.

Clio searched every inch of the floor and walls, finding nothing. Not even so much as a crack or knothole. The wardrobe had no false back or bottom, and held only some of her own clothes. The villain had planned well for his crime.

She dragged a chair over to the wall beneath the window. Standing on it, stretched on tiptoe, she could just peek outside. And all she saw were trees. Rocks and trees. She seemed to be in a clearing of some sort, and, no matter how her ears strained, she could not hear a single sound.

She slowly lowered herself into the chair, feeling profoundly alone and lost. Trapped. As she wrapped her arms around her chest, she noticed a bowl of fruit on the desk, glistening red and gold and purple, like a Dutch still life. There were no pomegranates, but she thought of Persephone all the same. She, too, had been snatched away from her life by a scoundrel on a black horse, borne down into the shadowy underworld just because some arrogant *man* felt like it.

A sudden flame of fury swept through Clio, burning away the chill of loneliness. How dare he! How dare Edward, the well-named Duke of 'Avarice', just lock her in here? How dare he—how dare he make her care for him? Want him!

'Idiot!' she shouted. She didn't know if she meant herself, or the Duke, or even the whole insane situation. Imprisoning her, as if they were caught in one of her friend Lotty's silly horrid novels. She reached out in a flash, shoving books and fruit and candlesticks into a clattering mess on the floor.

She pounded her fists on the table, relishing the ache of it because it was *real*. She didn't know why Edward had done this, though really she should not have been surprised by it. He was a strange man. But she did know he would not get away with it. Not this time. She was just as determined as he was. She would escape, and then she would...

Well, she didn't know yet what she would do. But it would be something terrible. Something to equal Artemis and Actaeon. Edward would be sorry he ever encountered her at all.

As she sat there, fuming, she heard a muffled noise from outside. Clio stood up on the chair again, peering into the clearing. Ah, there he was at last. Her Hades, astride his black steed. He studied the house cautiously for a moment before he dismounted, taking a package from his saddlebag.

'You *should* be cautious,' she muttered, watching with clenched fists as he approached. 'It will avail you nothing in the end.'

Tense, every nerve alert, she heard a door open somewhere below her chamber, heard the click of his boots on stone floors. On tiptoe, hardly daring even to breathe, she crept off the chair and scooped up the empty fruit bowl. It was bronze, light and thin, but she was stronger than she looked. Maybe if she took him by surprise, she could knock him unconscious and run away. Steal his fine horse.

Oh, yes. She would like that.

Holding tightly to the bowl, Clio took up her position by the door. She held her breath, listening tensely as his footsteps made their slow way up some stairs. Her heart pounded, and she couldn't breathe. He was almost there; she heard the metallic rasp of keys.

She raised the bowl high…

Chapter Twenty

Thalia knocked softly at Clio's bedroom door, leaning close to listen for any hint of sound. She didn't expect an answer, but half-hoped anyway. All she could hear was the echo of her father and Cory talking together downstairs.

She pushed open the door, slipping inside. It was dim, the curtains drawn over the windows, the bed neatly made. Even after only a day, there was the dusty air of disuse, of abandoned places.

Or maybe playing actress had only made her fanciful. Made her see drama and mystery where there was none.

Her father thought there was certainly no mystery. When they returned from a day's work at the villa to find a message saying Clio had decided to go to Motya with the Darbys after all, he had taken it quite in his stride. Clio had done such impulsive things before, going off to Agrigento, for instance, and he considered that it would be good for her to leave Santa Lucia for a while.

But Thalia was not so convinced. Yes, it would be good for Clio to get away, to be far from the Duke of Averton, and she did like to do things on the spur of the moment. Yet she never went away with only one hurried message.

Something was going on, something Thalia didn't understand, but a deep-seated feeling told her that all was not right.

Calliope and Clio had often concealed things that were unpleasant from her, trying to protect her. To shield her sensibilities, because they saw her as their baby sister. A silly little blonde who could be trusted to do nothing but play the pianoforte and dress up in pretty clothes.

She had had *enough* of that. Enough of being shielded and protected, of holding secrets. She was nineteen now, not a baby, and not a fool. Clio was up to something more than sightseeing, and Thalia wanted to find out what it was.

She quickly searched Clio's dressing table and wardrobe, finding that her brushes and perfume bottles, her soap and bath salts, and many of her clothes were missing. Just as if she *had* gone on a voyage. Her knapsack, which she carried to her farmhouse site every day, was also missing, which was a bit strange. It held picks and spades, not usually needed for a spot of genteel tourism. Her books and notebooks were still on her desk.

It did look as if Clio had gone on a short holiday, but Thalia was not convinced. Her sister had been acting oddly, ever since that Count di Fabrizzi had appeared in Santa Lucia.

Thalia went to the window, drawing back the curtains to peer down at the street. It grew late in the day; the walkways were full of people hurrying home to their supper, to the cosiness of their own hearths. A young Sicilian couple strolled past, the man carrying the woman's market basket, their heads close together as they laughed at some secret joke. How they *fit* together, Thalia thought as she watched them. How assured they looked in their belonging.

She wondered wistfully how that felt, to know that you

belonged somewhere, with someone. To find a true safe place. It must be glorious indeed. It must be something worth fighting for.

She thought of the Count's dark eyes, of his teasing, dimpled smile that hid so very much. He had tried to flirt with her, had danced with her all night at the *feste*, a round of wine and laughter and giddiness that still revealed nothing of him to her. Even as she longed to know more, to know everything, she could tell he was not like other men of her acquaintance, English men who gave her what she wanted with one pleading glance from her cursed blue eyes. One coquettish flutter of her fan.

The Count was not like that. He was wise to her wiles, as she was to his. But she was certain he knew Clio, knew her from before that tea at Lady Riverton's. Thalia had one great skill from all her theatrical studies—she could read people. Could tell when they had secrets, good, bad, guilty. She saw when they tried to hide those secrets behind polite smiles and pretty compliments.

Count Marco di Fabrizzi had secrets. Many of them. Thalia admitted she had almost been blinded by his charm, his fine looks, by the heady way she felt when he took her in his arms to dance. But not entirely. He was not here just on 'business', not just to call on his old friend Lord Riverton's widow. She was sure of that.

Was he here because he was in love with Clio? Thalia narrowed her eyes on the whispering couple below the window, remembering how Clio had flushed when the Count had entered Lady Riverton's drawing room. Was Clio in love with him?

Had she eloped with him?

Thalia sighed. How complicated things became, when one

was never told the truth about anything! It consumed so much time having to snoop around, ferreting out secrets. But it could also be vastly rewarding.

It was a valuable thing at times, being thought a pretty bonbon. No one ever guessed at her treasure trove of scandalous discoveries. If she wanted to give up music and theatre, surely she could make a fortune as a novelist!

But before she could become the next Maria Edgeworth, she had one more discovery to make. She had to find what had really become of her sister—before it was too late.

Chapter Twenty-One

The scraping of the key in the lock sounded as loud as cannon fire in Clio's ears. She couldn't even breathe, her throat was so tight. Her arm muscles ached as she held the bowl high above her head. Time hung suspended.

Then it sped up in a great, roaring blur. The door swung open, and she lunged forward, bringing her 'weapon' down in a swinging arc. She aimed for his thick, stubborn head, but even her agile quickness was not enough. He was a fraction faster, grabbing her wrist just before she could make clanging contact.

His grip tightened until she dropped the bowl, and he kicked it away. She tried to kick *him* in turn, forgetting that she was not wearing her boots until her toes crumpled achingly.

'Ow!' she cried, startled. He pressed her back against the wall, his hands on her shoulders deceptively light. They felt like the merest caress, feather-soft, but Clio knew she couldn't get away even if she tried. She leaned her head back, staring at him tensely. The air hung heavy and static between them.

She couldn't speak. Her throat was still tight and aching, and she feared if she started shouting at him she would never stop. Her fury would bring the roof down on top of them.

He, too, stared, his face white and strained, his lips set in a hard, determined line. 'I'm sorry, Clio,' he said hoarsely. 'I didn't want things to come to this.'

'To *this*?' she answered, finding her voice at last. 'To kidnapping? I think that is a crime, even for dukes.'

'After this is all over, after I know you're safe, you can do whatever you like,' he said. 'Go to the authorities, denounce me, have me transported—shoot me. But for now I will do what I must.'

'And I'll do what *I* must!' Clio cried, her temper beyond all control. The arrogant blackguard! She twisted in his grip, breaking his hold so she could shove him away. She couldn't bear the heat of his nearness, the piercing green light of his all-seeing eyes, for another moment.

She dashed to the other side of the room, gripping at the bedpost until she thought she would snap the thick wood in two.

'You have done crazy things in the past, your Grace,' she cried. 'But you must be mad indeed to think you can get away with this! My family has surely missed me by now.'

'I think not, my dear,' he said, still so infuriatingly calm. 'They think you've gone to Motya with the Darbys, and I know that family plans to go directly home to England after their excursion. It will be a few weeks before you are missed.'

Clio opened her mouth, then closed it again, nonplussed. It was a rather good ruse, she had to admit. Everyone knew she had gone off on impromptu jaunts before. Her father and Thalia would be busy with their respective projects; they wouldn't question her whereabouts for a while.

'How did you get my clothes and things?' she asked.

He gave her a gentle, disquieting smile, more fearsome than any shout. 'I have my methods.'

Of course he did. The man could surely coax the very birds

from the trees, if not with his title and money, then with his fine looks. The intense charm that affected all women, even Clio, no matter how she fought against it. Denied it.

She fought against it even now, when she was his prisoner

'Do you think to compromise me?' she asked, more and more puzzled. 'Why would you do that, when dozens of women would happily be your wife or mistress?'

Edward laughed wryly. 'No one will know you're here, so you won't be "compromised". I would be a fortunate man indeed to have you for my wife *or* mistress. But I'm not fool enough to think that will happen.'

'Of course it won't, after this ridiculous escapade! I don't understand it at all. I don't understand *you.*'

'Then we are even, my dear, for you are a mystery to me as well. Why could you not have heeded my warning, have stayed away from your blasted farmhouse?'

'You surely know me quite well enough to know I never do what I'm told, unless I am given a good reason. Why did you want me away from there so very much? So you could send in your *tombaroli* unobstructed?'

'I am no thief, Clio. Remember what happened last time you suspected me of such crimes?'

Clio remembered all too well. She had been caught in her own thievery. The one failure of the Lily Thief.

She shook her head, not able to look at him.

'I should ask what sort of scheme you and your good friend, the so-called Count di Fabrizzi, are up to,' he said. 'So convenient, him turning up like that in Santa Lucia. I must say he is more convincing a count than he was a gypsy.'

'You won't distract me like that,' said Clio. 'We aren't talking about my sins now, but yours. At least I have never kidnapped anyone.'

'Perhaps, then, I could distract you like this?' he said. Before Clio could tell what he was about, he swiftly crossed the room, reaching out to clasp her by the waist. His lips descended on hers in a quick, crashing kiss.

Clio arched back, startled, still angry. But all her fury and confusion, her frustration, flashed out, colliding with her desire for him like alcohol meeting a flame. It burned away all rational thought, all memory of their tangled, complicated past, and left only pure emotion. Pure need.

She threw her arms around him, her fingers wrapped tightly in his hair, holding him to her as her lips parted for his kiss. He groaned, a primitive sound of need to equal her own, his tongue meeting hers, their mouths and bodies and even thoughts enmeshed. He was caught as surely as she was, bound by this push-pull, cat-and-mouse game they could never be free from.

He did terrible things, but then so did she. Kidnapping, theft. Would they each be into such irredeemable mischief without the other? Clio didn't know, and at the moment she didn't care. She only knew, only wanted, his kiss. His touch. How could he make her forget, with only a glance, a touch, how very bad they were for each other?

Pulling him with her, Clio stumbled backwards until she fell across the unmade bed, sinking into its feathery softness. She drew him down on top of her, their kiss frantic. She wrapped her legs tightly around his hips, kicking her skirts out of the way. Her stockings abraded against his soft breeches, and she felt the heavy proof of his fierce desire against her thigh. But it wasn't enough, not nearly enough. Not any longer.

Clio let her head fall back against the tumbled sheets, revelling in the shivery sensation of his lips against her jaw, the arc of her throat. The hot rush of his breath, his heartbeat, all around her, part of her. How *alive* he was, how vital and real! She had lived too long among ancient artifacts, lives long over, and now she wanted his heat and life. His passion. No matter how angry he made her! No matter what happened after.

When she was with him, she knew real emotion, the true urgency of existence and craving and passion. When she was with him, no matter if they argued or kissed, she was alive herself. She couldn't give that up.

Her eyes still tightly closed, absorbing every feeling and sensation, she slid her touch over his tense shoulders, his taut chest, until she found the buttons of his waistcoat. She made quick work of them, pushing the heavy cloth back so she could unfasten his shirt. The lacings grew tangled under her desperate touch, and she sobbed in frustration. She had had *enough* of half-measures, of broken kisses furtively snatched. She wanted to touch him, feel his bare skin under her hands.

Now!

She caught at one of the knots and tugged hard, breaking it open. She parted the placket of the soft linen, shoving it away from his shoulders. Edward groaned, his face buried in the curve of her neck as her fingers traced the naked skin of his chest.

Clio had only ever seen the nude male form in cold marble statues or flat paintings, had only been able to wonder how Edward would compare to them. How real, living flesh would feel. The curiosity and fantasy had sometimes been quite— intense. But it could not compare with the reality. Not even close.

Her fingers traced over hot, smooth flesh, roughened by a sprinkling of coarse hair. His heart pounded under her caress, his breath quick, yet he did not move away, no matter how much he might want to. He did not try to snatch control from her. He lay wrapped in her caress, his lips against her shoulder, and let her explore.

She smoothed her palm over his flat nipples, the sharp arc of his collarbone, his muscled shoulders. She would have thought an English duke, waited on slavishly, swathed in ease, would be soft. But his skin was taut over lean, powerful muscles.

Clio tightened her clasp on his shoulders, rolling him to the bed as she rose above him on her knees. She could hardly breathe, hardly think! All she could know was him, the unbearable need that had been building inside her for so long. She had tried so hard to deny it, to push it away, fight against it.

She just could not do that any longer.

Her dress was loose, and she grasped it by its rucked-up hem, pulling it off over her head. Her chemise quickly followed, and she knelt above him clad only in her stockings, gartered above her knees. She shrugged off the temptation to hide behind her hair, pushing the long, tangled strands down her back. She held her breath, staring down at him in what was suddenly a crackling and profound silence.

Edward's bare chest, sun-golden and touched with the red-blond of his hair, rose and fell with the force of his own breath, the heartbeat that stirred the small amulet on a thin chain. She saw it was a tiny cameo, Clio the Muse of History's scroll, on ebony.

She knew that he wanted her, as she wanted him, could see the proof of it straining his breeches, but he lay still. His green eyes, dark as a primeval forest, watched her closely.

'You see, Edward,' she whispered, 'I have no weapons. I give in. I surrender.'

He stared at her for a long moment, still wrapped in that heavy silence. Clio started to feel cold, to feel the strongest urge to cover herself. To run for her old shelters of anger and reserve. Was she hideous, then? She was tall and thin, she knew that, and her breasts were small. But she had always assumed that men were not so picky as all that—a naked breast was a naked breast, after all. And Edward *did* seem to want her. Had he not kissed her in London, at the farmhouse, at the *feste*?

But maybe now that she was naked before him in all her thin boniness, now that she offered herself to him, he had changed his mind.

She felt the itchy prickle of tears behind her eyes, and tilted back her head to hide them. *Men*—they were absolutely incomprehensible!

Then she felt the slide of his touch around her bare waist, easing her away so he could sit up. So they were eye to eye. Clio wrapped her legs tightly around him.

'On the contrary, Clio,' he said roughly, 'it is *you* who demand *my* complete surrender.'

'And do I have it? Do we have a truce between us, if only for today?'

'You have every part of me. You know that.'

Clio tipped her head back, laughing in a sudden rush of utter exaltation, hotter and wilder than her anger had ever been. 'Oh, Edward. I only want *one* part of you right now. Now, do be quiet and kiss me.'

He claimed her lips again, their mouths meeting in a desperate clash that held nothing of artful romance or subtle seduction. Only a deep, primitive need that had been too long repressed. Too long denied.

Clio could certainly deny it no longer. Love him or hate

him—or both—he was a part of her. They were like two halves of an ancient coin, mirror images too long separated.

They couldn't be parted now.

She broke their kiss only to pull off his shirt, then wrapped her arms around him again, leaning into the sharp curve of his body to feel the press of naked skin to naked skin. Heartbeat to heartbeat. They tumbled down to the bed, limbs entangled.

'Clio,' he gasped, rearing back from her. 'You are a lady, and I'm—we shouldn't do this.'

'I don't think we really have a choice,' Clio said, suddenly desperate at the thought that he might leave her now. Walk away from what they both needed, and had wanted for so long. They *had* to exorcise each other from their blood, or they would never be free.

'This has been coming for a long time,' she said. 'We can't stop it now. No one will know, and I—well, I know how to prevent complications. You see, I might be young, and, yes, a virgin, but I am not such a *lady* as all that. Now, be a gentleman, and finish what you started!'

He gave a startled laugh, and she dragged him back on top of her, silencing his words with her kiss. Soon there were no words at all, not even rational thought, just emotion, feelings, hot sensation. The joy of being inevitably joined at last.

He quickly shed his breeches, sliding into the welcome of her parted legs as if he was always meant to be just there. Their bodies *fit*, their movements perfectly coordinated like the most beautiful dance. Clio closed her eyes, revelling in the feel of his mouth at her breast, the delicious friction of their damp, hot skin, the frantic need that built and built inside her.

Through that white-hot haze, she felt the press of his

fingers against the seam of her womanhood, parting her for the heavy slide of his penis as he entered her. She tensed at the slight burning, the unfamiliar stretch and ache of it. Her breath caught in her throat, and she gave a tiny whimper.

But even as he drew back she arched upwards, sliding him even deeper inside her, so deep she could vow he touched her soul. As she held him there, the ache subsided, and there was only the deep satisfaction of being part of him. That delicious joy building up again.

'Oh. That *is* nice,' she whispered.

Edward laughed roughly. He drew slowly out, then back again, faster and deeper, that wonderful friction expanding, growing, until Clio felt she was soaring up into the sun itself. Surely no one could survive such intensity, such overwhelming, frantic ecstasy!

She held tight to Edward, calling out to him incoherently as at last she touched that sun, and flew apart in a million flaming fragments. A shower of bright release that sent her tumbling back to earth, weak and trembling.

He caught her as she fell, holding her safe in his arms as she suddenly, inexplicably, burst into tears.

'Oh, Edward,' she sobbed. 'That was—marvellous.'

He cradled her against his chest, and she felt the deep rumble of his laughter as he kissed her hair, her temple. 'Marvellous, my dear,' he muttered, 'doesn't even begin to describe it.'

Chapter Twenty-Two

'You are such a *duke*,' Clio said, laughing. She sat on the worn brocade couch in the cottage's only parlour, wrapped in her dressing gown and watching Edward attempt to light a fire. She had just finished drinking her infusion of smart-weed leaves and rue—vile, but Rosa had solemnly assured her it would prevent pregnancy—and Edward's efforts were an excellent distraction from the bitter taste.

He glanced back over his shoulder, grinning at her. He wore nothing but his breeches, his hair carelessly tied back, and he looked—happy. Happiness was certainly not something she ever associated with him, yet it certainly looked good. His eyes, his smile, the golden glow of his skin, it was so very beautiful. Her bright Apollo.

She felt quite happy herself, light and giddy, as if her feet floated right off the ground. Despite being a prisoner here, she couldn't remember ever feeling quite so carefree.

Sex certainly wasn't overrated, then.

'I've been called worse,' he said, trying again to light his haphazard pile of wood and kindling. 'What about me is particularly duke-like right now? My fine raiment?'

'The way you can so handily kidnap someone, yet you can't light a fire,' she said.

'Would you care to try, then, madame? Not that *you* live daily with a houseful of servants, of course, I'm sure you have far more experience with domestic chores than I would…'

'Oh, here, give me that!' Clio pushed him out of the way, taking the flint from his hands. She studied it carefully. She had certainly watched the maids light fires dozens of times—surely it could not be so hard?

Edward leaned back against the abandoned couch, his hands behind his head as he watched her with smug satisfaction. It made her all the more determined to build the best fire ever seen!

'Surely I am not so completely useless,' he said. 'Even dukes have their advantages.'

'Oh, yes? Like what?'

'Did I not carry in vast quantities of water, just so you can have a bath?' He gestured toward the buckets lined up on the hearth.

Clio laughed. 'So you did.' And he had also brought a shining brass hip bath, piles of fluffy towels and her own lily-scented bath salts and soap. All the finest *ducal* luxuries. Yet it would do them no good if they could not heat the water.

At last she got the flint to catch, and lit some of the kindling. She pushed it under the wood with the poker, watching with a great sense of accomplishment as the flames caught and built.

'I'm exhausted.' She sighed. 'And famished! What have you brought for my supper?'

'So very demanding,' Edward teased. 'Build me a fire, find me some rue, give me supper.'

Clio laughed, snuggling back into his welcoming arms as the fire heated the room. His embrace surrounded her, warm and safe, and she felt his chin nestle atop her hair. She thought she could surely stay there for ever, curled up next to Edward with a good fire and a soft bed. They seemed to be the only two people in all the world.

It could not last long, she knew that. It was far too sweet, too perfect. She would have to escape soon, to find out what was happening in the wide universe outside their little cocoon. But not yet. Not tonight. It had taken her and Edward too long to come to this moment of understanding; she had to enjoy it to the fullest.

While it lasted.

'As a matter of fact, I did bring supper,' he said. Not letting her go, he reached out with his bare foot and hooked a covered basket, dragging it close. 'Bread, cheese, olives, prosciutto. Some fruit and lemon cakes. Wine.'

'Hmm, so there *are* advantages to being a duke,' Clio said, rummaging in the basket until she found a loaf of bread. She tore off a soft white bite, popping it into his mouth before eating the rest herself. 'Delicious.'

'A true ducal repast, one worthy of you, my dear, would have at least twenty courses.'

'Served on golden plates?'

'Of course. And ruby goblets.'

'With an orchestra from Vienna to serenade us while we eat our roasted swan and lobster patties.'

'And doves to soar overhead, carrying banners embroidered with your name, "Clio the Most Fair", as they dropped diamonds and pearls into your lap.'

Clio laughed at their silliness as she poured out the wine, not into ruby goblets but into plain pottery. 'Knowing doves, it would *not* be pearls they dropped, but something far less glamorous.'

'Not ducal doves.'

'So, even birds do your bidding?'

'Certainly. The only creatures who don't are Muses.'

'We don't do anyone's bidding, I fear.' Clio dug about among the food, laying out the meat and cheese, the glistening lemon cakes. At the very bottom of the basket was a small nosegay of Sicilian wildflowers, gold and purple and sage-green, tied up with white satin ribbons.

'For "Clio the Most Fair",' Edward said quietly. 'I wish they were diamonds.'

She shook her head, inhaling the crisp, clean scent of the flowers. They smelled of nature, of wildness, of freedom. Of everything she had found here on this ancient island, with him. 'Flowers are surely far better than any diamonds.'

'I knew you would say that. So I sent those earrings back to my jeweller…'

Clio laughed, falling back into his arms. 'Oh, Edward. I can see now that even dukes might make good husbands, given the proper training.'

He held her close, his breath stirring the loose curls at her temples. She felt the quick press of his kiss on her ear, and it made her smile. 'You could find a hundred better husbands than me, Clio.'

'Oh, undoubtedly. A kind husband who would do my bidding without complaint, and not lock me up in funny little cottages with no servants to prepare my bath.' Men who weren't somehow involved in shadowy antiquities deals…

'Italian counts with handsome faces and hand-kissing manners?'

'My goodness, Edward, are you jealous? Of Marco?' For some reason, the thought that he might be just a little bit jealous gave her a twinge of satisfaction. Edward had surely been in love, or at least in lust, many times in the past, whereas she had only him. But he didn't have to know that just yet.

'Marco and I are merely friends,' she said airily. 'Colleagues, I suppose you could say.'

'And where did you find this *colleague*? Skulking around a gypsy camp in disguise?'

'Of course not,' Clio said, laughing. 'He wrote a very stirring pamphlet, on the sad fate of some Italian antiquities, stolen from Florence and Tuscany and hidden away in foreign private collections. He's very passionate about such things, about culture and heritage.'

'And you approved of his views right away, I'm sure.'

'I did. I had often despaired of many of the more, shall we say, unscrupulous collecting habits I saw in some of my father's acquaintances. I just had no idea what I could do about it. So, when I read Marco's pamphlet, I wrote to him about it.'

'You wrote to a strange man?' Edward said incredulously.

'It wasn't a romantic letter at all! And really, Edward, are you surprised I would disregard propriety in such a way?'

He gave a rueful laugh, his arms tightening around her. 'I suppose I should not be. Nothing you do ought to surprise me any longer.'

'No, it should not. I have ceased to even surprise myself.' Though, in truth, she was rather surprised at herself at this moment. Sitting alone with Edward in an isolated cottage, half-naked, chatting casually about her most closely held secrets. A month ago, even a week ago, she couldn't have imagined it. 'But that is how I came to be friends with Marco. And when I devised the idea of the Lily Thief, I knew who to turn to for help.'

They were silent for a long moment, nibbling at their

repast to the crackle of the flames, the whistle of the night wind outside their cottage refuge.

'You're really not in love with him, then?' Edward said at last.

Clio laughed. 'Not at all. He is far too charming for me.' She turned in his arms, looping her hands around his neck. He watched her cautiously, and she pressed tiny, light kisses along his jaw and cheekbones until he smiled at last. 'I much prefer mysterious, taciturn dukes.'

He held her against him, cradling her to his bare chest as he buried his face in the curve of her neck. 'Oh, Clio,' he muttered. 'We're two of a kind, whether we want to admit it or not.'

Two of a kind? Before Clio could say anything, could question him or demand that he finally stop being so blasted mysterious, he kissed her lips and she forgot everything else. She just knew that kiss, his breath and skin, the now-familiar way his body felt under her touch. The hot, sharp need their lovemaking had created rose up inside her again, more urgent than ever.

Could she ever have enough of this man? Could her yearning ever truly be satisfied? Clio feared the answer was *no*. Never. The more she had, the more she wanted. She wanted every part of him, his body, his spirit, his secrets. For he surely possessed all of *her*.

They tumbled back on to the floor, the heat and smoke from the fire wrapped around them as they shed their clothes, the last barrier to their touch. Clio welcomed him into her body, into her very heart and soul. Even as she lost herself in their lovemaking, she feared he would stay there, locked in her heart, for ever.

This time out of time, with the world shut away from their secret bower, was a rare and fleeting gift. She wanted to make the most of every second, every touch and kiss.

Because it surely could not last long.

Chapter Twenty-Three

Thalia glanced down at the slip of paper in her hand, then up at the house. It seemed to be the right address, yet she wasn't sure. It didn't look like the residence of a count.

She didn't know what sort of abode she expected for Marco di Fabrizzi. A vast white baroque palace, with stucco flourishes and wrought-iron balconies? A medieval castle, cold and forbidding, bound in ancient stone and overgrown ivy? Whatever she imagined, this wasn't quite it. A tall, narrow town house in a part of Santa Lucia tucked behind the palazzos, inhabited mostly by shopkeepers. Neat and respectable enough, but not grand.

Thalia's estimation of him went up a small notch. He was not a snob, then, like his friend Lady Riverton. But that did not mean she intended to leave him alone. She had come here for answers, and answers she would get.

She drew her cloak's hood closer about her face, staying in the night's shadows. Chase Muses were known for being daring, for being fearless bluestockings, yet coming to a man's house would be too much even for daring young ladies! Luckily there was no one on the street; respectable shopkeepers probably retired early. And there were no lights to be seen in the Count's windows.

If she was fortunate, he would be out and she could rifle his desk in search of secret papers and letters without being hurried. She wanted to discover something, anything, to tell her where her sister really was.

Unless—unless they had gone off together. Eloped. Was there some form of Gretna Green in Sicily?

Thalia knew that Marco was not all he pretended to be. No, he was definitely more. More than a charming, peripatetic, not-too-bright Continental aristocrat who cared only to flirt, dance and acquire artwork. When he had talked to her, in the dark of the masked ball, she saw such fierce intelligence in his eyes. Saw the intensity he tried to hide. He held secrets, many of them. He had a purpose here in Santa Lucia far beyond going to parties. Yet she—and Clio—seemed to be the only ones who saw that.

That was the thing about great beauty, Thalia reflected. It was a blessing and a curse for those who possessed it. A blessing, because most people seldom looked past it to see the ugliness and pain, the secrets and plans, hidden beneath. There was always a certain power to being underestimated, as she well knew. Yet it was a curse, too, because most people also didn't *want* to see past fine eyes and glowing skin. They wanted only the fantasy.

She knew Marco was up to something, something hidden behind the glory of his face. He thought himself well disguised, but he had not reckoned with her.

Thalia hurried back behind the quiet row of houses, counting until she found the right one again. A set of shallow stone steps, set behind an iron railing, led down to the kitchen. It, too, seemed quiet, as if the servants were out. Or perhaps he kept no servants, all the better to hide his secret deeds.

She tiptoed down the steps and carefully tested the door, finding it unlocked. When she peered inside, she found a narrow corridor piled with crates of produce and wine bottles, but no noise or movement. No people. From the gloomy light coming through the open door she dashed through the kitchen to the servants' stairs.

How thrilling it all was, she thought, to be doing something so very *wrong*! She could see now why criminals, like that Lily Thief who had struck London last year, kept on doing it, despite the danger. Thalia suddenly felt so very alive, tingling with excitement and fear all at the same time. It was like a suspenseful play, and she held her breath to see what would happen next.

She pushed open the door at the top of the stairs and found herself on a landing, a high-set window illuminating two partially opened doors. She glimpsed a dining room and a drawing room, simply furnished and dark. The whole place had a chilly air of disuse about it, an abandoned quality that made her think of ghost stories.

Her hand trembled, but she kept moving. She had to; she had come too far to turn away, to miss what the next act might hold.

She crept up the stairs, higher and higher into the darkness. Finally, along another narrow corridor, there was one door with a thin line of light around the edges. She could hear no sound, no murmur of voices, no screams or shouts. Just the enveloping silence of the rest of the house.

Steeling her nerves, Thalia ran forward, shoving open the door with a great bang. At first, she dared not look, dared not see what horrors she might have found. But when she peeked, she saw—well, not much at all.

It was a small bedchamber, well lit by lamps and a cosy fire in the grate. Marco di Fabrizzi sat at a desk by the heavily curtained window, papers and books scattered before him. He wore a brocade dressing gown, his black hair rumpled over his brow, yet as he glanced up in shock his hand shot to a wicked-looking dagger resting on the desk. He held it balanced expertly on his palm, prepared to do battle.

Thalia's gaze darted around the room, but she saw no one else. Marco appeared to be alone.

He came slowly to his feet, still holding the dagger. 'Signorina Thalia?' he said incredulously. 'What are you doing here?'

'I came to find my sister,' Thalia cried. 'Where have you hidden her?'

'Clio?' he asked. He watched her closely, his lovely dark eyes full of wariness, suspicion, and—and laughter? 'Is she not at your house?'

'Of course she isn't, or I wouldn't be here looking for her, would I?'

'I'm sure I could not say.'

'I am not as big a fool as all that.' But she was, Thalia realised with a horrible sinking sensation, something of a fool. Once again, she had dashed into things without pausing for thought. Without thinking of the consequences. Now she was alone in a silent house, with a man in possession of a dagger.

'I thought she had eloped with you,' she said weakly.

He gave a startled laugh. 'I do not believe so.' He went to the wardrobe, opening the doors to show her the interior, empty of everything but clothes. 'No ladies there, alas.' He knelt to peer under the bed. 'Nor there. Though I must speak to the maids about dusting.'

Thalia watched him, more and more chagrined, as he stood up and smiled at her. It was a beautiful smile, of course, carving unearthly dimples into his whisker-roughened olive cheeks. But it was also careful, as if he humoured the crazy lady who had broken into his house.

Thalia stepped back, pressing her hands to her burning cheeks. 'Then you don't know where she is at all?'

'I fear I have not seen her since your dinner party,' he said gently. 'Has she really disappeared?'

'Yes. No. I don't know.' Thalia groaned. She felt the most ridiculous, childish urge to stamp her feet and sob! But was this whole exercise not another way to make her family see she was grown up now, not a silly child? Not someone to protect? So, she kept her shoes firmly on the floor, determined to stop and think for once in her life. Now that it was too late.

'Here, *signorina*, sit down,' Marco said. He put down the dagger and moved slowly toward her, holding his hands out as one would to a skittish horse. Thalia let him take her arm and lead her to a chair. 'Have some wine, and tell me what has happened.'

'I really don't know *what* has happened,' she said, watching as he poured out a glass of wine and pressed it into her cold fingers. She sipped at it automatically, but it was indeed bracing. It helped her slow her racing thoughts.

'You say your sister has vanished?' he asked, sitting down beside her.

'I thought she had. She sent us a message saying she had decided to go to Motya with the Darbys after all. But things have been so very odd lately…'

'Odd?' He spoke quietly, as if he feared to scare her, but she heard the concern in his voice.

'Yes. Clio has been rather, I don't know, moody. Quiet. Especially since you arrived. I thought perhaps you two had decided to elope, and I was angry she was keeping secrets from me. I decided to find out for myself.' She took another fortifying sip. 'I see now I was wrong.'

He smiled wryly, as if amused she could think him a seducing eloper, even though he himself seemed to want to appear a heartless flirt. 'Why would you think I would run off with your sister?'

'I saw the two of you on the terrace at our party, talking together so intimately,' she said. 'And did you not know each other before?'

'Before?' The dimples vanished.

'Before Santa Lucia. In England, even.' Thalia laughed. 'You needn't look so surprised. There are some advantages to looking like a silly blonde bonbon, you know. I see things my sisters think I do not.'

'I *am* surprised, Thalia,' he said. 'Yet I should not be. I knew you were dangerous the very first time I saw you.'

'Not half as dangerous as you, I'm sure—Count.' She put down the empty glass with a sigh. 'But I am no closer to finding my sister.'

'Is it possible she really did go to Motya?'

'It is possible, of course. She has gone off on such excursions on short notice before, and my father doesn't seem concerned. Yet...'

'Yet *you* are concerned?'

'Yes. It doesn't feel right to me somehow.'

Marco shook his head. 'Nor to me. She would not go now. You are right to be concerned.'

Reassured by the fact that he seemed to take her seriously, and did not just laugh her fears away as her family would, Thalia turned to him, reaching for his hand. 'Tell me. What do you know of the Duke of Averton?'

Chapter Twenty-Four

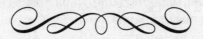

Edward roused slowly from sleep, a deeper, sweeter rest than he had known in a very long time. A dreamless, healing slumber that seemed to wrap all around him like a soft velvet blanket, bringing such beautiful dreams.

Only the dreams were real. He opened his eyes to find himself lying on a pile of cushions on the cottage floor. The air was warm, scented with woodsmoke, wine and lilies. As he gazed up at the dark rafters high overhead, he heard the splash of water. And a humming sound. Loud and distinctly off-key.

'"It was a lover and his laaaaasss, with a hey and ho and a heeeyyy nonny no",' the voice sang, all warbling and wavering. And very, very happy. '"Nonny nonny no!"'

Grinning, Edward sat up to find Clio in her bath, splashing her feet in the water in time to the song. Steam rose up in curling wreaths around her, dampening her pinned-up hair and flushed cheeks. She was truly the most beautiful thing he had ever seen.

'Thomas Morley would roll over in his grave, if he could hear what you do to his song,' he said.

Clio smiled at him over her shoulder, giving one more great splash that sprayed water over his bare chest. 'I confess I am not the musician Thalia is. But everyone is a great singer in the bath. I'm glad you're awake. You can hand me that soap over there.'

Edward pushed himself to his feet, stretching luxuriously in the heated air. When had he ever felt so very—free?

Never. And surely he never would again. But he would always have this time with Clio. Even if he had had to resort to kidnapping to gain it!

'It is no use trying to tempt me with your body, Edward Radcliffe,' she said teasingly. 'I am taking my bath, and that's that. I can't be distracted. Now, soap please.'

Edward laughed, and scooped up the ball of white soap from the table. It, too, smelled of lilies, summer-sweet, just like Clio. He walked slowly toward her, the soap held out like an offering, to see if she could indeed be tempted.

Her eyes widened, but she shook her head. 'Would you be so kind as to wash my back?'

'With pleasure, madame. I am yours to command.'

'Well, that's a first,' she said, leaning forward in the tub. 'Why do I suspect you are mine to command only in things you already wish to do?'

'You know me too well.' Edward rubbed the soap between his hands, working it into a frothy, scented foam. He studied in fascination the elegant arc of her bare back, the curve of the nape of her neck, the damp curls that escaped their pins to cling to her skin. So beautiful, yet so vulnerable.

'On the contrary,' she murmured, shivering as his finger-tips touched her spine, 'I don't really know you at all.'

She knew him, deep-down knew him, better than anyone

ever had. 'What do you want to know that you don't already?' he said, tracing a soapy pattern over her skin.

Clio leaned back into his touch. 'Everything, of course. Everything you love, everything you hate. All that has ever happened to you.'

'That's a great deal to know.'

'Of course. So, start at the beginning.'

He laughed. 'From the day I was born? I fear I don't remember it well.' He kissed the nape of her neck, breathing deeply of her lily perfume.

'Then tell me what you do remember,' she whispered.

He ran the flat of his palm over her shoulder, the curve of her arm, the slickness of her wet skin. He felt the pulse beating in her wrist, strong and alive. 'I grew up much like you, I suspect.'

'Not with a passel of sisters!'

'I fear not. Only with an older brother. A perfect older brother.'

'Ah, so you *were* like me. For no one could be a more perfect older sibling than Calliope.'

'William was.' Edward gently urged her forward, slipping into the tub behind her. It was a tight fit, but he wrapped his legs around her, holding her close, and she curved her body back to fit against his, her head on his shoulder. The lily-scented water lapped against them.

It was easier for him to talk about his family, to voice their long-unspoken names if she couldn't see him.

'William was always good at his lessons, and he never, ever got into trouble,' he said.

'As you did?'

'Oh, always. I never could resist getting into mischief. William, though, was my parents' fine classical son. Their Hector, they called him. He followed in their scholarly footsteps, did well at school, at university, at everything. He joined the Antiquities Society, found a perfect lady to become his fiancée.' Edward paused. 'He would have made a fine duke.'

'But you, too, must have learned your classical lessons well!' Clio exclaimed. 'Everyone admires your great scholarship, even my father.'

'Oh, I learned eventually. One could hardly avoid it, with tutors and my parents ramming Plato and Aristotle and Herodotus down my throat every day. Yet I did not care. Not until much later. Only then, when it was too late for William and my poor parents, did I see the true value, the wonder of it all. They knew only my wild youth.'

Clio was quiet for a long moment. Then she leaned over the edge of the tub and caught up their goblets from the remains of their supper. She held them up, hers empty of wine, his still full. 'Does this have anything to do with it? I noticed your glass was full at our dinner party, too.'

Edward plucked the cup from her hand, studying the ruby-red liquid as if it held vast secrets in its depths. He placed it gently back on the floor, and leaned his head on the edge of the tub. 'You asked me once why your brother-in-law hates me.'

Clio thought this seemed as if it might turn into a rather serious discussion. She stood up from the water, reaching for one of the fluffy towels and wrapping it tightly around her torso, as if the thick cloth could be an armour to ward off words. To keep the truth away from their idyll, even as she knew she had to hear it.

'Yes,' she said quietly. 'Cameron is so very amiable, I don't understand his fury with you.'

'Amiable, yes. He always was, even with me. We were friends of a sort, when we first met.'

Clio sat down on the couch, still wrapped in her towel. Edward leaned his arms on the tub, watching her. His hair was damp, slicked away from his handsome features. 'You were friends?' she said, surprised.

He smiled humourlessly. 'You are startled, I see, and who could blame you. People less observant than you, my dear, have noticed the strained manner of our recent meetings. But when we first met at university, he was like no one I had ever encountered before. He had spent his life travelling, seeing places, meeting people all my other friends had thus far only read about. He was serious, serious about his studies and his family, yet also—kind. Always ready for a jest.'

'And you were not? Serious and kind, that is.' She couldn't picture him jesting, either.

'I was not. I was spoiled, always seeking the next pleasure, the next novelty. My friends were the same way, a useless, debauched lot whose lives did no one any good. Least of all themselves.' Edward rose from the bath and reached for the other towel. His breeches were soaked through, his amulet gleaming on his wet, naked chest. The stone floor around the tub was covered with soapy puddles, but he didn't seem to notice. He was far away from her, deep in his own past.

'A friendship with Lord Westwood might have been a good thing for me then,' he continued. 'After all, *he* has come out a worthy husband for a Chase Muse. Yet I was too caught up in drinking and whoring, gambling away any money I had, or didn't have. Showing my parents how little I cared for their scholarly ways, for what was important to them.'

'Did you truly not care?'

He laughed harshly. 'Of course I cared. But I was tumbling downhill too fast to stop myself. I was drunk all the time, living in a haze, in danger of being sent down and disgracing my parents even further. That was when it happened.'

Clio felt a cold, clammy dread creeping over her, yet like Edward she felt she could not stop anything. There had to be truth between them if they were to move forwards. Even if the truth was like daggers. 'What happened?'

'There was this woman. Isn't there always? But she was girl really, she couldn't have been more than seventeen or eighteen.' He sat down on a bench by the fireplace, not close to her, not looking at her. He stared only into the past, to a place where she could not go. 'She worked as maid in a tavern where my useless friends and I liked to go. She was pretty and sweet-natured, and she seemed to like me a great deal. Heaven only knows why.'

Clio swallowed hard, her throat dry. 'You had an affair with her?'

'An affair? I swived her in the alley behind the tavern, if that's what you mean. Several times, if I remember correctly. My—relationships back then were always of that sort.'

'Then what was special about that one girl?'

'Your brother-in-law liked her. Not in the debauched way I did. I think he saw her true vulnerability, in a way I could not. He warned me to leave her alone, but I just laughed at him. Told him who knew the Greeks were really such priggish puritans, insulted his mother in a way I'm ashamed to remember. He was right in the end.'

'What happened?'

'She came to me one night. I was drunk, as usual, and had just lost my entire quarterly allowance on the turn of a card. I was in a foul mood. And she said she was pregnant.'

'With your child?'

'Yes. I did not believe her. I disavowed that the brat could be mine, declared I was sure the father could be any one of a dozen men.' His voice was low, expressionless, but tight with an emotion long suppressed. 'She fled in tears. Two days later she was discovered hanged in her room. And it was Cameron who found her.'

'Oh.' Clio felt she had had the air punched out of her. She crossed her arms tightly over her chest, closing her eyes against the rush of tears. That poor, poor girl.

'Once you told me I could not possibly have been worse than any other young nobleman, gadding about in my misspent youth,' he said. 'Perhaps I was not. I'm sure my so-called friends got plenty of tavern wenches and house maids with child. But I have been haunted for years by that girl. I murdered her, and my own child, and I was too drunk and callous to care. Cameron broke my nose the day he found her body, and he should have done worse.'

Clio shook her head. 'What could he do that is worse than what you have done to yourself? It was a terrible thing, true, but you don't drink now. You don't debauch serving maids.'

He smiled ruefully. 'Only young ladies of good family. After kidnapping them, of course.'

'*This* young lady practically forced you to debauch her! As for kidnapping—I am still not happy about that. But I know you did it because you believed you had to, to protect me somehow. You work for the Antiquities Society; I have heard you are ex-ceedingly generous to charities. You are trying to make amends. And your old friends are probably just as useless as ever.'

'Better late than never, eh?'

'Of course. None of us is a lost cause until we're dead.'

He laughed, no longer the harsh, humourless sound she so hated, but a real laugh. 'Clio, who knew you were such an optimist?'

'Well, I am not a lost cause, either. At least I hope I am not. We all have lessons to learn; yours was harsher than most. It made you see you had to abandon your old ways. Turn your life around.'

'Not *just* that.'

'What do you mean?' Clio wondered if he had yet more terrible secrets in his past, and she shivered. But she, too, had made a choice when she made love with Edward. She had made the choice to let him into her life, for good or ill.

'You remember Lady Riverton's game of Truth?' he said.

'Yes.'

'This is my truth, Clio. After that girl died, I spiralled even further into trouble. More drink, gaming in ever-rougher establishments, even experiments with opium. I told myself it was because of the pain of my broken nose, but that was not so. I loathed myself; I wanted to destroy myself, end what I was doing. Not even my parents could stop me, though they tried.'

'What *did* stop you?' she asked softly.

He came to sit beside her on the settee, reaching for her hand. His fingers entwined with hers. 'A muse. For are they not figures of great inspiration?'

'So I've heard,' she whispered. She touched his bare arm with her other hand, tracing a sinuous line along his tense muscles. 'What did this muse inspire in you?'

'She inspired me to change, once and for all. To seek to alter my course before it was too late.'

'An extraordinary muse indeed. Don't they usually just inspire a sonnet or a play?'

He smiled at her. 'This was a more far-reaching muse. An ambitious one, you might say.' He pressed a kiss to her temple, lingering there as if to savour her taste, her feel. 'That game at Lady Riverton's…'

'Oh, yes,' Clio said, remembering his words that night. 'You said you lost your one true love.' She had been intrigued then by his hinted-at secret. Had even been jealous of that unknown woman.

Could it have been that poor, lost tavern maid? Was that part of his torment? Or…

'I did not lose her so much as she was never mine in the first place. Muses can't truly belong to anyone at all, I am coming to realise.'

'And where did you find this—muse?'

'Where does one find anything important? At the British Museum, of course.'

Clio gave a startled laugh. Of all places, she did not expect that. Gaming hells, brothels, taverns—those fit his story. Not the British Museum. 'When did you find time to go there? Getting drunk and losing your allowance must have been very time-consuming.'

'So it was. But after one particularly lurid night, some of my friends thought it would be amusing to go the British Museum, to scandalise all the high-in-the-instep scholars. I agreed, thinking news of my behaviour would surely reach my parents. But I got more than I bargained for.'

Clio remembered that long-ago day now, surely the very day he talked about. She and her parents, along with Thalia, Cory and baby Urania had gone to the museum to look at a new black-figure vase just donated to the collections. As they went in, she stopped to peer into one of the sculpture galleries, drawn by the sound of raucous laughter.

She had known who he was, of course. Everyone knew the Radcliffes, their great interest in antiquities and philanthropy—and the trouble they had with their younger, prodigal son. Her own parents commiserated about it, laughing about how fortunate they were to have only daughters. But Clio was only fifteen then, still practically in the schoolroom, and she had only seen Lord Edward Radcliffe from a distance, riding in the park or at a play or concert. From that distance, he was terribly handsome. Terribly intriguing.

Up close, he was still handsome. But so very—careless. Looking at him she had felt so terribly angry. Here was someone who had things she, as a female, could only dream of—a university education, the chance to travel, to study, to do important things. And he did not seem to even care. Did not even see the beauty all around him at the museum.

She had been angry that day—and sad.

'You saw *me*,' she said softly. 'That day when I was fifteen.'

'I saw you. And you were so very disdainful, so beautiful. I had lived with my family's disappointment for years, yet I could not bear when I saw it in your eyes. I found I wanted to be worthy of someone like you.'

'Someone like me?' she said incredulously. 'Someone angry and confused, always searching for something that can never be found?'

'Someone sure of themselves,' he contradicted. 'Someone willing to fight for what they care about. *That* is what I admire in you. That's what I wanted to be like then.'

Clio felt that ache of tears behind her eyes, and she fought them back. Fought not to fall into his arms and sob like a lost child. All those lonely months and years of feeling no one understood, no one shared her burning desire for more. More than a privileged, civilised life. And here all along was someone who had shared her wandering spirit. Her quest for transcendence.

'I, too, have done things I regret,' she said. 'But I have

found that no one is really lost. Some of us are simply on a different path, a new, undiscovered trail. And redemption can surely be found there in the wilderness, if we seek it.'

'Or if we are willing to accept it when *it* seeks *us*?'

Clio kissed him, their hands still entwined. It was a slow, sweet kiss, a kiss that said what she could not. All her yearning, all the old pain and uncertainty, everything she longed for. She sought to take away *his* pain, too, to give him forgiveness that was not hers to bestow, to ease the ache of the past. She clung to him, to this moment that meant so much. Meant everything.

She drew back, studying the elegant angles of his aristocratic face in the dying firelight. She traced the line of his mouth, the sweep of his jaw, his crooked nose. Memorising every inch of him so she would always, always remember. His eyes were closed, his jaw clenched as if pained, yet he did not move away. Not even when she softly kissed the corner of his mouth, the pulse that beat at the base of his throat.

'I think,' she whispered, resting her forehead on his chest, 'that we should go to bed now. It's late.'

Without a word, he wrapped his arms around her, lifting her high in the air as he stood up. Clio held tightly to his neck as he carried her up the stairs into the darkness of the bedroom. *Their* bedroom.

Once she had fought him, feared him. Now—now she trusted him to lead her anywhere. Even into the fearsome unknown of a game of Truth.

Chapter Twenty-Five

Edward lay propped on the pillows of Clio's bed, *their* bed, among the tumbled blankets. Clio slept beside him, her arm flung over his chest as if to hold him there. She sighed in her dreams, burrowing deeper under the sheets. The whole chamber smelled of her lily soap, the sweet smell of her skin, the warm, dark presence of *her*.

He smoothed her tangled hair back from her brow, wrapping the long, auburn strands over his chest and throat.

It was possibly more than he deserved, yet he savoured it all the same. Beings like muses were mercurial indeed; she would fly away at any moment. But for now, she was his to hold.

He studied the starlight blinking in the small window, growing ever fainter in a sign that night would soon end. But it was a night that had changed so very much. He had never talked of that tavern maid before, of the terrible thing he had done. He never talked of the drinking, the opium, the wild friends, all the things that had carried him so far from what he owed to his family. Carried him away from himself.

It was all years in the past, the work of a heedless, angry boy. The man he was now, the Duke, worked every day for scholarship and antiquities, for charities and his estates, yet it had never been enough to erase the past. Not until tonight, when he had looked into Clio's eyes and seen forgiveness. Seen understanding, and the first rays of hope.

Like all muses, she looked on human folly and weakness and saw everything. Saw what drove people to the desperate things they did, and understood and pitied. Her kiss was an absolution, if he could just accept it.

Clio stirred in his arms. She blinked her eyes open, staring out into nothingness as if still caught in dreams. Then she focused on him, and smiled.

'Are you all right?' she asked.

'Of course I am. Better than "all right", as a matter of fact.' He slid down among the sheets, still warm with her sleep, and wrapped both arms around her as she curled into his body. 'I have never felt better.'

'Neither have I. Who would ever have imagined it?'

'Imagined what?'

'That you and I would be here now, like this. And no one has even been knocked unconscious or pushed out of a window.'

He laughed. 'I think one would be hard pressed to push so much as cat out of such a tiny window. But I must say I'm grateful for the lack of bodily harm. It's more than I deserve, I think.'

'Indeed it is. Kidnapping is a capital offence, and I will certainly get you back for it one day.'

'When I least expect it?'

'Revenge is pointless when it's looked for, isn't it? But you are right about one thing.'

'Just one? And here I've fancied I'm right about many things.'

'So conceited, just like a duke. You're right that this cottage is in need of a cat.'

He gave a surprised laugh. Whatever he expected her to say—and really, Clio could be counted upon to say anything—it was not that. 'A cat? So you can push it out of the window in lieu of me?'

She slapped his shoulder indignantly. 'Certainly not! I have always wanted a cat, but they make my father sneeze. When I was a child, we could only have fat ponies as pets. And a barn owl Cory took in once, fancying herself Athena. This cottage needs a cat, a fluffy grey one. To sleep beside the fire and purr cosily. That would make this place completely perfect.'

'You like this funny cottage, then?'

'I adore it. Can we stay here for ever and ever?'

That was a most tempting prospect. To stay hidden here with Clio, to just be Edward and not a duke for the rest of his days. To forget. To be happy. 'Do you not think we would be missed before "for ever"?'

She frowned, her fingertips tracing light, enticing patterns over his shoulder. She lifted his amulet, studying it in the starlight. The scroll of Clio, Muse of History.

'I suppose we might be missed,' she said. 'My father is absent-minded, but he still might notice if I never came back. So, we just have—how long?'

'I don't know yet,' he answered.

He was afraid she would ask questions about his task, about what drove him to bring her here in the first place. He had no answers for any of that yet. But she just let the amulet drop.

'So, for ever might still be a possibility,' she said.

'What else did you want when you were a child?' he asked. 'Besides a cat.'

'Many things. A library of my very own where I could

work, without my sisters running in and out making noise and distracting me. A lake to go swimming in the summer and skating in the winter, though we actually did have that. Oh, and no music lessons. I could never do better than Thalia at the pianoforte and the harp, and I hated that!'

'Ah-ha! One thing the muse can't do.'

'I also can't dance well,' she said, laughing. 'But I can ride, and swim, and pick locks.'

'I have ample proof of that one. I'm surprised you didn't pick the lock on this door and run away.'

'I didn't have time. And now—well, it's rather nice here.'

'Nice enough to stay for ever.'

'Even if there is no cat. And that would be easy enough to obtain.' She was quiet for a long moment, so quiet Edward thought she had fallen asleep. But then she said, 'What happened after?'

'After?'

'After that day at the British Museum. Did you immediately reform? Swear off drink and courtesans?'

'I had to. For when I left the museum I heard my brother had died, fallen from his horse and snapping his neck. My parents' Hector was gone, and all they had left was poor, unsatisfactory Paris.'

'With no Helen?'

'Alas, no. My parents tried to get me to marry William's fiancée, but I could not. I tried to make it up to them in other ways, by sobering up, resuming my studies. Going off on a Grand Tour to find antiquities to add to their collection.'

'What did they think of your efforts?'

'I don't know. They died of a fever when I was in Rome. I'm sure they had their doubts, though. It must have troubled my father's last hours to know I would soon be the Duke.'

'But if they could see you now, surely they would be proud. They would see that their legacy is in safe hands.'

'Perhaps not if they saw me right at this moment. In bed with one of the Chase daughters, so very scandalous,' he said with a laugh.

Clio laughed, too, pushing herself up against the pillows, the sheet drawn across her naked breasts. 'Perhaps not right this moment, no. But if they saw your work with the Antiquities Society, the monographs you write on your travels and the history of the Punic Wars. The way you don't drink and don't—well, you know.'

'Debauch women?'

A dull pink flush spread across her cheeks, and he almost laughed aloud with the rare wonder of it. Clio Chase, blushing!

'I wouldn't know about that,' she muttered.

'Of course you would. You are the only woman I have *debauched* in quite a while.'

'Oh, Edward. You great, romantic fool,' she said between kisses.

'So, for all that, do I not deserve a reward?'

In reply, she cast off the sheet and pushed him flat on his back to the mattress, climbing atop his naked body. She kissed him again, a hot, heady flurry of embraces that drove away all thoughts and doubts. Drove away everything but the knowledge that he was making love with *Clio*. That he was hers, and she was his.

'Clio…' he muttered.

'Shh,' she whispered, stopping his words with her kiss. 'I'm giving you your reward.'

He fell back on to the bed, his eyes closed as he lost himself in the feel of her lips, her hands. Her fingertips swept lightly, enticingly over his shoulders, his chest, the sharp plane of his hipbones. Her mouth followed, trailing a hot ribbon across his skin.

Her teeth scraped over his flat nipples, and he sucked in his breath. His hands tangled in her hair, the tangled strands gliding through his fingers as her kisses moved ever lower.

He felt the light touch of her tongue over his ribs, her lips on his taut abdomen. He dared not move, dared not breathe, for fear this dream would vanish. That Clio would be just a vision again, a fantasy.

But Clio was very real, and ever surprising. Her hair tugged at his grip as she knelt between his legs. Her fingertips skimmed over his thighs before alighting, ever so delicately, on his erect penis. The merest brush, but it was like a bolt of lightning, flashing with sizzling heat all through his being. She traced its hard, straining length, her nails gently scraping over the tip.

Edward arched up. 'Clio!' he cried hoarsely. Did he protest—or beg her not to stop? He hardly knew; he couldn't think straight at all with her touch *there*.

'Be quiet,' she murmured. Her gaze was rapt on his body, her touch growing more sure. 'I haven't done this before, I have to concentrate.'

He gave a strangled laugh. 'Please, my dear. Concentrate all you like.' He collapsed back onto the pillows, surrendering utterly to her caress.

She lowered her head, her hair trailing over them both in a dark curtain as she kissed his hip, the top of his tense thigh. Her breath was warm on his skin. Slowly, tentatively, the tip of her tongue touched the veined length of his manhood.

'Blast it, Clio!' he groaned. It was almost unbearable.

'Did I do it wrong?' she said worriedly. 'The fresco at Pompeii…'

'On the contrary. You did it far too correctly.'

She laughed and kissed him again, her tongue sweeping down the length of him as she balanced him lightly in her hand. Finally, he could bear it no more. He clasped her shoulders, pushing her away from him as he rolled her to the bed.

'Clio, you are *killing* me,' he said. 'No more trips to Pompeii, I beg you.' She parted her legs, welcoming his desperate lunge into her body. She arched up to meet him, thrust for thrust, her arms and thighs wrapped around him until they were as one being, one person. Everything else vanished.

'Then we'll die together,' she gasped.

'Is that not what romantic fools do?'

'Oh, yes. And I'm the most foolish of all.'

He found his climax, a hot, bright flash of light that obliterated all before it. Nothing mattered but the heat and scent of *her*.

'Clio!' he shouted out. 'Clio.'

'Yes,' she whispered, her own body tensed with the rush of her orgasm. 'I'm here, my darling. Yes.'

Chapter Twenty-Six

'Where are we going?' Clio asked, laughing. Edward held one of her hands; with the other she touched the edge of the silk scarf covering her eyes. The darkness made her very sensitive to the rough ground under her feet, the scratching noise of leaves and pebbles. To the smell of fresh air, warm and tinged with the earth and green, growing things. It was a whole new world.

Edward laughed, too, his hand tightening on hers as he led her onwards. He also seemed new-made after their late-night revelations. Younger, freer somehow.

She did not know how *she* felt. Not shocked or surprised by his old mistakes. Surely she had heard of worse. But sad that he had been buried with the guilt of it for so long, unable to forgive himself. To put the past behind, and move into a future full of possibilities.

She, too, had not let the past go. It was always with her. But it seemed there *was* something magical about this hidden place, their fairy-tale cottage. Something that lifted a blinding veil and allowed her to see new truths at last.

'Where are we going?' she asked again. 'Are you trying to kidnap me all over?'

'I should have kidnapped you long ago, if I had but known what delights my latest crime would lead to,' he said. 'But I won't tell you where we're going. You just have to find out for yourself.'

'I knew it,' she said. 'You're taking me to the underworld!'

He laughed. 'And here I thought I was finally emerging from the darkness! Like Orpheus and Eurydice.'

'That didn't turn out well at all.'

'Ah, but in *my* version of the story, it is Eurydice who does the leading, and they emerge safely into the light.'

'Just like a woman,' Clio said. 'We are far too sensible to look back when told not to.'

'My dear, there are many words I could think of to describe you,' he said. 'But "sensible" is not one of them.'

'Ha! I tell you, I can be quite sensible indeed when needed. Have I not resigned myself to being your prisoner when there was no hope of escape?'

'Only because I bribed you with books, and cakes, and baths.'

'And other things, too.'

'Other things?'

'Come now, your Grace. You must not underestimate your own attractions.' She stumbled over a tree root, and his arm came swiftly around her waist, keeping her from falling.

Clio held on to him, the darkness heightening even her awareness of his nearness, the heat and clean scent of him. The way his muscle-corded arms, clad only in the thin linen of his shirtsleeves, felt under her avid touch.

'So, you think I'm attractive,' he murmured in her ear.

She shivered, despite the warm spring day. Her body knew his well now, craved its pleasures and intimacy. Craved the closeness. 'You know you are.'

'I know no such thing. But I'm glad to know one lady—the most important lady—finds me so.'

Suddenly, he swept her up in his arms. The world tilted dizzily as her feet left the ground, and she clutched at him, laughing giddily. 'Edward!'

'Don't worry, I won't drop you,' he said. 'We're almost there, and then you can satisfy your curiosity. Both about our destination *and* my "attractive" body. If you are so inclined.'

'I hardly think so, with my stomach so queasy,' she gasped.

'It's all those infusions you've been drinking,' he teased. 'Not to mention the vast quantity of bread and cheese you consumed at breakfast. Shocking.'

'I worked up a great appetite last night. All your fault.'

'Feel free to call on me whenever you feel the least bit peckish, my dear.'

She felt his steps turn, heading down a slope, and she tightened her clasp on his neck. The shadows at the edges of her blindfold grew closer, as if they entered a dense grove of trees. She heard the wind sing overhead, rustling leaves and birds stirring into flight. He turned again, the new ring of stone under his boots. They seemed to be descending stairs of some sort.

Then she heard an unexpected sound, the soft lapping of water.

'Is it the River Styx?' she whispered.

Edward laughed, and lowered her gently to her feet. 'See for yourself,' he said, untying the scarf.

For a moment, Clio's gaze was unfocused from being in darkness. She blinked hard, and found that they *had* entered the underworld. An enchanted realm.

She gazed around in wonderment. They were in a cave, rough stone walls rising steeply to a skylight high above that streamed pale yellow sun down to where they stood on the bottom riser of a steep flight of flagstone steps. Below was a pool of clear blue-green water. It shimmered in the faint light, curls of silvery steam rising from its surface.

'It's not exactly a lake,' Edward said. 'And I doubt anyone could ever skate on it. But I thought you might like it.'

'What is it?' Clio murmured, entranced by the water, the rough designs painted on the stone walls. Sheaves of wheat and baskets of fruit, she saw, along with heavily pregnant animals and red poppies, the emblem of Demeter.

'The Grotto of Demeter,' he answered. 'I was told about it when I leased the cottage. They say in ancient times acolytes of Demeter performed rites here, asking for the bounty of the harvest and a fruitful season.'

'It is beautiful.' She knelt down to trail her fingers through the water. It was warm and soft, as befitted a life-giving goddess. She had the sudden undeniable urge to dive into the pool, to feel its essence all around her, its promise of a bountiful future she could not yet believe in. 'Can we swim in it? Or is that forbidden?'

Edward smiled. 'I doubt Demeter would mind. It's *your* grotto today. A new realm for the Muses.'

Clio laughed, and sat down to tug off her shoes and stockings. Her dress and chemise quickly followed, and she eased herself into the welcoming embrace of the waters. The pool wasn't very deep; she could rest her feet on the sandy bottom, letting the waves lap over her shoulders. Her loose hair floated around her, and her limbs felt buoyant, as if the water held her up, above all the cares of mortal life.

'It is wonderful!' she cried, her voice echoing around them. 'You come in, too, Edward.'

He smiled at her delight, kneeling down by the edge. His gaze was tender, and strangely wistful. 'In a minute.'

She eased down until she could float on her back, staring at the sky so far overhead. It was their own underworld indeed, a magical place of old ritual and prayer. A place where all truths were revealed and forgiven. Loves lost and won—and lost again.

But for that moment, she felt only a sweet lassitude, a healing contentment that washed over her with the water.

'When I was a girl, my sisters and I used to go swimming in a pond at Chase Lodge,' she said. 'My mother forbade us to do it, but we would sneak off and do it anyway when she and my father were in town. We couldn't help it, it was the most fun! We would swing out over the water from a tree branch and dive in, pretending to be mermaids and pirates. But it was cold and murky, nothing like this.'

As she floated there on her back, she heard the soft rustle as he shed his clothes and slid into the water. The waves splashed, signalling his swim to her side. She felt his touch on her bare skin, holding her aloft.

'I missed having lots of siblings when I was a boy,' he said. 'Brothers and sisters to swim and ride with, to make up games and tell ghost stories with on rainy nights. William was so much older, and not much for games anyway.'

Clio laughed. 'We certainly did all those things, true, but we also argued and fussed, and pulled each other's hair and called each other names. Well, Thalia and I pulled each other's hair; Calliope was too good. She was our peacemaker. I sometimes wished I was an only child, so I would have time to study in peace.'

'Would you really have been able to do without your family?'

She dove down under the water, getting her feet beneath her before she plunged back upwards. She pushed her hair back over her shoulders, smiling at him. 'No, of course not. I adore my sisters, though they also drive me mad sometimes.'

'Drive you mad?'

'They are always *there*, you see. We aren't ourselves, we're a collective—the Chase Muses. Part of each other for all time. It means we always have each other to rely on, but it also means we are obligated. Always and for ever.' Clio paused. She had never spoken of such things before, never even really thought about them. But somehow, here with Edward in their sacred grotto, she felt she could say anything at all. That all her thoughts and dreams and fears would be understood by him, and him alone.

'I think perhaps that is one of the reasons I decided to become the Lily Thief,' she said.

'Because of your sisters?' he asked quietly.

'Yes. Oh, there were the antiquities, of course—that was the most important. To save them from people who did not care for them, to make sure they went to where they truly belong. But also it was something *I* could do. A cause just for me, a secret. It was wrong, I see that now. I went about my ideals in entirely the wrong way. Seeing the disappointment in Calliope's eyes was the most horrible feeling. But for a while…'

'For a while you felt truly alive.'

'Yes,' Clio said, surprised. 'How did you know?'

He gave her a wry smile. 'Because I know what it is to feel numb, dead inside, to try to feel something, anything, by doing things we're told are wrong. But it didn't work, not for me or for you. It was as if I watched the world in shades of hazy grey, never vivid, clear colour. Not until now. Your red hair is the first real colour I see.'

Clio feared she might cry. She had gone through years with

no tears, only to become a veritable watering pot when she was near Edward! She swallowed hard against the dry, hard knot in her throat and said, 'It is *auburn*, I will thank you to remember.'

Edward laughed, catching her around the waist and lifting her high, twirling her through the frothing water. 'It is red! Everything about you is painted in the most vivid of hues, Clio Chase. Red, and emerald green, and sun yellow. You're all the heat and noise and passion I've ever known.'

Clio laughed, too, giddy with the emotion of it all. She braced her hands on his shoulders, staring down at him as the steam rose around him in a silver veil. She had thought him handsome before, but in that moment he looked so young and free, his beauty positively incandescent. Her golden Sicilian god. 'I *am* noisy, that's true.'

'You are life itself,' he insisted, lowering her slowly back into the water. They stood there entwined, part of each other in the ancient magic of that place. 'You saved me.'

'No, no. You saved yourself.'

'I turned myself from a careless boy to a semblance of a duke, I suppose,' he said. 'I gave up taverns for the dusty halls of the Antiquities Society. Yet I could not have done it without your disapproval.'

'Ah, well, I am good at disapproval. I managed to keep it up with you for years.'

'I know. I still feel the stinging effects of it,' he said, laughing as he reached up to touch the faint white scar on his brow where the Alabaster Goddess had once landed.

Clio kissed that scar, filled with a sudden rush of remorse at the violent memory. 'I'm so sorry, Edward! I never—'

'No, I deserved it. My wooing of you was—rough, to say the least. But do you still disapprove of me? After everything?'

She shook her head. 'It's true that you should not have snatched me away like that. It's surely something the "old" Edward would have done! I know that you have your reasons, but you could have talked to me. Explained things.'

'I only wanted to keep you safe. And time was, is, so short. I couldn't come up with anything else. I'm sorry.'

'No, I don't want your apologies.' She laid her hands gently against his face, holding his gaze on hers. There could be no running away now, for either of them. No more deception. 'I want to know what is really happening.'

'Clio.' He pressed his fingers over hers, holding her to him. 'It is dangerous.'

'Come now. You know me better than anyone ever has. You know I do not shrink from danger. I want to help you, if I can.' She studied him closely. 'I know it's to do with the silver. Are you here to take it for yourself?'

He shook his head, turning to kiss her wrist. 'Surely *you* know *me* better than that. I have given up adding to my own collection, though pieces like the silver would be tempting indeed.'

'Then what? You're working with the Antiquities Society again, like in Yorkshire?'

'I am trying to.' He was silent for a long moment, as if weighing his options, weighing her words. Finally, he nodded. He took her hand and led her to a stone bench cut into the wall beneath the waterline.

'The bowl that I have,' he said, 'it came to the attention of the Antiquities Society last year, along with the information that there was certainly more where it was found. Could be an entire temple's altar set, the likes of which have never been discovered before. But it was in danger of being lost before it could even be seen.'

'Who discovered it?'

'Mr Darby, who is, as you know, also a member of the Antiquities Society. He is taking a report back to London. Soon before you arrived here, an informant brought Darby the bowl and told him of the search for more.'

'What sort of informant?'

'A former *tombarolo*. He claimed he sought more legitimate ways of making money, but I think he just wanted to play both sides for greater profit. It availed him naught, as he was soon after found dead. But his information seemed legitimate, and I was asked to come to Sicily and help investigate further. We had to hope it was not too late.'

'And did you know I was here?'

'No. I knew you were travelling with your family in Italy, but not in Sicily. I assumed you wanted to be as far from me as possible, after what happened in Yorkshire.'

Indeed she had, Clio remembered ruefully. Had longed to run from him, from what she felt and yet could not understand. Her father's suggestion they go abroad for a time was a godsend. 'Would you have stayed away if you had known?'

He laughed. 'On the contrary. I would have travelled here even faster.'

Clio laughed, too. 'Perhaps you should have! We've wasted so much time being angry. Not—not seeing. But tell me the rest of your tale. Have you found the silver yet? Any piece of it?'

'Not yet, but luckily it seems that neither have the thieves. You have got in their way.'

'Me?'

'Your work at the farmhouse. That is where it's thought the silver will be found. Before your arrival, no one ever went there, and the thieves could work in leisurely peace. When they could find people willing to brave the curse, that is. Now…'

'So, that *is* why you warned me away!'

'Of course. These are ruthless men. They would get you out of their way however they could.'

Clio shook her head, furious that thieves would dare defile her farmhouse! Dare sully the lives of those who had lived there, had buried that silver in fear and frantic hope so long ago. *This belongs to the gods.* 'The English buyer grows impatient,' she said, remembering the conversation she overheard at the *feste*.

'Yes. That's why you are now in greater danger. Why I kidnapped you.'

'Who is the English, then, that has the money to command such a flock of thieves?' Including, it seemed, Rosa's Giacomo.'

'At first we thought Ronald Frobisher.'

'Lady Riverton's cicisbeo?' Clio said, somewhat surprised. She would not have thought of him; he always seemed merely concerned with his neckcloths and planning parties, staying in the good graces of Lady Riverton. She should have remembered appearances were almost always deceiving.

'He seems to have the money, and he's quite an ardent collector, if something of a neophyte. Possessing a silver altar set would gain him attention and respect among other collectors. And with Lady Riverton.'

'Very true. No one else has anything like that, not that I know of.'

'If you *had* known, would the Lily Thief have struck again?'

Clio laughed. 'I told you, my thieving days are behind me. Except for the night I broke into your palazzo, of course. But you said you *did* suspect Frobisher. Do you not any longer?'

'Oh, he is part of it. It seems, though, that he is acting on behalf of someone else.'

'Of course,' Clio breathed, feeling suddenly foolish. 'Someone he wants to impress above any other. Lady Riverton.'

'Indeed,' Edward answered. 'When I first came to Santa Lucia, I did not suspect her, either. Lord Riverton was a great collector, but she never really seemed to share his interest.'

'No. Only hats and parties. I should have known no one could be *that* interested in bonnets without having something to hide.'

'I couldn't understand why she was in a quiet place like Santa Lucia, and not in Naples. Only people with a great interest in history and antiquities come here.'

'I just thought she wanted to play social queen for a while, in a place where no one else has time to throw lavish parties,' Clio said reflectively. 'Father and Thalia enjoyed her entertainments well enough, and I didn't think of it all very much. What a cabbage-head I was!'

'Then we are cabbage-heads together, surely.'

'Are you quite certain it is Lady Riverton?'

'Not completely. But the list of suspects is short, and she and Frobisher are at the top.'

Clio tipped her head back against the stone wall, staring up at the skylight as her thoughts whirled. 'We have to find out for sure.'

'*We?*' He shook his head. 'No, Clio.'

'Yes!' she cried. She turned to him in growing excitement, clasping both his hands in hers. 'You said yourself you cannot lock me up to keep me safe.'

He shook his head again, his lips set in a stubborn frown. 'That does not mean I will put you right on the path of danger.'

'I am not like the silver, you know,' she insisted. 'You cannot hide me away. I may not have seen the truth of Lady Riverton, but I can help you. I have worked with people like that, I know how they think. How they act.'

'No! If you were hurt…'

'I won't be hurt! Did anything happen to me when I was the Lily Thief?'

'Only because you were lucky.'

'Lucky, yes. But also I was not stupid. I won't be stupid now, either! Please. Let me help you find the silver. We can't let it be lost.'

He stared down at her, his green eyes dark and full of stern doubts. She did not turn from him, just held on to his hands, willing him to believe in her. To see that she could be strong, and they could achieve so very much together.

'I am not a porcelain doll,' she said. 'I don't crack easily, and you know that. I *can* help you, if you will just give me a chance.' She pressed kisses to the white scar on his brow, the crooked line of his nose. 'You will be there to protect me, I know.'

Finally, finally, she sensed him wavering the merest bit. He shook his head again, but said, 'Very well. I know that your help will be invaluable. I have seen what you can do. But you must promise me you will be careful, that you will take cover at the first hint of any danger.'

'Thank you!' she cried, kissing him again in a burst of jubilant excitement. 'You will not be sorry. We will find the villain, whether it's Lady Riverton or not, and they will lead us to the silver. You must promise *me* something, though.'

'What is it?' he said. He still looked most wary, but she knew that would soon change. Once he saw the full potential of all they could be together.

'That you will also be careful. For you are quite precious, as well.'

He caught her in a fierce embrace, his mouth finding hers in a kiss full of passion and desperation. Clio wrapped her legs tightly around his hips, feeling his manhood lengthen and harden against her, as he walked up the sloping ground to the dry side of the grotto. Passion born of danger and anticipation blossomed between them, undeniable as a tidal wave. He pressed her back against the wall and entered her, fast and full of need, lust, fear and—and hope.

Clio arched against him, melding him to her even deeper, until she didn't know where he ended and she began. They were, and always had been, as one. And there, in that ancient grotto, she gave him her whole heart. In that moment she was his.

Not that she would tell *him* that, of course. He would only take that as a sign he should marry her and lock her up for all time. And she would make a terrible, miserable captive-duchess.

But for that instant, as their bodies and kisses and souls melded, she loved him. And it had to be enough.

Later, Clio lay at the edge of the pool, revelling in the feel of the warm water lapping at her feet, the broken sunlight that fell over them from high above. Edward's head rested on her naked stomach, and she ran her fingers through his loose hair, smiling at the absolute perfection of that moment, the gentle, sweet lassitude that had stolen over her in the wake of their lovemaking.

She laughed in a sudden burst of irrepressible merriment, kicking out at the water and sending a blue-green spray high in the air. Edward rolled over, grinning up at her.

'I love the sound of your laughter,' he said. 'It's much too rare.'

'No doubt it sounds rusty with disuse,' she answered. 'We are far too serious people, you and I.'

'True. We don't do anything casually. Nothing by halves.'

'All for one, eh?'

'If you would only let me.'

'Hmm. It's—difficult for me, you know. To trust, to share. I'm used to living in my own head.'

'Keeping your own counsel?'

'Indeed. Like someone else we know, *your Grace*.' She splashed water over his handsome head, making him laugh in turn. 'You're infuriatingly close-mouthed when you want to be.'

'Oh, not always. Not now, for instance.' He pressed a warm kiss to her abdomen, the curve of her ribs. 'Or now…'

Clio shivered, tangling her fingers in his wet hair. 'You are trying to distract me.'

He grinned against her skin, leaving a string of yet more kisses just under her breasts, the arc of her shoulder. 'Is it working?'

Of course it was. She could hardly remember her own name when he touched her like that. She tightened her clasp on his hair, drawing him away from her so she could think again. 'You know I am trying to get you to promise not to keep secrets from me any longer.'

He groaned, and rolled over to lie by her side. Only their hands touched. 'I have no more secrets left. You know everything.'

'Not quite everything.'

'Everything that matters. You know more of me than anyone else ever has. But I am not the only one with secrets,' he said.

'I have also told you everything,' she protested. 'You know all. Even about the Lily Thief.'

'Oh, come now, surely I cannot know *all*. You are a very complicated person, Clio Chase. There must be a great deal hidden in the dark corridors of your soul.'

Clio laughed. 'Dark corridors of the soul? Are you perchance a secret novel reader, your Grace?'

'I have been known to indulge in a Minerva Press tome a time or two, if you must know my very last secret,' he said. 'Purely for cultural research.'

'Oh, yes, certainly.' Clio squeezed his hand.

'So, tell me,' he said. 'What would Clio's truth be?'

That she loved him to distraction, of course. Her beautiful, strange, horrible, wonderful duke. She couldn't say that aloud, though, for she *did* still have some secrets she locked away. 'I told you, Edward. You know them all. Every last shocking thing. The wonder is that you are still here with me.'

'I don't scare that easily,' he said. 'The only thing that could have made me run away would be discovering that you are actually an empty-headed débutante. One of those dreaded gigglers in white gowns.'

'No fear of that. None of the Chases are *gigglers*.'

'I'm very glad to hear it. So, giggling is not your secret.'

'Indeed not.'

'A propensity to read fashion papers? Secret tippling?'

'I have enjoyed a grappa on occasion,' she admitted. 'One of our cook's many sons distils it, you see, and it's quite good.'

'Ah-ha! I knew there was something.'

'Now you truly do know all,' Clio said lightly. But the memory of that grappa made her think of Rosa's other son, Giacomo the *tombarolo*, and she felt a deep pang of sadness for people she had come to care about. 'I have been thinking…'

'Oh, no! Never that.' He laughed. 'Terrible things come of thinking, Clio. Thefts, night-time break-ins, things of that sort.'

'Well, you are just going to have to become accustomed to thinking. I do a lot of it, you know.'

'I do know. What are you thinking of right now?'

'Of finding the silver, and ferreting out the thieves.'

'I see.' Edward sat up, suddenly serious. 'Well, surely no one would know better how to go about such things. What are your thoughts?'

'I've been hearing quite a bit about vengeful spirits, curses and such. They often seem to take matters like that seriously here, and it seems my farmhouse is ringed with them.'

'I have heard such tales, too,' he said. 'That your site is guarded by ghosts who keep away interlopers. It's probably one of the reasons the hoard has stayed safe so long.'

'Hmm, yes. The local thieves would be scared of the spirits who guard the silver.' Clio remembered the warning inscription on the bottom of the bowl. 'Silver that belongs to the gods.'

'You think we can use these curses in some way?'

'Not on Lady Riverton, perhaps. But maybe on the thieves who do the actual work. Giacomo for one seemed to be convinced.' Clio frowned in thought. 'Lady Riverton and Mr Frobisher couldn't get the silver themselves. They wouldn't know how to do it. They rely entirely on their hired *tombaroli*. If the thieves thought the curse was upon them…'

'They might lead us to the cache, or at least refuse to dig up any more.'

'Hopefully, yes.'

'How do you propose we implement this curse? Ghosts are notoriously unreliable.'

'Well, for that we may need some assistance. *You* are certainly dramatic enough for anything, but you are so well known. I don't think we two can do it alone.'

'Exactly what kind of "assistance"?' he said suspiciously. 'Your friend Marco?'

'I hadn't thought of Marco! I'm sure he could be of valuable use, though. He's quite good at disguises, and he knows more about local customs than I do.'

'Yes, I know about his disguises. Then, if not the Count, who? We don't want too many people involved.'

'I agree. The more people, the more likely the scheme will be discovered. But Thalia is entirely trustworthy, and always ready for mischief,' Clio said.

'Your sister?'

'Yes. She is an excellent actress; you saw her at the theatricals. And she is also something of a playwright. She would be the best one to help us concoct a play about ghosts and curses.'

'I don't know,' he said, the stern Duke again. 'I agreed to accept *your* help. I cannot put all your sisters in danger, too.'

'It is only one sister! Believe me, Thalia is ideal for such a task. She might look fluffy and fashionable, but she truly is quite talented. And she has even more "dark corridors" in her soul than I do, I would vow. If anyone is ruthless enough to spring a trap on Lady Riverton, it is Thalia.'

Edward was quiet for along moment, then said grudgingly, 'Very well. Your sister, then, and perhaps that blasted Count. That is all.'

'That's all I need,' Clio said, satisfied. For the moment.

'Where shall we "spring this trap", then?'

'Where else, my darling? The ancient theatre. I'm sure all manner of ghosts dwell there.'

Chapter Twenty-Seven

Clio peered through her spyglass at the amphitheatre below her rocky perch. It grew late in the day, but Thalia was still there, her script open in her hands as she paced the length of the old stage. The sun was an orb of shimmering burnt-orange behind her, beginning its long descent below the horizon and casting Thalia's white draperies in stripes of bright colours.

Already Clio felt the fairy-tale magic of her little cottage fading away into mist, dispersed by the cold winds of life and plotting. The soft cocoon that enclosed her in that small bed-chamber, the grotto, fell away, leaving her shivering and exposed, aching for dreams she hadn't even realised she possessed. They were all gone now, vanished in the face of the real world.

But even as she lost her idyll, she felt a new, hard-steeled sense of purpose she hadn't known since the end of the Lily Thief. There were treasures to save, and this time she was not alone in her mission. She had Edward.

Edward. She smiled just to think of his name. Months, even just weeks ago, she would have scoffed at the idea that they could work together and not against each other. That they could even see things from the same angle. Yet here they were, joining forces.

Oh, she knew very well he was still reluctant. She could see it in the troubled depths of his eyes, feel it in the tension of his embrace as they had kissed goodbye on the road into Santa Lucia. He still had his silly, wonderful chivalric ideas about ladies and their place, about keeping her safe. But he would see soon enough. Would see that she would not be kept in an ivory tower, or a cosy cottage.

It all hung on the safe recovery of that silver.

Clio gazed through her glass again, watching Thalia as she drew a shawl up over her robes against the breeze. For an instant, Clio saw her sister not as she was, a beautiful, wilful young lady of immense talent, but as she had once been. A golden little cherub, their mother's favourite, who toddled everywhere after Clio and Calliope, screaming to be allowed into their games.

Clio sympathised with Edward's driving desire to keep everyone safe. Thalia was her little sister, the loveliest of the Muses, but also, in many secret ways, the most vulnerable. It had always been her older sisters' task to protect her. How could Clio put her in danger now?

She nearly turned and fled, running home to hide all her secrets away from her family again. To come up with a new plan, one that put no one but herself in danger. Yet even as she glanced back over her shoulder to the open path, she knew she could not. Thalia would not take kindly to being 'protected', any more than Clio had. Thalia would want to be involved, and indeed was truly the best person for the task.

Clio had vowed to let the past go. Perhaps that included letting her sister grow up.

"'I have heard tell the sorrowful end of her, Niobe",' Thalia said, her voice strong, carrying on the wind. The resolute voice of the tragically principled Antigone. "'How strong shoots upgrown like ivy bonds enclosed her in the stone. With snows continuous and ceaseless rain her body melts away...likest to hers the bed my fate prepares".'

To Clio's surprise, another voice joined Thalia's, this one deep and resonant. Touched with the music of a Florentine accent. "'She was of godlike nature, and we are mortals, of human race. And it were glorious odds for maiden slain, among the equals of the gods in life—and in death—to gain a place".'

As Clio watched through her glass, she saw Marco appear from the stony wings. He and Thalia stood together against the brilliant glow of the sun, hands held out to each other, but not touching. Golden day and darkest night.

"'Ah me, unhappy!'" Thalia said. "'Home is none for me. Alike in life or death an exile must I be".'

"'Thou to the farthest verge forth-faring, o my child of daring",' Marco said. "'The cause is some ancestral load, which thou art bearing".'

Clio held her breath. She felt she was not watching Thalia and Marco at all, but ancient Greek figures, caught in unbearable, inescapable struggles. Dragged down by fate. No, she could not protect her sister, no matter how much she longed to. Not from anything. They were all bound by their own 'ancestral loads'.

She put away her glass, scrambling down from the rocks and hurrying along the path to the old agora and theatre. As she moved closer, she saw Thalia and Marco still stood together at the edge of the stage, not speaking, not touching, just gazing together out over the sunset-lit valley.

Perhaps it was her own heightened emotional state, the

deep feelings of being with Edward, making love with him, but she sensed a new tension between Thalia and Marco. A shimmering, tenuous tie between them that made the very air taut.

'I still don't think you said it right,' Thalia said suddenly, snapping that tie in a shower of sparks.

'Of course I said it right!' Marco argued. 'You wanted more emotion in the words, and I gave you more emotion. Italians are good at that.'

'But now it is too much emotion,' Thalia insisted stubbornly.

'May the gods save me from obstinate Englishwomen!'

'And may the *goddess* save me from men who think they can act! Marco, I do believe that—Clio!' Thalia cried. She dashed to the edge of the stage, her script fluttering from her hands. She ran down the path to throw her arms around Clio, nearly knocking them both from their feet. 'Clio, you're here! You're alive.'

Clio laughed in surprise, patting Thalia's shoulder. 'Of course I am alive.'

'I was so worried.' Thalia drew back, her gaze sweeping over Clio as if to be sure of her wholeness. 'You're back very early.'

'I turned back before we reached Motya. There's too much work here for me to waste time sightseeing.' Clio glanced over Thalia's head at Marco, who had come to the edge of the stage and watched warily. 'I see you have been busy.'

'Marco, you mean?' Thalia said carelessly. She laughed, but Clio thought it was a tense sound, unlike Thalia's usual exuberant chuckle. Her sister also wouldn't quite meet her gaze.

What was going on here?

'He has been helping me with the play,' Thalia said.

'Only the play?'

Thalia shrugged. 'He has also been working with Father at the villa. Father is most impressed with his knowledge of ancient architecture.'

'Well, I see you have *all* been busy while I was gone!'

'We had to do something to occupy ourselves. Lady Riverton hasn't been entertaining at all, and the Duke of Averton was gone. To Palermo, they say.' Thalia peered closely at her. 'Did you know about that? The Duke being gone, I mean.'

'I…' Clio instinctively opened her mouth to deny any knowledge of the Duke's whereabouts, but then she shook her head. Had she not determined to stop sheltering her sister? To stop lying, and admit when she needed help. Admit everything.

Almost everything, anyway.

'Actually, yes. I did know,' Clio said. She took Thalia's hand, turning with her back towards the stage. 'I need to talk to you and Marco about something important.'

'I can scarcely believe it!' Thalia exclaimed.

'It is indeed a strange tale,' Clio admitted. Her sister and Marco sat in rapt silence as she told her story, minus the personal bits in the cottage, of course. Now they burst into questions. 'Lady Riverton, the Duke asking for help…'

'Oh, no, Clio,' Thalia said. 'The wonder is that *you* ask for *my* help.'

'Why would I not? There is surely no one else who knows more about putting on theatricals.'

'That is true,' Marco agreed. 'She is a stern stage manager indeed. But how did the Duke come to suspect Lady Riverton in the first place?'

'Did *you* suspect her?' Clio asked him. 'Is she the reason you came here to Santa Lucia?'

Marco shrugged. 'I thought she might know something of the silver. Such a find would be very valuable, and there are rumours she has considerable debts. People say she was in Florence for a time, but had to leave in a great hurry.'

'Probably she owed her milliner,' Thalia said wryly. 'It will be a vast pleasure to help see her come to justice!'

'You will do it, then?' Clio asked.

'Certainly. I already have an idea for a scene we could use. But…'

'But what?'

Thalia glanced at Marco from the corner of her eye. 'Nothing. We should get home, Clio, before it grows even darker. Father will be surprised to see you.'

'You're right, of course. We can meet here tomorrow to finalise our plans.' Clio watched as Thalia gathered up the scattered pages of her script, her white skirts and red shawl fluttering in the breeze.

She noticed that Marco watched, too, his dark eyes solemn as they followed Thalia's pretty figure.

'If you hurt her in any way,' she whispered fiercely in his ear, 'I shall make you very sorry.'

Marco gave a startled laugh. '*Cara*, when it comes to your sister I think the one you should worry about is *me*.'

'I mean it, Marco. Thalia likes to flirt, but she has a good, kind heart, and she cares so deeply. She's not like you, with your great causes and sacrifices.'

'What makes you think I do not care deeply? I can see the worth of a person, Clio, just as well as I see the value of an Etruscan vase.' He pushed himself to his feet, stalking over to help Thalia gather her papers.

Clio stared after them, feeling suddenly dizzy. A lot *had* happened in the short time she had been gone, in the world around her as well as in her very own heart.

Whatever would she find at home? Her father married? Cory betrothed? She shuddered to think of it all.

Chapter Twenty-Eight

Clio leaned out of her open bedroom window, gazing out over the burnt-red rooftops and white church spire of Santa Lucia. Everything was blanketed in the usual dusty purple-black of Sicilian night, as quiet as ever. No one was betrothed or married, after all, yet something had definitely changed. A new tension in the air, a feeling of waiting, watching for something. She did not yet know what that *something* would be, what would happen tomorrow or the next day. When the peace would be shattered.

Perhaps it was not the town that had changed, she thought, but her. Maybe her too-short days with Edward had altered everything she saw and did.

She drew in a deep breath of the clear, cool air, curling her hands tightly on the windowsill. Before, when she had become the Lily Thief, she had felt no fear. Nervousness, of course, that tight fluttering inside whenever she broke into a library or gallery. Yet never cold fear, like the sense that came over her now. She had much to lose before; now she had everything. She had Edward.

Well, she did not *have* him exactly, she thought with a

laugh. He wasn't a statue or ivory box she could tuck safely away, much as she might want to. But he was her lover, her other half, and she knew so well that the work he did was dangerous. He faced people who were ruthless in their pursuit of riches. They would not let art, history, or even human life stand in their way.

She could see now why he had lied to her, why he had tried to lock her up to keep her out of harm's way. To risk one's own life was easy. To see a loved one leap off that cliff was quite a different matter.

And she found that she hated that worried feeling, that cold pit in her stomach. It gnawed at her, making her feel so tense she feared she might jump out of her skin at any sudden noise. At dinner, it had taken all of her willpower just to sit in her chair and listen to her father talk. To look at Cory's new sketches, and pretend all was well. All was the same as it had ever been.

Was this love, then? This deep craving, this hollow feeling when he was out of her sight? Was this what her father and mother had felt all those years, what Calliope and Cameron felt? If so, how did they ever survive?

How would *she* survive?

'Oh, Edward,' she whispered. 'What are you doing to me?'

As she stared out at the street beyond, she noticed a shift of movement, a ripple in the shadows. She straightened, reaching for the nearby table where she had left her dagger. That tension inside her grew and expanded, until she feared she would snap and go shooting off into the night.

She tucked the blade close to her, hidden in the folds of her silk skirt as she peered closer to the shadows. That movement slowly coalesced into a tall, cloaked figure. A thief? Or one of the cursed spirits?

'Clio,' she heard a voice call. A voice as familiar now as her own.

'Edward!' she answered. Her fingers loosened on the dagger's hilt. She had to smile despite her fear, her taut apprehension. Surely all would be well, if they faced the unseen foe together. 'What are you sneaking about like that for?'

He stepped closer to the wall beneath her window, shaking back his hood. The lamplight fell across the tumble of his bright hair, making it shimmer. 'I thought your father might not appreciate me calling after midnight.'

Clio laughed. 'Perhaps not. He does seem to like you, but he also likes his rest. Stay there, I will come down.'

She caught up a black shawl, wrapping it over her head and shoulders before she dashed down the stairs. The house was dark and quiet, except for the soft sound of the piano from behind the closed drawing-room door. Thalia was still awake, too, pouring out her own hidden emotions in Beethoven.

Clio slipped out of the front door, running around to the side of the house where she had seen Edward. He was not there, though, the garden seemingly empty.

Had she just imagined him, then? She spun around, scanning the darkness. Suddenly, a strong arm caught her around the waist, dragging her close to the wall. Her startled cry was buried in a hot, hard kiss. Edward's kiss.

She seized him by the shoulders, holding on to him tightly as she returned that kiss with a desperation of her own. They clung to each other as if it had been a year and not just a day they had been parted for.

'I've missed you,' he said roughly.

'I missed you, too,' she whispered. 'And I miss our cottage. My bed here looks so big and cold…'

He groaned. 'Don't remind me! I should have kept you my captive even longer.'

'But you couldn't, I know. While we basked in our grotto for weeks and months, the villains would certainly escape.' She pressed one more kiss, a soft, alluring caress, to his lips. 'Once the silver is found, feel free to kidnap me any time you like.'

'I will be sure to remind you of that offer later,' he said, laughing. 'Did you speak to your sister, then?'

'Yes, and, just as I suspected, she is up for any mischief. She and Marco will help us. I'll send out invitations to our own little theatrical evening tomorrow. Everyone will surely want to be there, as Thalia tells me Lady Riverton is not entertaining so much now.'

'Everyone?'

'The Elliotts, the Manning-Smythes. All the English visitors. Rosa and her vast family. And Lady Riverton and her faithful Mr Frobisher, of course. We will make it the event of the Season. With a fabulous finale, of course.'

'Not as fabulous as *this*, I hope,' he muttered, kissing her again.

'Hmm,' Clio moaned, arching into his body. 'Nothing could be as wonderful as this.'

'Then let's go back to the cottage,' he said, taking her by the hand and tugging her teasingly toward the gate. 'Right now. We'll hide in bed until this is all over.'

She laughed, shaking her head. 'I would run back to our cottage in a moment, Edward. But none of this can be over without us. We have to finish it, find the silver.'

'Oh, my dear, how sadly, sensibly right you are.'

'I'm always right.' Except when it came to him, of course. There she had been terribly, wonderfully wrong. 'Almost always.'

'I shall have to remember that.' He took her other hand, gazing at her with that steady stare that always seemed to see everything. 'What about after?'

'After we find the silver? I don't...'

'Will you come to the cottage then?' His voice was suddenly serious, deeply so. Clio tensed, yet did not pull away. She couldn't run, not any more. No matter how much she wanted to.

She tried to laugh. 'Why, your Grace. Are you propositioning me? Shocking.'

'I'm asking you to marry me.'

Clio didn't know what she had expected him to say, but it was surely not that. She shouldn't be surprised; all he had told her in the last few days, all she had discovered, made her know he was a changed man. A man with his own sort of honour. They had made love, she was supposed to be a wellborn lady, therefore he thought he should marry her.

As she stared at him in the moonlight, at his beautiful, solemn, scarred face, she felt a deep yearning unlike any she had ever known before. A longing to be permanently joined with this man, her other half.

But—but she did not want him like this, she found. Obligated and honourable.

'I would make a terrible duchess,' she said, trying to be light despite the tightness of her throat.

'You couldn't possibly be a worse duchess than I am a duke,' he answered. He held to her hands, not letting her run from him and the inescapable behemoth of the future. 'Yet I have found that dukes are given great indulgence for their eccentricities.'

'Like swimming naked?'

'Like doing whatever we—you and I—like.'

'Edward, I just—I can't think about that now. My mind is too full of the silver, the play, everything.'

He nodded. 'I understand, my dear. I'll give you time. But after this is over, I will come back and ask you again. And I will keep asking, until we are both old and grey, if need be.' He kissed her hands, and let her go to melt back into the night. 'Think about it, Clio. That is all I ask.'

'Yes. I will think about it.' As if she could think about anything else now! She stood there for a long time after he left, leaning against the wall with her shawl drawn up against the wind. Yet she did not feel the chill, or even see the darkness that wrapped around her. She heard only his words, echoing over and over in her mind. *Marry me.*

Yet how could she? How could the magic of their time here, the ancient enchantment of Sicily, ever translate to England? To the reality of their lives there, especially Edward's with his vast myriad of responsibilities.

She would surely end by disappointing him. And that she could not bear.

Clio shook her head, pressing her hands to her aching temples. 'Don't think of that now,' she ordered herself sternly. 'Think of your work here. That is all that matters right now.'

The rest of it—well, it would surely be waiting for her later. Unless Edward changed his mind.

'Clio? Is that you talking to yourself out here?' she heard Thalia say.

Clio quickly wiped at her damp eyes, pasting a smile on her lips before she turned. Thalia was leaning out of an open drawing-room window, still dressed in her pale blue muslin dinner gown, an Indian shawl tossed over her shoulders. Her gaze was curious, and very concerned.

'Are you quite well, Clio?' she asked.

'Of course,' Clio answered. She sounded far too cheerful, even to her own ears. 'I just needed some fresh air.'

Thalia didn't look convinced. She climbed straight out of the window, tugging her skirts impatiently behind her, and hurried over to Clio's side. She didn't say anything, just leaned against the wall next to her. But Clio was suddenly glad of her presence, her silent sympathy.

'You are up late, too,' Clio said.

'I couldn't stop thinking about our scheme. Playing the piano helps me sort out my thoughts, work out the play in my head. I thought I heard voices out here.'

Clio smiled. 'So, of course you had to investigate yourself. No time for summoning the footmen or anything like that.'

'The servants have already retired! Why should I disturb them just because my sister takes it into her head to wander about the garden talking to herself?'

'I suppose we are neither of us behaving as we ought.'

'Do we ever?'

'No. Especially since Calliope left.' Clio paused. 'You have been spending a great deal of time with the Count lately?'

Thalia shrugged, not quite meeting Clio's gaze. 'Not a *great* deal. We have met once or twice, and he kindly offered to help me with *Antigone*. You were gone, so he had to make do with the second-best Chase.' She added in a soft, barely audible voice, 'As usual.'

'Thalia,' Clio said warningly. 'I'm not certain the Count is someone you ought to—'

'Oh, Clio!' Thalia waved away all warnings with a laugh. 'I am not like Susan Darby, I won't lose all signs of intelligence at the sight of a handsome man. I know what Marco di Fabrizzi is. He's fun to flirt with, of course, and an excellent co-conspirator in our little scheme. But I won't take him seriously. I probably won't even see him again when we leave here.'

Clio had seen the way Marco looked at Thalia, and she was not so sure of that 'never see him again' business. But she knew when Thalia was set against discussing something, and her sister had that mulish look in her eyes now. So, Clio merely nodded.

'I am more worried about you and the Duke of Averton,' Thalia said.

'The Duke? Whatever do you mean?' Clio said. But she was not quite as good an actress as Thalia, and she found her bright, innocent tone fooled no one.

'I mean he is working on finding this lost silver, too, is he not? You must have met him recently, become friends even, if he has taken to confiding in you. Asking for your help.'

Clio tugged her shawl closer around her. 'He knows how much the Chases care about antiquities.'

'Hmm, yes. He could hardly miss that little fact, I think. But you two have always quarrelled in the past! And he is so—so strange.'

Clio could hardly argue with that. Edward *was* strange. He was like no one else she had ever known. 'Sometimes we have to put aside past differences for the good of the future,' she said weakly.

'That is very good, Clio. You should write it down,' Thalia said. 'Speaking of writing, I must go begin work on our new play. It will be ready to start rehearsal day after tomorrow, I promise.'

'It will be suitably Gothic, I hope.'

'Of course. Thunder, lightning, quite horrid. Our friend Lotty would love it.' Thalia turned back to her window, eschewing doors. Before she climbed back inside, she glanced back over her shoulder and said, 'Don't stay out talking to yourself all night. It's turning cold.'

'I won't.' As Clio gazed up at the hazy stars, she reflected that even when she felt alone, she never truly was. Someone, somewhere, was always watching. Knowing.

Once, that feeling would have frightened her, made her angry. Now—well, now it was strangely comforting. She was no longer alone in her work, but then neither was she alone in the danger of it. There was Edward, and Thalia and Marco. And *that* knowledge made her shiver more than any cold night wind ever could.

Edward lingered in the shadows just beyond Clio's gates, watching as she talked to her sister. Making certain she went safely back inside.

For was that not what he must do now? Make sure Clio was always safe. That she came to no harm, both here in Sicily and...

And always.

When he had come to Santa Lucia at the request of the Antiquities Society, come to find the elusive altar silver, that was his one goal. All he could see, think about. The presence of Clio Chase was a distraction, a danger. But then, slowly but certainly, it became something else entirely. Something deeper, richer—stranger. She became a partner in his task.

A partner in his life. She said she would make a terrible duchess. But she was wrong.

He watched Clio follow her sister into the house, the windows and doors closed firmly behind them and the lights flickering out one by one. Only then did he turn towards his own house, towards the work that waited for him.

When he had kidnapped Clio, he had wanted only to keep

her out of the way, safe, until everything here was finished. He should have known better, of course. Clio was like no other woman he had ever met. Her fierce intelligence, her steadfast independence—the determination that led to the Lily Thief—would always be there. She could not stay quietly at home when action was needed over a cause she believed in, no more than he could. And that was why he had come to love her so very much.

Edward stopped just outside his house, suddenly astonished. Not that he loved Clio, but that it had taken him so long, so many turns, to admit it. He *loved* her! Loved everything about her, even the stubbornness that drove him to madness. She was his other half. His helpmeet. His duchess, whether she believed it or not.

There was just nothing else for it. She would have to marry him, even if she continued to protest. Honour demanded it, after what had happened between them in the cottage. And love…

Love demanded it, too. She would surely come to see that, just as he had.

They *would* be wed, the moment danger was past. And he would keep her safe.

Chapter Twenty-Nine

Clio peered out from behind a screen, hastily erected at the back of the amphitheatre stage to provide effects for their play. The theatricals hadn't begun yet; the audience was just arriving, trickling to their places on cushions scattered about on the stone benches. The sun was setting over the valley, illuminating their fine clothes, the silken gowns of the English ladies, Rosa and her Santa Lucia friends in their best black dresses. They all seemed to be talking and laughing as if it was a normal evening out. No one suspected anything.

'Is everyone here?' Thalia asked.

Clio glanced back, and smiled at her sister. Thalia wore her costume, a fanciful creation of cheesecloth and white muslin. The ragged hem and the ends of the draped sleeves were tinted pale silver, a colour that would catch the flickering lamplight and glow with an otherworldly illumination. She did not yet wear her headdress, and her golden hair fell loose over her shoulders.

Thalia didn't seem nervous at all, Clio thought. In fact, she seemed far calmer than usual, her blue eyes serene as she mouthed her lines one last time.

Clio, on the other hand, felt all alight with nerves. The anticipation, the calm before the theatrical storm, vibrated all through her. They had had to prepare everything so hastily, she wasn't sure any of it would work. What would become of the silver, of all of them, then?

And what, oh, *what*, would she say to Edward's proposal? That was the greatest uncertainty of all.

She pressed her hand tight to her fluttering, aching stomach. 'No, not everyone is here yet,' she answered Thalia. 'Mr Frobisher and Lady Riverton are nowhere to be seen.'

She peered again past the screen, and saw that Giacomo was not yet there, either. There were a few men from the village she had heard might be involved in a bit of recreational pottery hunting. But Rosa sat with just Paolo, a couple of their daughters and some grandchildren, and a few of her friends. The children scampered up and down the tiered stone steps, scandalising the English guests with their playful shouts. Sir Walter sat with Cory and Lady Rushworth in the front row, where Clio could keep an eye on them.

'Never mind. We still have lots of time before curtain. I'm sure they'll arrive at any moment,' Thalia said. 'Come and help me finish getting ready?'

'Of course.'

Thalia had set up a small mirror in the corner, with a table scattered with an array of brushes, hairpins and theatrical maquillage. Clio had no idea where Thalia had procured those strange little pots and bottles. Probably she had broken in backstage at Drury Lane one night and insisted some hapless actress sell them to her.

'Here,' Thalia said, handing Clio a pot of what appeared to be chalk and a little brush. 'Sweep this over my forehead and cheeks, like so. It will give me a wonderful pallor. I'll look quite dead.'

Clio shuddered, spilling some of the white stuff on the table. 'Don't say such things, Thalia.'

'Clio! Never say you have become superstitious, too.'

'No sense in taking chances.'

'Well, let's hope your *tombaroli* are of the same opinion. No one wants to anger the spirits.' Thalia turned her face up to the fading light, holding still as Clio dusted a thick wash over her skin. The roses-and-cream complexion quickly turned to ashes.

'What is this stuff, anyway?' Clio asked. 'It's quite good.'

'Isn't it? I heard Mrs Thompson uses it at Covent Garden whenever she plays a spectre. I have some lip salve, too.' Thalia reached for a tiny bottle, rubbing a bit of grey over her lips. 'Do I look frightening?'

'Terribly,' Clio said truthfully. She longed to scrub away every bit of the grey and white from her sister's pretty face, to make her alive again, but Thalia spun away from her. She stood before the mirror, fitting on her headdress of more cheesecloth and white feathers.

'Don't worry, Clio,' she said. 'Everything will go perfectly. You won't be sorry you asked for my help.'

'Of course I won't. If anyone could scare the truth out of Lady Riverton and her thieves, it's you. Just promise me you'll be careful.'

'Certainly she will be careful,' Marco interrupted. 'She will be with me, won't she?'

Clio turned to find him emerging from his own 'dressing room' behind yet more screens. He wore the costume of a peasant shepherd, rough russet-coloured wool breeches and waistcoat, a cap on his raven hair. He carried the 'cursed object' his character stole from a tomb, a fake Etruscan vase painted with the large letters 'Belonging To The Gods'. Just like the inscription on the silver.

Thalia rolled her eyes, but Clio could see the shadow of a smile on her grey lips. 'I can take care of myself, thank you very much.'

Clio could tell that Marco longed to argue. Honestly, every time she saw those two together they were arguing! They seemed to take a strange delight in it. But there was no time now. She held up her hand, forestalling any quarrelsome words, and said, 'Go practise your lines, both of you. It's almost dark.'

She peeked around the screen again. The amphitheatre was filling up, as it had not since ancient days, and Giacomo was now with his family, fidgeting in his seat as he glanced nervously around. Ronald Frobisher was also there, holding his little court with the friends who always gathered around him and Lady Riverton. But of the lady herself, there was no sign.

Clio's gaze swung over the audience. Servants were lighting the torches along the stone steps, and the lamps on the stage that served as footlights flickered in the soft breeze. The glow illuminated laughing faces, the sparkle of jewels.

Along the very top row of seats, half-hidden in the darkness so far from the torches, she glimpsed Edward's bright hair. He, too, surveyed the crowd, tense and watchful.

Reassured by his presence, Clio turned back to Marco and Thalia. 'I think it's time,' she said. 'If we wait too long the audience will become restless.'

'And perhaps throw rotten fruit at us,' Thalia said. 'That would quite spoil the mood, I fear.'

Clio smoothed the skirt of her amber-coloured muslin gown one more time, before she slipped around the screen and stepped to the edge of the stage. As she held up her hands, the audience shifted into expectant silence.

'Good evening, everyone, and thank you so much for being here on such short notice,' she announced, gaining new strength and confidence from knowing Edward was out there beyond the blinding lights. That soon this would be over, and they would have the truth at last.

'As you know, my sister Miss Thalia Chase is very talented at amateur theatricals,' Clio went on. 'What you may not know is that she is also a playwright. We have not before been able to persuade her to share her work, but she has been so inspired by this beautiful place that we were able to convince her to perform this little scene. Because we know that you, too, love Santa Lucia and its intriguing history.'

Clio stepped a bit closer to the lights. 'My sister's tale is based on stories she has heard, *true* stories of a violent past, brave deeds and hidden treasures. Long ago, this Greek settlement was invaded by a Roman army, which laid all to waste and enslaved the people. What had been a prosperous, idyllic town, with a marketplace, baths, theatres and fine villas, was ruined.

'But a few people managed to flee. They left behind them beautiful objects, sacred things. They did not, however, leave them unprotected…'

Clio stepped back behind the screen as Marco took his place on stage. He began the tale of the shepherd who finds a vase buried behind the walls of a ruined Greek farmhouse, and determines to steal it. Thalia waited in the wings, a truly fearsome sight in her make-up and draperies.

Clio stood where she could continue to watch the audience unobserved. Was Giacomo shifting even more nervously in his seat? Was Frobisher looking guilty? And where was Lady Riverton, the centre of it all?

Yet there was no time to worry now. Action was needed. The plan was in motion. As Thalia glided on to the stage, her arms raised as she crept up behind Marco, Clio reached for her own costume. It was made of cheesecloth and muslin like Thalia's, and with a deep hood to hide behind.

Once covered, she crept out through a hole in the back wall of the amphitheatre, dashing up the hillside and around to where the main entrance led to the old agora. From there, she could peer down on all the activity with her spyglass.

Thalia was cursing Marco quite enthusiastically for taking that which belonged to the gods, the vase that had been buried so long ago and ringed round with spells to keep it safe. Marco's tormented screams were all too convincing, quite terrifying really. Clio wondered if Thalia had pinched him under her draperies. The audience members either looked on in wide-eyed, delicious horror, or giggled nervously. Frobisher peered back over his shoulder, a handkerchief wound tightly in his hand.

And Clio found she was, strangely enough, rather enjoying herself.

As Marco's torment went on, she was so caught up in the scene that she almost missed what she had been waiting for. Giacomo emerged from the theatre, glancing frantically both ways through the deserted old marketplace. His brow glistened nervously in the moonlight. As he took off running toward the ruins of the temple, Clio followed, glad of all the recent hill-walking that made her sure-footed and fast on the bumpy pathways. *And* glad of the fact that Giacomo's fear seemed to make him clumsy, unsure of his direction.

She scrambled up atop a large boulder that lay by his meandering path, and held her arms up. The breeze stirred her draped sleeves in a gratifyingly eerie manner.

'Halt! Thief!' she cried, in as deep a voice as she could summon. 'You have stolen what belongs to the gods.'

Distracted and frightened by her shout, Giacomo stumbled just long enough for Edward to tackle him from the shadows. The timing on this part of the plan, on the entire plan really, was so delicately balanced. But this bit came off just right. Clio watched in satisfaction as Edward leaped up, dragging Giacomo to his feet and holding him fast even as Giacomo struggled desperately to escape.

Clio clambered down from her perch, crouching behind the boulder to keep a watch on the distant theatre entrance. Surely the other players would soon make their appearance, if all went well.

And if Giacomo's thieving cohorts didn't interfere.

She pressed her palm to her leg, feeling the reassuring weight of the dagger strapped there beneath the muslin and cheesecloth.

'It's very rude to leave the theatre before the final curtain,' Edward said calmly, almost conversationally. Clio peeked around the rough corner of the boulder to see him holding the frantically twisting Giacomo as if the thief was naught but a rag doll.

Surely no one would recognise the indolent Duke of 'Avarice' now!

'Why were you running?' Edward said. 'Did Miss Thalia's play strike a chord with you, perhaps? Remind you of some previous obligation?'

Giacomo babbled something in quick, rough Italian. Clio couldn't catch it all, something about warnings and how he had 'told them' it was not safe. She could hear the raw edge of cold fear, though. The panicked sense of the line between reality and dream blurred.

Good. Maybe it would keep him away from tomb-robbing in the future, and reassure Rosa at last. But in the meantime they still had to find the silver. And stay out of danger themselves.

'I know you found part of that silver hoard,' Edward said, also in Italian. 'Did you find the rest? Where is it?'

'The altar set, *sí*. We found it.'

'And sold it?' Edward said, his voice tight with fury. Clio certainly did not envy Giacomo his current predicament. 'Illegally?'

'I should not have! I know the legend, the curse. My mother warned me…'

'But ancient ghosts were nothing to modern coin, eh?'

'It said it belonged to the gods, and I should have listened! Like the Count.'

'Count di Fabrizzi? Is he part of this?'

Clio tensed as she waited for the answer.

'No, no,' Giacomo said. 'He knew better. You saw him tonight.'

'Then who did pay you?' Edward demanded. 'Who is your English customer? Frobisher?'

'Of course. He is the one who first approached us. Yet the money does not come from him. He's hired, just as we are. He pretends he is not, but we all know the truth.'

'Lady Riverton,' Edward said slowly. 'She is the one who hires you and Frobisher, then, just as we suspected.'

Before Giacomo could answer, could give them the confirmation they sought, Clio saw Ronald Frobisher himself emerge from the theatre. The play was not yet over; she could hear the echo of Thalia's voice. Yet Frobisher seemed intent on his own errand, hurrying toward the pathway to Santa Lucia. He didn't run or babble, like poor, frightened Giacomo, but he was obviously in a great rush all the same.

Clio cast off her robes, shoving them into a crevice at the base of the boulder before she darted out and grabbed Edward's arm.

'There he is,' she urged him. 'We have to go!'

Edward nodded brusquely. He let go of Giacomo, who sank to the ground with his hands over his face.

'Shame on you, Giacomo!' Clio shouted back at him, as she and Edward ran off after Frobisher. 'What would your parents say?'

'And what would *your* parent say, my dear, if he could see you now?' Edward said. She marvelled that he could go from menacing to teasing in an instant. She was so very excited she was sure she would scream at any moment! 'Running off with a man into the night?'

'He would say we have to save the antiquities, of course. He *is* Sir Walter Chase. Now *hurry*!'

They ran up the path, trying to keep Ronald Frobisher in sight, but he was surprisingly quick for someone who professed complete indolence. Clio's lungs burned, her legs ached, yet she did not slow down. She held tightly to Edward's hand as they dashed through the village gates into Santa Lucia.

The town was quiet, as almost everyone was gathered at the theatre. The evening breeze blew clouds of dust across the square, bits of paper and leaves over the cathedral steps. Frobisher was nowhere to be seen.

'Have we lost him?' Clio panted, dismayed.

'I'm sure we can guess where he's gone,' Edward answered.

'Lady Riverton's palazzo?'

'Where else? I have a guard on his lodgings, though, just in case.' He squeezed her hand, leading her down the street toward the grand palazzos. 'Well, my dear, shall we pay a call on Lady Riverton? A rather unorthodox hour, I know.'

'Somehow, I think we will be expected anyway.'

The house, like the rest of Santa Lucia, was quiet and dark. No sound escaped from the shuttered windows. Without the life and noise of one of her parties, it seemed a gloomy and ominous place. Clio half-expected to see more ghosts, flitting in and out on their ethereal, sinister errands.

'Servants' entrance, I think,' Edward said, as they studied the courtyard. 'Those doors are usually unlocked, and people like Lady Riverton don't think of securing belowstairs.'

They found the servants' door at the side of the palazzo, down a short flight of steps. Clio cracked open the door and peered carefully inside, in case some stray footman or maid was not enjoying their evening off at the play. It was as silent as the rest of the house, though, the stone floors cold with no fire in the kitchen grate.

Hand in hand, they hurried up the steep stairs and through a doorway into Lady Riverton's realm. They stood there for a moment, Clio hardly daring to breathe as she listened for any sound at all. Any clue as to where Frobisher might have gone.

Then, at last, it came. A faint, faraway crash. They immediately followed it, running along a corridor and down more steps to the grand drawing room.

It was far from the lavish, welcoming space where Clio had sipped tea and applauded Thalia's *Antigone*. Only one branch of candles was lit, perched on the marble fireplace mantel and casting a circle of light that didn't reach the corners and high ceilings. But Clio's eyes were used to the dimness now, and she quickly saw Ronald Frobisher.

He stood by a table, its hinged top hanging open, broken and fallen on its side. The large, velvet-upholstered chair Lady Riverton had used to preside over her gatherings also lay toppled on the floor. Its rich cushions were viciously torn open, no doubt by the wickedly sharp dagger now in Frobisher's hand.

He swung toward them, the blade held aloft. 'Don't come any closer!' he shouted. All signs of the foppish, fawning Frobisher had vanished. His entire being fairly vibrated with anger and desperation.

For the first time, Clio thought he might really be descended from the Elizabethan pirate. She reached slowly for a fold of her skirt, ready to draw it up and pull out her own dagger.

But Edward clasped her arm, pushing her partly behind him so that he alone faced that blade.

'We only want to find Lady Riverton,' Edward said slowly, softly. 'We know that she is the one behind this whole scheme.'

Frobisher laughed bitterly. He gave the fallen table a venomous kick. 'I would certainly like to *talk* to her myself. But she isn't here. She's gone.'

'Gone?' Clio said sharply. 'To the theatre?'

'She sent me to your ridiculous play, told me she would meet me there. But she's taken her jewels and several of those wretched bonnets,' Frobisher answered. 'So, I dare say she has gone somewhere rather further away. The *witch*! She said we were partners, she promised me…'

'Promised you what?' Clio said, peering over Edward's tense shoulder.

For a moment, Frobisher was mutinously silent. But then he shook his head, and said, 'I might as well tell you now. She's gone, and I will be the one who pays. She said we would take that silver and go away together, to Naples or Rome. There would be plenty of money then, an easy life for both of us. "Just help me, Ronald," she said. "You're my only friend." And I believed her. Fool!' He kicked again at the poor table, reducing one carved wooden leg to splinters.

Clio nearly kicked out herself, in sheer frustration. Why had she not thought of that, of Lady Riverton fleeing while they were all distracted by their own scheme? She should have set someone to watching this house days ago.

'Now she is gone, and left me nothing but this,' Frobisher growled. He held up a small silver bowl, the twin of Edward's with its fine etchings and embossing, but more battered, its edges dented. 'She took all the rest: the incense burner, the ladles, the other bowls. The *witch*! I hope she burns in hell, I hope…'

Clio watched, appalled, as he raised the bowl above his head, prepared to dash it to the marble floor. She cried out, breaking away from Edward and lunging towards Frobisher, grasping for the precious bowl. All they had left now. She caught it, falling into Frobisher and knocking him back against the wall. His arm came down, the dagger in his hand nicking her in the shoulder.

But she barely felt the sting as she crashed to the floor, clutching the bowl tightly in her numb hand.

Then the pain flooded down her arm, her whole side. She stared down at her torn sleeve, the blood on her shoulder, in hazy shock. She barely heard Edward's frantic shout, the clatter of Frobisher's boots as he fled. She felt Edward's strong arms around her, helping her sit up.

'Clio,' he cried, his voice full of fear and panic. Strange— she hadn't known Edward *could* be afraid. 'Clio, darling, don't faint. Stay with me.'

'Did he open a vein, then? Am I going to bleed to death?' she murmured. She felt the sticky, warm, disgusting trickle of blood along her arm. Her head swam, and she could barely focus on his face above her. Who knew she, the Lily Thief, was afraid of blood?

'Never,' he answered. She heard a ripping noise, then he wrapped a length of soft linen around her shoulder. He had removed his coat and torn a piece of his shirt hem off for a makeshift bandage. 'I won't let you.'

'I've never been wounded before,' she said, bemused.

'Then you are profoundly fortunate, with the damn foolish risks you take,' he said fiercely, tying off the end of the linen. 'What possessed you to leap at a man holding a knife?'

'I was afraid he would damage the bowl. It's all we have now, to help us find the rest.' She gazed down at the bowl in her lap. So tiny to cause so much trouble. 'But he'll get away! What if he *does* know where Lady Riverton and the rest of the hoard is?'

'He won't get far, don't worry.' Edward cradled her gently in his arms, rocking her gently as the sting faded and she felt only weary. Weary—and safe, with him. 'We have to get you home, where you can be nursed properly.'

'And where you can lock me up so I don't get into any more trouble.'

He laughed, and kissed the top of her head. 'My dear, I don't think there are any locks strong enough.'

'But the silver is gone!'

'Clio.' Edward drew back, gazing down solemnly into her eyes. For that moment, there was only the two of them. 'Don't you know? I would never, ever leave you bleeding on the floor to chase after any criminal, any antiquity. I would never leave you at all.'

Clio curled against his chest, inordinately content. She should not be—Frobisher, Lady Riverton and the silver were

gone. She was wounded, lying on a cold floor in an abandoned house. But she was wildly happy.

Edward would not leave her. And, for that night, that was
all she ever wanted.

Chapter Thirty

'I vow, England is going to be dull after all this!' Thalia declared. Clio sat with her on their terrace, sipping tea and enjoying the sunny afternoon with her arm bound up in a sling.

She stared out over the garden, at the bright spring green turning dry at the edges. Soon it would be summer, and the intense southern sun would blast everything to brown. Days would grow long, drowsing in the heat. But they wouldn't be here to see it.

'I fear you're right,' Clio said. 'Our work here is almost done. Even Father thinks so.' At breakfast that morning, Sir Walter, appalled that his own daughter had been set upon by 'footpads' walking home after the play, declared that they would head to Geneva for the summer. 'But we can look forward to boating on the lake, and perhaps a spot of mountain climbing in Switzerland.'

'Mountain climbing!' Thalia pulled a face. 'That's all right for you, you're half-mountain goat anyway. But what will I do?'

'You could write a new play. An Italian tale of angry gods, stolen jewels…'

'And valiant heroines, wounded as they try to defeat the

villains?' Thalia gently adjusted the shawl over Clio's shoulders, careful of the sling.

Clio laughed. 'Your heroine will have to be far braver than to fall apart at a mere scratch. She will have to be *truly* wounded.'

'It is hardly a "mere scratch"! The bleeding would have been quite dangerous if not for the Duke's quick thinking.'

Clio sipped at her tea, remembering last night's haze of pain and confusion. Remembering Edward tearing his own shirt to make a bandage, carrying her home through the night. *I would never leave you*, he had said, and last night she believed him.

'Will there be a hero in your story?' she asked.

'Of course. And a romance. A play must have a romance. Passion and devotion that surmounts all danger, even death itself,' said Thalia.

Clio smiled at her. Thalia's blue eyes gleamed with the birth of a new tale. 'A dark Italian count in disguise?'

'Or an English nobleman with a secret errand! He has been in love with the heroine for years, of course...'

'Yet she, the stubborn chit, has never seen it before.'

'Not until he saves her life, sacrificing that secret errand to do so. Because love is more important.' Thalia nodded decisively. 'You catch on to this storytelling business, I see.'

'Love, danger, sacrifice, all the required elements.'

'Perhaps I will add in some gypsies who steal the cursed object. Bits with gypsies are in all the best plays.'

'Oh, yes. Though I don't recall any gypsies in *Antigone*.'

'The only thing it was missing, I assure you.' Thalia drew a notebook from her workbox and started scribbling away.

As Clio settled back in her chair, Rosa came out bearing fresh tea and a plate of cakes. She didn't say anything, didn't even look at Clio, but she tenderly tucked a blanket over her knees before gathering up the old tea things.

'How is Giacomo today, Rosa?' Clio asked quietly.

'Well enough, *signorina*. He sometimes suffers from nightmares, ever since he was a baby, and he was up with a very bad one last night.'

'I hope there is something that can be done about these—nightmares.'

'*Sí, sí*. He is going to stay with my brother in Palermo, who owns a grocer's shop. We have been trying to persuade Giacomo to learn the trade for years, and now at last he has agreed.'

'I'm sure he will do well there.'

Rosa nodded. 'Don't sit out here too long, *signorina*. You need to rest,' she said, bustling back into the house.

Clio turned back to the garden, to the endless expanse of blue sky. At least someone had found a new beginning out of all this. All she seemed to have was more questions.

Thalia lowered her notebook to her lap. 'I just don't know what will happen at the end.'

'I fear a play's audience would be most unhappy if the tale ends with "who knows what will happen"!'

'True. The actors would likely be pelted with rotten fruit.'

'They have to rescue the treasure, of course.'

Unlike in real life. All they had were two small bowls, and the rest was who knew where with Lady Riverton. 'And love? Will it triumph?'

'It depends. Do I write a comedy or a tragedy? And that reminds me…' Thalia drew a folded letter from inside her notebook. 'This came for us this morning, from Marco. In the excitement over your arm, I almost forgot.'

'What does it say?' Clio asked. 'Does the Count declare his most tender feelings for you?'

'Don't be silly,' Thalia said, shoving the note into Clio's

hand. 'We have no tender feelings, only quarrels. Remember? He says he is leaving, going to Pisa to search for Lady Riverton. It seems he visited Mr Frobisher in the Santa Lucia gaol and discovered that was her first destination. Why would she go to Pisa, of all places? If I was trying to hide a stolen treasure, I would go to Russia. Or maybe India. Somewhere very far away.'

'Why does anyone go anywhere?' Clio muttered. 'I would wager that sooner or later Lady Riverton will wash up on England's shores. And Marco will end up chasing her across the whole continent.'

'How very exciting, to go dashing across Europe on a gallant errand!'

'Indeed.' Clio felt a sharp pang that she, too, could not just dash off after the silver. That she had to stay home while the treasure retreated further and further away.

But then she looked at Thalia, and thought of Cory and their father, Calliope and Cameron, all their little sisters in England. Of everyone she loved. Edward had let Frobisher flee while he stayed with *her*, had declared that she was always more important than any antiquity. She could not do any less. Her family needed her, and she needed them. She would stay with them all, and let Marco do the dashing into danger.

For now.

But would Edward go after the silver, too? Would she lose him when she lost this place?

'But Switzerland will be interesting, too,' Thalia said reassuringly, as if she sensed Clio's melancholy. 'Lots more adventures wait for us there, I'm sure.'

Clio smiled at her, her heart still aching. It was time to begin a new chapter, yet she wasn't sure how. So much had happened here in Santa Lucia, so much had changed. *She* had changed, in ways she couldn't yet understand. It was as if the old Clio had been washed away in Demeter's grotto, been newborn in Edward's kiss. How did this new Clio move forwards?

'Signorina Clio,' a footman said, coming out on the terrace. 'There is a package for you.'

'A letter *and* a package in one day?' Clio said with a laugh. 'We are certainly popular. Thank you, you can bring it out here.'

'I fear it may be too large to fit through the door, *signorina.*'

'Too large?' Curious, Clio tossed back the blankets and shawls and hurried into the house, Thalia close on her heels.

In the foyer stood a massive parcel, thickly wrapped and bound until it was shapeless. The servants all stood about and stared, just as bemused as she was.

'It can't be a diamond,' Thalia murmured. 'Or pearls.'

'Unless it's the biggest diamond in all India.' Clio took the kitchen knife a footman handed her and sliced through the binding ropes, impatiently pushing back the wrappings. As they fell away, a wonder was revealed.

Artemis. The Alabaster Goddess.

She stood there in their small foyer, her bow upraised, her silver-white stone gleaming beyond the light of any diamond. Without her base, she stood almost as tall as Clio.

Clio laid a gentle touch on the intricately carved swirls of her hair, the crescent moon bound there. She was cold and perfect, her serene eyes refusing to divulge any of her long-held secrets.

'It's the Alabaster Goddess,' Thalia breathed in wonder. 'He's given it to you, Clio.'

Had he given it to her? After all they had been through over this one statue, over everything?

The statue was surely the most elaborate gift possible. Was she a sign of farewell? Of contrition, forgiveness?

Clio swung toward the footman, suddenly frantic. 'Was there anything else? A note or message?'

He shook his head. 'Just the statue, *signorina.*'

Clio ran towards the door, hardly noticing the painful twinge in her shoulder or hearing Thalia calling after her. She hurried out to the street, ignoring the startled glances of the people she passed, not stopping until she found her goal. Edward's palazzo.

She stopped at the open gates, out of breath. Not from her mad dash through town, but from what she saw there, servants carrying out trunks and cases. The windows of the house were all open, the curtains stirring in the breeze, adding their sinuous satin whisper to the bustle and dash of the courtyard.

He *was* leaving, she realised in shock. Going away and leaving Artemis to say farewell.

A flash of hot anger burned away the cold shock, and her hands tightened on the wrought-iron bars of the gate. Run away from her, would he? *No!* Not now, not after everything. She wouldn't, couldn't, let him. Couldn't lose him.

That anger chased away all doubts, and her insecurities, too. Only as she stood there, watching him go, did she see the one and only truth that mattered. She loved Edward. He was the only person who had ever seen and understood *her*, as she really was. Because they were cut from the same cloth, two of a kind. It was hardly important that the world would think her a poor excuse for a duchess. She would be *his* duchess, and that was what counted.

If she could just keep him from leaving now!

Clio hurried through the gate, asking the first servant she saw, 'The Duke! Where is he?'

'In his chamber, *signorina*, but I don't...'

She pushed past him, and the butler who tried to stop her at the door, and all the servants carrying their boxes down the stairs. She remembered well where his chamber was, and she didn't stop until she reached it.

Edward sat at his desk, writing. All the antiquities she had seen the night she had broken in were gone, packed away, leaving only the locked box on the dressing table. The one that held the silver bowl and the silken scrap from her old Medusa costume.

He did not even look up from his work, just smiled as if he had been expecting her all along.

'You are looking well today, Clio,' he said.

'Thanks to you. You saved me there, in Lady Riverton's drawing room.'

'It was my fault you were in such a dangerous situation in the first place.'

'No, it was my fault. I insisted on being involved.'

'And now that you have seen how it all ends, would you do it differently?' he asked.

'Certainly not.'

'I didn't think so.' He laid his pen down at last and looked up at her, his arms folded on the desk. 'I have learned a most valuable lesson in all this, my dear.'

'Just one?'

'Oh, no, indeed. But this was the most valuable. You will never be the sort of lady who stays safely at home, out of the way of trouble. If you see a wrong to be righted, you will leap into a fight, come what may. I cannot stop you from that. I can't keep you safe, even by resorting to kidnapping.'

Clio gave a choked laugh. 'It took you this long to decipher that? And here I thought you knew me so well.'

'I do. And that is why I know this—your fierce determination is one of the things I love most about you. If you stayed home embroidering by the fire, you wouldn't be Clio.'

'You—you love me?' she whispered.

'You know I love you. I love everything about you, even that stubbornness that drives me to insanity. I think we have to marry.'

'Why is that?'

'So that when we run into danger again, as we assuredly will, we can save each other. And because I just can't envision my life without you. I have asked you before, Clio, and I ask you again. Will you marry me?'

'Yes!' Clio cried. She threw herself into his lap, kissing him again and again through a storm of laughter and tears. He kissed her, too, holding her so close they could never be parted again. 'Yes, I will marry you. I will make you the most wonderful duchess ever, eventually. I promise. Now, when is the wedding?'

'As soon as I can arrange it, my dear. I told you there were some advantages to being a duke. I'll make the wedding so quick you won't be able to escape me again.'

'Or *you* will not be able to escape *me*! Is that what you were trying to do in leaving Santa Lucia? In sending me the Alabaster Goddess?'

'I am moving to other lodgings. This palazzo has become a bit oppressive, I think. And you can consider Artemis a wedding gift of sorts, if a rather ironic one, considering how fiercely she defended her virginity. But, yes, I am leaving soon. To help your friend Marco find Lady Riverton and the silver.'

'Another adventure, then?'

'But not without you, Clio. Never again without you.'

'I will hold you to that promise,' she said, kissing him again. 'For many, many years to come. All our adventures will be together.'

'Oh, my dear…' he laughed '…when we are together, the world will never, ever be the same.'

* * * * *

MILLS & BOON®

Want to get more from Mills & Boon?

Here's what's available to you if you join the exclusive **Mills & Boon eBook Club** today:

✦ *Convenience – choose your books each month*
✦ *Exclusive – receive your books a month before anywhere else*
✦ *Flexibility – change your subscription at any time*
✦ *Variety – gain access to eBook-only series*
✦ *Value – subscriptions from just £1.99 a month*

So visit **www.millsandboon.co.uk/esubs** today to be a part of this exclusive eBook Club!

MILLS & BOON®

Why shop at millsandboon.co.uk?

Each year, thousands of romance readers find their perfect read at millsandboon.co.uk. That's because we're passionate about bringing you the very best romantic fiction. Here are some of the advantages of shopping at www.millsandboon.co.uk:

* **Get new books first**—you'll be able to buy your favourite books one month before they hit the shops

* **Get exclusive discounts**—you'll also be able to buy our specially created monthly collections, with up to 50% off the RRP

* **Find your favourite authors**—latest news, interviews and new releases for all your favourite authors and series on our website, plus ideas for what to try next

* **Join in**—once you've bought your favourite books, don't forget to register with us to rate, review and join in the discussions

Visit **www.millsandboon.co.uk**
for all this and more today!

MILLS_WEB